DOPE IS A D.E.A.d MAN'S GAME

ISBN-13: 978-1461039884

The diversity of the cop business never ceases to amaze me. Just a mere sixteen days ago I was going to my office in a one-hundred year old building in the downtown area. There was no place to park the stinking, dilapidated detective-car. My little desk was ancient: the drawers didn't lock, the surface was pock marked, and the walls were coated with nicotine and cheap paint. The typewriters were ancient. The office was thick with smoke and the windows didn't open. It had to be that way so the murder suspects couldn't toss contraband, or themselves out of them.

I dealt daily with desperate damaged people; victims who were dead, victims who were left behind to try to piece their lives back together after losing a loved one. There was never a happy moment. Murder quickly became mediocre and there was no escape from it.

I had been trying to escape mediocrity for the entirety of my life, but despite my efforts, I dug myself deeper into it. I had a mediocre name, Ray Arnold. I was born and raised in a mediocre and infamous town, East St. Louis, Illinois. I had a dangerous job with mediocre pay, so I reluctantly accepted mediocrity, but I still continued to fight it from within by constantly trying to better myself. I worked at being fit and well read and semi-educated. It was the East side curse, a cur dog, and it followed me across the Mississippi to the big city.

I wondered if the mediocrity cur would follow me to Clayton, the county seat and business hub of the metropolitan area. I had a new assignment: a federal appointment, a federal supervisor, a seized Corvette to drive, a parking spot inside a tiered garage, an open modern office with computers, and a great view of a bustling business street from four stories up. The flea-bitten monster-hound hadn't found me yet, but I had brought something else with me, a dossier. The feds knew my demeanor, authority and conformation, I had problems in both fields. I was beaten up on my first drug deal. Set up by some Feds. Now I was being lectured by a Fed while my damaged brain played tricks on me. The humility was overbearing.

I never liked Feds. I could sometimes muster up a little respect for FBI agents but not very often. I had worked with them, on and off for fifteen years, having been a detective with the P.D., but I could never say, you know, I like that FBI agent.

But when it came to narcotics Feds, the most I could dole out was a total lack of respect. I could never say I liked any of them. They were intense to the extent of being annoying. As far back as I can remember, I have been able to read people and know their intentions. For most folks, especially cops, it's a skill they acquire and then polish. But it was pure bred in me. I believe I was born with it.

DEA Feds are just like us cops, but they feel they are superior. They aren't overly educated like FBI agents. They aren't smooth and smart like Treasury agents, and they aren't sophisticated like CIA agents. They present a false persona, that they are the top of the food chain in Federal Law Enforcement. This causes distrust amongst local law enforcement because we as cops read people for a living. We know what we see. It is one of our most revered traits.

Cops know nuts when we see them. We can walk into a room and without fanfare, spot a troubled individual. It is what keeps us alive, because mostly what cops do is go into people's homes and try to help them solve their problems.

We don't go uninvited. We answer our police radio when someone calls to report a domestic dispute. When we walk in we nonchalantly look around and we catalogue, subconsciously, who and what the dangers are to us.

So when we come into contact with a federal drug agent, with their winking eyes, and toothy smiles, we local cops put up our guard. And when you get to know the agent, and maybe drink a beer with him, after two beers he or she starts talking you and your department down, and talking themselves and the Drug Enforcement Administration up. They start by talking about pay.

Feds make more money than local cops. That's a fact, but who cares? The local cops don't care. We can work overtime, or a second job and make federal-type cash. And drug agents are always acting like they want to sell you something. They are used car dealers with federal credentials and a gun.

It sends up an alert for a local cop. "Danger, nut in presence. Take precaution." It's just like going into a domestic disturbance home where the male is drunk and the female has a mouse under her eye. You know you're going to have to fight the drunk.

DEA guys and gals are part of the Department of Justice, just like the FBI, but they, as agents, are fearful of that agency. They are the little brothers of the FBI. They fear the FBI is constantly monitoring them: listening to their telephone calls, reading their reports, auditing their cash seizures, interviewing their informants, placing agents under surveillance, and they have reason for their paranoia. The FBI is monitoring them, constantly.

Cops have names for the people they hate. Internal Affairs Division investigators are referred to as creeps, snitches, back-stabbers. DEA folks refer to FBI folks as Feebs, and they usually spit on the ground when the say it.

This morning was lecture time for Detective Ray Arnold and it reminded me of junior high school. I had the same numb feeling in my gut telling me I had to conform and do what I was told or the new infraction would be stacked upon my East side curse dossier and used against me in this life and the next one.

I was sitting in the office of DEA group supervisor, Special Agent Doc Penrose, and he was lecturing me on the perils of being a federal drug agent. My head was pounding from the beating I had taken the night before, and I was groggy, adjusting an ice-pack on my puffed up face, drifting in and out and having a difficult time focusing on Doc's drone about team-playing and the DEA creed, "All for one and one for all."

I was watching two television screens; one with Doc preaching, and one with my old neighborhood in the East side. My left eye was watching the neighborhood and my right eye was watching Doc. And while this was transpiring my inner eye was walking to the elevator in the police headquarters in downtown. The brain is so fragile.

"The problem with you is that you're an individual," he droned on. "We don't have individuals here at DEA, we work as a team." I had had brain concussions on and off during my youth, usually inflicted by an enraged parent or school teacher and I knew the symptoms. Inability to focus was just one of the problems.

When your brain is damaged, one doesn't concentrate on the intricate things needed to learn. Instead, the injured brain reverts to the basic instinct of survival, and the victim delves deeply into the persona of the person, or group who inflicted the injury upon him.

I blamed Doc Penrose for the beating. I was too old for the DEA Task Force. I was older than Doc, and I was slightly younger than the Special Agent in charge, the one they referred to as the SAC. But I had burned out in homicide, and there was no other place for the chief to put me.

It was a strange little drug deal. The kind DEA folks do all of the time, and get away with. I was with the other task force guys and gals, but Doc conveniently wasn't there. I wondered about his absence, but it was none of my business. My business was to do three years in the task force and then take a retirement from the police department. It's what I had scheduled for myself and I wasn't going to be dissuaded by a brain concussion. I had had worse experiences. My brain would heal, and my face would go back to normal in a couple of weeks. Right now I looked and felt terrible.

Nausea is one of the side effects of brain damage, and as I watched Doc and listened to his drone, I felt like I was going to vomit on his desk. But I didn't. Instead, I dissected him as an individual. Tall, about thirty five, full head of hair. A big guy and an ambitious Federal Agent. A federal bureaucrat on the fast track. He was married and had kids, but he was a womanizer and he didn't try to hide it. There was a picture of him and his wife and kids on a shelf behind him, and there was a picture of him and his younger girlfriend beside it. Obviously his wife didn't visit him at the office.

Doc droned on about DEA and the police department and how we are trained to be individuals at the P.D. because we are alone so much of the time patrolling in one-man cars and how different it is here at the task force. "We are brothers in arms here."

He was selling me a used Porsche, and I was obliged to make him think that I wanted to buy it. He was my supervisor, conning and pimping me in the Federal way. If I had let him know that I knew the drill, and that I was as educated as he was and much more aware, I would be on his hit list for my duration at DEA.

I had been on his hit list, and I had suffered the consequences. Someone had told him I wasn't a team player. It was a congenital problem. It was the kiss of death in DEA. As Doc pimped me my mind drifted back to the day before, where this saga began. I had just gotten back from DEA school in Kansas City.

The DEA offices were in fashionable Clayton, the business hub of the metropolitan area. It was all class, beautiful women, great restaurants, and the offices were in a bank building, a new structure of chrome and glass and architecturally perfect. Things downtown were archaic, and so was police headquarters.

I had been in homicide for too long, about fifteen years. Homicide gets everybody sooner or later, and I admit it got me. I started getting too involved in my cases. I was taking them personally, and that is something you can't do in a high-stress cop investigative job. You have to take them one at a time and then allow them to slip away if there's no way to solve them.

I wasn't doing that. I had a case I had dwelled on. A gorgeous young woman killed downtown. She had been abducted, abused, raped, murdered, and dumped back out onto the streets. There was no DNA, no witnesses, no evidence.

I had taken this murder home with me. My live-in cop girlfriend, Gloria, who was constantly monitoring me, picked up on my obvious dilemma. "You need a different assignment," she said.

The victim was blonde, and her blue eyes were staring at me as I rolled her over to examine her wounds. She had been beaten to death, blunt trauma caused by someone's big fists.

I've got this thing for beauty, a fixation with it. A beautiful woman is sacred to me, something to be worshiped, placed on a pedestal. When beauty is abused, I get strange. The guy who did that to her enjoyed it. He used her as a human punching bag after he had his way with her.

I vowed to myself that I would even the score for her. Her big blue eyes asked me to get revenge for her and I told her I would. Being talked to by stiffs is the first sign that you need to get out of homicide. Answering them is the second, and making a pact with them is the third. The chief sent me to the DEA Task Force.

Gloria, AKA Big-Boned Gloria, my cop girlfriend, had been studying me too closely, and I could tell she didn't like what she had seen. My obsession with the murder of the young woman turned Gloria off. She was twenty years younger than me, and there had always been a generation gap. Now the gap was as wide as the Mississippi River.

But I had been through romances with scores of women, and they always ended the same way. Penetrating stares, looks of distrust, dissatisfaction. Eventually, they move out of my house with the view of the Mississippi, and I continue on with my meager existence as a cop investigator with my dog, Tyrone. You can trust a dog.

Gloria came along at the right time for me. She was as solid as a rock, big breasts, shoulders, buttocks, and strong as a man. And she didn't have any fat on her; she wasn't gross to look at in the nude; in fact she was beautiful, in a large way.

I had liked her for about six months, and we were great in bed, and out of bed, but the end was near. I knew it. She wasn't happy about the DEA transfer. I think she wanted me to take an office job. I'm not that type of a cop!

I continued to backtrack as Doc droned on, selling me used Porsches. "There's a deal tonight," Doc had told me on the previous day. "There's a deal almost every night. You casual with that?"

"Yeah," I said smiling and watching.

"You'll need a car," he continued. He tossed me a set of keys. "It's a red Corvette Roadster. It's parked in the garage, level three. It's where we park. It's the United States

Government's garage." He watched my every move, and I watched him.

"You can roam around today and get to know the group. We've got cops and Special Agents. You'll get the hang of it. Weird hours, weird dope dealers. Be prepared for tonight. It's a buy bust and we need every hand we can get. That's all."

A large-breasted, creamy red-head named Carla showed me to my desk. I sat there all morning, trying to make eye contact with some of the city officers. I got the cold shoulder. The special agents ignored me, too. I got up, went to the garage, and located the Corvette. I cranked it and drove around for four hours.

It was early spring in St. Louis, but the weather hadn't broken into warmth. It was the growing season; rain at night and sun during the day, but chilly.

I had high anticipation about the changing of the season. I could see the green sprigs coming out on the trees, and there were patches of green on the ground, but there would be another hard freeze and all of the spring vegetation would die. It was Mother Nature's way of letting us know she could kill us whenever she wants.

The heat would be here soon. I had a casual lunch, then went back to the office. I sat there in limbo for another hour. Doc came in and addressed the group.

I regressed into flashback land. "It's a simple little buy bust," Doc began. "TFD Carl Robinson is the undercover. He'll be wired and we'll all be listening to him on channel three. Be in the downtown area in one hour and monitor channel three. Any questions?"

No one asked any so I didn't either. Doc walked out and everybody else made moves toward the door. Fat TFD Clete Jones walked by my desk and sneered at me. He was a city cop like me, and I had worked with him before in City

Intelligence. He had always been overweight, but he was past redemption now. He must have been three-hundred pounds, and it wasn't muscle.

There were a few other cops in the group I had had contact with throughout the years, but none I had ever considered as friends. Most of the rest were real young, early twenties, and from different departments than mine. I felt out of place.

We all headed downtown in our DEA-seized cars: Caddies, Corvettes, Lincolns, customized pickup trucks talking to each other via the two-way DEA secure radio, and calling each other on cell phones upon request. It was cold and dark, and I thought about the Mammas and the Papas singing "California Dreaming."

"Mamma's been dead for thirty-years," I mumbled to myself. I shook it off. We rode around in circles, block after block while one of the young-looking cops set up a meeting with a dope dealer.

"Go to channel B," a voice said on the DEA radio, so I changed the channel and listened. The deal was going on in Carl Robinson's "G" car right in front of me on a closed gas station parking lot. I parked on the street, watched and listened.

TFD Carl Robinson, (Task Force Detective is what they call us) was speaking with the dope man. "Are you Bob?"

"Yeah, are you Carl?"

"Yeah! Where's the dope?"

"Where's the money?"

"I've got the money, but you're going have to show me the dope."

There was a pause. The dope man was paranoid. "How do I know you're not the cops?"

"How do I know you're not the cops?" Carl Robinson had an answer for everything.

"Show me the dope and I'll show you the money."

"Here's the dope, but you can't have it until you give me the money."

"Here's the money."

"Here's the dope."

"It's as good as gold," Carl said. "You're under arrest, DEA."

The dope man jumped out of Carl's G car and ran toward a White Castle on Broadway. Monica Rose, a DEA Special Agent, ran him down and tripped him up. He went down face first. TFD Pat Brown and I had been running after Monica while she was pursuing the dope man. We jumped on him and handcuffed him behind his back, hoisted him up and waited for someone to bring a conveyance to our location.

We were at the rear of a closed tire business, in the dark, huffing and puffing in the chilly damp weather. Pat Brown started beating the handcuffed prisoner with his fists about the midsection.

"You filthy dope-dealing bastard," Pat said, "don't you ever run from the cops again." Pat had taken the wind out of the prisoner with the beating, but the dope-dealing miscreant wasn't objecting to the beating. It was as if he figured he deserved it. A nondescript cargo van pulled up and we tossed the federal prisoner into it and climbed in after him.

I observed Clete waddling up to the van through the porthole window. He tapped on the door, we opened it and he climbed inside. He slapped the disheveled Italian-looking dope man, forward and backhand, then choked him a little, just to get his attention.

"Who are you selling the dope for?"

"Phil Williams," the dope man mumbled.

"You've got only one minute to decide if you want to spend fifteen years in jail or fifteen months in jail." He was timing him with his wristwatch.

"Fifteen months," the dope man said.

"Where is Phil Williams?"

"At a downtown hotel, Fourth & Washington, Trader Vic's, waiting for me to bring the eight-thousand dollars to him."

TFD Carl Robinson tapped on the door, I slid it open and he climbed in. "He's gonna make a controlled delivery for us," Clete advised Carl. The inept dope dealer stared at Carl's boyish face in disbelief. Clete got on the air and advised the cops and agents.

"Trader Vic's Hotel, Fourth and Washington, presidential suite." I climbed out and got into the Corvette. "We're all going to meet at Fourth and Washington," Agent Mike Schweig repeated with authority. "Park your G cars and meet in the hallway of the fifth floor."

I drove to Fourth and Washington, parked the Corvette, and slowly walked to the lobby of the hotel. I was mentally dissecting the impending deal. Why would one person have the presidential suite? We didn't have enough manpower for this deal.

I was carrying my trusty 357 Smith & Wesson, which has saved my life on two separate occasions, my Susan gun, named after an old girlfriend. The agents were carrying Glock, semi-automatics. I reluctantly took the elevator to five and met up with the troops.

They had their pistols out and were lining the walls on both sides of the presidential suite. Carl Robinson was checking the wire on the dope man and giving him last-minute instructions as he handed him the eight thousand dollars, wrapped in a ball with rubber bands about the size of a softball.

"Go directly to Phil Williams and say, 'Here is the money I got for selling the coke for you.' That way it'll be recorded and the United States Attorney will realize you've cooperated with us. Got it?"

The dope man, who acted like a man who was taking his first parachute jump at thirty-thousand feet with a parachute that his girlfriend's ex-boyfriend had packed, nodded in acknowledgment.

I kept my 357 in my waistband and got in line behind the door. I could feel the tension and animosity directed at me, from the other cops, mixed with the danger of the deal. I was the outsider, the new guy, and I didn't like the feeling. I didn't like surprises either. Cops weren't supposed to be surprised. Surprise in law enforcement equates to death.

The dope man banged on the door. It opened with the blare of hard rock. The room was soundproof, a surprise for us. The door was standing wide open; forty partying, dancing, coke-snorting weirdos stared at our little band of undercover cops standing in the hallway. A small surprise for them. A big surprise for us.

Carl Robinson pushed the dope man into the suite and we all stormed in shouting, "DEA, GET DOWN, GET DOWN. GET YOUR HANDS BEHIND YOUR HEADS." The softball of cash went flying into the room as I pulled my lucky three-fifty-seven and scanned the room for weapon-wielding dopers.

A large man covered with tattoos and obviously mentally incapacitated by drug ingestion sneered at me with his hands in the air. Agent Mike Schweig shouted, "ON THE WALL, EVERYBODY ON THE WALL." Some were face-first on the floor, some were grabbing the walls; all were confused.

It was a typical cocaine and booze party, men and women, rich and poor, ignorant and educated, professional and blue collar. Everybody was stoned. There was powder cocaine and shooters, metal tubes dopers use to snort dope into their noses, on the modern glass tabletops; and weed and hashish tossed around the room.

They all had the look of Satan in their eyes as they stared at us and slowly went to the walls with their hands up. The large tattooed man grabbed my 357 and tried to wrestle it from me.

I grabbed him by the throat and squeezed his larynx with my left hand as I snatched the little weapon away from him. I felt stupid for playing the federal gun game, but when in Rome. I got my handcuffs on the stoned muscleman and stuck my 357 back into my waistband.

I suddenly recognized the muscled dope man who I had just gotten the handcuffs on. He was a teamster nose-bender and leg-breaker, a semi-pro boxer and a professional bad-ass. His job in the teamsters was to intimidate whomever didn't go along with the ruling local six-hundred leaders, and to beat them if intimidation didn't work. I had interviewed him before. We knew each other and we were enemies.

That is the problem with being a cop for so many years in a town like St. Louis. Everybody you come into contact with knows you for life. They never forget a cop investigator. They remember your name, where you are assigned, and what your specialty is.

At the time of our first interaction, I was a detective in Intelligence, working organized crime. He was a person of interest. He recognized me immediately, but it took me a couple of minutes to identify him. It is why he grabbed my gun. He wanted to kill me with it.

Special Agent Ross Milton, who held the responsibility for the eight-thousand dollars of federal cash, made the first query. "Where's the money?"

The TFD's and the agents made see-no-evil, hear-no-evil moves and milled around the room looking under furniture and searching the stoned party monsters. Ross

Milton held a huddle in the middle of the room, one that I wasn't invited to attend.

"We're going to strip search every person in this room if somebody doesn't come up with the cash," he announced. "And we're going to start with the women." The stoned dopers mumbled to each other; the stoned females whimpered; the muscled tattooed man turned around and sneered at me and the other cops and agents.

I could see the wheels turning in Ross Milton's eyes. He could see the hate in the eyes of the big man. "What's your name?" Ross asked him.

"Phil Williams," the big man spat out.

"TFD Arnold, bring him back to the bedroom," he said to me with truculence.

Agents Monica Rose and Mike Schweig intelligently chose to guard the stoned party monsters while the rest of the crew retreated to the bedroom with me and Phil Williams, who was handcuffed behind his back. Ross Milton and Carl Robinson were exchanging glances. Clete was standing in the shadows. Pat Brown stood at the door. Ross was smiling and glancing at me.

Ross Milton and Carl Robinson beat the muscle-man Phil Williams with their fists and feet. They beat him like he was a punching bag in a YMCA gym until he could hardly stand. He was bent over and spittle was coming out of his mouth. "Carl, take the handcuffs off of him," he said in a low animalistic tone. Carl complied.

Phil Williams was like an unleashed wild animal as he turned toward Ross and Carl. They stiff armed him, simultaneously sending all 250 pounds of him to me. I tried to fend him off, but he was on me like a werewolf on a streetwalker, pounding and tearing and swinging wildly.

He caught me with a solid right cross and sent me reeling toward the king-size bed. I landed with force and bounced off and landed on the carpet. He was on me, pounding my face and trying to choke me. I covered up and waited for the beating to stop, or to lose consciousness, or to have my alleged compatriots pull the stoned giant off of me. Finally, he was off of me and I was standing, blurry eyed and wobbly kneed, with no punch left.

They had him down on his back by the door. Pat Brown and Carl Robinson were stomping him and pistol-whipping his face between kicks and stomps. Agent Ross Milton and TFD Clete Jones stood back and watched. I grabbed the house phone and beat him on the face when I could get to him. The phone disintegrated in my hand after about four licks. He was trying to stand and fight to the death; he got to his knees and took the punishment rendered, just like I did when he was beating me on the carpet, but there was nobody to save him. I started beating him with my fists, because I knew what was coming. Somebody was going to put a bullet in Phil Williams' brain on this fine night, justifiably.

Carl Robinson had my handcuffs. He knelt with his knees on the giant's back and handed them to me. I got one handcuff back on his right wrist and pulled on it hard. It knocked his face down onto the carpet as I forced it behind his back. Pat Brown got a cuff on his left wrist and jerked; we had his hands cuffed behind his back again. He was back on his knees with his face in the carpet getting kicked and pistol-whipped and stomped. "ENOUGH," I shouted, 'HE'S DOWN, STOP!"

Agent Ross Milton calmly walked to the living room and dialed 911 on the suite telephone. EMS showed up in ten minutes. Phil Williams was down, but not out. He was breathing like a wounded Tiger, shot but not killed, his breath gurgling, covered with blood. The medic glanced at him. "Who shot him?"

"He wasn't shot," I replied, "just beaten."

Agent Monica Rose walked back to the bedroom. “Here’s the money. A guy out here had it stuck in his sock,” she said as she tossed it to Ross Milton. She gave me the once-over, took my arm, and led me to the bathroom. My nose was bent sideways and my face was starting to swell. I could feel my eyes closing and my face getting thick. My lips felt like I had golf balls under them.

Monica made an ice-pack out of a bath towel and handed it to me. I stayed in the bathroom applying the ice-pack. I glanced out, watched, listened as Clete and Agent Ross Milton kibitzed about the turn of events. They were happy, whispering to each other. TFD’s Carl Robinson and Pat Brown looked concerned, like they had done something they felt guilty about, but they had no other choices.

I looked at my nose in the mirror, bleeding and crooked. I blew real hard in a towel and twisted it back into shape. It made a terrible sound, but the bleeding stopped and the nose looked straight.

I glanced at Phil Williams as they were wheeling him out on a stretcher. He was going to die. Humans aren’t made to take beatings like that, but I had taken a good beating, and I was standing and walking and talking. I wasn’t dying on this night! You didn’t get Ray Arnold tonight.

But why were they trying to get me maimed or killed? The night was full of surprises. The biggest surprise was on my compatriots. I didn’t die. I didn’t run. I wasn’t leaving.

Monica Rose escorted me out of the hotel and placed me in the front seat of her Lexus G car. We drove to Barnes Hospital, a place I’m familiar with, where I was told to “Take aspirin,” and continue to pack your face in ice.

I was happy to leave the emergency room and happy to be alive. I’d had some close calls in the past year and I was questioning my mortality. Maybe it was time for me to retire. Big-Boned Gloria thought it was.

Monica drove me back to the Corvette. "Don't come back to work until your face is normal." She kissed me on my swollen lips before I climbed out of her Lexus which I thought was strange, but she is a pretty gal with a killer body, and I liked her.

I climbed into the Corvette and headed south, driving through slits and blurs and taking my time, thinking about Gloria. I wasn't sure how she was going to take this turn of events. She had been a uniform cop for five years. Uniform cops are there for each other. Rarely does one of them get beat up.

I guided the Corvette through the pin oaks to my secluded home overlooking the Mississippi River and St. Clair County, Illinois, and parked in the circular drive in front of the house. I climbed out, unlocked the front door and walked in with the ice pack on my face.

I watched Gloria through the slit of my right eye. She was dressed for speed, see-through gown, no bra or panties, smiling. The smile stopped as she studied me. "What happened to your face?"

"I got beat up at work," I mumbled.

She pulled my hand and ice pack away from my mug which was about the size of a soccer ball, and gasped as she backed away. "Who did this to you?"

"Dope dealer."

"Where were the other detectives, didn't they help you?"

"No. Not at first. Not until I was beat up."

She led me into the kitchen and sat me at the kitchen table and stared. "I need some fresh ice in this pack." I handed it to her. She poured the water out and refilled it with cubes and handed it back to me. Tyrone, my blue eyed mastiff, Siberian husky came up to me and whined as I petted him.

I had to let this play out, see where it was going, where it was going to end. She was recoiling from me, repulsed at the sight of my smashed face. I thought back to Special Agent Monica Rose, a black woman. The woman who had kissed me on the lips just twenty minutes earlier. The culture gap was as wide as the Mississippi River from St. Louis to St. Clair County.

"Is it like this a lot? I've heard narcotics work was the most dangerous." Gloria was speaking in the little girl tone that she used when she was stressed or conniving. It was erotic to me and I loved it. It made the strapping sexy woman seem vulnerable.

"It can be."

"But you're an investigator," she exclaimed, a senior officer. Shouldn't you be insulated from the violence?"

"No one is insulated from violence. This thing tonight? It could have been an initiation. I'm new to the unit. Or, maybe somebody was trying their best to get me killed or maimed. I'm not sure why it happened."

She got up from the table and climbed the ladder to the loft. I stood and let Tyrone out the slider and watched the lights of the tows going up and down the Mississippi, fifty yards below my yard. Gloria came down and was dressed in Levis and a sweat shirt. "Are you going back there?" she asked.

"Yes."

"When?"

"Tomorrow." I was trying to smile but couldn't get it done. I pushed harder on the ice pack.

"Must you return to federal narcotics?"

"Yeah. That's where I'm assigned; it's where the Chief of Police sent me."

"For how much longer?"

"I'm not sure yet. Probably three years."

"Will you retire after that?"

"Maybe."

She was trying to look into my eyes but the swelling wouldn't allow it. "Ray, I'm going to my mother's for a couple of days." She dropped it like a hot potato and stared for effect. "You aren't angry, are you?"

"No, Gloria," I mumbled and pushed the ice pack into my face.

"Call me in a couple of days, would you, Ray? We can talk then. I want you to retire, Ray. I don't want us to go through this anymore. I can still be a cop, but I don't want you to be one."

She grabbed her leather coat out of the closet and sailed out of the room. I heard the front door open and close and her Mustang starting. She was gone. No surprise for Detective Ray Arnold. I'd been through it with every lover. Sometimes they come back, sometimes they don't. At least I still have half of my life, Tyrone. I shook off the flashback and tried to act like I cared about Doc's DEA spiel.

Doc had been droning on for the past two minutes while I regressed in concussion-land. He didn't know I had been mentally dilly-dallying. I figured he had never been a recipient of brain trauma.

"You've got some big shoes to fill, TFD Arnold. TFD Jack Parker was one of our best TFD's. All I ask of you, TFD Arnold, is to go out there," he used his thumb as a pointer, "and to be one of the boys. Can you do that?"

Jack Parker, the missing cop. I had heard of his disappearance. So, I was taking his place. Doc was intently waiting for my answer. Any answer other than, "yes," would mean the end to my DEA experience. I was compelled to commit my allegiance to the group, and to DEA. "Yes," I sincerely replied.

Doc stood and smiled, then offered me his hand. That was a cue that the meeting was over. I stood, shifted the ice-pack to my left hand, wiped my right hand onto my Levis, and shook hands with Doc. He sat back down and put his head down to study a report as I wandered out into the open office and plopped down at my desk.

All eyes were on me. I was the transfer kid, the one who‘d gotten beaten up on the playground by the schoolyard bully, after I was lured by the other kids to a part of the playground where the teachers couldn’t see me being beaten.

I was supposed to forgive and forget. Maybe I could do it. Maybe not. Only time would tell.

2

Carla, the task force secretary, was walking to her desk checking her wristwatch. The rest of the special agents and TFD's were sitting at their desks with laptops opened and waiting like students in an entry level computer class for the instructor to tell them to begin. All eyes were on me as I sat the ice-pack on my desk and opened my laptop, waiting for the command.

"We have a lot of work to do this morning," Carla said with her large breasts swaying and her red hair tossed back as she spoke. "As usual, I will monitor you all. You may begin."

She walked over to me, bent over at the waist and whispered in my ear, "Not today TFD Arnold." She closed my lap top and took my ice-pack, then walked out of the office. She returned in three minutes and handed me the ice-pack filled with fresh ice.

The others were banging on their computers with their heads bent down. I looked across the room, about forty feet away. There was a gorgeous young woman, and she wasn't typing. She was a classy Hispanic with a tan, dark shoulder-length hair, Levis, and a sweatshirt.

She moved with grace as she adjusted items on her desk and opened her laptop. She glanced at me and saw me catch her looking. She didn't roll her eyes; she was sure of herself and her glance turned into a stare.

I blinked and looked down at my desk top then looked back up at her. She recognized my insecurity and smiled. My heart was pounding. I had always had a weakness for Hispanic women. There is a mystery to them I cannot resist. She got up and walked out of the office.

She was in shape like a body builder. V-shaped upper body with no bulges. I watched her derriere swing as she walked away from me and visualized those long lovely muscles that women get when they work out rippling under her soft, moist bronze skin. She was tall, about five-ten I guessed, and she walked like a gymnast at a meet, with long flowing graceful movements.

I got friendly vibes from this beautiful mystery woman, so I pushed away from my desk, stood and headed for the door after her with the ice pack at my face. I walked by Carla. She put her hand out for me to stop. I took it as if I was going to shake hands with her. She stood, came around the desk and got real close to me. “You okay?”

“Yeah!”

She touched the exposed half of my swollen face and went back to her chores. I walked out, searching for the mystery Chicano. I checked the lounge but the Hispanic beauty wasn’t there so I walked out of the offices and made the short trek to the Club, the restaurant-bar where the special agents, the TFD’s and the office workers hung out. I had heard about it from some of the detached cops. It was the in-place in Clayton.

She was sipping a cup of coffee at the bar and watching as I walked in as if she knew I would follow her. The place had just opened; it was just us and the barmaid and the morning bar stench of spilled booze and rotting citrus products. “Black coffee,” I said as I sat next to her.

“I’m Ray Arnold.” I offered her my hand, “I haven’t had the pleasure.”

She gave me the once over and giggled as she firmly took my hand. I was instantly mesmerized. Her teeth were perfect and glowing like a screen star. She had dimples when she laughed and she tossed her hair back like all gorgeous women do when they’re interested.

“I know who you are, Ray Arnold, everybody in the St. Louis field office knows you TFD Ray Arnold. How are you feeling?"

I watched her as she sipped before answering. "I'm fine. I mean, the swelling is going down and the soreness is leaving. I'm having trouble focusing, but the nausea is starting to subside. I'll be alright. I tossed the ice pack onto the bar."

There was a lull in the conversation as we sipped hot coffee and watched each other. "I'm Special Agent Heidi Anderson," she said with a smile.

I shook her hand again, "Why haven't I seen you before? You weren't here yesterday."

"I've been down south on an undercover assignment. I've been in town for a while, but I just got back to work."

"Is that where the tan came from?"

"Yes," she said tossing her hair back again, "I take the sun very easily, I tan quickly, and I keep it."

"You look Hispanic, Anderson, what's up with that?"

"My dad is German American, my mother is Puerto Rican." She paused and looked at me through the bar mirror. "We should get back. I don't want to upset Carla."

I had a good impression from her, not just because of her good looks, or her charm. She reeked of sincerity. She was sincere when she said she didn't want to upset Carla, the task force secretary. I was wondering if she was the one I could communicate with in this strange world of violence, conspiracies, and missing city cops. I needed to get into my agenda, and I didn't want to be clumsy doing so.

"I noticed the empty desk across the room. I wondered whose it was. I guess it was yours. For a while I figured it was TFD Jack Parker's desk. I heard he vanished into thin air."

It came out clumsy, but there was no other way to get into the subject of a missing young narcotics detective cop on loan to the federal government. She studied me for a millisecond and shot down the last drop of coffee in her cup, then smiled at me as the bar maid refilled it.

"No, you took Jack's desk, and yes he did disappear, but probably not into thin air. Everybody in the St. Louis field office thinks he's probably on a beach with a large-breasted blonde drinking himself into oblivion."

"Oh," I mumbled. "Was he a big womanizer?"

"Oh, yeah, and a big drinker, too." She was smiling again and I was staring like a lovesick kid.

"Why run away? Couldn't he practice that lifestyle while he was actively assigned to the Drug Enforcement Administration?"

"Yeah, I guess he could have. But there's no beach in St. Louis. He loved the ocean and the beach and I know for a fact he was stressed to the max. He had too many women, too many beers, and too many cases. The lifestyle eventually destroys you if you don't have an out. His was the beach so we all surmise he went to the beach. There's no other logical explanation."

"Oh," I replied with a puzzled look.

"The cases devour you. When you start a case it controls you until the last bad guy is arrested. Even then, you have federal court to contend with, and with big wealthy dope dealers, the kind we take off, court is no picnic. These multi-millionaire dopers hire the best attorneys money can buy. The case always involves a confidential informant, and we have to deal with them. We have to protect them, pay them, deal with their relatives, hide them. They're a pain in the ass, but without them there would be no cases."

"I get it," I reluctantly said. She paused and studied me.

"You think you get it. You don't have an understanding of the drug culture yet. The TFD's are undercover cops, and eventually the dirt of the job rubs off on them. The other guys and most of the agents truly believe that Jack made a big score and instead of sharing it with his pals, he just disappeared. That's a druggie mind-set; it's putting the square block into the square hole."

"Oh, yeah," I mumbled to show her I was interested in her observation.

"It's the logical thought process for somebody in this business, and it's safe to assume. That way life goes on as usual. The guys work hard for Doc because he allows them to do their own thing. Doc is interested in career enhancement. Washington checks on the statistics of every DEA group on a regular basis. This task force has the highest statistics, arrests, money seized and vehicles seized. We're the best, statistically. That means soon, Doc will be promoted and move on in his career. He can attribute his success to the hard work of the TFD's."

"So what happens to the TFD's?" I asked.

"They eventually burn out, get sent back to the P.D., become depressed, and quit law enforcement, or disappear like Jack Parker," she replied. "Doc doesn't even like them. He just knows how to manipulate them and get the most out of them. That's what DEA is about. It's what we are trained to do with informants and it's a natural thing to do with the TFD's. Is it wrong? Yeah, it's wrong, but it happens. Special Agents build their federal careers on the premise of manipulation."

We paused and drank coffee. I continually glanced at her through the bar mirror. She had it all, looks, smarts, moxie.

"So, tell me, has anyone heard from Jack Parker? Is he still alive?" She didn't answer immediately. She sipped coffee and coyly glanced back at me. I wondered if she was thinking about me like I was thinking about her. I was the opposite of her. Too old for this job, damaged, confused and alone in a new and dangerous environment.

"No, nobody that I am aware of. These guys are as thick

as thieves, pardon the pun. I would think they'd know where he is, but I've been gone for a month, so I really wouldn't know for sure. His G car was found down in the city, by the Mississippi, near the President Casino, parked on the cobblestones. His dad's a retired cop and he works as a security guard at the casino. It's your G car now, the red Corvette."

"So, I inherited his desk and his G car?"

"Yeah."

The bar maid re-filled our cups again as we continued to shoot glances at each other through the bar mirror. There was a lull in the conversation and I was mentally dissecting her statements about the task force. "We have the highest statistics?"

"Yeah," she said watching me, then diverting her eyes.

"Doc manipulates them?" It was an honest question; she'd started with the manipulation aspect of law enforcement. She didn't answer. "In order to manipulate someone you must have something that the person or group being manipulated desires." She studied me and sipped coffee.

"You've never worked drugs before, have you?"

"No."

"Have you ever been undercover?"

"No," I muttered.

"Drug dealers have cash to burn. They don't work for it, it's easy come, easy go. These young cops are supposed to be acting like drug dealers in order to catch drug dealers. That's the persona they need in order to perform for Doc. It takes cash to act like you're rolling in drug proceeds. The federal government isn't going to give a bunch of young cops carte-blanche to spend money on booze and broads. Doc makes sure the TFD's are happy. The final product is high stats and an illustrious federal career for the group supervisor, the ASAC and SAC. They only care about their careers. They wouldn't give a TFD a ride to the hospital if his mother was on her death bed."

I covered my puffed up face with my swollen hands and moaned. I was too old to be in this unit. I wondered why the chief had sent me here. "What about the other special agents? The ones in the other groups. Do they know what is going on?"

"In the task force?"

"Yeah."

"Hell yeah," she replied. "We all just sit back and watch the show. We get good stats and good reviews from Doc, our group leader. For the guys who are on the government fast track, it's a for-sure promotion. A lot of the guys and gals just want to get to GS-thirteen, the journeyman grade, and stay in the same field office for as long as they can. St. Louis is a good place to be assigned. Real estate is reasonable here and it's a good place to raise your children. We all reap the benefits, but it causes a rift between the special agents and the TFD's. The agents despise most of the cops. They consider them thieves and ne'er-do-well's, even though they live off of their stats. Doc hates all of you guys! He wouldn't admit it, but he does."

There was another lull. I wondered why she gave me the task force scenario. But it is typical in this business. Everyone has an opinion of their associates, usually a jaundiced opinion. She gave me her opinion as a Special Agent in the Drug Enforcement Administration, clear and simple.

She was staring at me inquisitively, not through the mirror. The straight-line questions were forthcoming. She was an investigator. It's what good investigators do, start with small talk, and then get down to business with straight-line questions. A blind person could tell I wasn't the typical candidate for TFD status. "Why are you here Ray Arnold?"

I didn't answer her. She was using physiognomy to categorize me. I use it daily; every investigator does.

"Why leave homicide to come to DEA? Did you burn out? Is this a management ploy to get you back into the rhythm? Is it a case that haunts you, Ray Arnold? What is it?"

"All of the above."

"Tell me about the case, Ray."

"Why?" I was staring back at her, trying to keep her at bay. I didn't want her getting inside on me, but I didn't want to lose her either. I had to respond or she would be gone. It's got to be a truthful response or I lose her, for good. She's smart.

"A waitress, a downtown waitress. Blonde, young, just twenty, almost angelic with her creamy features and perfect bone structure. Sexually assaulted, beaten to death. Tossed to the side of the road like a piece of trash. No witnesses. No evidence. Tip money in her pocket. That's where it started. I needed to solve it and I didn't. It began there and spiraled to here. That's it."

"Was her name Lynn Stewart?"

She had thrown cold water in my face with the question. How could she have known that? Why would she follow the crime stories in the city so closely? Why would she remember the victim's name? "How did you know her name?" I coldly asked.

"Newspaper, Ray. And when I'm out of town, I use the internet. I read all of the major publications daily. I like being informed, and I have a great memory."

The lunch trade started drifting in, secretaries with their bosses, secretaries with their boyfriends, secretaries with secretaries. Some enchantingly made up and dressed to draw attention, a few who were mediocre, the majority outstanding. They were the graceful wildlife at the watering hole, enticing and vulnerable as they crouched to drink from the enticing waters of the Club.

The TFD's filtered into the restaurant: brash, muscular and young with no fear. Flush with testosterone and confidence, they approached their prey, the secretaries. They handled themselves like characters in a smooth screenplay. There was the coy foreplay, the whisper in the ear of the prey and the laugh with the quick exit, the hug, the long stare, the promise to meet this evening for a friendly drink in the Club after business hours. Heidi was reading me as I watched the show. I could tell she was amused at my powers of observation.

The prey was mesmerized by the cocky young cops. The pack of dogs noticed Heidi and me at the bar and approached us. Pat Brown, the cock-sure country cop, shook my hand and hugged Heidi.

Clete Jones, the fat thief, king of the TFD's, nodded and walked by us. Bill Yocum, strong and big-boned with hands like a German carpenter, hugged me and Heidi, then moved on to a table with lonely looking ladies.

Special Agent Mike Schweig smiled and stopped as he ordered a whiskey and coke and shook like a street hobo as he drank it and tried to be friendly to me. Heidi ignored him. Carl Robinson plopped down at the stool next to me. He checked my swollen face and shook his head.

"I want to apologize. Clete told us you were a Feeb snitch. I hope you'll forget about this and let us all get on with our job, locking up dope dealers."

I didn't verbally respond. I just nodded. He offered his hand and I took it and smiled.

"What was the outcome on the Phil Williams case?" I asked.

"He's in the federal hospital in Springfield, Missouri,"

Carl replied.

"Did he come in on the big dope man?"

"Nope."

"Was he the dope man?"

"Nope, just a little puppy dog running for his master. He'll probably plead and get some time and it'll be over, if he lives. He was in critical condition for a while. Almost died on the way to the hospital."

I nodded again and watched Heidi's reflection. I liked looking at her and she knew it. The barmaid asked if we wanted lunch. We both ordered cheeseburgers and watched the show behind us through the mirror.

Doc Penrose, Special Agent Ross Milton, and group secretary Carla Copeland slowly walked in and took a table by a window at the rear of the room. They didn't acknowledge Heidi or me.

Special Agent Monica Rose came in alone and walked directly to us. She kissed me on swollen lips again and stood next to me, rubbing and touching me. Heidi gave me a weird look through the bar mirror and Monica caught it. She hugged me again and walked toward a table of cops and lonely secretaries.

I chomped my cheeseburger and watched the TFD's networking and hustling, jumping from table to table setting up the evening liaison at the Club. The lunch period was over and the restaurant emptied out, except for the DEA folks.

A big brash man sauntered in. He was foreign looking, like a Russian, but dark, with dark eyes and strong Slavic features. His hair was combed straight back and he had a big bushy mustache that came down below his bottom lip when his mouth was closed.

I watched him in the mirror…, because he was a predator. The other TFD's were also watching him. He was a body builder, and he had layers of muscle bulging under his Polo sweat- shirt. I was a body builder, also, and I knew humans didn't get that big unless they used illegal substances.

Body building is a sport, and it is fun and positive, but when a person gets obsessed with size and starts using steroids, it becomes dangerous. Not just for the body builder, but for anyone he comes into contact with. They become aggressive, almost insane. This insane mass of humanity was standing behind me, towering over my seated, aching body and staring at me. "Is this the Feeb snitch?" he loudly said.

The room became quiet. "We'll take care of you better the next time," he said and then turned and walked out of the restaurant.

I could see the TFD's in the mirror. Fat TFD Cletus Jones was trying to stifle a laugh. The other TFD's were white-faced and quiet. Doc acted like nothing happened. "What was that about?" I asked Heidi.

"Special Agent Jim Schwartz. He's from another group. He hates Feebs, and he apparently…, thinks you're friendly with them. It'll pass. Just ignore him. He was under cover with the El Foresteros in Texas for a couple of years. Their ways rubbed off on him and he can't seem to shake the persona. He loves being a one percent guy. He allowed himself to be brainwashed by the bikers."

I was feeling nauseous again. I drank a Coke, belched, then Heidi and I returned to the task force office and sat at our desks. All of the desks had new paperwork on them to be converted into federal reports, DEA six forms, surveillance reports, and informant debriefings.

I needed to get my mind off of the Jim Schwartz encounter. Doc shouldn't have allowed an agent from another group to terrorize any of his TFD's, even though I was an outcast. But he did, which meant Heidi was correct. Doc hated us.

The other TFD's and agents were also afraid of Jim Schwartz. Who wouldn't be? He was six-four, two-hundred and sixty, and crazy. Clete Jones must have told everybody in the St. Louis field office that I was an FBI snitch. He laid out the unwelcome mat for me. My day will come. Payback will be a bitch for Clete.

I told Carla I wanted to do some reports. She smiled and stacked a pile of handwritten reports on my desk that needed to be converted to official DEA six computer reports. I went through them before I started typing, and got the rhythm of what Jack Parker had been doing.

I was doing reports that the missing TFD Jack Parker should have done before he went missing. He had been a busy federal covert cop for the two years he had been here. Most of the reports were about undercover buys of more than a kilo of cocaine at a time.

It seemed unusual to me that so much cocaine is readily available in the St. Louis region. It isn't a North American product; it's grown and processed in the jungles of South America, smuggled into the country, and eventually brought to St. Louis and a thousand other cities like St. Louis.

This kid Jack Parker was buying it like candy on the streets of this fair city. Even stranger to me was the well-known fact among narcotics detectives that the illicit drugs are given in bulk to the American brokers on consignment by the drug kingpins in Colombia.

I regressed back to my homicide detective days. In so many easily solved drug-related murders, somebody screws up the dope money and there's a murder. No conversations, just a violent death. Life's a bitch and then you get murdered.

I typed into the laptop, nonstop. I finished and Carla,

standing in front of the group said in a loud clear voice, "Okay, you can close your laptops. You've been wonderful today. I thank you for catching up on these reports."

A large black man in a three-piece pin-stripe suit walked into the office, glanced at the group, and walked into Doc Penrose's office. I recognized him as the Special Agent in Charge of the St. Louis field Office, SAC Willie Mitchell. He swore me in when I first came to the unit which was just days ago. I felt like it had been months.

"Cocaine is devastating this country," he told me as he stared at me inquisitively before giving me the oath. "It affects the same part of the brain as orgasm."

He continued to stare as he raised his right hand and read the Federal oath, stopping at each sentence for me to repeat with my hand raised which declared my allegiance to the federal deity and the Drug Enforcement Administration, so help me God. He shook my hand and gave me some paper federal credentials. I read his look: physiognomy, why are you doing this?

"Square Bidness is a remarkable man," Doc Penrose said to me as we exited the office and walked toward the task force office. "Came up poor, struggled to get an education went up the ladder at DEA. Remarkable!"

"Square Bidness?"

"That's what the troops call him," Doc remarked.

"We're gonna have a pep talk," TFD Bill Yocum said. "I bet you twenty bucks that Square Bidness can't talk for more than sixty seconds before he says, Square Bidness."

"You're on," Pat Brown said.

"I want some of that," TFD Carl Robinson said.

Doc and SAC Willie Mitchell came out of Doc's office and stood in front of Carla's desk. Doc looked as if he had just been chastised. "SAC Mitchell has something to say to the group," Doc said.

"Good afternoon, ladies and gentlemen," SAC Mitchell began. "I just have a few words to relay to you all this afternoon. I want to remind all of you that safety on the job is one of our main concerns here at the St. Louis field office. We had an unfortunate incident last evening, and luckily, no one in the DEA family was seriously injured. Our mission is to incarcerate drug dealers. Our goal is to do it without any other DEA personnel being injured, and that's square bidness."

Someone started clapping and the group followed suit. Doc Penrose shook the SAC's hand and thanked him for his words of wisdom as they stood before the task force personnel, smiling and nodding. Willie Mitchell walked out of the office waving, with Doc following him as Carla closed the door.

Bill Yocum had the second hand on his wristwatch frozen and was showing it to Pat Brown and Carl Robinson. "Fifty-nine seconds, you both owe me twenty, pay up." They both tossed twenty dollar bills at him and gave him the finger as Doc came strolling back in. He stood in front of the group again and everyone stopped their grab-assing and looked at him.

"I'd like to add something to what SAC Mitchell said," Doc began. "We're all here for a purpose and that purpose is to destroy dope dealers. Thank you for your hard work." He walked into his office. The group was subdued as I walked to Heidi's desk.

Monica Rose turned on her desk radio and tuned in an oldie R&B station. Bobby Bland and BB King were singing a duet of "Let the Good Times Roll." Monica was swinging and swaying in her chair and singing along with them as the winter sun was rapidly falling, giving the office a romantic hue.

Mike Schweig pulled a bottle of bourbon out of his desk

drawer, spiked his machine Coke and ice, sipped it and smiled as he smoked a Marlboro and gyrated to the music. He was a happy guy at that moment in his life. He smiled and rubbed his hand through his sandy, combed-straight-back hair, then pulled on his face and made fish faces, pursing his lips and acting like a goldfish begging for food.

Pat Brown, the country boy nark, muscular, dark hair down to his shoulders, cheap sweatshirt, pointed-toe cowboy boots and Target jeans, sauntered over to Monica's desk and grabbed her arm to help her up.

He gently swung her and they danced to the rhythm & blues. Slowly and seductively he swung her around the carpeted office, her denim-covered bottom sashaying in our faces as we all watched the floor show. They were a contrast. White country cracker and dark city slicker. Two completely different people enjoying each other at the federal trough.

Mike Schweig killed his bourbon and Coke, butted out his Marlboro, stood, and then walked out of the office. He returned with a fresh paper cup of Coke, spiked it, sat down and fired up another Marlboro, smiling, sipping and puffing as he watched Pat Brown and Monica Rose dance around the office. He gulped it and belched and coughed, "I've got to go to the rest room," he said as he stood and walked out of the office. All eyes were on him.

Pat Brown danced over to Mike's Coke, swooped it up and danced into the undercover telephone room. He danced out in fifteen seconds zipping his fly, returned the Coke and bourbon cup to the desk and continued to dance with Monica. The song changed. T-Bone Walker was singing "Confusion" and Monica and Pat were still dancing around the room.

Mike Schweig returned and continued sipping and smoking. All eyes were still on him as he downed the drink, belched, and walked out of the office. He returned with another Coke, spiked it and fired up another Marlboro. He was making a face like a fish out of water, half-gagging and half-coughing. He turned to Ross Milton, "Did I ever tell you what my dad did for a living, Ross?"

He answered his own question before Ross could respond. "He was a dog catcher, the lowest rung on the law enforcement ladder. I'm at the pinnacle of law enforcement. It's strange the cards life deals you, isn't it?"

Ross showed his disgust with a look on his yuppie face. I could tell he didn't want to be with these misfits. He felt like he was above them. He acted the part of a Harvard graduate who had been misled at some point in his life and wound up at DEA in mediocre St. Louis.

He wore his blonde hair in a Princeton, and wore Polo sweatshirts and jeans. His Bass Weejuns had tassels on them, and even though it was eighteen degrees outside, he didn't wear socks.

"Yeah, Mike," Ross sarcastically replied. "You tell me the same story every time you get three drinks in you. If you ever tell me that story again I'm going to jump off of the roof of this building."

Mike gave Ross a cursory look. "What's up? You're upset, what's up?"

Ross handed Mike a letter. Mike read it to himself, then started smiling. He couldn't contain himself so he started laughing and guffawing. Ross was embarrassed and he covered his face with his hands and moaned. "A colonoscopy," Mike said with a guffaw.

"Give me my damn letter back, Mike." Mike shoved the letter back at him still giggling. "The damn silver Cadillac," Mike muttered, "Every DEA agent's nightmare."

"The silver Cadillac," Pat Brown shouted as he danced with Monica. "Who's getting the silver Cadillac?"

"Ross is," Mike said with a chuckle.

"Whoa," Pat Brown shouted. "That dog will hunt." He spun Monica and she came back to him and ground her thighs into his then danced away.

"I ain't interested in no silver Cadillac," Monica shouted, "I want that white Jaguar." She danced the frug and the watusi and pointed at Pat's fly.

"I was thinking," Bill Yocum said. "They never give us TFD's the silver Cadillac. What's up with that?"

"Because the government don't care if our assholes rot out and fall on the ground while we're chasing some damn dope dealer," Pat Brown said as he danced the twist and the bugaloo. "We're machines, man, not federal bureaucrats. They want cases and stats out of us, that's all. When one of your snitches gets sick, you don't pay for his doctor visit, do you?"

"Ah, no," Bill Yocum said with a stammer.

"Case in point, brother," Pat said, doing the shuffle while spinning Monica Rose.

"I've had enough," Pat said. He walked to his desk and sat down. Monica came over to his desk purring and kissed him on the neck. She straddled him in his desk chair and humped him. Pat stared at her.

"Maybe later," Monica said as she got up. "You're a good sport, Pat."

Pat stood and walked toward the door as if he was going to the rest room. He had a strange mischievous look on his face. He walked by Mike Schweig's desk as Mike was taking a long drink.

Pat's hand shot out and he had Mike's whiskey bottle. He jogged around the room holding the bottle like he was Kurt Warner at the Super Bowl, dodging tackles and scrambling. He pumped and looked out at the field.

TFD Carl Robinson was standing in the end zone, Carla's

desk. “KURT IS SCRAMBLING,” Pat shouted. “WHO IS THAT IN THE END ZONE? IT’S TASK FORCE DETECTIVE CARL ROBINSON. HE’S WIDE OPEN, KURT PUMPS AND THEN THROWS,” Pat threw the bottle at Carl who grabbed for it and touched it with his fingers knocking it goofy. He juggled it until he got it under control. “TOUCHDOWN, TOUCHDOWN,” Pat screamed as he ran around the room high-fiving the agents and TFD’s.

“If you fuckers break my whiskey bottle, I’m going to make you buy me a case of Jack Daniels,” Mike Schweig calmly said. “Place it back on my desk, please.”

“You know,” Ross said while he adjusted his ascot, “I was talking to an FBI agent before court the other day and he told me that they don’t have to get the damn silver Cadillac colonoscopy. He said DEA is the only federal agency that’s required to get it. Fucking Feebs, they always make out. DEA’s always getting fucked by them.”

“I know why,” Monica shouted. “It’s because when they hire those pricks they take out their colons and replace them with galvanized pipe. They’ve got no colons and they’ve got no souls.”

“I think I know why we have to get it,” Mike said. “DEA probably took off some Democrat’s kid whose daddy is no doubt a congressman or a senator, and the politician probably called the White House and told some damn closet Democrat up there that DEA had a case on their darling little dope dealer kid and that the agency should have to pay for this indiscretion. Then the damn under cover democrat probably said , hey, you know what? Every DEA agent should have a silver Cadillac rammed up his or her ass at least once a year. Fucking Democrats!”

“Fucking Feebs,” Monica Rose shouted.

“Fucking silver Cadillac,” Ross exclaimed.

Mike Schweig was swilling his highball chuckling and

pointing at Ross. "Silver Cadillac," he muttered, swilled, and laughed some more.

"You shouldn't be laughing at me, Mike." Ross had a smug look on his face, and he leaned back in his chair and placed his feet up on his desk.

"Oh, yeah, Cadillac man, why?"

"Because Pat Brown pissed in your drink." Mike stopped smirking, looked at his empty glass, started burping and making fish faces, stood and ran for the restroom.

3

"CLETE," Doc shouted from his corner office. Clete went bounding toward the office door like a rabid Saint Bernard, belly shaking like Jello, walked inside and closed the door. Two minutes later he strolled out with Doc behind him.

"We're all going to the Club," Doc announced, "for dinner and drinks." He was waving his arms as if he was directing traffic, motioning for us all to follow him out of the office and to the Club, which was a mere thirty feet away. Everyone complied. I brought up the rear with Special Agent Heidi Anderson.

We strolled into the Club en masse. "Table for twelve," Doc said to the hostess which was weird because there were only ten of us.

"Yes, sir, Agent Penrose," the young girl said as she rushed to the rear of the room and pulled three tables together next to a giant window with a view of downtown Clayton. We were semi- private and stumbling over each other as we all tried to figure whom to sit next to. Doc and Carla sat at the head of the table and left two empty settings between them. Heidi headed toward the other end and I followed her; the rest of the group filled in and plopped down.

"Beer," Doc ordered. The waitresses brought pitchers of draft beer and pilsner glasses and distributed them around the table. Mike Schweig, who had just returned from the restroom, started the festivities by pouring himself a glass, then pouring everybody around him a glass.

He chugged his and poured another, belched, and commented about a chili dog he'd had for lunch that upset his stomach.

I poured Heidi and me each a glass and sat back and

waited for the entertainment to play out. Menus were brought, "Order anything you want," Doc said. Most of the crew ordered steak, so I did too. Heidi ordered fish.

We ate our salads and the conversation got loud as the beer went down, and the inhibitions went with it. A pair of young ladies approached our table: a tawny blonde, semi-cute with an okay body, big boobs; and an Asian lady, probably Manchurian by the look of her.

She wore her dress to her ankles and wore no makeup. She was foreign looking, due to her demeanor, cautious and mysterious and quite beautiful in a Manchurian sort of way, alabaster skin and shiny hair, reserved and demure.

Heidi observed me watching them as they sat down, at our table after hugging Doc and smooching him. Heidi whispered in my ear, "AUSA Sue Lee, that's the Asian chick. Works for the United States Attorney's Office. She tries the dope cases the TFD's and the agents bring into the office. She's a TFD groupie. Gets the boys out of trouble when they screw up on deals which is all of the time."

"Oh, she covers for them because she likes them?" I asked.

"Yeah, something like that. Tina Monroe is the other girl, she's Doc's main squeeze."

"I saw her picture on Doc's back desk shelf. Is Doc separated from his wife?"

"No, he's big time married, with two kids," she countered.

I thought about Doc. He was a federal bureaucrat, a future leader of the war on drugs in Washington D.C., a decision-maker for the United States Government. "Is that unusual?" I muttered to Heidi.

"Not in the dope business. It's all part of the game. Tina works for Sue Lee. She's her secretary. Everything's connected in the federal government. Everybody works together and plays together. We're just a big happy family." I stared at her. She wasn't smiling. Her sarcasm came through to me.

They brought the steaks, strips with the trimmings; the clamorous conversation turned to a hum as the group devoured them. Five minutes passed and the boisterousness continued. More pitchers of beer were delivered and the group was attempting to party again. They flopped. The beer was getting warm and stale in the pitchers. Doc picked up on it. "Check please."

I tried to figure the bill in my head, I figured between three and four hundred with the tip. The waitress brought it to Doc who unabashedly handed it to his right-hand man, TFD Cletus Jones. Cletus glanced at it and rolled off six one-hundred-dollar-bills and tossed them on the table without remorse.

People were drifting away, Doc and his entourage quickly got up and exited. Clete wasn't far behind. Mike Schweig was trying to finish off the beer left in the pitchers, chugging and belching and making fish faces, then smiling and smoking his Marlboro squares.

He and the TFD's moseyed to the bar where several lovely, lonely secretaries were waiting for the ultimate party. Somebody plugged the jukebox while Pat Brown enticed a cute secretary to dance with him. The lights were low and the view was great and everyone was full of steak and beer and power.

I stood as if I was going to leave. Heidi gave me an inquisitive look so I sat back down. "Are you married, widowed or divorced?"

"Divorced," I replied.

She had a frown. "Recently?"

"God no, about twenty years ago. When I was a kid."

She kept staring at me. "You're in good shape, buffed

and firm, and you might be a good looking guy when your swelling goes down. I like your style. I just thought I'd tell you that."

"Thanks, I like your style, too."

"This is only Tuesday. We've got three more days before the weekend. I live for the weekends. What do you do on your days off, TFD Ray?"

She was staring and sizing me up, for what I wasn't sure but I was sure she was gorgeous and not a kid, either. I figured her as late thirties.

"I go to the gym some of the time. I work on my house, play with my car and my dog and I travel when I can afford it. Sometimes I play golf." I paused and she picked up on it.

"What else?"

"I go to the Art Museum," I muttered. She didn't respond and there was another pause in the conversation. "It helps me to relax," I muttered again. "I escape into the paintings and sculpture. I can actually leave my body and enter into the piece of artwork. While I'm inside, I sometimes look out and see my mortal being standing there like a stupid skin-covered mannequin. It's what we are, you know. Hunks of flesh." I told her too much about myself. I was embarrassed. She was pausing again. She studied me.

"Sounds like a plan to me," she said. "I have to go." She stood and I followed her out of the restaurant into the hallway and onto the elevator leading to the parking garage. We got off on the third floor, and she walked to a red BMW convertible. "It was nice meeting you, TFD Ray."

She offered me her hand. I took it, it was warm and dry. She was in complete control of her emotions. She looked up at me, her eyes were teasing me. I pulled her to me,she closed her eyes with her head tilted upward as I kissed her full on the mouth. She pushed her breasts into me and ground me with her hips.

Things were too perfect. The gorgeous agent was inviting me to play games with her, and we just met. The cars, the office, the Club with its view of Clayton. The scene was from a movie set so why was I thinking about Big-Boned Gloria?

Heidi felt my reluctance, turned sideways and opened the door of the Bimmer. She shot me a movie-star smile, climbed in, fired it, put it into reverse and backed out of the parking spot. She waved as she spun the tires while heading for the garage exit.

I drove home mentally dissecting the task-force experience. It appeared it was an "anything goes" atmosphere, that there was no control and few rules to worry about. Nothing like the law enforcement experience I had with the St. Louis Police Department.

The power these young cops had was scary and unhealthy. Everybody has to come down sometime. Being sent back to the police department could be traumatic. I wondered what happened to Jack Parker.

I thought about TFD Cletus Jones. He had always been my nemesis, and I knew he was unconscionable, but most cops and agents are. I had worked with him before. In the past the badge gave him a license to steal. Skim drug proceeds from one dope dealer to get to another at a higher level; righteous in theory, hideous in application.

I idled into the circular driveway in front of my old house with a view, climbed out and used the key to enter the front door. I looked out of the sliding glass door to the massive deck and saw my hound, Tyrone, climbing out of his insulated dog house with his blanket draped over his broad back. I laughed at him and opened the door. He stormed in and stood on his back legs and stared at me, eye to eye. He was smelling Heidi on me and looking confused. "I'm confused, too, old buddy."

I petted and rubbed him. "Big-Boned Gloria left us; I guess I've got a new girlfriend now."

4

I walked into the task force office and went directly to my desk and plopped down like a high school kid. It was 0845. I glanced over at Heidi's desk. She was in attendance, head down toiling over a report, banging on her laptop. She knew I was there but purposely didn't look up, I could feel it. Today was business. Last night was role playing.

Carla was standing in front of her desk, trying to act nonchalant but nervously biting her lip as she checked the clock. She was looking especially attractive this morning. Her red hair was pulled back and loosely formed into a ponytail.

She was wearing a low-cut navy blue dress, tied at the waist. Her creamy white skin shined off of it and her humongous breasts shook when she moved. The cleavage was driving me crazy and I felt conscious and embarrassed of my staring. I glanced at Heidi to see if she saw me ogling Carla.

I had always had a weakness for red-heads, but I knew deep down inside they were bad luck. She was so intense and professional. What kind of parents produce offspring like her?

She went through the same ritual every morning the holding of the picture. Everybody was in it, except me. It was taken at the Club and everybody was holding up their glasses and grinning like possums. Jack Parker was centered between Heidi, Monica Rose, Carla, and an unidentified lonely secretary. Carla would ogle it and then carefully set it back on her desk then get on with the business of the day.

They started stumbling in, Pat Brown and Monica Rose, hanging onto each other. Mike Schweig, still intoxicated, stumbling and making fish faces, wearing a tweed sport coat that I wouldn't let Tyrone lie on, and that probably came from a garage sale, plopped down at his desk and loudly moaned. Carl Robinson, Ross Milton, hung over and hurting, slowly walked to their desks, and Cletus Jones, belly shaking as he tried to look human as he walked across the floor to his desk.

Bill Yocum strolled in nodding to all of us, his big hands swinging to and fro, his iron forehead red and perspiring, a wry smile on his face, like a little boy who did something mischievous on his way to school and got away with it.

Mike Schweig climbed out of his chair, waddled to the coffee urn and drew himself a cup, returned to his desk fired up a Marlboro, smoked and sipped coffee and made fish faces. The rest of the crew made periodic trips to the coffee urn and spilled coffee on the carpet as they made their way back to their desks.

Carla was watching and waiting, allowing them to get settled before she gave the command to open their laptops. They were zombies, brain dead from partying at The Club.

"CLETUS!" Doc screamed from his office behind Carla's desk. Clete stood and clamored toward Doc's office, hesitated, and stood at the door. "We need some deals today, Clete if you want to continue with your lifestyle. The stats are down. Get moving on it."

"Yes, sir, Doc," Clete mumbled and made his way back to his desk.

He was on the telephone, calling confidential informants, demanding information, anxiously awaiting return telephone calls. He called police officers, and lawyers, and bondsmen. I knew his demeanor. In his mind the case, the deal that would satisfy Doc was in the works and would come to him through his contacts. He had connections. That's why Doc gave him "favorite-confidential-informant-with-a-badge" status.

"I have contacts. I have friends in law enforcement," I

muttered. I telephoned a sheriff in Jersey County, Illinois. "I need a drug case," I told him.

He paused. "You working drugs now?" He was in disbelief. I was the sport-coat cop detective, trendy and relaxed amidst the blood, guts, and mayhem of the little city. He was trying to picture me as a nark and it wasn't working for him.

"I'm detached federally to DEA," I advised him. It was too foreign to him and he continued to pause. I thought he was going to balk. Drugs in the sticks are as common as drugs in the inner city. He had the problem and he needed help with it. It's expensive to investigate drug dealing in small rural communities.

When I told him I was working federal drug investigations his mind opened. He knew federal meant money. His department would get most of the drug proceeds if the DEA seized cash, jewelry, cars, or property.

"I've got one," he replied. He gave me the gory details.

"We'll be over in two hours."

Clete was still waiting for the promised telephone call. "I've got a deal," I said to the group. They slowly made their way to my desk and stared at me.

"Where's the deal?" Monica Rose asked. "Madison County, Illinois," I replied.

"Give us a briefing."

"A buddy of mine is the sheriff of Jersey County, Illinois. It's up north--- by Grafton." They stared inquisitively. "Pere Marquette State Park? The Great River Road?" They nodded finally in acknowledgment, and I continued.

"He arrested some gal for stealing in the Grafton area and released her on her own recognizance with the promise that she'd show up for her court date. This gal's live-in boyfriend is a big time dope dealer in Madison County, Illinois, an adjoining county. Her court date came around;

the doper gal doesn't show up for court. The sheriff telephones her and she tells him to screw off then hands the phone to her boyfriend. The boyfriend tells the sheriff to screw off, too, so the sheriff takes it like a man and waits his turn. As luck would have it, another gal cruises through his county, drunk, driving on her rims and crashes into a ditch and passes out. The sheriff and his boys get her out and take her to jail for DWI. She comes around and makes the realization that she's incarcerated and looks for a way out. She tells the sheriff that she can do the biggest dope dealer in Madison County for a walk on the DWI charge. The sheriff says, 'Who?' 'Freddy Ellis,' she replies. Turns out this drunk gal is the ex-girlfriend of the same dope dealer who told the sheriff to screw off. The sheriff's got a state search warrant, and he's waiting for us to come over and debrief the DWI lady and do the warrant with him."

"I like it, I like it a lot," Monica Rose said.

Clete, who had been standing at the rear of the group broke from the pack and headed for Doc's office. He and Doc emerged, walked to my desk, and listened to the continuing conversation.

"I've got the transmitter in the trunk of my car," Bill Yocum said. "We can wire the DWI lady and listen for the right time to kick the door."

"Okay," Monica Rose said. "We're taking separate cars. Let's all meet in the parking garage and go over in a convoy. Ray is the only one who knows where we're going so keep him in sight and everybody stay on the air."

"I don't want the Corvette burned over there," Doc Penrose said. "Leave it here."

I nodded in acknowledgment.

"You can ride with me," Bill Yocum said, "I'll need some help with the transmitter anyway."

"You can ride with me," Monica Rose said, flirtatiously."

Heidi raised her head from the laptop and glanced at me. "No, that's alright, I'll help Bill with the transmitter."

"Okay," she said flippantly, "There will be another day."

"We're going to meet the sheriff in a parking lot behind the Alton State Hospital," I advised the group. The state crazy house, how fitting I said to myself. "He's going have the warrant and the confidential informant. He'll be in a big van."

"Saddle up," Clete shouted.

"I can't go," Heidi shouted, "I've got to have this report ready for the United States Attorney." I locked eyes with her; she smiled and went back to typing.

The group armed themselves with semi-automatic Glocks, a Colt machine gun, and a sawed off twelve gauge. We trekked to the elevator and went down together, trudged to our government cars, while the lawyers and insurance executives parked their Lincolns and Bimmers and made for the elevator, staring at us and shaking their heads.

Bill and I slid into his Camaro SS convertible and pulled out into the garage traffic lane and waited for the rest of the crew. "Nice ride."

"Yeah, took it from a fat Canadian," Bill replied. "Fool sold me a kilo in it. Seat's screwed up though and the back is broken or something. It sits crooked. I'm getting it repaired tomorrow."

Monica Rose was the last car in the formation,

"We're ready," she said over the radio.

"Tell me where to go," Bill said.

"Take one-seventy to two-seventy, go north. Take three-sixty-seven, north to Alton. I'll give you more directions after we get there."

"Roger!"

We were crossing the Lewis & Clark Bridge in thirty minutes. "It's neat being the cops," Bill mumbled.

"Yeah."

"Where to?"

"Turn right and go to College Street, turn up the hill, and go straight; is the gang still with us?"

"Yeah," he said.

"What kind of a town is this?"

"It was an industrial town: steel, glass, paper, bricks. People here made a good wage. Most of the industry is gone now. Like in most towns, there's a certain percentage of the population who's shady. Dope is the thing now and there is a lot of it here. Lawyers are gods over here. People depend on them for their existence, divorce, lawsuits, criminal defense. If you're a lawyer in Madison County, Illinois, you are placed on a pedestal. I'm not sure, but I don't think it's like that in other parts of the country."

We pulled into the state hospital parking lot; the sheriff climbed out of his green cargo van, belly first. He hoisted his gun belt up and smiled as we locked eyes and he leaned against the truck. Bill stopped the Camaro, the rest of the crew parked around the van, and everybody got out.

I shook the sheriff's hand and he slapped me on the back. He noted my appearance, which hadn't changed, except for jeans and leather jacket instead of harder attire. He smiled, "You investigating drugs. I can't believe it."

"Yeah," I replied with a grin. "You never know where law enforcement is going to take you." I couldn't believe it, either.

The group gathered around us. "This is Sheriff Josh Edwards," I said. He was a funny looking guy, dangerously overweight, chain smoking, bright red face with a full head of brown hair, a look of mischief on his face. He was likeable.

The crew acknowledged him and stared at their surroundings. We were in a courtyard at the rear of the

Alton State Mental Hospital, an insane asylum, and it was chilly in the shade of the large buildings. The inmates were staring down at us from six stories of barred windows, making faces and giving us the finger. Some of the trusted inmates walked around us, staring and asking for cigarettes

The undercover narks were spooked by the location. Sheriff Josh picked up on it. "Everybody into the van," he instructed. We all climbed in through the side cargo door, hitting our heads on the low steel ceiling. The DWI vengeful confidential informant was sitting in the rear seat of the ten-passenger truck.

We all eyeballed her as we climbed in. The sheriff was the last one inside; he slid the cargo door closed with a whoosh and bang. "Mickey Masters," he said as he motioned the introduction with his hand. "Tell these folks what you can do, Mickey."

She was a dried up thirty year old country doper with scars on her arms from shooting heroin and a bulbous red nose from snorting cocaine. She was probably attractive when she was younger, maybe when she was in her teens, but the drugs had drawn the life out of her.

Her blonde hair and fair skin had no life to it and could have belonged to a dead person. She was no different than the city junkie prostitutes who work the strolls. The drug problem in the country is the same as in the city; if you're a loser, you're going to get hooked.

"I can go to Freddie Ellis' house and buy cocaine from his girlfriend, Vicky Bass," Mickey said with a twang. "There's four kilos in the bedroom safe, and there's at least twenty-thousand in cash in the safe and other cash spread all over the house." She paused and watched us.

The sheriff patted her on the arm and told her it was going to be all right and that she was doing well. "The house is up on a hill," the sheriff began, "It's a modern A-frame kind of a place. There's a long driveway that winds up to it, and there's a locked gate at the bottom. It's got an electric lock on it that can be unlocked at the house. I don't know quite sure how we're going to get by it."

"The lock's broken," Mickey said. "I was there just yesterday and the gate was unlocked." "Yesterday," I said, "The dope might not be there today."

"It's there," Mickey said.

"We want you to telephone the house and tell Vicky Bass you are coming to buy," I said. "Find out if Freddy is there. We're going to tape record the conversation, okay?" She nodded.

Mike Schweig hooked up a tape recorder to his cell phone and gave me the thumbs up. "Okay, Mickey, I need to ask you some questions. How much do you usually buy?"

"A couple of ounces at a time," Mickey replied. "I cut them into eight balls and resell it, then use what is left over. That way I've always got enough money to buy some more." I handed her the phone and she dialed it as the narks looked out of the porthole windows at the crazies walking around the van.

"Hello, Vicky," Mickey said with a Tammy Wynette twang, "I'm coming over to buy; you got what I want in stock?"

"When you coming?" the whiskey-voiced female on the phone asked.

"Maybe in a half hour."

"I'll be watching for you. The lock on the gate is still broken; you can just drive up to the back of the house."

"Will it be just us girls?"

"Yeah," Vicky replied, "Freddy's out doing something. But he'll probably show up while you're still here. Bye, bye."

I looked at the sheriff, "Where's Mickey's car?"

"They're putting tires on it, should be here in a couple of minutes."

"There's something I need to tell you guys," Mickey said. She was stone-faced and we all looked at her in anticipation. "She has three big mean dogs, a Doberman, a German shepherd and a pit bull. They're trained attack dogs and they're always at her side. You'll probably have to shoot them because Vicky will give them the command to attack."

We gave each other goofy looks. "It's your deal, Ray," Mike Schweig said. "What do you want to do?"

"Let's cross that bridge when we come to it," I replied. "First, let's get Mickey on the inside and be sure the dope is in the house. I don't want to storm in there and kill those dogs and then come up empty. Monica, if you would, please, put the wire on Mickey."

Monica duck-walked to the back of the van, "Stand up and pull your blouse up." Vicky stood, crouched, and raised her blouse, showing her pasty, scarred stomach.

"Mickey," I continued, "When you see the dope, I want you to say, 'It's as good as gold. Got it?'

Mickey nodded.

"We'll execute the warrant when you come out. Are there any weapons in the house?"

"Yeah, a bunch of them," she replied. "It's a country home in Madison County, Illinois. There's rifles, shotguns, and pistols all around the house."

We heard a car drive up and a horn sound. "Mickey's car is here," the sheriff said as he slid open the cargo door. He stepped outside and motioned for Mickey to join him.

Monica climbed out and turned on the transmitter. "Testing, testing," Monica said.

"It's coming over loud and clear," I informed her from the van. I climbed out with the rest of the narks behind me.

"Here's two thousand dollars," Mike Schweig said to Mickey. "Sign here." She signed the government form and took the cash. "Buy the dope, come out, and we will go in," he continued.

Mickey nodded.

"There's a logging road just north of where Mickey is going to turn in to Freddie's house," the sheriff said. "I think we should set up there and listen to the conversation. Okay?"

"Yeah," I replied. Mickey got into her Chevy and waited for further instructions.

"Okay," Mickey," the sheriff said. "Take off, do your thing, we'll be listening." She drove off in the beat-up Chevy as we all climbed into our cars and followed a safe distance after her.

We drove through the country scenery for five minutes then she turned right and stopped at the metal bar gate. Mickey got out, swung it open, reentered the Chevy, and drove up the hill around to the back of the house. We drove past the driveway for about fifty yards and turned right onto the logging road.

We spun the cars and the big van around and faced away from the house, our cars pointed toward the main road and waited.

Everyone was monitoring the activity on their car radios. Mickey's Chevy stopped and the engine was shut down. "Here I go," she said as we heard the sound of the car door opening, then slamming shut, and the rustle of her clothing brushing against the microphone. We heard her feet on the wooden steps, the dogs barking and envisioned her on the porch and at the door. Vicky Bass was apparently waiting for her.

"Come on in," the whiskey voice said, "sit down and make yourself comfortable. Do you want to do business first or would you like to sit and talk for a while. It's been a long time since you and me had a good girl talk. Can I get you a beer?"

"Yeah, a beer would be great," Mickey replied.

We heard footsteps and the refrigerator door opening and then closing and the sound of bottles being popped, then footsteps back toward the wire. Vicky's dogs apparently sensed trouble, "You boys stop wandering around this house," she commanded, "Get your asses over here and sit next to me."

"So how are you and Freddy getting along?" Mickey asked.

"Pretty good," Vicky replied. "I should apologize to you for taking your man, but I figured you weren't getting along anyway, the way he used to beat you and all."

"Does he beat you?" Mickey asked.

"Oh, he's slapped me a couple of times," Vicky answered, "But nothing like he used to do to you. I can always tell when it's a-coming. When he gets high and starts getting paranoid. He imagines I'm going to nark on him and that he can't trust me, he starts arguing.... he makes the dogs go outside and then he slaps the shit out of me and it's over, then he's alright. I cry about it. It hurts like hell, but he has never hit me with his fist, not like he used to do with you."

There was a rasping, snorting sound coming over the speaker. "What the hell is that?" I asked.

"They're snorting cocaine," Bill Yocum replied.

"Why doesn't she just buy the damn dope and get the hell out of there?"

"When she comes out I'm going to beat her with my fists," Mike Schweig said over the air.

"We got to make a plan," Mike Schweig said. "It would be advantageous to us to take the place before Freddy comes home, and we definitely got to do it before it gets dark in about two hours. Let's give her a little more time and if she isn't out with the dope, let's make it. We'll take her down too, act like she didn't know anything about it."

There was another pause and the sound of someone blowing their nose. "That's it," I said over the air. "All of you guys come up to the van, leave your cars parked." The sliding door opened and they all piled in.

"Bill and I will man the shotguns, Carl, you take the Colt machine gun. Mike, you drive the van. Bill and I will jump out first. If the dogs give us a problem we'll eliminate them with the shotguns. Okay, Mike let's roll."

Mike drove out of the brush and turned left onto the main road, then gunned the van and drove past the open gate and up the winding driveway. He stopped abruptly in the barnyard directly behind the house. We slid open the cargo door, and Bill and I jumped out into the country air.

"Freddy must be home," Vicky said as she walked to the front door. She observed us as we came running for her porch with the shotguns. The attack dogs ran out of the door and stood by Vicky on the porch. We pointed the shotguns at the dogs and Vicky. "Attack, kill," Vicky shouted. The dogs looked at Vicky, then cowered down to the porch deck and whimpered.

"A dog will always take the winning side," Bill Yocum shouted as we ran up the steps of the porch and grabbed Vicky Bass. I was surprised, but Vicky was attractive in a country sort of way. Good body, blue eyes, dressed in jeans; and a button shirt. She took a wide roundhouse swing at me, "You dirty mother-fucking narks," she shouted. I ducked and tossed her to the ground…where I cuffed her.

"DEA, ma'am," Mike Schweig said. "You're under arrest for distribution of cocaine." The rest of the crew ran into the house and took off Mickey Masters for show, gently placing her on the floor and handcuffing her, then led her past Vicky Bass on the way to the van.

Vicky figured out the scenario, “Nark, you fucking nark,” she shouted at Mickey. The dogs wandered around the house while their mistress was shackled and lying on the floor. Satisfied they had done their job, they rolled up on the floor beside her and took a nap.

We began the search. The house was like a Colorado ski lodge: knotty pine, circular stairway leading to an upstairs loft, rock fireplace with a master suite right off the family room, and a large walkout basement.

Piles of dog waste was scattered throughout the house along with cocaine in plastic bags and cash in various denominations. I located the safe in the closet in the master suite.

“Car coming up the driveway,” Mike Schweig shouted. I ran to the porch and waited. It was Sheriff Josh, smiling and pulling his gun belt up over his gargantuan belly as he climbed out of his Ford and waddled up the steps of the porch.

Vicky Bass rolled her bleach blonde head around and looked up at him as he grinned at her. “Oh, fuck,” she said and turned away.

“Afternoon, Miss Bass, I see we meet again.”

“As I said on the telephone, go fuck yourself.”

The sheriff walked inside with me, and we made our way to the safe in the master bedroom. “Any idea how we can get into it?”

“Nope.”

“Monica,” I shouted.

She meandered into the room. “Anybody at DEA capable of busting this safe?”

“Yeah, but we’ll have to take it to the field office.”

I pushed and prodded it, “It weighs a ton. It’ll take four

men to move it to the front door."

"Car coming up the drive," Mike Schweig shouted. I grabbed the shotgun and we ran to the porch. Freddy Ellis was making the curve toward the barnyard when he observed the van and the sheriff's car. He stopped abruptly and placed his old Ford pickup into reverse. I bounded off of the porch and placed the shotgun in his face.

He looked up at me and the muzzle of the scattergun and smiled. "Where's my dogs? You didn't kill them, did you?"

"No, they gave up without a fight. You should do likewise." He nodded in compliance.

"Keep your hands in sight and get out of the truck."

He was still smiling as he climbed out.

"Turn around and place your hands on the truck roof." Mike Schweig spun him and roughly placed him on the truck as he quickly frisked him. Freddy had a .25-automatic in his field jacket pocket.

Mike showed it to me and pocketed it, then cuffed Freddy behind his back and marched him up the stairs to the porch, past Vicky Bass, who was still prostrate on the living room floor, cuffed behind her back.

"It was Mickey Masters," she screamed, "She's a damn nark."

We escorted him into the master bedroom. I grabbed a kitchen chair and placed it in front of the safe. Mike placed Freddy in it.

"I'm going to take the handcuffs off of you, Freddy. I want you to open the safe."

"Nope, I won't do it. Who are you guys with, anyway?"

"DEA."

We were studying each other. He was unkempt but not dirty. He had a two-day growth, a Marine Corps field jacket, Levis, and engineer boots, a typical guy who answers to no one because he doesn't have to. He had an intelligent sparkle in his eyes. He wasn't panicked or frightened by his fate on this winter day. I could smell beer on his breath and estimated he'd had four or five right before he drove up. I figured he was in the practice of relieving himself in the woods whenever he wished and he was probably due.

"We can get someone over here from Clayton to open it," I bluffed, "But it's going to take a couple of hours. You willing to sit there for two or three hours and wait for them?" He stared at me and I could tell he was weighing his options.

"You guys got a warrant for the safe?" Freddy asked

"Yeah, I replied."

"Let me see it." I held it up for him to examine. He read every word.

"Okay, I'll open it. Take these handcuffs off, but I need to go to the bathroom before I open it." I un-cuffed him and he walked into the bathroom and relieved himself leaving the door open.

He walked back out and stood in front of the safe. "Can I ask you guys something?"

"Yeah."

"You're going to seize my cash, right?"

"Yeah," I said.

"The cash in the safe, right?"

"Yeah!"

"Okay," he said as he dialed the combination and swung the door open.

"Sit back down and put your hands behind your back again." He complied and I cuffed him, then rifled through the safe. I pulled out a large manila envelope and opened it; it was full of hundreds.

"There's twenty thousand in there," he said. I pulled out four kilo bricks of cocaine and laid them on the bed, then rifled through the safe some more.

"That's it," he said. There's nothing more of importance in there. I continued to search and proved to myself that he was telling the truth.

"I can set up the guy who sold me that dope," he said nonchalantly. "We can make some kind of a deal, can't we?"

"Maybe," I replied. But you're still going to do some time."

"But cooperation is beneficial to me, right?"

"Ycah. What's the guy's name?"

"Hold on, I don't want to get ahead of myself, but I do want to cooperate. Can I call my lawyer?"

"Hold that thought."

I huddled with Mike Schweig and Monica Rose in the next room. "We should get clearance from Sue Lee," Monica said, "I'll call her."

Mike and I walked back into the bedroom. He stared inquisitively, "What's the story?"

"We're working on it."

Monica stuck her head into the room. "Sue Lee wants to know what his lawyer's name is."

We looked at him, "Harvey Goldman," he said.

"Harvey Goldman," Monica repeated into the receiver. Monica came back into the bedroom; "Sue Lee says okay. She had to square it with the United States Attorney for the Southern District of Illinois, but it's squared."

I removed the handcuffs and handed him the cordless. He dialed and waited, "Harvey, please. Freddy Ellis. Yeah, I'll hold."

We waited and stared at each other. He was constantly testing us, feeling us out, trying to gauge what kind of guys we were. I had an inner feeling he was smarter than us, and he was leading us down the road to hell. The guy knew the game, and the most worrisome part about the scenario was that he wasn't scared.

"Harvey," he said into the receiver, "I've run into a little trouble out at my house, I've been taken off by DEA, search warrant. Yeah, yeah, state warrant, not federal, but DEA came on along for the ride with Sheriff Josh Edwards from Jersey County. DEA guys talked to Assistant United States Attorney, Sue Lee, she okayed me working for them for a deal to get some of the pressure off of myself. I'm willing to do my source. Yeah, yeah, I just wanted you to touch base with AUSA Sue Lee, in St. Louis and find out who she cleared this with within our district. I don't want to work for nothing. Right, right, I'll be waiting."

He punched the button and ended the conversation, "He's going to call me back."

"You been practicing this? You know the system pretty well."

"I had a good civics teacher in high school," he replied with a stare. He was studying me, trying to get a take on me personally. I couldn't figure out why. I attributed it to his predicament. When people are arrested they turn into trapped animals. I figured he was using animal instinct to try and figure out a way to get out of his troubles. I was the person who shackled him. I was the object of his instinctive concentration.

"You're new to this game, aren't you?" I didn't answer him but he knew he had pulled my hole card. "I could tell," he continued. "You're not grungy like the rest of the cops, and you're older than them. You probably had a desk job someplace. Maybe a sensitive investigative job, and then somebody, some damn bureaucrat, felt that you should see the seedy side of the world. What's more seedy than narcotics work? I'm right, aren't I?"

I still didn't answer him. He was the prisoner, and I wasn't going to allow him to interrogate me. "You know my nickname?"

"No," I muttered.

"It's Buckle. You ever heard of me?"

"No."

"When I was a kid I always wore a fancy cowboy belt buckle. The name stuck. Only my relatives and my closest friends know that I go by Buckle. A casual friend wouldn't know that."

"Okay," I muttered.

"You know, this wasn't supposed to happen to me." He was still studying and gauging and prying into my psyche.

"How do you figure?"

"I paid for protection. A couple of months ago. Twenty thousand dollars worth of it."

I saw the light of a conspiracy slightly burning at the end of a long tunnel. I had to pursue it. "Who did you pay?" He knew he had me then. His face lit up and he smiled, wryly, like a professional poker player.

"A guy who knew my nickname. He called me and told me that if I wished to continue in my drug venture that I'd better have twenty thousand dollars in a gym bag, and that I should drop it in Rock Springs Park, near the golf pro shop in the parking lot. I did that, and I drove off which is what he told me to do. But, I'm a country boy, and I don't like getting ripped off, even though I rationalized my way through it. It was a cheap price to pay."

"So what happened then?"

"I parked my truck and doubled back through the woods as fast as I could. Some big dude, dark hair, looks like a professional wrestler rides by on a Harley and snatches the gym bag with the twenty thousand in it. You know the guy I'm talking about?"

"No!"

"I'll know him if I ever see him again." He stood and

went to the bedroom door. His intelligent eyes scoured his house as Clete and the crew searched and prodded his personal belongings. "There's no need for them to do that," he commented as he stared at me.

I stared back trying not to show my embarrassment at Clete and the boys pillaging his home. Freddy, the country dope man, was smart and he had done what he'd set out to do. He had placed a mental barrier between me and the rest of the DEA guys. His power of perception and his reaction was brilliant. He was a scary guy.

"You've got all of my dope and all of my dope money. There's a couple of grand in house cash stashed around, but it's not dope money. Are you guys going to take that, too? I saw that fat guy take some of it and put it in his pocket."

I didn't answer him, but he read me. He knew the system better than most cops. He knew he was being ripped and he wanted to humiliate me. He had read me well enough to know that I was a straight shooter.

His insight was amazing. If this goes to court, his lawyer's going to have a lot to chew on, but we are cops and special agents. He's a dirty dope dealer. He'll lose, maybe. This is Madison County, Illinois. The bad guys win most of the time.

The telephone rang and he answered it. "Yeah, yeah, okay, I'll let you know where I am. Yeah, the deal is the same for Vicky. Right, right, okay." He punched off and tossed the cordless onto the bed. "I'm ready to set something up. You guys want my source? You want me to have him bring a couple of kilos over here? Let me know what you want, and I'll do it, but it's got to be done tonight. As soon as word gets out that me and Vicky been busted, I got no play here, and word will get out. This is Alton, man. Nothing is secret or sacred here." He stood and stared as if to say, it's your turn now. Make a plan. I'm ready to work.

"Sit down," I commanded. He plopped back into the straight-back chair and placed his hands behind him. I cuffed him and went to the next room with Monica and Mike. "He wants to do this tonight. Says he can get his source to deliver two kilos here. What do you say?"

"I'll have to call Doc," Mike said. "He'll have to okay it." He flipped open his cell phone and walked to the porch as the cell waited for a connection. He came back in two minutes. "Doc wants to know who his source is. And Doc says to videotape the deal."

We walked back into the bedroom. Freddy's eyes were gauging us. "You want to know who my source is, right?"

"Yeah!"

He was smug, tightly smiling as he watched us. "Mark Lingo," he said, staring at us. "Don't you guys recognize the name? You've busted him before. He's a big heroin and cocaine dealer from here to California." Mike Schweig was rubbing his forehead, concentrating and turning in circles.

"He's a black guy, right?"

"Yeah, now you're on the right track," Freddy said.

"They call him little Marky," Mike said.

"Yeah," Freddy confirmed.

"I know him," Mike continued, "He's been through the St. Louis field Office before. Heroin sales, did some time, pled. I didn't know he was out. You want to call him and talk some dope?"

"Yeah!"

Mike hooked up a tape recorder to the cordless as I unhooked Freddy, again. Freddy dialed, "Hey man, I'm in need of two packages. Yeah, man, yeah, okay, how's your old lady doing? Cool, it's about time for you to go west, isn't it? Yeah, how about seven tonight? Still ten a package? Cool, I'll be waiting, later." We stood and stared. "He'll be here at seven with the dope."

I checked my wristwatch. "That's three hours. We've got to set up a surveillance camera."

Mike and I walked to the living room with Freddy following us. Vicky was still on the floor cuffed behind her back, sleeping with the dogs. "What part of the house do you usually do business with him?"

"Me and Vicky always sit on the couch. Marky is in that chair right there," he said pointing. I looked above the back of the couch. The loft was a great place for a surveillance camera.

"I've got a camera in my trunk," Mike said. "I'll go out and get it."

He left with his cell phone to his ear, I heard him say Doc, and then he was off of the porch and walking to his car. In three minutes he was back.

"Doc said we should use the seized twenty grand as flash money, which is actually the United States government's cash. Doc won't let twenty grand walk. It's got to be a buy bust. It's your deal, you cool with that?"

"Yeah." He handed me the miniature camera and we climbed to the loft and set it up. It was concealed behind a table leg with the mini-lens pointing at the back of the couch, the massive coffee table, and the front of the chair.

The crew joined us in the living room. "We're doing his source tonight," I informed them. "We've got about three hours to kill. You guys want to drive into town and get some food?"

"Great idea," Bill Yocum said, "Everybody ready?"

"Yeah," they chimed in simultaneously and headed for the door like a pack of wild dogs.

"Be back in two hours," I said.

"Yeah, right Ray. We'll see you then."

"Monica, Mike, you guys want to take a break?"

"No," Monica said, "I'll stick with you. You feeling

alright, Ray?"

"Yeah," I lied. Freddy perked up and stared at my puffy face.

"I'm not leaving you alone on a deal," Mike said. Freddy had grown tired of monitoring me and was watching Vicky sleeping on the floor.

"I should get her up and clue her in on what's going down," he said. "She's stoned, right?"

"Yeah, beer and cocaine."

I knelt down and removed her handcuffs. She stirred and rubbed her wrists, then looked at Freddy. "This was all a bad dream, right?"

"Nope, it's for real," Freddy assured her. "Get up, there's something I need to explain to you."

He helped her to her feet, and sat her on the couch. "There's a way we can help ourselves through this mess." She was staring at him through clouded lenses and damaged brain cells. He shook her. "Look at me. Wake the fuck up!"

"I'm looking," she screamed.

"We're going to set up Little Marky." She looked around the room and fixated on me.

"You fucking nark. You filthy fucking nark," she snarled.

Freddy slapped her and then backhanded her. "We're working with them tonight," he shouted. "We're the fucking narks now, understand? It's our only way to leniency. We've got to play the game."

He raised her up to her feet. "Clean this dog-shit up and straighten this house up. Then get your ass in the bathroom and clean yourself up. Put on some makeup and do your hair. Make yourself presentable to Little Marky, just like you always have. If he sees you like this," he said motioning with his hand, "it'll fuck up the whole deal." They glared at each other. She walked away and started cleaning.

"How's this going down?" he asked. "Who's going to be where?"

He was still angry but in control of his emotions. "You and Vicky will be on the couch," I began. "That's the way it has always been, right?"

"Yeah!"

"Mike and I will be in the loft near the camera. If anything goes wrong, hit the floor behind the coffee table. That'll give us a clear shot at the chair in front of the coffee table. Does Marky come strapped?"

"Probably. He's a big-time dope dealer; I would assume he's always strapped. I know I am."

We slowly migrated our way to the big open kitchen with a view of the barnyard and the wilderness. Freddy opened the fridge and pulled out a beer, popped it and slugged half of it down. "You guys want a beer?"

"No, thanks," I said.

"I'll take one," Mike Schweig said with a grin.

"Help yourself. I just put a case in there this morning." Mike opened the fridge and grabbed one, popped it and downed it, then got another one out. He patted his pockets looking for his squares, found the pack and pulled it out. He fired one up and looked out of the kitchen window at the weak spring sun sinking into the forest.

Freddy popped another one and they were instant buddies in the ski lodge atmosphere: both narks, both working for the federal government, both making a fine living off of cocaine.

Vicky Bass wandered into the affray. Her bleached hair was styled and she was sober and made up. She looked like a different person. Her good body got better with a bra holding her boobs up, she had on clean clothing, a red shirt with the top three buttons undone, showing cleavage, and tighter, clean jeans.

Her eyes still looked doped, but they were real blue behind the red, and I could see that she could be sexy if she applied herself. She was pouting and trying to be nasty to everyone: to Mike and me for being narks, and to Freddy for beating her and being a nark, and worst of all, making her a nark.

Monica wandered in and perused the situation. "Want a beer?" Mike asked.

"No, but I could use some food. You all got anything?"

"Peanut butter and jelly," Vicky said, "Help yourself," she said with truculence.

Monica fixed herself a sandwich and was eating it while standing at the sink. "Ray, you want one?"

"Yeah, got any milk?"

"Next to the beer," Vicky said, "Glasses above the sink." We ate and drank and watched the barnyard for about forty-five minutes. The rest of the crew drove up. Mike wandered out and instructed them to hide their G cars in the barn, then come in.

They drifted in with smiles and bulging bellies, carrying six packs and drinking a cold one as they laughed and grab-assed. "Man," Pat Brown began, "We found this little steakhouse downtown, in Alton. The steaks were good and the beer was cold. I ate so much I think I'm going to blow up."

I glanced at their eyes; they were all over the limit. "You guys going to be alright? We can blow this off if you want to."

"No, Ray," Carl Robinson said. "We do our best work when we're a little tipsy."

The TFD's laughed, slapped each other on their backs, shoved one another and slammed beers. I glanced at Monica Rose. She got close to me and whispered in my ear. "Welcome to the task force."

I checked my wrist watch; "Here's how it's going to go down. Me and Mike and Monica are going to be in the loft. We'll be videotaping the deal for any court proceeding. The wire is going be set up in the living room so you guys can listen from your posts. When Freddy says, 'it's as good as gold,' the deal is down. Take Little Marky off in the barnyard as he's leaving. He's probably armed. He's been through this before with DEA and did federal time. He's a professional dope dealer. Don't play him cheap."

"Yeah, yeah," they mumbled. "Let's get this deal down, I got some place to be tonight," Bill Yocum said.

"Me, too," Carl Robinson said.

"Yeah," the rest of the crew chimed in.

"Okay, go and hide and listen to the wire conversation," I said.

"There's a heated room in the barn," Freddy said, "It'd be a good place to hide." They wandered out and disappeared into the barn.

"We've got about thirty minutes, Monica," I said. "Please set the transmitter up somewhere in the living room and activate it."

"Roger."

"Mike, Freddy, Vicky, let's have a dry run." They looked at me like I had two heads.

"Want some Crown Royal?" Freddy said to Mike.

"Yeah."

I walked out into the living room. Monica had the wire set up. My radio barked, "Target is driving into the courtyard now, black male, forties, driving a black BMW with California plates."

"He's early," I said as I ran back into the kitchen. "He's early. It's going down. Everybody get to their posts.

I grabbed Mike by the arm, ushered him to the loft ladder and pushed him up. Monica was behind me, the last one up the ladder. The shotgun was lying on the bed. I checked it and cranked one into the chamber as Mike sat on the floor next to the TV monitor and played with the knobs. The dogs were going crazy, running around the house, barking and jumping on the furniture. "Shut up," Freddy shouted as he kicked at them.

Vicky was wringing her hands and pacing, on the verge of tears. There was a loud knock on the front door. Vicky opened it and smiled real big. "Marky." She got into character and hugged him and kissed him on the lips.

He grabbed her left butt cheek and squeezed it, then palmed her breast with the same hand. He was carrying a grocery bag in his left arm and kept it close to his body while the greetings were taking place.

Freddy shook hands with him and called him, "My man, and the greatest," and other lies and they took their seats. The dogs were still restless, roaming and staring.... with hair standing up on their backs. Freddy kicked at them again and they crawled to the side of the couch and plopped.

The fifty-pound black pit bull stayed within striking distance in a crouch at the end of the couch watching every move Marky made. Marky took off his leather jacket. He wore a black muscle Tee. His biceps were bulging and the veins in his neck were protruding like a true body builder. I didn't see a weapon in his waistband and was relieved.

"Crown Royal?" Freddy was pointing as he asked.

"Yeah, brother, that would be cool."

Freddy walked into the kitchen and Marky started flirting with Vicky. "When you going to leave that cracker and take up with me? I'd take you to California and get some color on you, baby." Vicky acted coy and Marky got off on it as Freddy came back into the room with the drinks.

Mike Schweig was making fish faces as he watched the monitor. He started with his head in an upright position with a little fish face. His facial contortions came in waves, with his head dropping down further after each grimace until he was almost in puking position; with his face red and his mouth all the way opened. Then he would catch himself and come back upright, then start the process again. I kept exchanging glances with Monica. She looked concerned.

"You got the dope, right?"

"You got the money, right?" Marky chuckled nervously.

"I'll get it," Freddy said as he stood and went into the bedroom, then returned with the manila envelope. He sat back down on the couch and emptied the envelope onto the coffee table. Marky's eyes got like saucers and he began counting it.

Monica and I were trying to watch the screen and watch Mike Schweig making fish faces. He was on fish face take number six or seven, and was real low in the process with his eyes half-mast and his mouth wide open, making puking motions when the unthinkable happened. A belch rolled out.

He jumped and covered his mouth, but it was too late. That belch reverberated off of the cathedral ceiling and right down to the couch and might as well have been a gunshot.

Little Marky jumped like he'd been hit with a cattle prod, "Somebody else in here? Somebody in the loft?" Freddy didn't answer him. Vicky was in shock. Little Marky reached inside the grocery bag and came out with a six-inch 357 and in one smooth motion he was standing and had Vicky by her collar and was pulling her across the coffee table toward him using her as a shield. "Who's up there? Who's in the loft? You'd better answer me, I got the bitch," he shouted.

Freddy took a dive behind the couch and froze in fear. Vicky's pit bull, who had been stalking Marky since he arrived, leapt in a blur of black muscle toward the gun wrist of Marky and clamped down like an alligator.

Marky screamed like a girl and the 357 started exploding and spitting rounds out around the house, destroying lamps and windows and knotty pine paneling, but the pit bull, who sensed he was finally on the winning side, wouldn't let go. Marky emptied the gun and continued to scream a high, shrill inhuman, surreal scream of terror as the pit bull chewed on his wrist with carnal lust.

I clamored down the loft ladder with the shotgun and pointed it at Marky. "DEA," I shouted. "Get down on the floor. You're under arrest."

He continued to scream, "I can't get down on the floor. This damn dog is going to eat me alive." He sobbed as he beat it on the head with his left fist. Monica was standing next to me. I saw Mike's shaking legs coming down the ladder, one rung at a time and he eventually joined us.

"I give up, man," Marky shouted, "Just get this damn animal off of me."

The pit bull was shaking his head, growling and howling like a junky's primal nightmare as he worked on Marky's wrist. Freddy grabbed the dog's head and tried to pull his jaws apart. Marky was going into shock and went to his knees, his head back and rolling on his shoulders, his massive muscular neck and veins vulnerable and inviting to the dog.

Freddy got a ball bat and started slugging the dog in the head and the back trying to break the trance it was in so it would loosen its grip on the wrist. The pit bull was looking into Freddy's eyes as if to say, what are you doing? I'm protecting my mistress. I'm on the winning side.

Freddy loaded up on the bat and slammed it hard on the crown of the dog's head. He yelped and fell to the floor, then regained his footing and ran to a corner, watching and waiting, frothing at the mouth from the excitement. The other two dogs ran into the bedroom and hid under the bed.

Pat Brown, Carl Robinson, Ross Milton, and Bill Yocum came bursting through the door with their guns drawn. Marky was down for the count on the floor going deeply into shock. I walked to the table telephone and dialed 911. "Dog bite victim, going into shock, it's off of the belt line in Fosterberg. Colorado-style house on the hill, circular road leading up to the rear of the house."

"I know where it is," the 911 dispatcher replied.

"Thank you!" I said as I hung up and returned to the group. "Ambulance on the way," I said. They had him laid out flat on the floor, his legs raised with a pillow. Vicky had a cold compress on his forehead, his belt and trouser waist loose.

The video camera was still rolling. I knelt down, secured the grocery bag, opened it, and observed two shrink wrapped kilos of something, hopefully cocaine. I poured the contents onto the coffee table and looked up at the camera. It was still recording.

Sheriff Josh walked in, breathing hard and perspiring in the twenty-five degree weather. "I heard the call come out for the ambulance. Madison County Sheriff's Department is on the way, too."

They arrived simultaneously, both with sirens screaming as they tore up the hill and came to a sliding stop at the steps to the porch. EMS technicians ran in with a stretcher and life support packs. A lieutenant from Madison County and a deputy sheriff moseyed in and stood at the back of the crowd, watching and waiting. EMS stabilized Marky and placed him on the stretcher. They were wheeling him out to the ambulance.

"That man is a federal prisoner," I informed them.

"He's going to Alton Memorial," a beefy female technician advised me. "You can have someone ride along if you wish."

I looked at Sheriff Josh, "Can you have one of your deputies go to the hospital and babysit him?"

"Yeah, consider it done." He flipped open his cell phone and dialed.

The tall thin sheriff lieutenant approached me and he wasn't smiling. "Who are you guys with?"

"DEA."

"Can I see your credentials." I handed him mine. He compared my face with the picture on the ID. Monica Rose intervened.

"I'm Special Agent Monica Rose, St. Louis field Office. I will answer any and all of your questions, Lieutenant." He handed me my credentials and pulled out a notebook as he and Monica walked away from the group.

The Madison County cops left with the ambulance. The TFD's were sitting around the house, restless and wanting to exit, giving what's-up looks. Sheriff Josh looked at me for guidance.

"Freddy and Vicky will have to be housed in your jail tonight," I said to him. "Can you transport?"

"Yeah," the sheriff replied.

"They'll be arraigned tomorrow morning at the courthouse in East St. Louis," I continued. "In order for the federal government to adopt this case from the state of Illinois, you'll have to be in attendance at the arraignment. Can you meet me there in the morning?"

"Yeah, ten o'clock okay?"

"Yeah," I replied. "Bring Little Marky Lingo with you, if he's out of the hospital."

The sheriff hooked up Vicky Bass. I put the cuffs on Freddy. We were walking them to the sheriff's van. The dogs were following us. "What about the dogs, Freddy? Is there someone I can call to take care of them?"

"No, just fill their bowls with food and water. When

that's gone, they can fend for themselves in the woods. They know how to survive. They can sleep in the barn and drink creek water."

I found a fifty-pound bag of chow in the kitchen, slit the bag up the middle and placed it on the front porch.

Monica and Mike gathered up the evidence, the dope, the money and the 357 and carried it to their car. I broke down the video camera and took it with me. We all walked out together. I was the last one out. I left a light on and slammed then checked the door.

Monica had Marky Lingo's BMW keys. She smiled as she slid into the driver's seat and fired it up. "Another one bites the dust," she said a she shifted into first gear and tore out on the gravel driveway.

The TFD's were headed down the hill in their G cars. Bill Yocum was in the Camaro SS, racing the engine, waiting for me. I took one last look around before I entered the car. The dogs were standing on the porch, watching, wagging their tails at me as I climbed in. We took off down the hill, turned left on the blacktop when Bill jumped on the Camaro.

He went through all six gears, and we were doing a hundred when he downshifted, braked, and made the curve to the belt line highway. He tore through Alton and jumped on the Lewis and Clark Bridge at eighty. We were cruising at eighty on three-sixty-seven when he popped a beer. "Want a beer, Ray?"

"No, thanks."

He was glancing at me as he drove. "Why did you become a cop, Ray?"

I didn't know where this conversation was going. Maybe the curiosity of a young intoxicated undercover nark, or maybe he just wanted to get to know me better, or he wanted me to know him.

"Fresh out of the Marine Corps. Had no other options. How about you?"

"My daddy was a St. Louis cop," Bill began with his story. "I always wanted to be a cop in St. Louis, but I never thought I'd make it. My dad always talked about the job at home, how dope dealers were ruining this country."

"Yeah," I muttered.

"We lived in the county, away from the city gangsters. We had a big house overlooking the Mississippi, and there was an amusement park there. Me and a buddy of mine got a job one summer at the park. Our neighborhood was starting to change. You know what I mean?"

"No, not really."

"The gangsters were starting to move into our neighborhood from the city. My dad was furious. He said we'd probably have to move. My buddy and me were both varsity wrestlers and we fought all the time. You work out, too, don't you Ray?"

"Yeah."

"You're in good shape for your age."

"Thanks."

He killed the beer and popped a fresh one. "We were working the tunnel of love ride one night at the amusement park when this Cadillac drove up with these two dope-dealing, pimp-looking street gangsters with killer girls. These dudes were all decked out with their pimp hats and their gold dangling off of them, and they were showing these bitches off, and they were fine. Where these low-life street pimps got them is a mystery, but money talks and bullshit walks."

"Yeah."

"Anyway, they get on the ride. We put the bar down on them and the ride starts. My buddy and me go into the tunnel and get our night vision. The cars with these two pimps and these killer chicks makes the turn and we're waiting for them. I took one; my buddy took the other one. We suckered them, beat them to a pulp. The chicks thought it was some kind of a joke, until the ride came out on the other side and those city assholes were beat to hell, unconscious, laying half in and half out of the cars. Somebody called the cops; they eventually took them away in an ambulance. We laughed until we cried. I had this strange feeling of accomplishment, like I'd done something worthwhile for the community and the human race in general. I knew then, I had to become a St. Louis cop."

"Neat," I mumbled. "Maybe I will have a beer, after all."

"In the back seat," he said. I reached over, retrieved a can and popped it.

"Oh, fuck, I'm being pulled over, and I just opened a fresh beer. It's Missouri State," Bill continued as he pulled to the side of the highway. "I'll just stick it between my legs, he won't look down there. It ain't macho."

The spit-shined, Sam Brown wearing Missouri State Trooper sauntered up to Bill's window. "Good evening, sir. May I see your driver's license?"

"Yeah, I've got it, what did I do?"

"You were doing a hundred in a seventy," the trooper calmly said.

Bill reached for his wallet, which was in his back pocket. The back of the bucket seat gave way, and he rocketed into the back seat of the mini-sports car. The beer, which was wedged between his legs, shot out onto his chest, saturating him with white foam. "Damn this piece of Detroit shit," Bill exclaimed as he attempted to regain his composure.

"I can explain all of this," he said meekly as he hoisted the seat back into position.

"Your driver's license, sir," the trooper repeated.

"I've got it," Bill said as he fumbled with his wallet. He

had three driver's licenses: Illinois, Missouri and Florida, all issued in a DEA funny name. He handed them all to the trooper.

"Why do you have three driver's licenses?"

"I'm an undercover agent with the Drug Enforcement Administration, sir. I was trying to keep up with some drug dealers who were right ahead of me. If you let me go, maybe I can still catch them."

"Show me your credentials," the trooper sternly said.

Bill flashed his credentials. The trooper carefully examined them and compared Bill to his picture. "Have a nice evening." He turned and walked away. Bill started the Camaro and merged back into traffic. "Man, it's great being the cops. And it's great being on the DEA task force." We were approaching our offices in Clayton. "We're all going to meet at the Club," Bill said. "Want to join us? There's lots of lonely secretaries there."

"No thanks, Bill I just think I'll head for home. I've got that arraignment tomorrow morning, but thanks for asking." I buzzed into the office and secured the camera and tape and was walking out the door. Heidi was walking in. "Hey," I said.

"Hey," she said back.

"Man, you missed a weird dope deal today."

"I heard about it, but that's why they call them dope deals. You have to be a dope to be on either end of them." We laughed.

"I've got the duty," she continued. "I've got to answer the telephone until midnight. Want to come over after that?"

She was tempting me again and I couldn't figure out why. "Love to, but I've got to get home, I'm beat; and I've got my dog to tend to."

"There's always tomorrow," she said.

I walked into the garage and made my way toward the

government Corvette. Lonely secretaries and TFD's and other sexual opportunists were necking against parked cars, grinding, laughing, making moves toward the back seats of Lincolns, Cadillacs and BMWs. The DEA surveillance camera was recording every move for posterity. Square Bidness critiqued the tapes every morning. Security was paramount in the dope business. Counter surveillance meant disaster and failure for the special agents and task force detectives.

I cranked the Corvette and headed for my old house with a view. I was thinking of Gloria. I wondered if I would ever hook up with her again. I was dreaming of our sexual escapades together and comparing her to Heidi. "Heidi," I said aloud. "That's why they call them dope deals. You have to be a dope to be on either end." Great explanation. I liked it. I liked it a lot.

I parked the Corvette and entered my house. Tyrone was wagging his tail and smiling at me from the deck. I let him in and he stood on his back legs and looked at me eye to eye. Someone had been in the house and had entered through the slider. It was unlocked. Had to have been someone Tyrone trusted. Probably Gloria. He was nervous. He smelled the other dogs, and strange smells. He couldn't put it together.

I walked upstairs to the loft. Gloria had returned and gotten her belongings. I felt sick and lonely, just like I did when every lover left me for good. I wished I had taken Heidi up on her invitation to come over.

It looks like she's going to be the one for me. I couldn't figure why I was balking. I was tired and bewildered. This nark job was taxing me, and my romance troubles were dragging me down emotionally. You have to be a dope to be on either end.

5

I walked into the task force office at three P.M. The TFD's and the special agents were still busy at their laptops, clicking away with Carla overseeing their work like a high school typing teacher. She gave me an inquisitive look. "Arraignment, Southern District of Illinois," I said as I made my way to my desk. "Freddy Ellis, Vicky Bass, and Little Marky Lingo." She nodded.

Monica Rose was staring and smiling. "How'd it go?"

"They're all being bound over. Marky Lingo has several broken bones in his wrist and severe lacerations. He's going to the Federal Hospital in Springfield, might even lose his arm below the elbow."

"Good deal," Agent Ross Milton said. "That filthy fucking dope dealer has been skating for too long. You think if they cut off his arm we can seize it and put it in a glass container, place it on a pedestal in our office? Every dope dealer should lose an arm."

"Maybe, Ross. You want me to call the hospital and ask them?" He adjusted his ascot and stared at his paperwork

"Hey, what a great idea. Cut the right arm off of every dope dealer," Pat Brown said. "That way everybody would always know who the dope dealers are in this world."

"We already know who they are," Carl Robinson replied. "They're almost everybody. Ninety percent of the population would be armless. There wouldn't be anybody to fight our fucking political wars."

"The fucking politicians would be armless, doctors, lawyers, teachers," Mike Schweig replied.

"Fucking football players, and basketball players, and baseball, too," Carl Robinson shouted with a laugh.

"You all are evil," Monica Rose said laughing.

I needed to access the DEA computer and get into the

Narcotics and Dangerous Drugs Information System. I walked to Carla's desk and asked her about it. "You'll need a password," she said. She made a telephone call to the administration office on the fifth floor, and wrote something down on a scratch pad. She handed it to me. "Your password. I'll show you how to access NADDIS."

We walked to my laptop and she took me through the process. I was in and entering the name, Freddy Ellis. It popped onto the screen. Freddy was already in NADDIS, which meant I didn't have to enter him.

I continued to read the entry. Madison County, Illinois, cocaine and marijuana dealer. Goes by the name, Buckle. Entered by Special Agent James Schwartz, St. Louis Field Office, group one. I pushed my way away from my desk and stared out of the window. The streets below me were teeming with people, even though it was twenty degrees.

I often wondered how other working people felt about their lives, their vocations and their avocations. What keeps us going? What drives us to get up every morning and do what we do to make money? For me, it's conspiracies. Why? I'm inquisitive. But for a secretary or a receptionist or a junior executive just starting out, I couldn't see what drives them.

I went back to the laptop and NADDIS. The entry by Special Agent Jim Schwartz was dated two months ago. How convenient. Freddy Ellis said he paid protection money two months ago. Schwartz knew Freddy's nickname. It was in the computer, Buckle. It was circumstantial, nothing more, although Freddy said the Harley rider was big, like a professional wrestler.

It still didn't prove anything. Schwartz was a Special Agent with the United States Government, Drug Enforcement Administration. He was a steroid nut, but I doubted he was a blackmailer of drug dealers.

My desk phone rang, it was Freddy Ellis. "I got out this morning," he began. "I wanted to thank you for taking care of my dogs." There was a pause. He didn't call me to give me accolades. He wanted to shoot another poison barb into my brain. I knew it, and he knew I knew it, but he'd read me well enough to know that I wasn't going to hang up on him.

I gave him the federal pause. "That guy I told you about that blackmailed me. He had a big mustache, covered his whole mouth. You know anybody like that?"

"Nope!"

"Yeah you do, Ray. You don't want to admit it. If you did, you'd be taking sides. Who's the biggest crook, Ray? Me, country dope man, or the DEA guy who went to the dark side? The blackmailer had a backup with him that night. It was a hog-headed guy, a lot like that guy Clete Jones you brought to my house when you arrested me. I think it was him, and that means he ripped me off twice. Once for twenty thousand, and then for a couple of grand when you guys searched my house. He was driving a Dodge Durango, a Hemi. So long, Ray, I guess I'll see you in court."

I hung up and stared at the pedestrian traffic again. It was a little conspiracy, now it's a big conspiracy. I went back to the laptop. I requested to view the names of the persons accessing the Freddy Ellis file. TFD Cletus Jones popped up. "Damn," I muttered as I zoned out of the window.
I got out of NADDIS, turned the computer off, and closed it.

My cell vibrated. I answered with a, "Yo."

Heidi was purring on the line. "I need to go to the courthouse. Want to come along?"

"Yeah. You think it's alright?"

"Your paperwork is caught up, isn't it?" We were watching each other from across the room as we talked in hushed tones. She was in heat. I knew the body language. It was instinctive to me. The line went dead so I walked to her desk. I was being monitored by the group. Carla was staring at me.

"Let's hit it," she said. I walked to my desk and retrieved my leather; Heidi was waiting for me at the office door. Doc came out of his office and stood by Carla's desk, watching us as we left. We took the elevator to the garage and emptied out into it.

"Which car?"

"Mine," she replied. We climbed in to her red government BMW convertible and slowly made our way east.

"Doc was watching us as we left the office," I began the conversation. "What's up with that?"

"He's the group supervisor. That's what they do. You don't understand the task force philosophy," she said with a smile. "Don't take this wrong, and I don't want to come off as crass, but there's something you must be made aware of. You city guys are brought here to assist the regular DEA guys. We need your help, there's no doubt about it, but if you're to be brought into the DEA family, you must realize that you're here to assist us." She studied me, looking for my facial expressions.

"I didn't know that."

"Some of the agents in the other groups refer to you guys as confidential informants with a badge. I feel that's rude. I personally don't feel that way. Most of the agents in the task force don't feel that way, either. Doc is able to get the most out of each and every one of us because he's constantly monitoring his children, looking for new avenues to manipulate us to make us turn flips for him so he can look good. If we can impress him, he can impress Square Bidness, and maybe, impress someone in headquarters, which will maybe get him his next promotion. He was measuring you and me as we walked out together, wondering if we can make a good team to make him look good to the other bosses."

"Oh, so it's the manipulation thing," I said, studying her.

"Yeah, like I told you. That's what this dope game is about, manipulation. That's how DEA agents start their careers, manipulation of informants to get to the bigger dope dealer. An introduction to a dope dealer who can take the agent to the top man. We just want the top man, the source of the dope in this country, the head of the cell. If wc can manipulate him, we can bag everybody in the dope conspiracy. The silent partners who supply the cash for the dope transactions, they are the ultimate goal. Wealthy Americans, pillars of the community, the ruling class. It all starts with manipulation."

"Oh. Doc didn't go with us on my deal in Illinois. What's up with that?"

"He's always with his little girlfriend from the United States Attorney's office."

"He has to go home sometime. No wife is that dumb. How does he get away with that?"

"He and his wife work separate shifts. Besides, DEA wives get used to their husbands not being around early in this game. It's a fact of life. The hours with DEA suck. Guys like Doc are married to DEA. Their wives and family come second. As far as the girlfriend on the side, it's an occupational hazard. The manipulators can't stop themselves from manipulating. They're constantly on the make for new victims. It's their obsession and they can spot a weakness in almost everyone they talk to. Every DEA agent sincerely believes that any person who has a successful, full life, with the toys that go with it, made their way through the dope business. In their minds, nobody can succeed without cheating. In Doc's mind, he doesn't feel he's doing anything wrong. He's conned and manipulated a sweet young thing, a lonely secretary. He's got sex, companionship, contacts within the United States Attorney's office, money, freedom, power, groovy cars, and it's all under the auspices of the federal government. It's their church, you see, their religion, their way of life. They're used car dealers who are out of control. They can't stop selling."

I visualized Doc selling me a used car. He looked the part: tall, long dish-water blonde hair, semi- mullet, shifty eyes, partial beer belly, and aggressive demeanor. I could see him walking toward me as I kicked the tire of an old Corvette, his aggressive gait, as if he was walking in a plowed field and using his knees as shock absorbers. Can I help you, sir?

He would be studying me, looking for my weakness for sports cars, testing how great my weakness was, knowing I was already partially hooked or I wouldn't have stopped and kicked the tires. I was no match for him. He had the car. I had the weakness.

We parked at a meter and took the elevator up to Sue Lee's floor. We didn't go into her office. We went to another office in a corner with a view of the Mississippi, the Arch and East St. Louis, my hometown.

Heidi went through a door with no inscription, unlocked by a buzzer while I sat in the dentist-sized waiting room reading the morning newspaper. I finished it, then read the "USA Today." I then read "Time," "Newsweek" and five car magazines. She came out looking frazzled.

"Let's go," she said. I followed her out, down and to the BMW. I wasn't going to ask her what was up. It was obviously covert government bureaucratic bull. I wanted nothing to do with it. I despised it for what it was. I despised it for upsetting her. But I couldn't help but wonder who was behind the locked door. I examined the problem. I figured the office was used by a government honcho from Washington, visiting for an interview: an interview of a Special Agent of the Drug Enforcement Administration. Why be so covert?

She cranked the Bimmer, filled her lungs with air, like an athlete preparing to swing a club or pitch a ball then blew it out. "It's three o'clock," she muttered. "I don't feel like going back to the office. Do you?"

"No."

"We could go on surveillance. Want to?"

"Yeah, sounds great. Who's the bad guy?" I asked.

"He's not a bad guy. He's a possible confidential informant, a C/I who has been calling me when I have the duty. Wants to snitch on some coke dealers. We've been telephone fencing for several evenings. He finally told me who he was. I ran his name in the computer and found out where he lives. Hortense Place. Know where it is?"

"Yeah. Just off Euclid. Private street. Exclusive. Take the Forest Park Expressway to Euclid, turn right. Take it down about six blocks. It's the street on the left. Gated, but the gates are rarely closed."

We cruised by the mini-castle, made from granite stones. It was a 1904 flashback with modern windows. It was the year of the world's fair in St. Louis. The city was at its pinnacle then. It has continually gone downward since then and has never stopped spiraling. The house was completely restored. Million bucks, I figured.

There was nowhere to set up so we cruised the Central West End neighborhood admiring the stately, restored mansions. I knew the area well. I was a rookie cop there. The day was rapidly disappearing. It was like a day off for me. No deals. Just riding around the Central West End with a beautiful woman.

"Where has the day gone?" She said with a smile. It's five o'clock. Is there a good place to eat around here?"

She was being coy. I admired that about her. "Dressels' Pub," I replied. "Euclid and McPherson."

"Groovy," she said as she drove toward the pub and parked at the curb.

We strolled in and got a booth in the back. She called Carla and told her we had been on surveillance. She spoke so low I could hardly hear her. Government work makes everything overly covert. We drank German beer and snacked on pretzels. We both ordered the Reuben. "Best I ever had," she remarked.

We sat and sipped beer for some time. I paid the check and we were back in the Bimmer heading toward the office. It was past eight o'clock. The proposition was forthcoming. I just had to be patient and wait her out: she liked to be the initiator. I was a sexual goal for her. I hadn't taken the bait she'd cast upon the water and it made her curious. It was a new experience for her. "Can you come over tonight?"

"I've got to tend to my dog," I clumsily replied. "He's been ill and I've got to tend to him." I was embarrassed at such a weak excuse. The dog-ate-my-homework excuse. I almost smirked after I said it.

"Are you romantically involved?"

"At the end of an involvement," I said. "Live-in girlfriend just moved out." I saw the look of acceptance on her face. We were communicating.

She dropped me off at the Corvette. I glanced into the surveillance camera as I fired it up and headed for home, thinking about Heidi and her aggressive demeanor. It's a cop/gal thing.

These gals come to law enforcement which has historically been a male-oriented profession, with ambition and guile. They're good students, most of them. Most men in the cop business aren't, so they've got the upper hand on us. But they want more. The only thing a man has is his masculinity. The female cops want a part of that. So, they become the aggressor.

I was satisfied that Heidi was smarter than me, but now she was intent on dominating me. I figured I would have to be careful of her. She desired more than sex. My cell rang and I answered with a "Yo." It was Heidi.

"This is federal law enforcement, Ray. We all work closely together. If something magical happens between two people, then it happens. It's just part of the game. Federal law enforcement trust other federal law enforcement folks. Outsiders aren't welcome into the club. That's why you cops are scrutinized so closely. Relax and enjoy the ride. It'll be the experience of your life. But you've got to loosen up a little. I'm patient, Ray, but I'll soon get tired of trying if you don't acquiesce."

She was preaching to me like Doc. "Are you a used car dealer?" I paused, not knowing what answer she would throw at me.

"No, Ray, I'm more like a used yacht dealer, same principle, higher class of victim. Like you, Ray, you're a classy guy and I like you a lot. We can have a very rewarding time together. Take care of your dog, Ray, and get some rest. I'll see you in the morning."

I pulled into my garage, walked into the kitchen and was greeted by Tyrone. I was certain he was my only friend. I opened the slider and he charged out to the backyard, ran near the drop-off and did his thing, then came bounding back in. I fed and watered him, petted and talked to him, then climbed the ladder to the loft. I was mentally exhausted.

I drifted off but kept having the same bad dream and jumping up and looking at my surroundings to acclimate myself. I dreamt I was back in the Marine Corps, living in the jungle, having Commanding General inspections during the short stay on base in Okinawa, and dancing with the Okinawa bar girls in the little town of Hanako.

Sometimes I would wake up fighting the other Marines over turf and bar control. Then I would collect myself and go back to sleep just to have another dream, talking to a bar girl, the one I'd had rights to when I was in town, Kimiko. She was a gorgeous mystery woman, probably only seventeen at the time, but she was the only one I could communicate with, dance with, and make love to; kind of like a girlfriend back in the states would have been.

In my dream, I was talking to Kimiko, explaining to her why I came back to Okinawa, why I joined the Marine Corps again but no words were coming out of my mouth. When I walked into the bar, Kimiko looked the same: young, vibrant, gorgeous, but as the evening wore on, as we danced and talked and drank, her appearance changed.

The Hanako clubs didn't have modern music. The girls behind the bar had stereos and L/P albums. The albums were vintage. I was dancing with Kimiko to a Johnny Cash tune and looking at us in the bar mirror; Kimiko turned old, her hair turned white, and her face changed into a puffy wrinkled prune and I pushed myself away from her and tried to look at her without the aid of the mirror. She grabbed me and held me and wouldn't let me look at her. We struggled and danced. My mouth was moving but no words came out.

I jumped out of bed and went into the bathroom and splashed cold water on my face. I wondered if the Reuben I ate for supper was tainted with something. I sat in the dark on the commode and went through the nightmare, psychologically deciphering the crazy dream.

The Marine Corps was a brainwashing machine, always there brainwashing, manipulating, controlling. The bar girls were an outlet for the Marines, placed there next to the base by the United States Government for the Marines to play with.

My brain was rebelling to the DEA brainwashing. I was being brainwashed by DEA, and even though I knew it, I had no choice but to allow it to happen. Heidi was there for me to play with, to assist and to make stats for Doc and Square Bidness, just like the bar girl, Kimiko.

And just like Okinawa, I would leave DEA someday, but the experience would stay with me forever. Uncle desires it to be that way. How fragile our little minds are.

6

I walked into the task force office at 0901. It was the last Monday in April and I was feeling good about it. May was the end of winter. The room was quiet for the entire morning as we typed our stories. Heidi and I went to lunch, and returned to the office. Doc was waiting for us.

"Heidi, Ray Arnold, come into my office," he sternly said. We slowly walked in. He sat down. I glanced at all of his family photographs. His young children, his blonde wife with the bad complexion, smiling, holding onto her man at a restaurant with tropical decor, maybe in Miami. A picture of his girlfriend at the top of the heap on his bookshelf. Damn hypocrite.

"There's a damn Feeb down in Square Bidness' office," Doc began. "Ray, that hillbilly over in Madison County says you stole four grand from him. The Feeb is going to interview you about it. I advise you to tell him nothing. If he presses you, which he will, tell him you made an official Department of Justice report, a DEA six, and that you'll stand on what's in the official report. He's in the interview room on the fifth floor. I want to know every word that's said in there. Okay?"

"Yeah, Doc," I replied. "I'm the only one being accused?"

"Yeah!"

"Is it David Moynihan?" Heidi asked.

"Yeah," Doc replied.

"He's filth, Ray," Heidi said. "He's a snake in the grass. He's capable of anything. Watch yourself."

I walked up the stairs to the sixth floor. Freddy, the Madison County dope dealer, knew me well from our brief encounter. He spotted the straight shooter. He relayed everything to his lawyer. They came up with this ploy. He's trying to stay out of prison. He feels I'm the weak link in the chain that will keep him out. He's wrong. I knocked on the interview room door.

"Enter," the voice said. I did. He was in his mid-forties, military haircut, getting white at the temples. Cheap clothing, a brown suit that probably came from Sears or Target. Square-faced and ruddy. He was big like a gym rat, but not on steroids like DEA Agent Jim Schwartz, and he didn't have the crazed look about him.

There was only one chair in the room and he was sitting in it. He leaned back in the chair with his head back and studied me, looking down his nose as I stood before him.

"I'm Special Agent Dave Moynihan." He tossed his business card on the table and slid it toward me. "You've been accused of stealing four thousand dollars from a drug suspect in Madison County, Illinois. Freddy Ellis. Do you know him?"

"I know who he is. Cocaine dealer. I arrested him. Do you know him?" I was being cute with him.

'I'M MAKING THE INQUIRIES HERE, DETECTIVE," he shouted. He was red-faced and out of control. We stared.

"I need a statement from you."

He pushed a legal pad and a pen across to me on the table.

"I've already written a statement," I calmly said. "It's in my original Department of Justice report, DEA six. I'll stand by that."

He stared, then smiled like he was my brother and wanted to help me through a bad time in my life. I didn't smile back. I just thought back to Heidi and Doc and how Doc said Heidi hated the Feeb and I wondered why. I should've asked her about it before I came into the room with him. I usually ask questions freely, but I'm a guest here and I realized quickly that I'm here to work and not ask questions. That was made clear to me in the hotel when I was getting my brain massaged by the crazed dope dealer.

The Feeb was running physiognomy on me, and again I was offended by it. It's what I do to adversaries, mostly criminals. He apparently thought I was less sophisticated in criminal investigation than he was. I resented his arrogance. He was underestimating me, everybody does.

"You're letting them brainwash you, Detective. Do you actually think I waltzed in here not knowing everything there is to know about you?" He was waiting for an answer. I stared without giving him one.

"I checked you out Ray, you're a high-profile guy. I can't believe a great investigator like you would accept an assignment with DEA. Why did you? Why are you really on the task force? Is it that waitress murder you couldn't solve?"

I didn't answer that question either. I just stared wanting this to be over as soon as possible.

"They're going to whore you out, Ray. They do it to everybody who comes in contact with them. These folks out here play for keeps, detective. They'll throw you to the wolves in a heartbeat just like they do all of their informants. To them, you're a C/I with a badge. Have you heard that terminology before, Ray?"

"Yeah."

"They just act like you're part of the family to get you interested in the drug business. Driving a Corvette roadster, huh? Like it? That's how they get you locals dedicated and involved, baubles and bangles, and a little romance from the lookers. You like that Special Agent Heidi Anderson, don't you, Ray?"

I continued to stare.

"You think she likes you? You think she might love you

someday, a man of your advanced age? Wrong, Ray. You know what she loves, Ray? She loves money and power and she's out to get as much of both of those commodities as she can. You're a promotion for her, if she uses you right. That's all, Ray, just a promotion. The next step for her is Group Supervisor, maybe in Miami or Phoenix or Los Angeles. Pretty heady stuff, huh Ray? Or does she already have her claws deeply embedded into your brain, Ray?"

"No. I've got nothing embedded into my brain from Heidi." He paused and continued to stare at me.

"Got a big automatic forty caliber? Big impressive gun, right? Stick it in people's faces'? It's what they do, Ray. They stick their big impressive guns in peoples' faces. And now, you're doing it too, right? That's something you never thought you'd do, isn't it? Violate the law enforcement creed to never un-holster your weapon unless you were going to kill someone with it or clean it. I'm right, aren't I?"

I didn't respond, I continued to stare.

"They're hotdogs, Ray! They make the Bureau out to be the bad guys, but we're not; they are. When they burn you up, you'll be back in the department looking for another investigative job. But there might not be any because none of your department peers will want to take a chance on you. They'll be certain you're a crook, or a doper, or a dope dealer yourself. So don't be smug with me, detective. If you don't wake up, you'll be a used car dealer when you leave here. Once you start the drug life, you can't stop, no matter what side of it you're on. If you aren't careful there won't be a life for you after DEA."

I stared at him, impressed with his speech, because I knew it was the gospel. He knew he had gotten to me and he was smiling.

"You may need me some day, detective. You'd better keep my card. I can be your lifeguard. Everybody gets in over their heads with DEA."

I stood and stared at him, reading his facial expressions. He pointed at me. "Physiognomy, right?"

I didn't respond to his question. "Are you finished with me?"

"Yeah, you can go."

I turned and walked out. I made my way back to the task force offices. Carla pointed at me as I walked in, "Doc's office." I walked in and Heidi was there, sitting in front of Doc's desk. She was smiling.

"How did it go?" she asked.

"As expected. Just like Doc said. I didn't make any statement, he wasn't pleased, but he excused me and I left. Now what?"

"It'll be an open investigation with you as the suspect," Doc replied. "Don't worry about it. This is the drug business. Everybody suspects us of being crooked. We all learn to live with it. The Feebs are just jealous because we have better stats than they do. We're a real investigative unit, they're just snitch developers. They rely entirely on snitches. This guy Ellis, he's a candidate to be a Feeb snitch. The Feebs would do anything to roll him." Doc gave me the concerned used Porsche dealer look. Anything else? You happy here, Ray?"

"Yeah."

"Okay, you're excused."

We walked back to our desks and resumed typing on the laptops. Seventeen-hundred was rolling around and the troops started moving toward the door.

"There's a deal tonight," Carl Robinson said. The agents stopped dead in their tracks.

"Deal?" Ross Milton said. "Nobody said anything about a deal tonight. I've got tickets to a hockey game."

"I'm taking my wife out to dinner," Mike Schweig said.

"Why didn't you warn us about the deal?"

"I can't go either," Heidi said.

"Me either," Monica said. "What kind of a deal is it?"

"Some Mexican is supposed to be coming to the Holiday Inn over in Edwardsville with a load of cocaine. I thought we'd get an adjoining room, drill a hole in the wall and watch him with a pin camera for a couple of hours. It might be nothing, you never know. The guy's name is Jesus Rangool from Tijuana. We haven't locked up a Mexican in a while."

"Who's the source?" Mike asked.

"An old C/I I haven't heard from in a couple of years."

"Who's going?" Ross asked.

"Me and Bill, and Pat, Clete, and Ray, if he can go. Can you go, Ray?"

"Roger," I replied.

"When are we going?"

"In about ten minutes," Carl replied.

The agents continued their push for the door; Carla was right behind them. Carl dialed the Holiday Inn. "I need room number one-seventeen," he said to the desk clerk. "One night. Yes, I'll pay cash, yes, be there in about an hour. It's done! Let's head over there. Ray, you can drive your Corvette. Clete, bring the Durango. Me and Pat will bring the Porsche. Meet you guys over there, room one-seventeen."

I drove home, had a long talk with Tyrone, and collected a long leather lead-loaded sap that I'd had for fifteen years, and headed across the bridge to Edwardsville, Illinois. I parked the Corvette and made my way to room one-seventeen, tapped on the door. It opened and I walked in.

The TFD's were huddled around a miniature television watching Tijuana dope dealer Jesus Rangool who was making his first mid-west appearance at the downtown

Edwardsville Holiday Inn. "What's up, guys?"

"So far," Pat Brown began; "This fat bastard, no offense Clete, has picked his nose eighty-seven times and scratched his balls one-hundred times. We haven't seen any dope yet, and we aren't sure if he's here to sell or to buy. I vote we knock on his door and act like we're his connection."

"I second it," Bill Yocum said,

"Aye," everyone said, except Carl Robinson.

"Let's watch him for a little while longer. We've got a couple of beers apiece left over from the case; when that's gone, we'll knock on his door."

"Who's going to do the undercover?" Bill Yocum asked. "That dude is pretty big."

"I'll do the UC," Carl replied. "It's my deal. Let's chug em." They killed the brew, belched and took turns urinating. "I'm ready," Carl said as he headed for the door with the group behind him.

We walked out of the room and lined the wall on both sides of the door, just like the fiasco at the other hotel when I got beaten goony by another overgrown coke dealer. They get oversized because they've got nothing to do but live the good life. Deal coke, delegate, threaten, intimidate, go to the gym, screw their coke whores.

They don't have to work and get bone-tired and eat shitty food and get stressed by some asshole boss. We had our hands on our pistols but we didn't pull them.

Carl positioned himself in front of the door so he could be seen through the peephole, then knocked on the door and gave his warmest door-to-door, working-myself-through-college smile. The door opened. Jesus Rangool stood in the doorway.

He was much larger than the video camera portrayed. He was 6'6, 300 pounds, with a nasty attitude to match. His face looked like a rugby ball that was being used in the final game of a twenty game tournament. His body looked like a mere human could not penetrate enough fat to do any harm to his vital organs.

"What you want? I don't call for any room service," Jesus said.

"I'm here to buy, I'm your connection," Carl said with a smile.

"Connection, huh? What's the password?"

"Money," Carl replied.

"That ain't it," Jesus attempted to slam the door. Carl's foot kept the door from closing.

"Oh, you want to come into my room, little gringo?" He picked Carl up by his jacket lapels and tossed him backwards into the room. We stormed in after him and jumped on Jesus trying to get him down to the floor. We were hanging on him like midgets on a giant, and he was throwing us off one by one.

Carl leapt from the floor and landed a hard right cross into Jesus' jaw. Jesus shook it off and continued to wrestle with us. I started bobbing and weaving in front of him and peppering his face and jaw with right and left combinations, which weren't phasing him.

I didn't want to get tagged by him. My brain trauma had been healing. One lucky punch could be the end for me. He was forcing us into a corner near the door and studying us as we grouped for our next attack.

I brought out the lead-loaded sap and showed it to the group. Jesus pointed at the blackjack and laughed, then started side-stepping around the room like a professional wrestler in a ring.

Pat started boxing in front of Jesus, jabbing and hooking. Carl leapt onto Jesus' giant neck and attempted to bull him down while Carl punched at his kidneys and liver.

I started slugging Jesus' leather head with the sap. We

were all wearing out, I was sapping and sapping, sap after sap after sap, and Jesus was starting to head for the floor. Blood was splattering on us and on the walls and furniture.

Over and over again I was nailing his head like a Mississippi chain gang inmate making small rocks out of big ones. Jesus was inching toward the floor. Finally, the fight left Jesus and he tumbled to the floor, unconscious.

We stumbled over each other, done in from the fight and the beer and the excitement, trying to get Jesus' hands behind his back so we could get handcuffs on him. He was so fat we had to use two sets of cuffs hooked together, but we finally got the job done.

"Somebody search him," Clete shouted. "He might have a gun."

"You search him, Clete," Bill Yocum shouted. "You're the only one who isn't done in from fighting with him."

Clete emptied Jesus' pockets and tossed the contents onto the bed. "Identification, Jesus Rangool, Tijuana, Mexico. Look at the roll of cash this bastard has," Clete said with a smile as his eyes got big. Clete counted the poke. "There's over six-thousand here. That's a thousand apiece and we'll still be able to leave him some cash to get back to TJ. I'll divvy it up." Clete started making stacks of hundred's on the bed and counting to himself as his lips moved.

"I don't want it," Carl responded.

"Me either," Bill said.

"I certainly don't want it," I said.

"I'll take some," Pat said.

He and Clete stuffed the cash into their jeans pockets as we started searching the room for dope. I walked into the bathroom and viewed myself in the mirror. I was covered in Jesus' blood. I looked at my teeth; they were blood-stained. My eyes were blurry with his blood.

I removed my jersey and started washing my face and

hair and rinsing my mouth out with warm water, filled the sink with water and submerged my face in it and opened my eyes. My black Tee wasn't bloody so I left it on and tossed my jersey into the trash receptacle as I reentered the main room where the guys were standing around with Jesus at their backs.

Jesus leaped from the floor and ran for the door, backed into it and turned the handle. He had the door open before we could get to him and he ran out into the parking lot shouting, "POLICIA, POLICIA," and was almost run down by a Madison County Sheriff's patrol car dispatched to the motel for a horrendous fight in room one-nineteen.

"They beat me, they robbed me," Jesus screamed and pointed toward us with his nose as we were filing out of the motel room to begin our search for him. The two deputies pulled their nines and pointed them dead at us, and I didn't blame them. I looked like a southern politician, the others looked like axe murderers. "Get down on the ground. Keep your hands where we can see them."

"Police officers, DEA," we shouted simultaneously as we raised our hands.

"They robbed me," Jesus shouted, "Look in their pockets. Those two, they've got over three-thousand a piece in their pockets of my money."

"He's a dope dealer," Clete screamed. "We're federal narks making an undercover buy. He's a Mexican, probably a wetback. You can't believe him."

"Search them," Jesus screamed. "I no dope dealer, If I a dope dealer, where's the dope?"

"It's probably in the room," Carl shouted. "Why don't you go in the room with me and we'll search for it."

Jesus started walking stiff-legged, like a drunk sailor on liberty in Manila. He laid his bloody head on the hood of the Sheriff's car and moaned. "I going to get you guys, you wait and see. Nobody does this shit to Jesus Rangool and gets away with it. I don't forget you," he mumbled as he slowly slid his gargantuan body down the side of the car and sat on the ground, rolling his head in circles and moaning.

"Get an ambulance started here while I search these so-called cops," an old salt deputy said. His partner, a young athletic-looking man, got on his radio and screamed into it for a priority ambulance for a head injury.

"Empty your pockets on the hood of the car here," the old deputy said to Clete and Pat. They tossed the contents of their pockets onto the hood. "It appears you boys have approximately three-thousand dollars apiece on you. You boys are under arrest for assault and robbery."

The deputy disarmed them at gunpoint, handcuffed them behind their backs, and placed them in the backseat of a lock-up patrol car.

"Oh fuck," Carl Robinson said. "I knew this was going to happen sometime," he moaned as he walked in circles with his head down in the parking lot. "Where are you taking them?"

"Courthouse, downtown Edwardsville," the old deputy replied. "Our office is in the basement."

Carl walked to the sheriff's car and spoke through the closed window. "I'll call Doc," Carl reassured them. "We'll get you out." Carl got on his cell. Doc didn't answer. He paged him. Five minutes passed and Doc didn't call him back. "I'll have to call Carla at home," he said as he dialed.

"Carla, this is Carl. Where's Doc? He is? Oh shit. Clete and Pat are in jail, over in Madison County. The deal went sour and we had to beat a guy, couldn't find the dope. Clete ripped a guy's poke and gave some to Pat. The guy ran out into the parking lot and flagged down a sheriff's car. He told them Clete and Pat ripped him. They searched them and found the guy's poke divided between Clete and Pat and arrested them. The guy is on his way to the hospital. No, don't call Sue Lee, yet. Maybe we can resolve this without alerting her. Nobody else to call? Oh, shit! Go ahead and call her and call me back on my cell phone." He stuffed the cell back into his jeans pocket.

"She's going to call Sue Lee. I kind of hope she turns us down. Then this whole game will be over and we can go back to living normal lives. It ain't worth it!"

Carl's cell rang and he answered it. "What? Okay. Tell her thanks and we'll make it up to her. Sue Lee's going to make some calls." He stuffed the cell again.

"Ray, if you would, go back into our room and get the pin camera and any other equipment belonging to us, then lock the room. We'll see you tomorrow morning at the office."

"Roger."

I took my time in the room, searching for the alleged dope, looking for a weapon, wondering how things could get so screwed up in law enforcement which, in reality, is a structured disciplined way to make a living. It's this undercover nark lifestyle that sends everything out of control.

The young narks were completely out of control, and I was turning into one of them. The unit couldn't go on like this, reacting to every nuance of a clue, overreacting on every deal. Somebody's going to get killed; it was only a matter of time.

The worst-case scenario is that a group of dopers sets us up as a unit during a deal and gets the drop on us. It wouldn't be difficult to do; most of the time the guys are drunk and feeling indestructible. Youth, gang mentality, big guns, ultimate power of the federal government behind them. Strange mix for young cops.

I envisioned the dopers pointing automatic weapons at

us, then taking our big Glocks away, laughing, punching, and kicking us as we backed into the nearest corner, waiting for the burn of the supersonic lead projectiles to tear through us, maybe killing us instantly. Maybe just wounding us so we could be tortured by many well placed shots. Every cop's nightmare, being disarmed by the bad guy.

An old cop once gave me a cloth holster that fits right below the belly button. Velcro straps hold it in place. I laughed when he gave it to me. I'll never be working undercover, I said to him. "You never know in this game." He was right.

I had tossed it in my dresser drawer and forgot about it, until now. My 357, titanium Smith & Wesson, my Susan gun, named for an old girlfriend, will fit it perfectly. It's undetectable, even with a frisk, bad guys and cops won't grab a guy down there. It ain't macho. I'm putting it into service tomorrow. Things are going downhill in the task force.

7

They were sliding into the office, all of them just a little late after their mid-week therapeutic extravaganzas. Carla was at the DEA super-secret computer. Clete, Pat, and Bill were standing in front of her desk. "Jesus Rangool, a filthy dope dealer from T J," Pat said to Carla as she typed the name into the memory bank. "I want to know everything about him. That scum sucker beat the system last night and I want to know who he is and what he's about."

"Here it comes," Carla said. "He's a dope dealer from Tijuana, belongs to the Mendoza Cartel, he's muscle for the cartel and an enforcer. Apparently he's trying to branch out on his own. He doesn't want to infringe on cartel territory, so he wound up in Edwardsville, Illinois, looking for new clients. He's a tough guy."

"We know he's tough," Pat responded. "Is he a killer? He threatened me and Clete."

"Let me put it this way, the morticians in Tijuana are driving Mercedes' thanks to him." Clete and Pat looked over to me at my desk for moral support. I nodded to them.

Monica Rose strolled in wearing skin-tight jeans and a Polo sweatshirt, singing "Porgy, don't let him take me." Mike Schweig stumbled into the office and fell into his desk chair. He sat at his desk and gave his impression of a fish out of water, smoked and drank cup after cup of coffee.

Ross Milton pranced in and surveyed the room. "I heard the little darlings got into trouble again last night," he said to Carla. "They're talking about it in the halls; How did they get out of it?"

"Sue Lee," Carla muttered.

"Oh, great, how charming."

SAC, Square Bidness, Willie Mitchell walked into the room. He was wearing a George Foreman scowl and a

Johnnie Cochran suit. “Where’s Doc?”

“In his office, sir.” Willie walked in and closed the door behind him.

Carl Robinson walked into the task force offices as Willie was walking into Doc’s office. “What’s Square Bidness doing in Doc’s office?” Carla shrugged.

Clete and Pat walked up to Carl and thanked him for getting them out of jail. Pat kept shaking his head and pumping Carl’s hand. “Can you believe them cops over in Illinois, man? They don’t know the difference between the good guys and the bad guys. They were going to break it off in our ass. I mean, we were looking at jail time, all for that piece of shit dope dealer from TJ.”

“Yeah, man, don’t mention it, but we got to have a TFD meeting sometime soon and talk things over. It’s supposed to be in the seventies today. Maybe we can take this afternoon off and play a little golf. Tomorrow is federal Friday; we can make a long weekend out of it. Is everybody in?”

“I don’t play golf,” Clete said.

“I’m in,” I said.

“I’m in,” Bill said.

“I’m in,” Pat said.

Square Bidness walked out of Doc’s office, stopped and glared at Clete and Pat with his I’m-going-beat-you-up stare, then walked out of the office. Doc walked out and stood in front of Carla’s desk.

“I need your attention. I’m sure everybody now knows about last night’s deal in Illinois that went bad. The SAC has informed me that this alleged dope dealer, Jesus Rangool, has a fractured skull and has been admitted to Barnes Hospital. I just called Barnes to get a condition on him and was informed that Jesus is in a rehabilitation apartment at Euclid and West Pine, down in the Central

West End. Apparently he's going to be in St. Louis for approximately six months while undergoing treatment. Stay away from him."

Carl raised his hand. Doc nodded to him. "Why is he allowed to stay in this country? He's a dirty Tijuana dope dealer and murderer. Why don't they deport him?"

"He's on a visa, and it's all legal. He has his own money and isn't dependent on anyone. He can stay here until he's recovered. You guys did him a favor. If he meets an American girl and gets married, he may be here forever. It's the American way. Anyway, you guys didn't find any dope. It's probably in a bus depot baggage locker. This guy is no dummy."

"It stinks," Pat remarked, "He threatened me and Clete, and he's a documented murderer."

"I'm just telling you what the SAC wants me to tell you. Obviously you have to protect yourself at all times just like you've always had to do. This is no different. Most of the characters we deal with have the ability to kill you at any time, before, during or after deals. Do what you have to do."

"Who's going to back us up?" Pat Brown shouted.

"Is DEA going to stand by us? It's for sure the police department won't," Carl shouted.

"Protect yourselves at all times," Doc reiterated, "That's all I'm saying, we'll figure out how to cover it after it happens. Besides, you guys have been threatened before. What's the big deal?"

"We've never been arrested before," Pat said. "For doing our job, and there was nobody around to get us out of trouble. If it wasn't for Sue Lee we'd be being arraigned about now."

"Okay, we're going to move on. The sheriff over in Madison County advised the SAC he doesn't want us over in his county anymore doing deals. The SAC quoted him,

'Keep your junior G men over in Missouri. If I see them over here again working, I'm going to lock them up and then let the Illinois State Court sort it all out.' We've got the rest of the country to work in. Let's stay out of Illinois for a while until this thing blows over. Okay, that's all I have. Get back to work."

"Okay agents and TFD's," Carla shouted. "It's a beautiful spring day in downtown Clayton and it's time to toil for the government. Laptops open, please." Like trained chimps we all opened our computers and started typing.

At 1100 hours Carl stood and gave us the high sign. We all strolled out of the office, except Clete, who stayed seated at his desk. We were on the elevator going down to the parking garage. "We'll meet at the central patrol parking lot in thirty-five minutes," Carl said. "We can take the Lincoln Towne car; that way we won't burn up our undercover cars."

"Right, okay," we said simultaneously.

I drove home like a madman, ran in, petted Tyrone, grabbed my sticks and shoes and made it to the parking lot in exactly thirty-five minutes. The boys were sitting in the big car drinking a cold one as I parked the Corvette. Bill hit the trunk release and I tossed my clubs and shoes on top of the heap and got in, closing the door as we were speeding off to the championship course at Forest Park.

We were on the second hole before Carl got loosened up enough to tell us why he called this meeting. He and I were in a cart, and Bill and Pat shared one. "Sue Lee is getting freaky," Carl began. She's growing tired of helping us get out of trouble. I can tell."

"We're city cops, we're supposed to get into trouble. If you don't get into trouble then you're not working," Bill said.

"I've been thinking," Carl continued, "Most of the

trouble we get into stems from fights with the bad guys. If we could control our emotions and not beat them up as often, or as bad, we might not need Sue Lee. The special agents don't get into any trouble."

"They don't make any cases, either," Pat said. "I've never seen any of them do the under-cover, except for Monica Rose. No offense, Ray, I know Heidi is a good gal and a good agent. Mike and Ross haven't made a case since I've been there."

"As far as DEA is concerned, the agents are the ones making the cases. They get the stats from our cases," Carl said. "DEA in Washington doesn't know we exist. We're building the careers of Mike, Ross, and Doc. Monica and Heidi carry their own weight. We are going to have to reassess and reevaluate our positions with the task force and come up with a plan for survival or we're going to be in front of a federal grand jury, or worse, working for the PD again."

"There's a guy coming toward us from number three," I said. "Maybe he left a club on the number two green," Pat said.

"Maybe," I replied as I looked over my shoulder at the green. We watched and waited as the cart got closer to us. "It's being driven by a giant," Bill stated, "And there's a little old man sitting next to him."

The golf cart came to an abrupt stop in front of us. The driver, who had the appearance of a retired football player, sized us up, then said, "Mister Likovelli and Mister Vitale want to be certain that you boys don't hit into them. They've asked me to advise you boys of their concern."

The golf cart with the giant and the little old man then tacked back toward the number three tee and joined up with another cart driven by another giant with a little old man next to him.

"That was ignorant," Pat exclaimed. "We had no intention of hitting into them."

"Those are two retired organized crime bosses," I replied. "I'm assuming the big guys in the carts with them are their bodyguards. I didn't think any of those guys were still alive. It's remarkable."

Pat grabbed a six pack out of the cooler in the back of his cart and tossed everyone a cold one. "Who's up?"

"Ray's up," they said simultaneously. I chugged my beer and hit an eight-iron six feet from the hole on the par three. Carl and Pat hit into the lake. Bill made the back of the green. We putted and moved onto the fourth hole.

"Beer," Bill said as he passed them around, "This case is almost shot. It's a good thing I brought another one. Who's up?"

"Ray," they said together.

"Hit the hell out of it, Ray," Carl said.

"I'd better wait. If I got into one, I'd probably put it into Mister Vitale's golf cart, then we'd have a fight on our hands."

"As far as I'm concerned," Pat began, "We ought to start shooting at them. They're old organized criminals, right? The Mafia started bringing dope into this city fifty years ago. Got all those inner city folks hooked on heroin. That's when they started tearing this city down, those hooked city street hooligans robbing and stealing to get money to buy more heroin from them Mafia assholes."

He put a cold beer to his lips, tossed his Charles Manson head back and killed it in three gulps. He crushed the can and tossed it into the golf cart and continued his tirade.

"Those Mafia bastards probably lived in Ladue off of the money those city assholes stole to buy more smack. They probably told their kids not to venture into the city because there were a bunch of dope fiends down there robbing and killing and it wasn't safe. Probably sent their kids to private schools so they could be doctors and lawyers, and it all started with those Mafia dope dealing bastards. Now we have to bow and scrape to these lawyers, so we can keep locking bastards up who sell dope so they can make lawyers out of their kids. I say we hit into them."

"Brilliantly put," I said.

"You're a genius," Bill said.

"Love you, man," Carl muttered.

I smashed my driver and the ball hit five feet from one of the giants. The two bodyguards glared at us while the little old men were preparing for their next shot. Carl hit his driver and the ball careened right at them and struck the back of one of the bodyguard's cart.

Bill smashed his driver and the ball went high and right. It bounced off of the asphalt cart path and then landed inside of the cart, ricocheting around like an errant twenty-two round in a wine cellar.

They came speeding toward us. The giant climbed out of the cart. "Who hit the first ball?" I raised my hand like a student wanting to ask a question.

"I'm going to teach you some respect," the giant said as he walked toward me, raising his hand as if he was going to bitch-slap me. I ducked under the swing and fired three short hard right uppercuts into the giant's heart. He crouched and froze for an instance. He was moving slower, but he came at me again, throwing wild punches at my head.

I slapped the punches away, palmed his right wrist and took him down with an arm-bar take-down body slam, which drove his face into the soft soil. I held onto his wrist as I kicked him in the ribs, then released his wrist and jumped on his back and neck. I backed away and waited for the next attack.

The next giant bodyguard, who was a look-alike for Hulk

Hogan, jumped out of the cart and charged Pat Brown. Pat sidestepped him and started throwing punches at the big man's head and face.

Carl got behind the assailant and thrashed him across the back and shoulders with an eight-iron. The man continued to attack Pat. Carl smashed the back of his head with the eight-iron. He went down face first with blood spurting out of his head.

The little old Mafia men were wearing looks of terror as they scrambled to get behind the wheels of their golf carts. Carl rushed toward one of the carts. "Not so fast, good fellas," he shouted as he took control of the cart.

Pat jumped behind the wheel of the other one. They drove toward the third hole, par three lake while the Mafia bosses were pleading for them to stop. As the carts got to the lake's edge, Carl and Pat bailed out. The runaway carts careened into the lake with their Mafia passengers and sunk. The two old men dog-paddled to shore and climbed through the muddy embankment to the grass where they laid out and clutched their rosaries.

"You fucking dope dealers," Carl and Pat screamed at the little old men as they were running to their golf carts. "Do you know how many lives you've ruined?"

We jumped back into our carts and sped toward the parking lot, tossed our sticks and coolers into the trunk of the big car, abandoned our carts, jumped in and tore out of the parking lot.

I was sitting in the back seat. I looked out of the rear window and observed one of the big bodyguards running in the parking lot with blood spurting out of the back of his head. He was writing down the license number of the car. "He's taking down our license number," I shouted.

"Big deal," Carl shouted, "These plates are issued to a vacant lot down in the eighth district to a guy named George

Brown; we've got nothing to worry about."

"We got those dope dealing bastards," Pat shouted. We gave each other high fives and toasted our victory with cold beer. "A toast," Pat said, "to beatings everywhere, so long as they are justified. Today, the beatings were justified."

I was having mixed emotions sitting in the back seat of the government car. I was one of them now. The feeling of being a member of the pack was reassuring. I felt indestructible, just like the testosterone-laden cop kids. It is what gets cops killed. I knew that. You start depending on the pack instead of yourself. Somebody in the pack makes a mistake and everybody goes down, either killed or indicted.

I felt the danger of the moment, the hapless disregard for anything but the feeling of brotherhood. It was suicide! Did Jack Parker have this feeling? Is he dead instead of missing.

Did the brotherhood dispose of him because of something he did or didn't do? I had no choice; I was compelled to hang tough and find out what happened to Jack Parker. I tried to figure out why I cared about the missing drunk, kid cop. It was a mystery. Quite possibly a conspiracy, and I had no defense against investigating them.

I didn't want to see these kiddy cops killed, and I didn't want to become a statistic. I figured I'd ride it out to the end. It's what cops are programmed to do.

8

After the fiasco in Illinois and the golf course incident the TFD's put the brakes on dope deals. I took some time off and some of the other TFD's did likewise. Doc was beside himself with deal anxiety and had started a rumor he was going to send some of the guys back to the PD. We all scurried back to the office.

We did some small deals; just to placate Doc and the weekend rolled around quickly. I took a Friday off and was beginning to feel like a normal person.

It was a gorgeous federal Friday late afternoon in May in beautiful south St. Louis. It was the first day of my three-day mini-vacation away from the task force. I awoke with the sun shining through my glass wall, barges and recreational boats plying the current on the Mississippi, and white pelicans zooming around like jet airplanes above the river surface.

The old house needed to be cleaned. Usually I had female companionship and the place was always neat and sparkling, but with hardly anyone ever here, except for Tyrone; It was losing its luster. I climbed out and made my way down the ladder, let Tyrone out and fixed my usual cereal and fruit, and two cups of coffee.

I read the paper in the sun on the deck while Tyrone romped. The Azaleas were coming up like magic. I wondered who planted them. It could have been a Union Army officer. There is no telling who camped on this spot hundreds, or even thousands of years ago.

I watched the river for a while, then cleaned the old house starting with the loft and working my way down. It was after one P.M. when I finished. I pulled my old crazy El Camino around to the back yard and washed it, put it back in the garage and then drove the Austin Healey around and washed it.

Tyrone was whining for a ride. I checked my cell phone for calls. I hadn't missed any. I expected Heidi to call me for a romp this evening. I was reluctant to call her; FBI Agent David Moynihan's speech hit home with me. I didn't want to be a total spineless jellyfish cop when it came to her or DEA in general.

I had to have some character in this DEA thing. A cop could lose control real fast here. Beautiful women, money, cars, power. It seemed like a dream for a city cop. I'm sure it could turn into a nightmare in seconds.

I pulled the Healey back into the garage and fired up the crazy El Camino again and backed it out. Tyrone hopped in with his Frisbee in his teeth and we were off toward Forest Park.

There are always loads of single coeds in the park on sunny days and they're all attracted to Tyrone and his athletic ability to catch a Frisbee while turning a 360, then running full bore back to me. The dog is a chick magnet.

I slowly drove to the park with Tyrone riding shotgun, parked on the street on Lindell and walked him to the exercise area with a lead. People were already following us, even before I took his lead off.

I unleashed him and tossed the Frisbee as hard as I could. Tyrone took off like a cheetah and ran it down, turned a 360 in mid-air, and headed back to me.

The crowd was exclaiming and commenting and applauding as we did the exercise over and over again. Tyrone never tired of it, and neither did the spectators. I kept my eye on the groups of people, looking for that right chick, that right look, the come-on smile, the green light that the female possesses for the male to make the move. I didn't see it.

The sun was going down and it was getting chilly. Most

of the spectators had made their way toward their cars. Tyrone ran to the lake and filled up on water. I waited for him to return as the last remnants of sunlight disappeared over my shoulder.

We walked to the crazy El Camino and climbed in. "Hamburger?" He nodded to me and I took off for a White Castle drive-through. We were eating our Castles on Seventh Street when I saw my nemesis, Clete drive by in the government Durango. He was crunched down in the seat and his jaw was set as if he was on a mission.

"Hang on, Tyrone, we're going to do some surveillance." I cranked the old Chevy and we took off after him, trying to stay at least a block behind the Durango. It had gotten completely dark, so I followed the tail lights south toward the Carondelet Police District. He took south Broadway to Bates, near my house, and went west on Bates, then made a left turn on Grand, and drove into Carondelet Park.

He stopped near a pavilion and sat in the Durango. My brain was going like a meth-head's dream. I parked the El Camino on Christy, told Tyrone I would be right back, then cut through the woods in the park until I came within muffled ear-shot of the pavilion.

I stood in the trees, in the chilly spring wind, and waited for Clete to make a move. He continued to sit in the Durango, in the warmth. I saw the lights of a vehicle, and heard it tearing through the park toward the pavilion.

The vehicle was a pickup truck and it pulled up with a sliding of the tires on the gravel; Special Agent Jim Schwartz climbed out, motorcycle leather, boots and jeans. He acted as if he was enraged. He stood near the DEA Ford four-wheel drive pickup and motioned for Clete to come to him.

Clete clamored out of the Durango and waddled over to the agent. When he got within arm's length Schwartz reached out to him and grabbed him by the collar. Schwartz was so big, it looked like an adult abusing a child. Clete was frozen in fear.

"You motherfucker," he shouted. "I told you to," then he lowered his voice. I couldn't make out the conversation. Schwartz shook him like a rag doll. Schwartz started shouting again, "and to add insult to injury, he does a search warrant on a client. Couldn't you stop that?" Schwartz was in Clete's face, screaming.

I inched my way closer to them. "It wasn't his warrant, Jim. It was a state warrant from some sheriff out in the sticks. Arnold knows him. It was a fluke, Jim."

Schwartz slapped Clete, a bitch-slap so hard that I felt it. Clete went down to the cold ground and stayed there. I knew what Clete was doing. He felt that if he stayed down, Schwartz would leave and allow him to live for another day.

But Schwartz wasn't finished. He did what DEA folks do. He pulled his forty caliber Glock and stuck it in Clete's face while he was on the ground. Clete was pistol paralyzed, his eyes frozen on the muzzle of the semi-automatic weapon.

Schwartz was crouched down with his gun in Clete's face for about thirty seconds. Clete wasn't begging for his life, or muttering, or praying. He was lifeless and waiting for the supersonic projectile to tear into his brain.

Schwartz laughed, stood upright, put the Glock back into his waistband, then walked to his truck, climbed in, cranked it, and tore away. Clete stood up, brushed himself off, yelled obscenities toward the truck, then waddled to his Durango, climbed in, and took off.

I walked back to my El Camino and Tyrone, climbed in and headed for home. I pulled the crazy El Camino into the garage and Tyrone and I went inside. I sat in front of the television wondering what to do with the information I had just gleaned.

Clete was a thief, but everyone knew that. He was a thief before he went to DEA; almost everyone in the department knew that, but it didn't hinder his upward movement in his profession.

So, now Clete's in cahoots with a federal agent. I wondered how these guys find each other. It's as if there is a crook resume that other crooks have available to them on their counterparts. Jim Schwartz had to have approached Clete with the blackmail scheme of Feddy Ellis. It was amazing that he felt he could trust Clete.

Now Clete's in trouble. His life might be in danger. Schwartz is unstable and a violent person. He could kill Clete. I thought he was going to do it this evening. He probably has plans to do it. Had he fired a shot this evening it would have been heard by hundreds of people.

There are houses lining the park, wealthy folks live in them. They're paranoid most of the time, and watch the park. Schwartz had to know that. That's all that saved Clete this evening. He was bound to get his sooner than later.

9

Spring was in the air in beautiful downtown Clayton. It was 0901, and the group wasn't at their desks pounding on their laptops. They were standing at the windows with surveillance binoculars watching the parade of young beauties tacking their way to their office buildings on the sidewalks below us. It's amazing what a little sunshine will do.

"Look at that snake," Pat Brown said as he zoomed in on a vivacious creature. "Hey, Ray, come and look at this one."

I got up from my desk and walked to the window. He handed me the binoculars. "Blonde, gorgeous," I said as I handed them back to him.

"That's the snake of snakes there," Pat continued. "I'm going to watch for her in the Club, she's going to be mine."

Mike Schweig came over to the window smelling of an all-night drunk, smoking and coughing and spilling coffee. "Can I see?"

"Yeah, Mike, but you'd better hurry. She's about to slither under a rock." Mike perched the binoculars on his face with shaking hands and watched the blonde as she walked out of sight.

Carla was standing at the front of her desk, clearing her throat and watching the clock. Everyone ignored her. Heidi came up next to me. "We've got to meet an informant tonight. You going be available?"

I glanced at her and checked her out before I answered. Black pants and a maroon low-cut blouse, showing cleavage. Pixy hair-do, moist skin glowing, just the right amount of perfume to make things interesting, just a waft to mesmerize the unsuspecting victim. Now I know why the TFD's call them snakes. Beautiful, but deadly. A venom there is no cure for.

Spring had definitely sprung. Or was I just going through the paranoid ponders because of the speech by FBI Agent David Moynihan. Baubles and bangles, and a little romance from the lookers.

Heidi is definitely one of the lookers. It's probably the same wherever a guy goes for a new job. Baubles and bangles and romance with the lookers? No, it couldn't be that way anywhere else. It has to be indigenous to DEA, and to St. Louis. Business, it's so damn weird here.

"Yeah, I'm available. Where did this come from?"

"It's the guy from Hortense," she replied. "Remember? I'll clue you in this evening. It has promise." She walked back to her desk.

Doc walked into the office; I caught his movement out of the corner of my eye, his gait threatening. I looked at him full. He scowled back at the group ogling at the window with the sunshine filling the big open room.

"Come into my office," he said to Carla. They left the door open and we were moving as a group toward Carla's desk, craning our necks, eavesdropping for clues.

"Read this." There was silence.

"Oh, my God," Carla exclaimed.

"It had to be a TFD," Doc said. "A DEA employee wouldn't have done it; it's a damn C/I with a badge. After all I've done for them. Damn, I can't believe it."

"What do you want me to do, Doc?"

"Find out whose laptop this came from. Can you do that?"

"Yeah," Carla replied, "but it might take some time."

They came out of Doc's office in a whoosh. We were standing at Carla's desk with our surveillance binoculars in our hands, our necks craned and our ears tuned. Doc was still scowling.

"I've got something to say to the group." We all went to

our desks and sat and waited as he paced in front of Carla's desk, scowling at us individually, trying to read us, running his right hand through his thick mullet, sucking in his encroaching mid-section.

"Somebody wrote a letter to my wife." He stopped and watched us as if we were drug suspects he was baiting, manipulating, leading. "Somebody in this room told my wife about my affair with my secretary friend in the United States Attorney's office."

He paused again, waiting and watching as we waited and watched him. "That's low down. It's despicable behavior for anyone at DEA. We're family. I've treated each and every one of you with respect. I'm going to find out who did this to me. I will get the person responsible for this betrayal. He will not go unpunished. I'm going to kick his ass." Doc turned and went back into his office.

"Okay," Carla said. "Open your laptops and start typing!" We were all typing with our heads down, like scolded children wrongly accused of committing an infraction in the schoolyard, wondering who the real culprit was.

There was another body coming into the office. We all stopped on cue and looked up. It was a county process server, serving Doc with a restraining order. He was now officially out-of-the-crib. We went back to typing.

Another distraction, movement at Carla's desk. Tina Monroe, Doc's concubine from the U.S. Attorney's office, walked in. It was damage control and re-group time. She probably wrote the letter. Everybody stopped typing and watched her as she hugged Carla and patted a tear.

I sized her up again, young, maybe twenty four, large rack, nice long thick blonde hair, good dresser, but she didn't have the bones, and she didn't have the skin, and she wasn't worth leaving the crib for. What she had was youth, and Doc was eighteen years her senior. Another ego thing in the dope business. You have to be a dope to be on either end of it, or in the middle. Tina's in the middle.

We typed in the subdued atmosphere, agents shooting glances at cops, cops shooting glances at agents, everyone wondering who the snitch of snitches was. Finally, seventeen-hundred rolled around and the group headed for the Club.

Heidi and I stayed around a little longer, writing and flirting. She gave me the high sign and I got up, locked my desk, and strolled over to her desk. She sent her work to the mainframe, closed her laptop and stood. "I can't wait to get out of here. This place is getting to me. There's too many crises. Every day it's something new."

I didn't comment but I knew what she was saying was the gospel. The place was a calamity waiting to happen. Law enforcement is that way, probably everywhere. I had always felt that way.

We headed for the garage without speaking, passing the lonely secretaries leaving their offices and heading for the Club for their rendezvous with the TFD's.

We were in Heidi's government Bimmer, cruising west on Lindell in the Central West End. I was waiting for her to clue me in, but she didn't seem to be in any hurry. "Want to clue me in now?"

"Oh, yeah, I'm sorry. I had my mind on this interview. When I had the duty last week the guy from Hortense calls me again, late. As usual, we fence. These people who call are always trying to give us some kind of a drug tip. Most of these calls are weird. Have you had the duty yet?"

"No."

"Anyway, I talk to this guy. He gave me his name a few nights prior; that's when you and I went by his house. But I could feel he was trying to feel me out, maybe to see what kind of an agent I was. He calls every night, and we talk. I find out more about him. He's a big-time chef. World renowned. That's one of the things I learned from listening to him ramble. He would never come clean and tell me why he was calling DEA late at night."

"You believe him?" I asked. "You think he's a big-time chef?"

"Yeah. So, we're talking on my last night of the duty, and he finally gives me his address: 4969 Hortense Place. He didn't know I already had it. For grins, I run him in the DEA super secret computer, and voila, he's in there as a world famous chef. His address is in there, too. House is worth about a mill five. Don't you think?"

"At least," I replied.

"The guy invited me over to his house for dinner. I tell him I can't come without my partner, that's you, and he says swell. So we're going to Sig Otto's mansion for a dinner. Okay with you?"

"Sig as in Sig Sauer?"

"No," she replied with a smile. "He's not a pistol, he's a human. Sig as in Siegfried. His name is actually Siegfried."

"Groovy," I replied.

She turned the Bimmer onto Hortense, a street that hasn't changed in a century. The mansions still looked new and the street had ornate working gas lights.

If it weren't for the modern automobiles parked in the driveways and on the street, a visitor would think he was in a time warp.

We pulled into the driveway of Sig's palatial granite Victorian house. An old black Oldsmobile 98 with blackwall tires and little chrome hubcaps was parked at the door. I wondered what kind of person would drive such a car. Surely he could afford to drive something more chic, like a BMW or a Corvette.

We climbed out and walked up the stone stairs to the massive porch and cherry wood door. It opened and he was there to greet us, "Welcome to my house, my new friends," he said as he hugged Heidi and then me. "I am so glad you have accepted my invitation. Please give me your coats." I mentally dissected him the way cops do. Full head of brown hair, thin mustache and goatee, solidly built, darting eyes, crafty smile, and the desire to please.

We peeled them and handed them to him. He shuffled around the massive foyer like a Chinese butler. He sported a dark red velvet dinner jacket with the butt of a 357 in a shoulder holster occasionally exposed.

"Tonight, my new friends, we are having beef tenderloin, but first allow me to serve you a glass of wine. This wine costs seven hundred dollars a bottle," he said as he poured it for us. Please help yourselves to the shrimp while I show you around my house. The house was vacant for years. Can you imagine a work of art like this sitting vacant?"

"No," we said simultaneously.

"Me neither," he continued.

"An architect purchased it and changed the windows and then he moved to Florida and the house was vacant again. When I purchased it, the fireplace mantel had been stolen and there was no heat. The furnaces had to be rebuilt and the floors had to be redone. Follow me to the third floor, I have my office there." He grabbed the wine bottle as he walked.

We trekked after him, sipping our expensive wine and giggling to each other as we climbed the massive curved and carpeted staircase. He ushered us into an open room with large windows at each end. There was a gigantic oak desk, computers, bookshelves, artwork, Indian artifacts, and copies of Gourmet magazine scattered everywhere. A glass trophy case was the focal point of the room. "I am so proud of my office. I spend most of my time up here."

"Those are neat trophies," Heidi said. "What are they for?"

"Okinawan Karate and Kempo. Are you familiar with the martial arts, Agent Anderson?" Heidi shook her head in the negative and intently studied Siegfried.

"What about you, Detective Arnold?"

"Somewhat," I replied, "I was stationed in Okinawa in the Marine Corps. I'm familiar with both disciplines. If I remember correctly, the philosophy behind Kempo is to get your adversary onto the ground and kill him, using your hands, feet, teeth, knees, head, or whatever is available. Okinawan Karate is a bit more refined."

"I knew I had you pegged. I could tell by the way you held yourself and by the way you moved that you were a warrior. It is an honor to make your acquaintance, Detective Arnold." He shook my hand again, as if we had just met.

"Please call me Ray."

"I have never killed anybody with my hands," Sig said. "But I look forward to it. I live by the rules of Kempo. Tread on me and you will die a terrible death." I nodded in acknowledgment.

"Feel my biceps, and my forearms and my chest."

Heidi and I reluctantly pushed and prodded Sig's upper body.

"Not bad for a sixty year old man, is it?"

"No," we said together.

"It's a fine place to work," Heidi said as we stood toe to toe with Sig wondering what was in store for us. The expensive wine was starting to take its effect on both of us. We had been doing paperwork all day and hadn't eaten any lunch, and Sig wouldn't allow our glasses to get empty.

I noticed two pieces of PVC pipe approximately three inches in diameter and four feet long on tripods at the dormer window in front of the house and two at the dormer window at the rear of the house.

"What are these?" I asked, pointing.

"Potato cannons," Sig nonchalantly replied.

"What's a potato cannon?" I asked.

"It shoots potatoes," Sig began to explain, "You stick your average red potato in the barrel and then prime the chamber with hair spray, pull the trigger, and a spark ignites the hair spray. The potato shoots out of the cannon. You can shoot a potato a hundred yards, and with the way I have them set up on these tripods, you can be accurate."

"Who do you shoot at?" I was hanging onto Heidi and laughing.

"When I first moved here, the neighborhood wasn't very good. I have wonderful neighbors, but they were afraid. We couldn't even walk down the street the street people had this neighborhood targeted. They would drive their cars down the street and look into the houses and then get out of their cars and break into them, or if my neighbors were in their yards or walking down the street, they'd rob them at gunpoint."

Heidi and I nodded, watched and listened.

"They were bold and nobody did anything about it. I set up my potato cannons and when a car comes down the street with their radio blasting some horrible music, I shoot the back window out of the car with a potato. I usually allow a car to cruise down the street one time. It's a dead-end street and they have to turn around. When they come near my house I let them have it. I put two potatoes through the back window at about ninety five miles per hour. The first potato disintegrates as it hits the glass and throws pieces of glass and potato all over the inside of the car. The second one bounces around the inside of the car and bangs up the occupants. It's neat, and the greatest thing about it is they do not know where the potatoes come from. They can not see up here because of the trees, but I can see them. I have a clear shot through the trees. It's the same way at the back of the house. Sometimes they drive down the alley when I get them in front. When they do, I blast them in the passenger side window."

He paused while Heidi and I smiled chuckled and hung onto each other.

"It blows the window right out of the door frame," he said laughing. "They leave and don't come back. I knocked a burglar off of a bicycle at eighty five yards last summer. Got that yahoo right in the back of the head. You should have seen that one. I laughed until I thought I was going to die. If they get in my killing zone, I get them. The neighborhood is much better now, and my neighbors love me for it. I didn't come to America to be a wimp. I want to kill the bad guys. That's why I love you guys so much. I love what you do."

Heidi and I glanced at each other with glassy-eyed stares, as if to say, Is this guy for real? He filled our glasses for the fourth time. We gulped and smiled.

"I saw a car drive down the street right after you guys got here," Sig said with a chuckle. "He went to the dead-end and stopped and turned his lights off. I never did see him drive back by. Heidi, turn those lights down. The switch is by the door. I'm going to look for that yahoo with these binoculars and see what he's up to."

Sig perused the street. "He's still sitting at the end of the street with his motor running. I don't like it. I'm going to give you guys a demonstration. As soon as he leaves and gets past my house, into the killing zone, I'm going to blast that desperado."

The wine had us warmed up. The lights were low and we were standing arm in arm while Sig was conducting neighborhood surveillance. Heidi raised her face to me and we necked while Sig hunted.

"He's moving," Sig shouted. "Here, Ray, take these binoculars. Watch this guy as I blow out his back window, and stick a couple of potatoes in your pocket so you can give them to me for a reload." He handed them to me and I stuffed them into my jeans pocket.

Sig primed the chambers with hair spray and stuffed one fist-sized red potato into each tube. He opened the dormer window and positioned the tripods for firing. I watched with the binoculars as the car slowly cruised by Sig's mansion. The cannons fired and the potatoes were sent on their way.

The first potato took out the rear window of the Chevy. The second one went straight through the car and broke the windshield from the inside. "We got him," Sig shouted. "That bastard will not be coming down this street for a while. Quick, give me another potato."

I dug into my pocket and handed him one then stepped back as he reloaded the cannon. I was looking at the car with the binoculars. It had stopped and the driver had gotten out. I zoomed in on him.

"Oh, oh!"

"What is it?" I handed her the binoculars. "What?" She said as she looked at the furious driver. "It's David Moynihan," she muttered. "Oh, fuck!" She handed me the binoculars and I continued to watch him. He was trying to determine where the projectiles came from.

He walked to the rear of the car and then stopped and surveyed the area, then scratched his head and walked up the sidewalk toward Sig's house.

"He's coming our way," I advised. Sig pulled the cannons inside and closed the dormer window. Moynihan stopped on the sidewalk in front of Sig's mansion and visually inspected the house, then turned and walked back to the damaged Chevy. He was sweeping the glass out of the inside with a newspaper, and smelling the remnants of the mashed potatoes. He had a wry smile, then got into the government Chevy and drove off.

"You guys know that yahoo?"

"Yeah, we know him," I said. "Apparently he was following us. I guess he got what he was looking for, trouble. I can't believe he'd follow us," I said to Heidi.

"Feebs have been following DEA agents since the creation of the Bureau of Narcotics and Dangerous Drugs," Heidi replied. "Moynihan even tried to follow me to Colombia on my last assignment. He didn't leave the country with me but he had me under surveillance after I got back to Miami. He's filth. They think we're all crooks. We think they're all nerds. He's a nerd and a crook, too. I know that as a fact."

"Is that the greatest thing you ever saw?" Sig asked. He poured more wine into our glasses. "Shall we go down stairs and eat? The beef will be ready, now."

"Yeah," we followed him down the stairway.

There wasn't much talk as we devoured the gourmet meal. Sig was attentive, filling our glasses and serving us second helpings. I wondered when the conversation was going to turn to dope. Heidi kept glancing at me and I figured she felt the same way.

We were having dessert, baked Alaska when Sig started talking. "In the food business, there are a certain amount of dead beats, much like other vocations. It seems this business has attracted a drug following. I've been privy to gleaned information concerning the cocaine trade in the greater St. Louis area. Does that interest you?" He was staring at us, reading us.

"Yes," I replied; Heidi was nodding in the affirmative.

"I despise the drug trade. I despise drug users. If I were in your profession, I would do my best to use my Kempo on every drug suspect I came across. I would teach them a lesson if they survived the beating I gave them." He was staring off into space as if imagining a battle for survival with him pounding a drug suspect.

He snapped back to us. "There is a shipment coming from Savannah, Georgia, tomorrow evening. Are you guys familiar with Savannah?"

"Yes," we replied simultaneously.

"It is a beautiful city, ornate and old, and it has some fine restaurants, he continued. "It's been infiltrated by some gangsters and ne'er-do-wells who've migrated there from south Florida. A pity."

"Yeah," we agreed.

"It is coming in by automobile tomorrow evening. I will write the address down for you." He obtained a pad and pen and wrote the address then handed it to Heidi. She glanced at it and placed it in her pants pocket then said, "Carondelet Park area," to me.

"The guy bringing the dope in is just a courier. He makes frequent trips from Savannah to St. Louis in a rental car. Brings kilos in the trunk. He puts the stuff in the garage behind the house and then takes the rental back to the airport rental company. This goes on approximately twice a month. That's a lot of cocaine for this area, but there's a lot of cocaine in this town. I hate it and I want it stopped. Can you guys do anything with this information?"

"Yes, of course we can," we said together.

"Come, let's go into the sitting room."

"No," Heidi replied. "Ray and I are going to help you clean up these dishes." She stood and started carrying dirty dishes into the kitchen, stopped and gave me a look, and I started carting them. Sig followed us with a pile of dishes, rinsed them, and placed them into the dishwasher. The table was cleared and the kitchen tidied up when we went to the sitting room.

We were still drinking wine and were completely relaxed and mellow. Sig was holding court. "Is there a chance that I could go with you guys on a drug deal?"

"Maybe someday," Heidi replied. "But not tomorrow. Your identity must be kept secret. Let's just see how this thing plays out. The information you've gleaned sounds great, but you and I don't really know if it'll be productive. In fact, I think we should go. Tomorrow is going to be a long day, and if your information is good, we'll be working most of the night." She stood and gave me the sign. I stood and so did Sig. He walked us to the door, gave us our coats and hugged us.

"I hope this will be a life-long friendship," he said as we were walking out the door. We smiled, and waved and entered the Bimmer. I got back out and walked to him and gave him my cell number on a card.

"Call me in a couple of months and we'll go on a deal together." He was beaming as I climbed back into the Bimmer.

We drove to the intersection, the place where Moynihan's G car got potato lashed. There was glass on the pavement; it scrunched under the tires of the Bimmer. Heidi started giggling. I thought of the escapades the evening had brought, and I started laughing. "What a night," I said still laughing. "We're not going to have to burn him, are we?"

"No. What makes you say that?"

"The Feeb, Moynihan, he says DEA always burns up their snitches. Is it true?"

"They burn up our snitches if our cases interfere with their snitches," she replied. "They'll tell their snitch who ratted on them. Our snitch turns up dead and nobody knows why. It's the Feebs!"

"No shit," I muttered.

"But most of the time, yeah it's true, we burn them, but we have no choice. Drug snitching is that way. The person snitching is usually a member of the conspiracy who got caught or who wants revenge on the co-conspirators. Naturally, that snitch is going to get burned. Most of the time he or she ends up testifying in federal court. We shouldn't have to burn Sig. Nobody knows who he is. I'm not going to tell Doc or anyone about him. He's our snitch, let's make it our responsibility to guard him."

"Moynihan is going to make it a point to find out who he is," I commented. "He isn't going to let his humiliation go unchallenged. He knows what house we went to. A police explorer scout could look in the directory and find out who lives there. I wouldn't be surprised if he doesn't knock on Sig's door and interview him. The Feebs work that way. The interview is their way to intimidate. They roll people that way. Their favorite ploy is, 'I'm giving you an opportunity to help yourself. It's ten o'clock AM, on whatever date. Special Agent Dave Moynihan is giving you the opportunity to help yourself. Are you going to refuse my help? Remember this conversation. You've had your only chance.'

"I know," she said. "It's gross."

"Have you seen that act before?"

"Oh, yeah," she said laughing, "many times. It's big-time sickening. They give up more information in their phony interviews than they ever get. They're fucked up."

We were driving south on Euclid, rehabbed mansions to our left and right, protected by ten foot walls. The streets were deserted. "We're being pulled over by a car with a red light on its dash." She pulled over to the curb; the car stopped behind us. The plainclothes driver walked up to the car.

"Oh fuck," Heidi exclaimed as she was watching the

person in her rear view mirror, "It's Moynihan." He stopped at her window like a traffic cop. She rolled the window down. "Hi Dave, want to see my driver's license?"

"Very funny, Heidi. What's with you guys shooting my fucking windows out in my G car?" Heidi looked at him like he was crazed.

"I know it was you guys, and I'm not going to forget it." He was red-faced and angry. "It's destruction of government property. I'll get to the bottom of it, even if I have to subpoena your new friend, Sig Otto. You just wait. Ray, I need to talk to you back at my car."

I got out and walked back to his G car. We stood toe to toe under a street light.

"This is the second time, Ray. You're falling into their grip. You're like a deer in their headlights. I can help you if you level with me. You can work with me to get these DEA freaks. What do you say?"

"I'm not following you," Dave. I'm a federal officer, just like you are. What do you want from me? I don't know anything about your G car windows."

"You're sworn federally," he said through clenched teeth. "You're correct about that, but you are just a temporary-play agent. You'll need me when you get back to the department. I can use you now. All I want you to do is to give me some information from time to time. Is that asking too much?"

"Information on what?"

"DEA information. There's something going on with your partner and your boss. I want to know what it is. It's no big deal. These people aren't your friends. They'll turn on you in a heartbeat. I can be your friend for a long time. I will not forsake you."

"You mean you want me to inform on my partner and my supervisor?"

"Yeah, they'd inform on you."

"No, thanks, Dave."

"Oh, I get it. I'm offering you friendship and protection. Are you turning me down?"

"Yeah, Dave. And fuck you, Dave!"

"Fuck me, huh," he muttered. He looked me up and down. My right pocket was bulging. He touched it, then rapidly went into my pocket and removed Sig's red potato ammo. He smiled and held it up for me to see.

"You know what this is, Ray?" He was sneering like he had won something important.

I didn't answer him.

"This is evidence, Detective."

I snatched it out of his hand and placed it back into my jeans. "It's not evidence, Dave. It's my potato. Since when is it against federal law to have one in your possession?"

I got back in with Heidi. I stared hard at her. "Is there life after DEA?"

"Doubtful," she replied.

10

I spent the morning with Tyrone, throwing his tennis ball at the cliff for an hour while I watched the boat traffic on the Mississippi.

I left the house at eleven-forty sharp and tried to hit Heidi on the secret car-to-car channel B. She didn't answer so I called her cell.

"Yeah?" she said.

"I wanted to let you know I was on my way."

"Oh, yeah, I'm on my way, too," she replied. "I snoozed late. I called Carla, told her we wouldn't be in."

"I figured. I'll meet you at the east side of the park, near Holly Hills Drive."

"Roger," she said.

Carondelet Park was playing big for me. It's where Clete got threatened and slapped by Jim Schwartz. It's one of the few nice parks left in the city. The residents of the homes surrounding it are mostly city players; lawyers, politicians, teachers, civic-minded folks. It's just a half-mile from where I live.

I parked at the curb and waited for Heidi. Ten minutes rolled by and she still hadn't arrived. I watched the civic-minded south-siders power walking, old timers slowly jogging in their shuffling rhythm, dressed in expensive sweat gear. Some were walking their dogs, talking to them as if they were human and expected acknowledgement. They all took mental pictures of me, my car, and my tag number.

I waited for a couple of more minutes and then drove toward the suspect's house. I drove slowly by and looked for a vantage point where the surveillance could be conducted without jeopardizing our activity. There wasn't any. It would have to be a rolling surveillance. We would have to circle the house via the alley, which was where the garage entrance was located. A twelve-foot chain-link fence was at either side of the garage and seemed to be the security measure of choice for the neighbors on both sides and across the alley. In the Central West End it would have been a ten-foot wall.

I drove back to the meeting place. I was drinking a cup of drive through coffee when Heidi pulled up. I climbed out, walked to her Bimmer, and climbed in.

The sleep did her good. She was vivacious, no makeup, hair brushed but not styled, blue pullover sweatshirt and faded jeans. She was all business. “The house is right down the street from here,” she began.

“I know I’ve been over there. It’s going to be hard to watch. We’re going to have to have a constant rolling surveillance. Street to alley. Want me to show you?”

“Yeah.”

I guided her to the site. We kept sliding by it, circling back and forth in the sunny spring landscape, sprouting trees and brown grass turning green, looking for something, not knowing what.

“The problem we have,” she continued, “is that we don’t know who or what we are looking for or what time he or she will be here.”

“Exactly. So we’re just going to have to watch for something that looks like an airport rental car. Ford, Chevy, or Chrysler.

“Yeah,” she replied.

“The other problem we have,” I continued, “is we’ve got to give them a chance to get the dope out of the trunk and cart it to the garage. We don’t have a warrant. And if he or she bolts and climbs the fence, we’re going to have to give pursuit. I can climb the fence. Can you?”

“Yeah,” she replied with a mean look.

"Okay, so that's the plan. We circle and watch until we see what we think is a rental car going into the alley. When the car stops in the alley, we watch it and try and figure if he's going to pull into the garage or unload the dope from the alley. We'll play it by ear after that. Sound okay to you?"

"Yeah," she muttered.

We took turns sitting in the park, one of us roaming, one of us sitting and watching. It had gotten dark, past eighteen-thirty, and the foot traffic in the park had subsided. I was cruising listening to a blues station in the G car Corvette. They were playing a Blind Blake song, "Boa Constrictor Blues." I sang along and tapped on the steering wheel. There was a maroon Chevy ahead of me, a rental insignia on its trunk. "Heidi?" I said into the microphone.

"Yeah."

"I'm a block away, headed your way. There's a maroon Chevy in front of me with a rental insignia on the trunk. Might be something."

"Ten-four."

I backed off and let the driver of the Chevy do his thing. He was heading toward the alley, slowing, and then signaling. "He's turning in," I said on the air.

"Ten-four."

The driver stopped midway, next to the garage door. He got out and raised it manually, then drove the rental inside. I parked the Corvette at the curb where the alley T's, got out and walked toward the garage. Heidi was slowly driving from the other direction with her lights out.

Heidi stopped approximately twenty-five yards from the garage, climbed out and was walking toward me and the garage. We carefully walked, glancing back from one to the other in anticipation. We didn't know what we would find inside the garage. It could be a lady with her infant, getting groceries out of the trunk. We could hear a car's radio playing country music as we walked. Heidi drew her Glock forty and had it at the ready. I had my hand on mine as we got closer to the music and the light in the garage.

We made a turn and were at the rear of the rental Chevy. The trunk was open and partially full of wrapped objects. The driver was making trips from the trunk to a wooden work bench. He looked up and observed us, then froze.

"Freeze, DEA! Get down on the ground," Heidi screamed as she pointed her Glock forty at him, point blank. He raised his hands and then bolted past us heading toward the garage door and the alley. He was running like a track star, hands straight out, arms pumping and legs driving.

I was right behind him, pushing myself to the limit to get to him before Heidi got a shot at him. There was no way she was going to allow him to escape. I was his only chance at survival.

He hit the chain-link fence on the other side of the alley at a full run and jump and was half-way up and hysterically clawing at the chain-link when I got to him. I grabbed his Levis and began pulling him down as he hung there and refused to let go of the fencing.

"NO, NO," he screamed as he clawed and hung. "LET ME GO. I'M NOT THE ONE YOU WANT." I made a strong pull and eventually got hold of his belt and yanked. He came down and landed in a pile of humanity, rolled up like a ball in the fetal position, crying and cursing.

Heidi walked over to us pointing her Glock at him shouting, "SPREAD EAGLE, SPREAD EAGLE. Show us your hands. GET ON YOUR BELLY AND SPREAD'EM."

I grabbed him by the scruff of his neck and pulled him out of his fetal position then forced him down to his belly and put my knee in the middle of his back. "Spread'em," I said in a calm voice. He obeyed.

I cuffed him behind his back then dragged him to his feet and searched him. "No weapons." I had him by the scruff of his neck and his left arm as we marched him back to the Chevy, the garage and the dope.

He was a wry little man. He wouldn't look at us; he directed his attention to the ground and kept it there.

Heidi counted the seal-wrapped kilos. "Forty!"

I emptied his pockets onto the hood of the rental. Heidi walked toward her Bimmer parked in the alley and drove it down to the garage entrance. She was back in four minutes. She got out with a digital camera and took pictures of the car, the garage, the dope, me, and the suspect and then an overall shot of the alley with us standing in front of the garage.

We loaded the kilos into the trunk of her Bimmer, and I placed the suspect in the passenger side of her car, tightly strapped him down, and took a handful of his greasy hair to pull his head upward. "You want to talk to us?" Heidi climbed into the driver's seat.

"Maybe. I haven't decided, yet."

I let his head go and his eyes went straight to the floor.

"I'm going to move this rental out to the street," I advised Heidi. "We can either tow it or contact someone from the rental company to come and get it." I pulled the rental out, climbed out and shut the garage door then climbed back into the rental.

"The U.S. Attorney may want us to seize it so keep the keys with you after you park it. Let's get out of here," she shouted to me through the open window of the Bimmer.

She followed me in the Bimmer to the T where I had parked the G Corvette. I parked the Chevy at the curb, locked it and pocketed the key, entered the Corvette and followed her to the front of the house. She took pictures from the car. It was a nice house: old, stucco, with French windows and big trees. We drove directly to the county jail in Clayton.

We booked him in, safekeeping, Drug Enforcement Administration. No cellmates, telephone calls, or visitors. He had two driver's licenses, one for the state of Florida, one for Missouri, under the name Henry Darby. I was pretty close on his age, I guessed him at fifty; he was fifty-two.

Nobody should have two driver's licenses, except for DEA agents and TFD's. The state always requests your old driver's license, and if you say you lost it, they want a police report for verification.

The fact that he had two was intriguing to me. He was a crook on the loose, which usually meant he was snitching for a federal agency.

"You an FBI snitch?" He looked at me and smiled.

"If I say, yes, would you let me go?"

"No."

His head went back down.

"I want you to think about something tonight while you're sleeping on the steel," I said.

"Yeah, what?"

"Try to figure how much time you want to do, two years, ten years, twenty-five years. Your level of cooperation depends on how much time you do in a federal penitentiary."

"I don't wish to go there," he muttered.

"Okay, we're starting to communicate already. We'll continue this conversation in the morning." The turnkey took him to a cell while Heidi and I exited the jail and headed for our G cars. She was looking at me with bedroom eyes. The thrill of the hunt and the capture aroused her.

"I'm going home," I said before she could ask me to spend the night.

"Okay, I'll see you in the morning. We've got to debrief

Henry Darby, It might prove to be interesting."

"Ten-four, over and out, I'll meet you in the office at 0830."

I climbed into the Corvette and headed south.

11

It was a relaxing ride to work in the government Corvette. The sun was shining, and the trees and foliage were greening. It gave me the feeling all was well with the world. We pulled into the DEA garage at the same time. I parked the Corvette and climbed in with Heidi, and we drove the block to the county jail. I signed the usual paperwork and the turnkey brought Henry Darby out to us.

He was smiling wryly as he approached us, kind of like we were old friends who were going to buy him breakfast. He studied us as we cuffed him behind his back and led him out of the jail and to the Bimmer. I placed him in the back seat and strapped him in, then climbed in at shotgun while Heidi started the Bimmer and drove out of the Sally Port and onto the busy Clayton Street.

"I could use a cup of coffee. Any chance you could drive through a McDonald's?"

"Yeah, we can do that," I replied. "You want a breakfast Mac, too?"

"Man, that would be great."

Heidi drove through the Mac and parked in the parking lot. I leaned over the seat and took the cuffs off of Henry, then re-cuffed him in front. He devoured the plastic food.

"Where you guys taking me, now?"

"To the court house," I said. "You'll be arraigned before a federal magistrate this afternoon."

"What about the cooperation thing you talked about last night? That still open for conversation?"

I gave Henry the federal pause. "Maybe; do you want to work?"

"Yeah. Tell me what you guys want."

"Whose dope is it?" I asked.

"It's a guy I know who lives in Georgia. Do you need me

to identify him right now? Shouldn't we work out some kind of an agreement before I give him up?"

Dope dealers know the system. It's as if they take a course "Dope Dealer Survival After Arrest." Henry didn't want to show his hole card until the pot got just right for him. I didn't blame him. Crime is a game where only the intelligent player survives.

Henry knew how to communicate with cops, another acquired trait which some folks are born with. He was making us like and appreciate him, even though he was just one click up in the criminal pecking order from a child molester.

Heidi had been silent as Henry the dope dealer tried to schmooze me. She broke the silence. "Who is the owner of the house where you were unloading the dope, Henry?"

Henry took a long pause. "I own it," he muttered.

"What is your profession, Henry? Other than dope dealing."

"I have a bar, a blues bar," Henry stammered. "I pay a lady friend to manage it for me. I tend bar sometimes." He was trying to smile and schmooze Heidi. She wasn't buying into it.

"The United States Attorney is going to want to seize your house as a drug profit, Henry, and your bar. They're going to ask Ray and me for our recommendation on the seizure. What do you want us to tell them, Henry?"

Henry cleared his throat. He wasn't smiling, he was sweating. "I get the dope from Viktor Agron," he said. "He has a little farm in Savannah, Georgia, on a deep water canal. I've known him since the early eighties. He's a Russian immigrant."

Heidi was stone-faced as she pulled into the Sally Port. I collected Henry from the backseat and marched him into the federal holdover. I signed him in, with the assistance of a united states marshal, Possession of cocaine with the intent to Distribute, and placed him in a temporary holding cell. Heidi went upstairs to the United States Attorney's office while I stayed in the office babysitting him.

I read the "Post-Dispatch" and drank coffee for two hours until she finally telephoned me. "Bring him up." I retrieved Henry from the holding cell, placed the handcuffs on him behind his back, and walked him out of the office to the elevator. We took it to the fourth floor and into Magistrate Saunders' outer office. Heidi and Sue Lee were waiting for us.

"I understand you have been cooperative with the agents," Sue Lee began.

"Yes, ma'am." He stared at her as if she was a novelty.

"Do you wish to continue to assist the United States Government?"

"Yes, ma'am."

"Do you wish to consult with an attorney before you continue with your cooperation?"

"No, ma'am."

"The judge will see you now," a receptionist said.

We marched into the magistrate's chambers. The judge didn't look up as we walked in; he was reading the information form that Sue Lee had prepared. He finally looked up. Henry was still looking down.

"Mister Henry Darby, you're charged with possession of cocaine with the intent to distribute. You'll be held without bond until a hearing. Said hearing will determine if and when you'll be allowed bond in this matter. Do you have an attorney?"

"Yes, sir."

"Any questions, Mister Darby?"

"No, sir!"

We marched out of the magistrate's chambers and to the

hallway. "This way," Heidi said. We followed her and Sue Lee to an office adjacent to the United States Attorney's office. There was a big oak table and six chairs and a view of the Arch. Heidi closed the door.

"I need to know your level of cooperation, Mister Darby," Sue Lee said.

Henry Darby looked at her as if he didn't understand her statement.

"Percentage, one hundred percent, fifty percent, twenty five percent. Do you follow me?"

Henry nodded, "one hundred percent, ma'am. My cooperation is one hundred percent."

"Okay, Mister Darby, these agents are going to interview you in my presence. I'll take note of your cooperation and be of assistance to you in your sentencing when you go before a federal judge. You may begin," she said to Heidi.

Heidi removed a Pearl tape recorder from her purse and activated it. "This is Special Agent Heidi Anderson, St. Louis field office, accompanied by Task Force Detective Ray Arnold, and AUSA Sue Lee, interviewing arrested subject Henry Darby. Mister Darby," Heidi began, "tell us the name of the person you are selling the cocaine for."

"Viktor Agron," Henry mumbled, "but can I ask a question?" Heidi nodded. "Is Ray Arnold a city cop detective assigned to DEA?"

"Yes. Any more questions?" Henry shook his head and stared at me.

"You previously advised TFD Arnold and me that Viktor Agron resides in Georgia. Is that correct?"

"Yes, Savannah, but that isn't where he's from. That's just where he settled to do his business." Henry looked around and smiled then got serious again.

"What is his business, Mister Darby?"

"He's a broker, a cocaine and weed broker. He travels around the world taking and filling orders for dope." He was smiling again, the bartender's smile, distrusting and disgusting.

"And where is Viktor Agron from? Where is his home?"

"He's from Russia. He came to the states when he was a kid and he and his parents settled in Brooklyn, New York. Brighton Beach to be specific."

"Little Odessa?" I asked.

Henry smiled, "Yeah, it's a neat place. Have you been there?"

"No," I replied. "It's the home of the Russian mafia. I'm familiar with it."

"Viktor isn't one of those guys," Henry said. "He's actually a nice guy, but he'd have me killed if he knew I was giving his name up. He's all business."

"You're going to have to do more than give us his name, Mister Darby," Heidi said. "This is just the beginning. I want you to realize that fact. Do you wish to continue with your cooperation?"

"You mean I'll have to go undercover with you and TFD Arnold?"

"Maybe, Mister Darby. You'll for certain have to give court testimony. Can you do that?"

"Does that mean I'll walk away a free man?"

"No Mister Darby. You'll have to report to a federal penitentiary for a while, but it will be a reduced sentence. Do you wish to continue?"

Henry pulled on his face and was deep in thought. "If I'm incarcerated then I won't be able to help you, or myself. He'll know I've been taken off. He's probably wondering why I haven't contacted him since I got back home. He's real cautious. He was in prison for dealing coke in Florida. He knows what he's doing."

Heidi walked to a telephone on a table next to the door, dialed It, and spoke to a federal Marshal. "Bring up Henry Darby's property, interview room on the fourth floor. Yes, immediately. Thank you."

Heidi turned off the recorder as we waited. No one spoke. There was a tap on the door, Heidi answered it and was handed the sealed plastic property bag. She handed it to Henry, "Open it and get your cell phone." He complied, turned it on, and waited for Heidi to instruct him.

"I want you to call Viktor Agron. Act normal and say what you would always say when you return to St. Louis with a trunk full of cocaine."

Heidi got a telephone wire device from her purse and attached it to the telephone. She connected it to the Pearl recorder, activated it and gave Henry a nod. Henry hit the auto dial and sat staring at the floor while the phone rang. The phone was cocked on his face so the room inhabitants could hear the ringing.

"Yes," a deep voice said.

"Viktor," Henry warmly said. "I'm back home in old St. Louis."

"Excellent. I'll expect two hundred thousand in approximately two weeks." There was a long pause.

"Okay, brother," Henry replied. He was anxiously looking at us.

"Ellen took off right after you left. I think she's gone back to the East side. The clubs have called her again. Check on her and let me know if you see her. Go by her house and see if there are any lights on, or if you see her car. Do you understand?"

"Yes, I understand. I'll get back to you. So long, Viktor." The call ended.

Heidi unplugged the recorder from the cell phone. She spoke into the recorder; "The recorded conversation was between cooperating co-conspirator Henry Darby and conspirator Viktor Agron, witnessed by Special Agent Heidi Anderson, Assistant United States Attorney Sue Lee, and Task Force Detective Ray Arnold." She put in a new cassette and activated the recorder.

"Who is Ellen?" Sue Lee asked.

"It's Viktor's wife. She's a stripper over on the East side."

"How did he meet her?" I asked.

"Viktor came to St. Louis regularly when he was just a kid, about twenty, I think. He came here to sell weed, but he also had some girls working for him."

"You mean he was a pimp as well as a weed dealer?" I asked.

"Yeah, he'd make the club scene downtown and on the East side and sell his dope and his whores. When he ran out of weed, he'd go back to Brighton Beach and the girls were on their own. Then he'd come back in a couple of months and resume business. It's how I met him. I bought weed and women from him."

"What year was that?" I asked.

"In the early eighties," Henry said. "He liked it here, it reminded him of Mother Russia; you know the winters and the old buildings and folks scrambling to make a living. He loved the architecture. He said City Hall looked like a miniature Kremlin. He met this young girl from Troy, Illinois, and he fell for her. That's Ellen. She later became a stripper. She's real independent. She stays with Viktor for a while and then she heads back to the East Side and resumes her career. She makes lots of money. She's a star."

"So you've known Viktor for over thirty years?" I asked.

"Yeah, more like thirty seven years."

"Where else has Viktor lived?" Heidi asked.

"Oh, he gets around. He lived in South Florida for a

while. Things got too hot for him. Dope dealers are tripping over each other down there." Henry was smiling again. "So he relocated to Southern Georgia. He travels a lot, internationally."

"Who are the other players in his organization?" I asked.

"He's got people who work for him, if that's what you mean. He's the boss of the organization. He hires people to do jobs for him. He's got a couple of guys who do his bidding. They're tough guys, street fighter kind of guys. They'd kill for him if the price was right, but they're just employees. They aren't affiliated with the business. Much of the time he has them guarding Ellen at the strip club. Viktor is tough in his own right. He can kill with his hands and feet. His specialty is kicking his opponent in the head and then grabbing his larynx."

There was a pause while everyone assimilated Henry Darby's description of Viktor Agron.

"Where does he get the dope?" I asked.

"He brokers it," Henry said. "He rarely handles the dope himself, except when I come down to get a load. He travels the world brokering dope. He's got a connection with a Colombian dope dealer. This guy's got a big freighter-type ship and he fills the order when Viktor contacts him."

"Give us an example," Sue Lee said.

"Okay. Let's say Viktor is in Copenhagen meeting with some local organized criminals. The criminal element Viktor is meeting with want some dope to sell. Marijuana is usually the drug of choice for the youth of the world. They tell Viktor to order them up a boat-load of weed. Viktor says fine, but I can't order weed without ordering cocaine with it. You have to buy both commodities. So the deal is struck, and Viktor contacts his guy in Colombia and tells him where to ship the dope. Viktor's usually on shore talking with the captain of the ship via cell phone when the ship arrives, somewhere offshore. Viktor gets the cash, the criminal element gets the dope themselves by meeting the ship out at sea, and the ship goes on its way waiting for another order from the broker, Viktor."

"What's the name of the ship?" Heidi asked.

"The" Corn Island," Henry replied. We were staring at him, awed by his information. He read us. "Viktor hates the "Corn Island." It's a scow, it stinks, and it's dangerous. He's been out at sea on it a couple of times and swears he'll never get on her again. He strictly brokers now, nothing more. His hands rarely touch the product."

"So the Corn Island sails the world with a hold full of illegal drugs and it never gets stopped and searched?" Heidi asked.

"It's in international waters most of the time. It's been stopped and searched but the dope is hidden in the bulkheads. It's undetectable. It was built to be a smuggling vessel. It's difficult to hide weed, but the coke is easily hidden. That's why the Colombian dope dealer keeps it. It should've been scrapped years ago."

"What is the name of the Colombian dope dealer?" Heidi asked.

"I don't know his name. Viktor doesn't cotton to answering questions about his business. I don't ask him anything except things that pertain to us and our business relationship."

"How long have you been doing this?" Heidi asked.

"For about five years."

"You've been transporting large quantities of cocaine for five years?" Sue Lee asked.

"No, the coke for only about three years. I used to pick up bales of marijuana from a locker when Viktor lived in south Florida."

"You transported bales of marijuana in the trunk of a

rental car?" Heidi asked.

"No, I used a van for that. A rental van."

"How many pounds of marijuana do you think you've transported to the St. Louis area from south Florida for Viktor Agron?" Sue Lee asked.

"Oh," he said as he pulled on his face, "Thousands of pounds, probably."

"How many kilos of cocaine?" Sue Lee continued.

"Oh, eight or nine hundred kilos."

"This interview needs to be moved to the DEA field office," Sue Lee said. "Group Supervisor Doc Penrose needs to be present before any more information is divulged."

"I concur," Heidi said.

I removed the handcuffs from Henry Darby's wrists. He acted as if his soul had been released from evil. He looked intensely at us for the first time, captors who were going to give him another chance at freedom, rubbing his wrists, and looking into our eyes, studying and gauging us as he rubbed and massaged his bony wrists.

"I'd like my lawyer present during the interview at the DEA office," he said. He nervously watched for our response.

"You can make those arrangements, Mister Darby," Heidi replied. "It's time to go. I'll meet you guys in the Sally Port."

Henry grabbed the property bag, emptied the contents into his pockets and tossed the bag in a trash can. We walked out of the room, took the elevator to the first floor, walked through the holdover and into the Sally Port.

We waited for Heidi on the platform above the entry area. She pulled in still stone-faced: Henry and I walked to the Bimmer and climbed in.

It was as if the investigation had been put on hold. Henry clammed up. He was thinking about his lawyer, no doubt.

Most good criminal lawyers advise their clients not to cooperate with the cops. He was probably going to be chastised for his partial cooperation.

We parked in the garage and strolled into the offices. Heidi stayed behind. There were two grocery shopping carts waiting for us in the office. “Dope in BMW trunk?” Mike Schweig asked. I nodded.

“Grab a cart and follow me,” I advised Henry. We wheeled our way back to Heidi’s Bimmer. She was waiting for us. We transferred the kilos of cocaine out of her Bimmer trunk and into the grocery carts then wheeled it to the drug vault on the fifth floor. Heidi stayed with the dope to check it in while, I took Henry up to the boardroom.

We sat and stared at each other. I could tell he wanted to converse with me, but there was nothing to say. He knew the game. He had gotten caught, and now he had to work. Talking about anything else would be ludicrous, and we had already talked about his cooperation.

Henry continued to watch me. The shock of the capture wears off and the captives turn into trapped animals, their senses keen for the demeanor of their captors, searching for a weakness. They are thug businessmen, and their instincts lead them, like ducks flying south for the winter and wolves howling at the moon.

Their instinct is communication; they want to know their captor, so they study you, waiting for the right time to begin the conversation. The pimp factor is their creed. They knew they were going to get caught; they know this day is always waiting for them.

I studied him wondering what makes normal looking and normal acting people turn into the lowest form of criminal, a drug dealer. He was dressed St. Louis blues club style: jeans, sweatshirt, old beaten Polo lightweight jacket. Reddish brown hair combed straight back like Elvis, clean shaven, not fat, not thin, no jewelry. He could have been a DEA agent, if looks had anything to do with it.

I stared and tried to figure him out so I could classify him. Demon? Weak follower? Addict? Manipulator? Manipulative? Greedy bastard? I settled on greed. Just another greedy criminal trying to beat the system.

"Do you know any FBI agents?" he asked.

"No," I replied. "Do you work for the FBI?"

"No. But some of the agents come into my bar. I give them draft beer for free. They sometimes ask me about certain crooks. Some I know, some I don't. I tell them what I know, sometimes, but I don't work for them. I'm not a paid informant for them."

We uncomfortably studied each other. "I need to use the rest room," he said.

"Okay, walk through the door and make two rights." I followed him. He went into a stall while I waited. He came out holding his side and shaking his head, "Nervous stomach," he said as he washed his hands.

He walked past me and made two lefts and walked back into the room. "You're treating me well. Does this mean you don't hate me?" He was smiling, a bartender's smile.

"No, it doesn't mean that."

He laughed, "That's good. That's good shtick," still with the bartender's smile.

Doc walked into the room. "What's your lawyer's name?"

"Preston Devon," Henry replied.

"In Clayton?"

"Yeah, just down the block." Doc walked out of the room and slammed the door.

"Who's he?"

"DEA big shot," I replied.

"Looks like a used Porsche dealer."

"Good analogy."

Another hour passed and I could hear talking outside the door. The voices were muffled but one of them was Sue Lee. There was a tap on the door and then it opened. It was Doc.

"Come out for a minute," Doc said. "The defendant's lawyer needs to confer with him in private." I came out and a young athletic-looking man with a long pony tail and horn-rimmed glasses walked inside and closed the door. I was standing with Heidi, Sue Lee, and Doc.

"I listened to this morning's taped interview from the United States Attorney's office," Doc said. "I checked Victor Agron in NADDIS. The confidential informant is right on the money. He's a class one violator. Everybody wants him. It would be quite a coup for DEA, the St. Louis field office and the United States Attorney's Office, and the task force, if we could bag him with a large amount of cocaine. Think you could work undercover, Ray?"

"You mean me and Heidi down in the Savannah area with Henry Darby as our sponsor?"

"Yeah," Doc replied, watching my eyes and gauging me.

"Yeah," I replied. "As long as Heidi is up to it."

"I'm ready to play again," Heidi said watching Doc. "I haven't been undercover in four months; I've actually missed it. Maybe when I retire from DEA, I can go to Hollywood and become an actress. I've done enough acting undercover to qualify for a screen actor's union card."

"I'm envisioning a one hundred kilo deal," Doc continued. He had an index finger on each temple and was swaying from foot to foot. "A buy bust, right here in St. Louis. If we can get Viktor Agron to trust you guys, we can probably include his connection in South America. You up for that again, Heidi?"

"Yeah," she replied, with reserve. She was zoning again,

mentally removed from us. I wondered where she was. Florida? South America? Something was menacing her, something about her previous assignment down south. That's all she ever said, down south. She never said where, just down south. But she had mentioned Colombia while we were at Sig's house.

I wondered if her statement was a poisonous barb shot into my brain, a manipulative potion to be used at a later date. She came back with a stupendous tan, the kind you get on a tropical island, not in Miami in March. It still gets chilly there and the sun isn't hot enough for her kind of tan.

The lawyer stepped out of the room and closed the door. "My client will cooperate one hundred percent."

"He will have to be debriefed in detail," Doc said. "Do you want to be present during the interview?"

"No, but draw up a proxy on what the government offers. If my client agrees, he'll sign it and he'll begin working for the government. My card." He walked away.

We moved to the big boardroom on the fifth floor next to Square Bidness' office. Doc was at one end of the table, Sue Lee was at the other end. Henry Darby was on one side by himself, and Heidi and I were across from him. A tape recorder was in the middle of the table. Heidi activated the tape recorder.

"This is Special Agent Heidi Anderson, Drug Enforcement Administration, St. Louis Field Office, conducting an interview with cooperating defendant Henry Darby. In attendance are Group Supervisor Delbert "Doc" Penrose, AUSA Sue Lee, and Task Force Detective Ray Arnold. I will be conducting the questioning of Mister Darby. "Where were you born, Mister Darby?"

"St. Louis, Missouri."

"What part of the city?"

"Old north side, near Calvary Cemetery."

"Did you go to public schools?"

"No, parochial."

"At what point in your life did you become involved in drugs?"

"I started smoking weed at about age twelve." He was smiling at us as if he was embarrassed.

"When did you start dealing in and smuggling drugs into the St. Louis area?"

He paused. He was gauging his audience like a stand-up comic telling a straight story. He had us in his grip and he loved it. "I answered that question this morning." He looked confused and uneasy. "Do you want me to answer it again?"

Heidi glanced at Doc and Sue Lee. "No, Mister Darby. So, for approximately five years you have been smuggling large amounts of marijuana and cocaine into the St. Louis metropolitan area, and you have been acquiring this contraband from Viktor Agron, of Brighton Beach, New York, somewhere in south Florida, and from his base of operations at this point in time in Savannah, Georgia. Is this correct, Mister Darby?"

"Yes, ma'am."

"And for the sake of clarity, Mister Darby, you have information regarding Viktor's source as a Colombian, name unknown, with a smuggling ship called the Corn Island, which circles the globe supplying Viktor Agron with an unending amount of illicit drugs. Is this correct, Mister Darby?"

"Yes."

"And also for the sake of clarity, Mister Darby, you have stated that Viktor Agron is of Russian descent. Is he naturalized?"

"Uh, I think so," Henry said with a smile. "I think he's a citizen of the United States."

"And Viktor Agron has ties with the St. Louis area,

excluding you, Mister Darby."

"Yes, he's been coming here off and on for thirty-seven years. And he's got a wife who strips in East St. Louis, Illinois."

"Tell us more about Viktor's wife."

"Ellen," Henry said with a smile. "She's always been his favorite. She was a kid when he took her in. She's only about thirty, now. Dark hair and eyes, a real beauty. She's Viktor's Achilles Heel. He's weak for her. When she leaves, he tracks her to East St. Louis and begs her to come back."

"Oh," Heidi said. She looked at the group as if to ask, "Are there any more questions?" The audience was subdued.

"We're going to release you on your own recognizance," Heidi said. "Be back here tomorrow morning at nine."

"I'll be getting another call from Viktor. I was off of the radar for a couple of hours, unaccountable. In Viktor's mind I could've been taken off. He'll call me soon."

"Okay," Doc said, "Tell him you've got a buyer for the whole package, the forty kilos, without breaking it up and distributing it. Tell him it's a couple you've known for a while from coming into the bar. Vouch for them, tell him they're righteous and that they want to get into the coke business, big-time. Family money, independently wealthy or some such shit. Anyway, get him to swim after the bait. Sue Lee, any questions?"

"No, but be here tomorrow morning for the continuance of the interview and the proxy."

Henry nodded.

"Get him booked, fingerprinted and photographed," Doc said.

It took thirty minutes for the booking, fingerprinting, and photographing. Henry activated his cell phone. It started beeping immediately. He activated his voice mail and held it up for us to listen to. "You get in trouble? You need help?

Don't make a statement. Call me immediately."

"That's Viktor. That's two times he's tried to contact me and my cell was off. That never happens. My cell is always on, unless it's dead," Henry said.

"Call him back," Heidi said.

Henry hit the speed dial, "It's me," Henry said.

"Who the fuck told you to turn your cell off? You get taken off?"

"No, my cell was fucked up. I didn't even know it, but I got it straightened out now. What's up?"

There was silence on the line while Viktor dissected the information. He was like a wild animal slowly walking through the forest sensing a trap one step ahead of him, his foot up ready to step, and then he stops and swerves and avoids it. His cunning instinct saves him to hunt another day. Viktor was poised with his foot up, breathing into the receiver, preparing to bolt sideways to avoid the inevitable.

"So," Viktor began, "How's your bar doing?"

"Fine."

"Did the load of vegetables get delivered okay?"

"Yeah, Viktor," Henry replied with sarcasm. "We already went through this, everything's okay."

"Your customers will love those fresh vegetables from sunny Georgia. You'll probably sell them quickly."

"Yeah, I may already have a buyer for all of them. Package deal," Henry said.

"Sounds interesting. Stay in touch and keep your damn cell on. And I sent Will to check up on Ellen. He just called me. He's staying at a motel on the East side."

"Okay, Viktor," Henry muttered. Henry hung up.

"Who's Will?" Heidi asked.

"Will Blanks, a leg breaker and nose bender. An ex-pimp from the sticks. He's Viktor's right hand man. He does what Viktor tells him to do." Henry looked worried. "Will's going to look me up, give me the third degree. Viktor probably already ordered him to intimidate me to see if I'll crack. He's paranoid and he feels I might have been taken off by you guys."

"Is Will Russian?" I asked.

"No, he's a swamp rat from South Florida."

"Where do think he'll contact you?" I asked.

"Probably at my bar. I go there once a day, just to check things out. Sometimes I stay and tend bar, but mostly I just harass my manager and then leave. He'll probably have the place under surveillance, and when he sees me he'll pounce."

"Where is your bar?" Heidi asked.

"On the Landing," Henry said. "Hot Toddy's Blues Bar. You guys ever heard of it? I get the best travelling blues bands there."

"We don't get downtown very much," I said. My brain tricked me. I flashed back to the angelic form of Lynn Stewart lying alongside of the roadway. The little girl look on her face, 'He hurt me Ray, please catch him.' I couldn't catch him. She was a downtown waitress. I shook it off. Heidi was watching me.

"We usually eat in Clayton," Heidi said. She was in deep thought. "We're going to wire you, Henry. You okay with that?"

"You mean so when Will pounces on me, you'll have some evidence pertaining to the case?"

"Yeah, Henry."

Henry was hesitating. "Does this mean I'll get preferential treatment from the United States Attorney? I mean like brownie points?"

"Yes," Heidi said, "brownie points."

"Okay, I'll do it, but can you wire me so that if somebody feels me up he can't detect the wire?"

"Yeah, follow me," she replied. We walked to the third floor. There was a small room with a locked door. Heidi used a key, unlocked and opened it and we walked in. A large table had transmitting equipment on it, used and placed there for the next agent to use. It wasn't the same type of equipment I had previously used with informants. It was small and state of the art.

Henry and I stood and waited while Heidi sorted through the electronic equipment. She separated certain elements from the pile and glanced at us. "Take off your shirt, Henry," she said.

He had been carrying his jacket. He tossed it onto a chair and pulled off his sweatshirt. He wasn't wearing an undershirt and he hadn't been to a gym in years. He was self-conscious in front of Heidi. She smiled and visually measured him for the wire as she walked around him.

She placed a transmitter in the small of his back. It had adhesive on it and it stuck to his skin. She plugged in a wire, then ran the minutely thin wire up over his shoulder and taped it to his right pectoral. It was the microphone.

The listening equipment was in a briefcase. She activated the transmitter and the briefcase equipment and told him to go out into the hallway and speak. He walked out, "Testing, one-two-three," he said in a normal tone.

"Okay, Henry, come back inside," she said. "It works."

He came back in, grabbed his sweatshirt and pulled it on. "So, I'm wired for sound. What now?"

"We take you home to get your personal vehicle, Henry," she said. "Then, you go about your daily chores, and we'll be within earshot of you. We'll give this operation a couple of hours and see where it leads us. Let's go."

We headed for the parking garage and piled into Heidi's Bimmer, then headed south toward Henry's house across from Carondelet Park. It had turned warmer, almost seventy and the sun was bringing life to good old St. Louis. We were closing in on Henry's house.

"Let me off here," he said from the backseat. Heidi pulled over and he climbed out. "Will might have my house under surveillance. I don't want him to see me with you guys just yet." He started walking down Holly Hills Street, swinging his arms and acting like he was power walking.

I rolled the window down and Heidi stopped. He stopped power walking and came over to the car. I handed him my business card. He took it and looked at it. "My cell number is on the card. Call me if you get lost, or if we lose you. I've got your cell. We've got to keep in touch."

He looked at the card and then handed it back to me. "I've got it memorized." He resumed the power walking and went through his yard and into his house.

There was a car parked on the street in front of the house. An old beater, an Oldsmobile. I ran the license number and it came back issued to Henry Darby. We sat and waited. He came out in five minutes and entered the beaten up Olds, then headed east toward downtown.

We followed at a safe distance expecting him to be forced off of the road by Will the nose-bender, intimidated, felt up, and abused. It didn't happen.

Henry made his way to the downtown area and headed due east toward the Mississippi river and Laclede's Landing, the nightclub area of the city. It was an old warehouse district, huge old buildings where fur, lumber, food, coffee, staples to live by were housed in the eighteen-hundreds.

It was abandoned until a developer thought it would be a good idea to rehab the buildings and make nightclubs out of them.

The area was quaint: cobblestone streets, gaslights, horse-powered buggies taking folks for rides. The bars and restaurants became more sophisticated as the project unfolded. Big-time money became involved, and the streets resembled the French Quarter in New Orleans.

We parked by the Mississippi River, near the casino, on the cobblestones. The windows were partially open and the musty chemical smell of the river was attacking our senses. "Hey, isn't this where my Corvette was found, I mean Jack Parker's G car?"

She gave me a short federal pause. It was short because she was smart and didn't need a lot of time to formulate her pimping of me. I had asked a leading question; that was her cue. Her expertise was fielding leading questions.

"Yeah, he'd park it here and walk to the casino and talk to his dad when he got drunk, which was almost every night, then weeble wobble his drunk-self back to the Corvette. That was his funny name."

"What?"

"Weeble Wobble," she said with a chuckle. "He was always weeble wobbling." She laughed as if she was imagining him walking drunk. "He'd get so drunk and spend all of his money, then go to the Taco Bell drive-through and barter for food. He'd barter knives, his wallet, nightstick, sap, pepper spray, anything he could use to get some greasy Mexican food to soak up the booze."

"You were with him?"

"Yeah," she replied. "Me and every other female he came in contact with. He was a whore just like the rest of the TFD's. Sluts and booze, that's all he wanted. No offense, Ray."

"None taken," I muttered. I was outclassed by her. She was smarter than me, and she had been trained by professionals to always be ahead in a one-on-one confrontation. Her focus was scary. I wondered if the DEA Academy trained her. Probably not. She wasn't like any DEA agent I had ever known. She was all class.

My cell rang. "Yo."

"I'm parking my car on the lot on Second Street and preparing to get out. I'll be walking on Second Street to my bar. Can you guys hear me okay on the wire?"

"Okay," I replied. "We can hear you loud and clear." He walked and hummed, his sweatshirt was rubbing against the microphone, cars were honking and people were making attempts at being friendly. Heidi and I stared at the Mississippi River as it rolled by. I thought about the Cahokia Indians. It's what they did, build mounds and look at the river, but from the East side. They're long gone.

There was some loud rustling: Henry shouted, "Hey." Heidi activated the tape recorder on the wire machine. "Will," Henry said, "What the fuck are you doing?"

"Get the Canon out of the trunk," Heidi said. I quickly exited the trunk as she hit the trunk release. I grabbed the camera, jumped back in, and she drove toward Second Street. The conversation was continuing.

"Viktor told me to check up on you. Did you get taken off?"

"No! What the fuck are you doing?"

"I'm searching you for a wire."

The rustling was getting louder as we approached Second Street. I had the camera aimed and ready. "Do you see them?" Heidi asked.

"Yeah," I replied. The whirr of the auto wind was screaming. I took a complete roll of film as Will was manhandling Henry. Will towered over him, unzipping his jacket and prodding his chest. Will was just as Henry described: big, a burly swamp rat. He was at least 6'6, went about 230, mullet haircut, jeans and a jeans jacket with a corduroy collar. The act had been played out before on this street.

The act is played anywhere there's a strong guy and a

weak guy. I saw it played out between Special Agent Jim Schwartz and city cop, Task Force Detective Cletus Jones in Carondelet Park, just across from where Henry lives. Except Will didn't slap Henry. That's reserved for agents and cops.

Henry held his own. He had moxie for a little guy. He eventually fended Will off. They stood looking at each other. Pedestrians were watching them. Someone was certain to 911. It appeared Henry was the victim of a strong-arm robbery.

"Let's go inside, Will," Henry said. "I'll buy you a beer. Viktor's way off on this one. I haven't been taken off. I just had a fucked up cell. Come on." Henry turned and followed him as they walked the half block to the Hot Toddy and walked inside.

We parked at the curb and pondered the situation. "When Will leaves we'll follow him," Heidi said.

"Sounds great, but in the meantime let's go inside. I'm thirsty. He's going to see us sometime, probably down in Savannah. We're playing the game of folks who are interested in becoming drug dealers. I'll buy you a Coke."

She backed the Bimmer up to a parking meter. We got out and she plugged the meter. We strolled down the street to the Hot Toddy. There was nothing modern about the building. It still resembled a fur warehouse.

We strolled in and made our way to the bar. Will was hanging around, killing time, nursing a glass of draft beer and using his animal instincts to get a feel for what was going on. We walked past him as he was leaning against the wall like a street pimp.

He gave Heidi the pimp stare and shot a look of intimidation at me. He sensed weakness, an older guy with a luscious chick. Everything was instinctive with pimps. He knew in his heart that he could take me and maybe intimidate Heidi, romance her, fill her with dope and eventually get her to make him some cash. It's how he had lived his life.

Cops live on instinct, too. He underestimated me and I loved it. I knew what he was thinking, and I sized him up eye-to-eye. I knew I could take him, mostly because he'd read me wrong. I mentally went through the moves. I looked at him in that instant as we walked by him. Big and scary, but not bright. Probably a big sucker-puncher who has always been lucky with the first punch.

He was weak in the solar plexus. One good shot there would render him bug-eyed, red-faced, gasping for air with none available. His knees would lock up and his hands would fall slightly. He would be vulnerable for a left cross to the temple or jaw. He would drop like a sack of potatoes.

His confidence was gigantic because he always had his reputation and his gang to rely on. But what if his big first punch missed? He would be trying to figure out why he missed.

His little pimp, dope-dealer brain would be trying to analyze the first punch and then it would be too late. I would take him apart with lefts and rights, body combinations and eventually get him on the deck and pummel him into sleepy time.

I knew it was going to happen; Will Blanks and I, and probably Viktor Agron, will be engaged in mortal combat before this deal is concluded. It is their nature, their instinctive criminal nature. I knew pimps. I knew what pimps do to young girls to make them work. They beat them and terrorize them and burn them on their buttocks with hot hangars to torture them.

I'll even the score with these two pimps, rest assured victims of these low life creatures. They have made the fatal mistake. They have underestimated the old cop. Their days of painless freedom are numbered.

12

It was 0900; we were making our way into the board room next to Square Bidness' office for the proxy between Henry Darby and the United States Government.

Sue Lee and Doc Penrose were again at the heads of the table. Heidi and I were across from Henry Darby. His attorney, Preston Devon, was sitting next to him. Coffee was being slurped by everyone in attendance, and throat clearing was the exercise of the morning.

Sue Lee handed a copy of something to Doc and Heidi. They examined it. I looked over Heidi's shoulder. It was the copy of the government's proposal. Heidi nodded her approval, Doc did likewise.

Sue Lee handed a copy to barrister Preston Devon. He read it and handed it to Henry Darby. Henry read it, sat it down in front of him and looked at the group. "It says I have to do five years. I only want to do two years. I can do two years and resume my life when I'm released. Is that a problem?"

"I agree with my client," Preston replied. "He's already worked for the government in good faith, setting up the deal to apprehend and put away for life an international crime organization. He's risking his life, for God's sake."

"You can have my savings," Henry continued, "which is about three-hundred thousand. My car is a junker, an old Oldsmobile. It isn't worth anything. My bar is on rented property, and it isn't doing very well, either. I've lived in the same meager house in the city for the past fifteen years. It's all I have!"

Sue Lee was studying him. "Do you have a safe deposit box?"

"Yes, here's the key." He slid it toward Heidi. "There's an additional fifty-thousand in it. It's got my attorney's name on it. I knew someday I'd be popped and I'd need to hire him. Are you going to take my lawyer money?" Heidi glanced at Sue Lee. Sue Lee shook her head in the negative. The event was scripted and choreographed.

It was Heidi's turn. "Where is your money?"

"Bad habits and poor choices," he replied. "I've been addicted to prostitutes my entire life. I gamble, too. I always had a drug habit. That's where it went. I feel lucky to still have three hundred thousand and my lawyer money." He was smiling his bartender's smile and talking with his hands again, patronizing the crowd, conning and pimping us. He continually glanced at me during his charade as if he knew I wasn't buying his story.

"Viktor Agron is expecting payment," Doc began. "When do you plan on giving him his take on this load?"

"Soon, he'll be dunning me for it."

"So," Doc continued, "When he comes to you for money, how much will he get?"

Henry was running and crunching numbers in his head. "After expenses, about an even two hundred grand."

The lawyers were glancing at each other apprehensively. Heidi's turn again. "Do you still have a drug habit?"

"No. I've been clean for years, I don't even drink beer."

"What were you addicted to?"

"Alcohol, heroin, cocaine, and marijuana," he said still smiling.

"We're allowing you to stay free, Mister Darby," Heidi continued. "to work for the government. How can we be certain that you won't relapse into drug addiction? There will be a lot of pressure on you, physical and emotional. You'll be spying and informing on your friends, setting them up to take a fall that'll put them in a federal penitentiary for the rest of their natural lives. Are you up to that task?"

"Viktor is not my friend," Henry said with a straight face.

"But you've had good times with Viktor, correct? You've considered him your friend for thirty seven years, correct? Can you set him up?" Heidi continued the badgering. "Can you set up Will Blanks? You've had good times with Will Blanks also. Correct Mister Darby? That's where the pressure comes from. Anybody can inform on somebody they hate or fear. Can you set up Ellen Agron? She has a part in this conspiracy."

"Ellen isn't part of Viktor's business," he snapped. "She knows about it, but that's all. She makes her own money. She's richer than Viktor." He was waffling as he sat slumped in the chair, not looking at the crowd, not patronizing or talking with his hands. "Yes," he finally said, "I can set up Viktor and Will. But when this is all over and I go to prison, I want to go to the Eglin Air Base Federal Penitentiary in Florida. Can that be arranged?"

Heidi glanced at Sue Lee who nodded in the affirmative.

"And I only want to do two years. Can you change the proxy? I want my attorney to read it before I sign it."

"It can be changed," Sue Lee said. "For your one-hundred percent cooperation, the government is going to seize three hundred thousand dollars in cash," Sue Lee continued, "place you in the Eglin Federal Correctional Center for a period of two years after you testify at the trial of Viktor Agron, et al. You'll be on supervised parole for a period of two additional years when you're released from the correctional institution. If for any reason you violate the cooperation terms of this agreement, this proxy will be null and void. Any questions, Mister Darby?"

"No, ma'am."

Sue Lee obtained a laptop from her purse and attached it to a small printer. She typed in the addendum to the proxy and printed it as we all watched. She handed a copy to attorney for the defendant, Preston Devon. He read it and handed it to his client. Henry read it, nodded in agreement, and signed it. The attorney signed it, and Sue Lee signed it.

"I want the three hundred thousand in this office on my desk in one hour," Doc said. "Cash, hundred dollar bills."

"Okay," Henry replied.

"Heidi, when he delivers the cash, I want you and Ray to copy the bills, and give him two hundred thousand back. Make him sign for it. They'll be government funds. Any questions?"

"No, sir," Heidi said.

"Nope," Preston Devon said standing to leave.

"I'll be back in an hour," Henry said.

"We'll be in the task force offices," I advised him.

He nodded and he and his lawyer walked out.

Heidi, Doc, Sue Lee, and I slowly walked to the task force offices. Doc was in deep thought. His head was down and he wasn't selling himself to Sue Lee for a change. He walked into his office and closed the door. Carla stared at us inquisitively. Sue Lee took a vacant desk and looked around the room while Heidi and I sat at our respective desks. "Where are the TFD's?"

"I don't know, probably at the club," Carla said. Sue Lee got up and walked out.

"We're getting behind on our reports," Carla said. "You guys caught up?"

"Yeah," I replied.

"Well, it looks like you guys are going out of town in the near future. I just don't want you to get too far behind."

"Thanks, Carla."

"She knows more than we do about our cases."

Heidi nodded, "Scary, isn't it? Coffee?"

"Yeah."

"Fly or buy?"

"Buy!" She handed me two bucks, I walked to the Club and ordered two coffees at the bar. Sue Lee was surrounded by the TFD's, flirting and laughing and eating a breakfast sandwich. Pat Brown was telling a story and making a downward striking motion with his hand as if he was busting a drug dealer's head.

I strolled back to the office. The receptionist called Carla and advised her that Henry Darby was in the waiting room. I sat the coffee on Carla's desk, went up and got him and walked him down to the task force office.

I tapped on Doc's door. "Enter."

Heidi joined us and we walked into Doc's office with our go-cups. Henry laid a briefcase on Doc's desk, opened it, and spilled the cash out. Doc started counting it. Heidi jumped in and helped him count and sort. It was in piles of hundred thousand. "It's all here," Heidi said.

"Can I have a receipt?" Henry asked.

"No," Doc replied.

"Heidi, you and Ray do the copying and then come back in here."

"Yes, sir!" We copied the notes and returned to Doc's office.

"Sign here," Doc said. Henry complied. "Give him the two-hundred thousand." I placed the bills in the briefcase Henry used to convey the cash to Doc's office and handed it to him.

Doc attached the receipt to the remaining one hundred thousand and placed it in his floor safe behind his desk. "Give me your cell phone," Doc said to Henry. Henry handed it to him. He placed a suction cup microphone to the receiver and attached it to a micro tape recorder, then handed it back to Henry. "Call Viktor Agron and tell him you've got his cocaine money. Mention a hundred kilo deal."

Henry nodded in acknowledgment and auto-dialed the cell. "Hey, Viktor, I've got good news for you, brother. Yeah, yeah, I've got your take on the last shipment. Yeah, yeah. I want to get rid of it. Yeah, yeah, okay. There's a big deal brewing, hundred kilos. Yeah. I'll see you in a week or so. Bye."

Doc took the cell phone from Henry and removed the microphone then gave it back to him.

"Make preparations to travel to Savannah, Mister Darby," Doc said.

"Yes, sir," Henry replied.

"That's all I have," Doc said. There was a lull while we all looked at each other.

"Let's hit it," Heidi said.

"I need a ride," Henry said. "I came here with my attorney. My car's at the bar."

"Okay, we'll take you," I replied. We walked out of the office and took the stairs to the parking garage. We piled into the Bimmer. Heidi drove, I rode shotgun, and Henry sat in the backseat.

13

Henry was like a little boy, sitting on one side and then changing to the other, and then sitting in the middle. He was gauging us, preparing to pimp us again. "Hey, this is kind of neat. We're going to be partners, the cop, the beautiful Special agent and the dope man. It'd make a good movie script."

I glanced over to him. Heidi was watching him in the rearview mirror. He was smiling his bartender's smile. "DEA always burns their snitches, don't they?"

We didn't answer him. "I mean, that's what I heard. Is it true?"

"You're going to be burned," I said. "You'll be testifying in federal court against Viktor and associates. It was part of your plea agreement. You're burning yourself."

"Oh, I know that. But if I wasn't in a plea agreement with the government, would you guys burn me?"

"No! Who told you that?" Heidi asked.

"FBI guy."

"One of the free-draft-beer guys?" I asked.

"Yeah, but they don't talk business on free draft beer. They started coming in after work and expecting to drink expensive bottled beer and Scotch whiskey for free. They're so damn cheap. They drink for free and they still don't tip the barmaid. I've got to tip her at the end of the evening. It's kind of hard for me to deny them anything because after two drinks they talk business. They didn't know I was a drug dealer. One of the things they talked about was DEA and how you guys always burn your snitches."

"They lied to you," Heidi said. "What's your point? Why do you ask?"

"Well, I figured since we were going to be working together." He paused and glanced at us individually, his head going back and forth like a bobble-head doll. "I thought you guys would tell me who set me up. I'm curious. I know you didn't take me off by accident. Somebody set me up. I'm not a violent person. I wouldn't try to get even. I'd just really like to know. Will you? Will you tell me?"

"No! It was an anonymous telephone call," Heidi said. "We acted on it and you got caught."

He was smiling, and then he laughed as he squirmed in the seat. "You guys are a piece of work. You play off of each other brilliantly. At first I had reservations about going undercover with you guys, but I'm okay with it now. I think this is going to work."

"Thanks for the vote of confidence," I said.

We were nearing downtown when he started pimping again. "You guys, I mean DEA, is under the Department of Justice, right?"

"Yeah," I said. He was silent for a while.

"You use the same computers? I mean, do you and the FBI use the same computers?"

"No," Heidi replied.

We pulled up to Hot Toddy's, Henry was preparing to climb out. "I wonder if Will Blanks is waiting for me. You guys took my wire. You want to give me another one?" he mumbled.

"No," I replied. We had the information we needed for conspiracy. I could tell he was anxious about another Will Blanks episode. Will had the ability to snap Henry's neck and leave him dying on the bar floor if he chose.

In the dope business the players never know when the end is going to come to them. There are no rules, just warnings. The most prevalent one is, "Don't get caught." Viktor and Will seemed to sense that Henry had violated the warning.

"We'll go in with you, if you want us to, Henry," I said.

"Yeah, that would be great," he replied.

Heidi parked at a meter and we ventured out into the sunshine, walking behind Henry the dope dealer toward his blues bar. It wasn't noon yet, just before the dream hour most workers look forward to. The cobblestones in the street and the fancy designed concrete sidewalks reeked of urine and vomit.

At night the streets and walkways were packed with cocky intoxicated young folks, fighting, cursing, puking before they entered their parents' cars for the drive back to utopia, the suburbs.

Coming to the Landing for a night of adventure was a young person's right of passage. Instead of going into the wilderness to fight Indians or to hunt for food, these modern barbarians go to The Landing to prove their ability to survive. It has always been played out in the midst of the Mississippi River, and it probably always will be.

Henry pushed on the old oak door and it came open. "hey, anybody here?" He shouted. The place stunk, and it was dirty. The huge bar had stale drinks and bottles on it, ash trays overflowing with butts, and trash was everywhere. The beer signs were still on and flashing. I looked down the bar and estimated it at ninety feet.

The stage was adjacent to the bar, just three feet off of the floor. A dance floor separated it from the giant bar. There were tables and stools, cigarette machines and a rail for drunks to lean on as they listened to the blues and got stoned.

A young woman came from the rear of the room through a saloon-style swinging door. "Oh, Henry," she said. "I was just going to start cleaning. I didn't expect you this soon. We worked late last night."

Henry was upset at the condition of his business. He was red-faced and his back was hunched.

"This place is a damn mess, Gina. Why didn't you clean up last night after you closed?"

"We had a great night, Henry. The crew was beat and so was I. I let them go home. I volunteered to clean up for them this afternoon."

"You're the manager, Gina," Henry continued. "I pay you to manage my business. I don't pay you to clean the place. If you're going to continue being my manager then manage. Do you understand what I'm saying?"

"Yes, Henry. It won't happen again." She was humiliated and staring at Heidi and me.

"Oh," Henry said. "These are friends of mine, Heidi and Ray. Guys, this is Gina my manager."

She shook hands with us, me first then we stood around awkwardly glancing at each other. She had a great body and she showed it in a blues-bar manager way. Tight jeans, revealing blouse, short dark hair, green eyes and too much makeup.

I figured she knew Henry was a dope dealer. He introduced us as friends, which probably made her assume we were also dope dealers, or some other type of degenerate. It made me uncomfortable.

"Are you alone?" Henry asked.

"Yes, Henry," Gina answered.

I took the cue, "We're leaving, Henry. Stay in touch. Nice meeting you, Gina." We walked out, strolled to the Bimmer, and climbed in. Heidi fired it and we were headed for Clayton. "I'm feeling weird about him wanting to know who turned him in," I said. "Think he could find out?"

"You mean could a drunk FBI agent find out for him and let him know?"

"Yeah, that's what I mean," I replied.

"Yeah, maybe. The Feebs monitor everything we do. They probably keep a log of every telephone call that comes into our office. An industrious Feeb could get the list through one of their super-secret computers and get issues on the numbers, and possibly come up with Sig's name and address, but he'd have to know Sig to connect it to us. The Feeb would have to know that I had the duty when Sig called. Unless it was Moynihan. He'd put it together immediately. He probably knows that Sig shot out his windows with the potato cannon."

I started laughing, Heidi joined in. "Man he was pissed," I said.

"He's a dangerous man to have as an enemy," Heidi said.

"And he's our enemy, right?"

"He's a Feeb, he's our natural enemy," Heidi muttered.

14

I awoke to a glorious spring day in beautiful St. Louis. There were boats on the Mississippi, birds circling and everything was in bloom. Tyrone was whining for me, coaxing me to climb out and let him outside. I rolled out and pulled on some Levis, then climbed the ladder down and let Tyrone out to romp. The foliage around my secluded yard was tall and thick, making it super private.

It was 0700 and I had an hour and a half to eat breakfast, read the newspaper in the sun and relax before leaving for the office. It was zero-eight-hundred before I had any action. My cell rang. I didn't want to answer it, but I did. It was Heidi.

"I can't find Henry Darby. I've been trying since about six A.M. and he isn't answering his cell."

"Try his bar," I recommended.

"I tried that."

"It's early," I said. "Maybe he's sleeping in."

"I'm going to drive by his house before going to the office," she said. "How about you going by the bar. Hit me on my cell if you find anything out."

"Roger!"

That gave me another twenty minutes to enjoy the sun. I showered and dressed and watched Tyrone from the kitchen as I slurped coffee and continually checked the clock. Zero-eight-forty-five, it was time to roll. I made sure Tyrone had food and water then walked out the front door to the Corvette, fired it, and rolled north on Broadway.

I was parking at the bar when I saw Gina the body, the restaurant manager, walking toward the entrance to the building. I quickly exited the Corvette, "Good morning," I said. She smiled a worried smile and kept on walking. She tacked toward the bar door with me in pursuit, unlocked it, and walked in. "I'm looking for Henry." She didn't answer, just stared at me like she was scared.

"Where is he?"

"I don't know, sir," she replied, looking down. She sat her cell phone and keys on the bar and ignored me by reading some order forms. I grabbed the cell and went through the caller I D.

"This number is almost like his home number," I said. "Where is it coming from?"

"It is his home number, sir. He has two phone lines."

"You mean he's at home?"

"Yes, sir. He has a safe-room, sir. He's in hiding. He doesn't wish to be disturbed."

She was stiff and frightened. I needed to get her relaxed. "Gina, please stop calling me sir. Okay? I need you to tell me what's going on."

"He called me at home late last night. He was drunk, or stoned, or whatever." She was speaking like a high school student, using her hands for emphasis, her voice to personify her indifference. "He told me he was going into the room and that he didn't wish to be disturbed. He's in hiding. When that happens, I'm in charge of everything. It's part of the plan we made."

"Plan?" I muttered.

"Yeah, when things get too much for him, he goes into his secret room and I take care of the business."

"Where exactly is the room?"

"It's in the attic of his house. There's a secret entrance in the hall closet. There's a dormer at the back. You can't see it from the front. It cost him a bundle. That's where he is. He'll come out in a couple of days."

"Do you have a key to his house?" She tried to walk away from me. I blocked her path. "I need the key to the house, Gina, and I need the key to the room." She went for her keys on the bar. I intercepted her and grabbed the ring. There were eleven keys on the ring. Two of them were almost identical. I held them up for her to eyeball. "Is this them, Gina?"

I could tell I had hit pay dirt. She had the look of a panicked girl who had just wrecked her dad's Jaguar roadster. "I'm trying to keep my job, sir," she said as she got up and walked out of the room through the saloon swinging doors.

I made my way to the Corvette with the two keys in hand, climbed in, and hit Heidi on her cell.

"Yes?"

"Meet me down on the cobblestones by the casino boat."

"Be there in five," she replied.

I tossed the top back and waited in the sun as she pulled up alongside me.

"What's up?" She asked.

"I think he's in a secret safe-room at his house. I got the keys from Gina the body, his manager." Heidi was thinking.

"What now?"

"Let's go talk to him," I said.

"You mean sneak into his house, find the secret room and then sneak into it and surprise him?"

"Yeah!" She was thinking again, staring out at the dirty Mississippi River.

"Okay, I'm game. You lead."

I drove off of the cobblestones with Heidi following me, headed west to Seventh Street, then south to Broadway. We slowly drove up Holly Hills and parked at the curb in front of Henry's house. The neighborhood power walkers were watching us.

They huffed and puffed their way around us, then turned and walked back, watching and gauging us as we climbed out of our expensive government sports cars and walked up the brick sidewalk, precisely centered in the spring lawn, to Henry's front door.

The French windows were bare and I stared through them looking for signs of movement. I didn't relish going unannounced into someone's home if they were going to be waiting for me behind the door. It gave me a strange feeling, like I was doing something wrong. But is there anything wrong in the dope game? The rules are made up as the doper and the investigator go along through the maze of deceit.

I took the lead since I was in possession of the door key. I slid it in and turned it and then twisted the handle and the door swung open without any noise, as if it had been recently oiled. "What kind of person would oil their door hinges?" I asked myself.

We strolled in, closed the door behind us, and stopped and listened. The place was as quiet as death. We were in the living room. The house was immaculately clean, expensively decorated in French provincial, and one wall was covered with a book case filled with hard cover books.

There were diplomas on one of the other walls. Henry had a degree in economics from the University of Missouri. He had graduated with honors. There were pictures of him in different stages of his youth, his high school diploma, and pictures of his high school and college graduations. A picture of him drinking in a bar with other young people. He was smiling an empty smile, showing his teeth but his eyes looked cloudy.

We continued our journey into the belly of the house, armed with holstered forty-caliber automatic pistols, snooping like burglars. The house had expensive wallpaper in some of the rooms and hardwood floors throughout.

The kitchen had restaurant-grade stainless steel appliances, granite counter tops and a stainless steel island. We continued opening doors and looking inside of rooms.

At the end of the main hallway there was a door. I opened it and rustled through some hanging clothing. There was another door. I opened it.

There were spiral steps leading up. We crept up them and came to a locked oak door. I slid the key in and unlocked it. We walked in.

He was lying on his side on the bed, a pool of vomit near his mouth, a look of excruciation on his green and white face, hair messed, long T shirt, hiked up showing his buttocks, dried tears on his face. He was moaning as he slept. I nudged him. He didn't respond. "Hey, Henry, wake up."

He stirred and glanced at us, then jumped and raised up as he pulled his shirt down. "How did you guys find me?"

"It wasn't easy," I replied with a smile. "What's up with you?"

I could see the wheels turning in his head. He knew he had to be communicative, although he was angry for being disturbed. He was wondering who he could blame for this breach of his security. He was certain it was Gina the body who had betrayed him. "It was Gina wasn't it?" He studied me for a response.

"No, Henry. We came looking for you and we found this room. It's as simple as that. I picked the locks. Gina had nothing to do with this." He wasn't buying it.

"Damn her," he moaned. "All I've done for her and she rats me out. I've made her rich, for God's sake."

"Money doesn't buy loyalty, Henry. Now tell us what's up." He looked at me with hatred, then turned his hateful eyes toward Heidi. He wanted to kill both of us. He looked like he had it in him, as if he had killed before for a lesser violation of his lifestyle, his space and his privacy.

But he was a money driven-organism. He knew he couldn't make money while incarcerated. We were his ticket to an early release. Communication and cooperation were his only options.

"Will showed up late last night with a couple of hookers," Henry began. "He terrorized me in front of them and then made me get drunk with him. We did some blow, too. That dirty mother fucker. I'm going to kill that bastard someday. I'll even the score with everybody who did this to me, I swear."

He was wearing a typical look: the look Ross Milton had when he was talking about having an unneeded mandatory colonoscopy. The same look Mike Schweig had when Ross advised him that Pat Brown had urinated in his bourbon and coke.

"How did he terrorize you?" I asked.

"Oh, man," Henry moaned. He rubbed his green face and scratched his chest. He placed his hands on his face at the cheeks and temples. He didn't wish to answer my question, but he knew it was still communication time and he had no choice.

"Viktor has always thought I've been stealing from him. You know, skimming dope money. He's not real smart with math, and he knows that I know numbers real good, so he gets paranoid and bitches to Will that I've been skimming. That's what went down last night. He knocks on the door and I, like a fool, answer the damn thing. He barges in and roughs me up. I didn't tell him anything. He can go back to Viktor now and tell him his story and they'll both feel like they've accomplished something. They're both pretty stupid."

"So the prostitutes stood there and watched this charade?"

"Yeah, they got off on it. It's part of the pimp, whore, trick routine. The whore Will brought for me played the part of protector and caregiver. I got off on it and so did she."

"That's real sick, Henry," I muttered. "Where did he get the prostitutes?"

"Friends of Ellen's," he replied. "Will found her but she talked him into telling Viktor he hadn't found her. She wants to be left alone for a while. She thought she was doing me a favor, sending the hookers, Will, and some blow. She almost ended my life."

He raised completely up and sat on the edge of the bed. "You hate me don't you?"

"Probably, Henry, but we've got work to do," I said. "Where's your cell?"

His jeans and shirt were heaped on the floor beside the bed. He carefully climbed off of the bed and rummaged through them until he found his cell. I took it from him and attached a suction microphone to it, then plugged it into a micro recorder and handed it back to him.

"Call Viktor," I ordered.

"I'm fucking sick, man," he balked.

"Hey Henry, I think this is all part of the game. Did you think you were going to get in and out of the dope game without some heartache? You're blaming Will? You're blaming us? You're blaming the anonymous caller? Blame yourself, Henry. It's payback time. Your chickens have come home to roost. Make the call. Tell him the deal's in the works. Tell him to contact the Corn Island skipper and order up the hundred kilos. Do it now!"

I turned on the tape recorder as he dialed the cell. He held the phone out so we could hear.

"Yes," the deep voice said.

"Hey, brother," Henry said. "How are you?"

"Hey, my friend, I was just thinking about you," the voice said. "Will told me you and he partied last night. Welcome back to the real world. How are you feeling?"

"Not well, but I'll survive," Henry said. "My friends are

chomping at the bit for the hundred kilo deal. Can you contact your friend on the Corn Island and order it up?"

"Hundred? Yeah, I can do that. When you want it?"

"Soon. What about price? I need a special volume price," Henry said.

"Like what were you expecting?"

"Maybe five a package," Henry said.

"That's a good deal for your client."

"I won't be charging them five," Henry said with a weak laugh.

Viktor was being cautious again. He was pausing, walking through the mine field of conspiracy. "I'll have to check with my people about the special price. Call me when you get ready to do the deal. I'll have my chickens in a row then."

"It's not chickens, it's ducks," Henry said. "It's ducks in a row."

"Oh, right, ducks not chickens. I don't know why I always call them chickens. Maybe because in Little Odessa we have many chickens and few ducks."

There was laughter between them. "Have you seen my lovely wife? Will hasn't caught up with her. She isn't dancing at any of the clubs in East St. Louis."

"No, I haven't seen her, Viktor. But I'm looking. I'm signing off. I'll call you when I'm en route. So long, Vik."

He gave us the look again.

"Okay, Henry, that was good," I said. "Now I want you to call Ellen, thank her for the prostitutes and the cocaine, and tell her Viktor is concerned about her well-being."

"I don't want to implicate Ellen," he said. "She isn't part of the conspiracy. She's just a girl on the fringe. Why do you want her?"

"For leverage somewhere down the road, Henry. Now do it."

"It's hard, man, I can't do it. I love this girl. You're asking for too much. It's too damn hard." He was on the verge of tears, sitting in vomit, his green face contorted, the veins at this temples bulging.

"Everything's hard, Henry, except sex, booze and rock and roll," I muttered to him. He realized he had no choice. He was good at counting cards but DEA controlled the deck.

He hit the auto dial, a sexy voice answered, "Yes, Henry, how are you this morning?" She was patronizing Henry and he was too mesmerized to know it.

"Oh, fine, Ellen. It had been a long time since I'd partied like that. I want to thank you for the blow and the chicks. It brought back old memories."

"You are very welcome, darling," Ellen cooed. "I want to help you in any way I can. Welcome back to the party."

"Viktor's been calling me wanting to know if I'd seen you. Why are you hiding?"

"I've had enough of Vik for a while. I'll let him stew, then I'll go back. It makes life more interesting." She loudly laughed.

"Okay," Henry said. "I just wanted to thank you for last night. "I'm signing off. I love you Ellen."

"I love you, too, Henry."

Henry handed me the cell and crawled back onto the bed. He got into a fetal position and stared at us. "See what you're making me do? She's probably the best friend I have in the world. She's a decent person. I'm a decent man. So we're freaky. Ellen does her thing for the money. I sell dope for the money. This is America, the free enterprise system. I should be able to pursue happiness in my own way and so should Ellen. Now, I'm doing my best friend and I'm sick. Fucking sick!"

He was shaking and heaving. There was a toilet adjacent to the room. He ran for it and slammed the door. "Henry," I loudly said to him through the door. “We’re going to take you to an emergency room. You need a doctor.”

“I’m not going,” he replied. “I’ve been through this before. First they diagnose you, ingestion of alcohol and cocaine, they’ll say. Then they lock you in a psyche ward for three days until you detox, and then they take your insurance card and kick you out into the parking lot. I can spend three days here detoxing. I hate doctors.”

“What do you think?” I asked Heidi.

“It’s his life,” she replied.

I opened the door to the bathroom. “We’re leaving, Henry. Contact us in three days. Understand?”

“Yeah, and fuck you,” he mumbled with his face in the commode.

We took our time driving to the office. Everyone was typing on their laptops as we walked in. Doc came out and eyeballed us, turned and walked into his office then came back out and stared at us again. “Come into my office,” he said as he turned and disappeared inside.

We followed him in. He sat back in his chair and zoned at us. “Did you find him?”

“Yes, sir,” Heidi replied. “He was in a secret room in the attic of his house. We had him telephone Viktor Agron. The deal is in the works.”

“When is he coming out?” Doc asked.

“Three days,” I replied.

“We’re all going to get promoted over this one,” Doc said with a smile. We smiled back on cue. Doc cleared his voice. “Ray, I need you on a deal for a couple of days. You were in the Marine Corps, right?”

“Yeah.”

“Heidi, you stay in the office and get caught up on the paperwork.”

“Deal?” Heidi asked. “What deal?”

"Monica Rose is the case agent," Doc said. "She's preparing the itinerary and should be giving the group the rundown about now. I'm trying to get her to G/S Thirteen, journeyman grade. She needs someone with Ray's expertise." Heidi and Doc stared.

"Okay," she said. I exited Doc's office. I figured I was insulated by the Viktor Agron case, but Henry Darby nixed that by getting stoned. I gave an inquisitive look to Heidi. She shrugged. At this point in time I was the utility TFD who could not hide in the big case. It had gotten up to eighty degrees. It was supposed to rain all night. Summer was here.

15

I made my way past Monica Rose, flanked by five big cardboard boxes almost as big as she, as she was giving her spiel to the group. She was dressed in Marine Corps camouflage from head to toe and she was all business. No dancing and singing and hunching, just DEA business. She had a stack of papers in her hand and was walking toward the group.

"I'm passing out a map of our next assignment. Pelican Island is the target. It's situated in north St. Louis County, right on the Missouri River at Highway three sixty seven. The island is owned by the State of Missouri, and it's uninhabited."

She paused while we stared at the map of Pelican Island, cleared her throat and continued. "This afternoon, we're going to be airlifted to Pelican Island to set up a hammer and nail operation to catch marijuana growers hopefully in the early morning hours when they come to their patch to water and fertilize." We all looked at each other quizzically while she paused again.

She approached the group with some eight by ten glossies and passed them out. "As you can see by the photographs, there's a sizeable patch of marijuana growing at the south center of the island. About a thousand plants, all about ten feet high, almost ready for a spring harvest, sinsemilla, meaning without seeds. It's a million dollar patch, folks. Somebody's growing it right under our noses, and our job this evening and tomorrow morning is to apprehend the growers and bring them to federal justice."

We continued to stare at her without expression while she paused. "It was an indoor operation this winter, and after the last day of any possible frost, the grower transferred them to the island by boat to grow in the rich soil there. It was a lot of work, folks, but it's probably better than punching a time clock at some factory. Sioux Passage Park is across the Missouri and within binocular range of a subdivision of expensive homes. Obviously, we don't know if the grower lives over there, but it's a possibility, so with that fact in mind, we've decided to land at the other side of the island and hike near the patch, set up a base camp and split into two squads in the morning and hopefully have a squad pursue the grower and chase him into the other squad for apprehension. Classic hammer and nail."

She paused again and waited for any questions.

"Groovy," Pat Brown shouted out. "I'm a camping expert, I've been in the woods my entire life."

"Lord save us," Ross Milton muttered.

"I've got a deal, I can't go," Carl Robinson said.

"I'm on his deal," Mike Schweig said, "I can't go either."

"I'm on the same deal," Clete said.

"Fuck it," Bill Yocum said. "I'll go to the woods and camp for a night. I've slept in worse places."

"All deals are off," Monica said. "We're going on the weed deal. We're leaving this afternoon from Spirit of St. Louis Airport, Hangar Twenty Nine, so make sure you all are there at 1500 hours or you'll have to answer to Doc. Anymore questions?"

"I've got a question," I said. She stared and waited. "Where did this clue come from?"

"St. Louis County Police. Their helicopter was flying over the island coming back from somewhere and the pilot observed the patch. She contacted Doc and Doc contacted me. I flew the island with our copter crew and took the surveillance pictures. Now everyone, come up here and get your gear."

We all got up from our desks and walked toward the big cardboard boxes and started digging into them. Marine

Corps camouflage, boots and caps, belts and holsters, canteens and packs, K-rations, rubber ladies (air mattresses), mosquito repellant, machetes, flashlights, Sterno, blankets and one twelve-man mesh tent. "Carla and I are leaving the room," Monica shouted, "so go ahead and get changed now. We don't have much time."

We dug into the boxes and found our sizes then walked back to our desks and changed clothes. I was lacing up my boots when it hit me. I was back in the Marine Corps. My nightmare had become a reality. I was wearing Marine Corps cammies, and I was preparing to climb aboard a helicopter and go to the jungle.

"Somebody tell me this isn't happening," Ross Milton said.

"They don't have my size," Clete Jones whined. "I can't go." He stormed into Doc's office and closed the door. Ten seconds later Heidi came out of Doc's office and walked out of the task force office. Ten seconds after that, Doc and Clete came out together.

"Where's Monica?" Doc asked.

"She walked out, Doc," Carl Robinson said.

Monica walked in and said, "What's up?"

"Clete can't go on the weed deal. There aren't any uniforms to fit him."

"Okay, Doc." Clete walked back to his desk and gloated on his victory while he watched us scramble to get ready for the deal.

"Y'all can leave for the airport now, if you choose," Monica said. "Ray, bring a shotgun, and Carl, bring the Colt Machine Gun, and everybody, stop by a grocery store and buy some provisions, unless you want to eat K-rations. We'll be on the island for at least one night so bring what you think you'll need. I'll see you at the airport."

"I can't believe this shit," Ross Milton said as he

adjusted his camouflage ascot. "My belly isn't as big as Clete's so I have to go on this torture run and he doesn't. It isn't fair. I'm a United States of America DEA fucking federal special agent for Christ's sake. He's just a cop, a damn C/I with a badge playing junior G-man. There's no justice in the criminal justice game. Everybody gets fucked."

"One more thing," Monica shouted. "Mike and Ross, bring the big tent with you. It's what's going to keep us from being eaten alive tonight."

"Oh, fuck," Ross exclaimed. "Now we're being turned on by one of our own. We have to be the lackies for the group bringing the damn tent."

"I'm bringing this shit up to the SAC at the next agent's meeting," Mike Schweig said. "We're supposed to be management here. The TFD's are supposed to be the lackies."

They tossed their packs on and emptied the big tent out of the cardboard box.

"It weighs a fucking ton," Ross said.

"Fuck," Mike Schweig exclaimed.

"We have no choice," Ross continued. "Monica is the case agent and she ordered us to bring the damn tent so we've got to bring the damn tent. Let's drag it to the Seville and toss it in the trunk and head for the airport."

"Airport, yeah. But first we've got to stop by a grocery store. I refuse to eat K-rations."

"Right!"

"Pat," Monica said. "You and Bill stop by a hardware store and purchase a five gallon gas can, fill it with low octane gas and bring it along. We need it to burn the weed."

"Roger!"

I walked into the supply room and picked out a Remington Wing Master, then decided I would pay a visit to the head before climbing into the Corvette. I did my business and was washing my hands as I looked into the mirror. The shotgun was slung on my shoulder and the Marine Corps cover was down at the base of my nose, just like I'd been trained to wear it a long time ago. I was having flashbacks and trying to shake them off, but I was proud of the fact that I could still fit into a Marine Corps uniform and actually still look like a Marine.

I walked out of the head and bumped into Heidi who was apparently waiting for me. She kissed me on the lips and hugged me as if I was going into combat.

"Be careful out there. I tried to get you out of this assignment but Doc said Monica needed your expertise. I told him I need your expertise, too, but he just laughed."

"No big deal. Doc's right, Monica does need my expertise."

"Make sure that's all she gets," she said with a stare.

"I read you," I replied. She kissed me again and walked toward the task force office while I took the stairs down to the parking lot, tossed my pack and the shotgun into the trunk of the Corvette and headed for a grocery store at Kingshighway and Euclid wondering why Heidi continually played me.

I parked in the lot and walked into the store without notice. No attire is unusual in the Central West End. I purchased bottled water and cans of pasta, beans, ham, bread, a big box of raisins, salt, toilet paper and mustard. For breakfast I picked up some Danish, some fresh strawberries, powdered milk, two small boxes of dry cereal and a cigarette lighter, paid for them and walked to the Corvette.

I loaded my pack with the food stuffs, opened the trunk, tossed the pack inside, slammed it, climbed in, cranked it, and headed for West County, enjoying the scenery and shifting gears.

I pulled onto the DEA hangar parking lot. The Porsche, Monica's three-fifty-Z and the Seville were parked in a line. Ross and Mike were fighting with the tent, muscling it out of the trunk, and dragging it toward the hangar. I parked the Corvette in the line and walked into the hangar and through it to the tarmac.

Monica and the rest of the crew were there milling around the helicopter. I walked up to them and slipped my pack and the shotgun off and admired the chopper. It was an MD-six-hundred jet helicopter, maroon with black trim. "Million bucks," I said, but nobody acknowledged my comment. I thought about the million dollar marijuana patch.

The grower, if he was lucky enough to harvest his cash crop and get it onto the market and get paid from the weed consignment he would have to do, and if he could avoid being arrested, or killed by a rival or a dope-man robber, like Detective Clete Jones, he might be able to afford one of these choppers.

The pilot was on board with the co-pilot. He gave Monica the thumbs up and began the process of starting the jet. The turbine was whining, then it got louder and louder, and the blade started turning and Monica gave the sign for us to climb in and get strapped down. We took turns getting on board, then I had to get back off and help Ross and Mike with the tent.

Bill and Pat muscled the five-gallon can of gasoline on board and then their packs and the Mini Colt Machine Gun. Finally we were all on board, looking at each other with "Why-me-man?" faces.

The chopper went straight up slowly hovered for an instant and then banked and headed for the Missouri River. The side door was open and I sat near it watching the changing terrain below me. There were houses, highways cars and people, then there was the muddy Missouri and islands and boats, then just green and mud as we got closer to Pelican Island.

We came in on the north bank near a backwater tributary and landed in a clearing beside the water. The island was in full bloom, milk-and-rag and horseweed ten feet tall guarding our landing from the subdivision miles away in a civilized community where someone might be watching the patch.

No one spoke; we just climbed out of the chopper, grabbed our gear, pulled the tent out, and the chopper took off. We were standing on the island in silence in forty seconds.

Monica took out a map and a compass and was looking at them as if they were something she had never seen before. I watched her and made the realization that she had never seen a compass or a field map before. "Ray, would you please help me with this?"

"Yeah." I took it from her. I studied the map and shot an azimuth and then looked at the terrain in front of us. The mosquitoes were starting to attack and everybody was going for the repellant, but we were sweating so much that the repellant wasn't working.

"We've got about a quarter of a mile to walk through the weeds to get to a place we can set up a camp and make a surveillance of the patch. If you want, Monica, I'll take the point."

"Yes, Ray, I'd appreciate it."

I pulled on my pack and slung the Remington over my shoulder and started whacking at the milkweed ahead of me with a machete that Monica had brought along. The stalks were an inch in diameter, and the milky fluid they emitted as I chopped them was flying over my head and past me at the group following closely behind.

I worked for half an hour and was obviously tiring out. "I'll take the lead for a while," Bill Yocum said.

"Thanks." I went to the rear of the queue and checked on Ross and Mike. They were breaking down, unable to walk any farther, on the verge of heat stroke.

"Drink water," I instructed them. Carl Robinson was sitting next to them, pale and shaky, with the five-gallon can of gasoline. They slugged water from their canteens, laid on the milkweed and moaned and dry heaved. "That fucking Clete," Ross moaned. "That fat fuck is probably eating a steak dinner about now."

"I can't go any further," Mike moaned. "Get me off of this island. I demand an evacuation. Call the damn helicopter, I need medical assistance."

The chopping stopped. Monica and Bill Yocum came back to our location. "We've got a place to set up camp," Monica said. "We need the tent so we can get it up and get these damn mosquitoes away from us."

I grabbed the tent and drug it toward Bill. He globbed onto it and dragged it toward the others as Monica and I sat on the chopped milkweed and evaluated Ross and Mike. They stared at us through hollow eyes as the mosquitoes attacked. "Get that tent set up immediately," Monica shouted toward the chopped milkweed. "Let's get them up, Ray," Monica continued.

We hoisted Ross up and he stumbled along the path toward the group. He left his pack, and I grabbed at it and sat it near me. Mike got up and wobbled his way toward the group, leaving his pack sitting near my boots.

I slung Mike's pack on my shoulder by one strap. It was heavy, maybe fifty pounds. I sat it back down and opened it. There was a case of canned Budweiser, iced down in a garbage bag with some cans of pasta around it. I looked in the other pack. Same thing, except it was Michelob Ultra.

Ross had to have the best.

I trucked them toward the group who had already started erecting the tent and came into the base camp. Pat Brown and Carl Robinson were finishing with the tent, tying down the ropes while Bill Yocum continued to chop the milkweed to give us some room to move outside the tent.

"It's up," Carl shouted.

We all moved inside and plopped onto the floor.

"My pack," Mike said. "Where's my pack?"

"Here," I said as I flung it toward him. He grabbed at it and hugged it, then used it as a pillow as he snoozed. Ross gave me an inquisitive look. I tossed his pack at him and he grabbed at it. I took off my cammie shirt and laid it out to dry, then took off my black T and laid it out.

I grabbed a towel from my pack and a bottle of water and doused myself and dried my upper body; Then I sat on the floor of the tent and tried to regain my strength as I ate raisins and sipped bottled water.

Mike and Ross were snoring. Monica was looking worried. Pat and Carl and Bill were lying flat out looking at the ceiling of the tent.

My strength came back quickly. I stood and looked south toward where the patch of weed was supposed to be. We were well hidden by the milkweed, but I couldn't see the patch. "Anybody seen the marijuana?"

"I haven't seen it," Monica said.

"It should be right over there," I said pointing. "Want to go look for it?"

"Yeah," she replied as she dug into her pack and retrieved a small video camera.

"Wash the sweat off of your exposed skin first," I instructed.

"Okay."

She doused her face and neck with bottled water, rubbed

it, then dried herself.

"Okay, load up on the repellant." I pulled on my cammie shirt and we both rubbed the mosquito repellant on then sprayed some near the door of the tent. We quickly opened it and ran outside and closed it. The mosquitoes were swarming around us but not lighting.

I started chopping again trying to make my way toward the alleged patch of expensive weeds. I was there in three minutes. We came out of the milkweed into a clearing. The plants were a vivid green, almost neon, as they swayed in the light breeze with the evening summer sun going down.

I estimated the plot was half an acre. It was cleared and raised and cared for, obviously by someone who knew what they were doing. It was harvest time; the plants were in their prime and full of dynamite.

The bad guy, would chop these plants and then take them to a spot for cleaning and packaging. The grower could plant another batch and then harvest it in the fall. Two batches a year, two million cool tax-free dollars. I hoped we can catch the guys who planted them.

The Missouri River was directly south of the patch, just like I observed in the surveillance photos. The grower had to live near the Missouri, and probably had a small boat pulled up on shore on the south bank. A plot like this had to be checked on every couple of days. "Beautiful," I muttered.

"The neatest patch I've ever seen," Monica replied as she filmed it.

"Let's go back," I said. "The grower has got to be in a position to observe his patch from somewhere on the south bank. I don't want him to see us."

We walked back to the tent. No one was stirring, but they had taken off their shirts and were lying in the breeze coming through the mesh camouflage tent and snoozing. I checked my wristwatch. "Seventeen-hundred hours," I said aloud.

Monica and I quickly ran back into the tent and zipped the door then sat on the floor and laid back to relax. “We’ve got to get a plan, Ray. Got any ideas?”

“Yeah. We’ve got to be listening for an outboard motor. When we hear it, that’ll be our cue that the grower is on the way.”

“An outboard? What if it isn’t him? What if it’s a fisherman?”

“It’ll be him. The Missouri isn’t a recreational river. People don’t even fish it. There’s no marinas on it and there’s no place to put a boat in. Would you come to this island if you didn’t have to?”

“Nope.” She called Doc on her cell. “We’re in position, Doc. We’ve got surveillance on the patch. Must be a thousand plants. Beautiful plants. I videotaped it. If we don’t make a pinch tonight or tomorrow morning, we’re going to chop it and burn it. Yes, Doc, I’ll talk to you later.”

We drifted off like day campers at a juvenile retreat after cookies and milk. It was dusk when I awoke. The group was starting to stir. I blew up my rubber lady and made myself a place to sleep for the night. Monica followed suit and placed her rubber lady next to mine.

I inspected and smelled the ham I had purchased from the grocery store and determined it was still fresh so I made myself a ham sandwich while Monica watched. I handed her the makings and she finished off the ham. We were eating bananas and drinking bottled water when the crew started coming back to life.

Ross Milton stirred, stood and stretched then reached into his pack and popped a beer. He slugged it, killing it in two gulps. Then he popped another one. The popping sound caused Mike Schweig to stir. He had his nose in the air smelling.

"Beer," he muttered. He stood and reached into his pack, and pulled out a cold can and popped it, slugged it and then opened another and gulped at it.

"I'm feeling better now," Mike said. "How about you, Ross?"

"Better."

Pat Brown stirred and got up. "The patch. Anybody seen the patch?"

"Yeah," I said. "Right down that path." He reached into his pack and came out with a beer, stuck it in his cammic pocket and then got another one out and popped it. "I'll be back, I'm going for a look-see."

Carl Robinson and Bill Yocum stood and both grabbed a pair of cold beers out of their packs. "Going for a look-see," they said simultaneously as they exited the tent. It was close to dark when the TFD's came back to the tent.

"Man, this place is wild," Pat Brown said. "I wish I would've known about this place when I was a kid; I'd have spent all of my summers here, just camping and fishing and drinking beer. What a place! We spooked a whole herd of deer over by the patch. Must've been eight or nine of them, a buck and some does. And there's a dead fawn just west of the patch. Hasn't been dead for long; the maggots are just now eating it. Wonder what killed it." He reached in and grabbed two more beers and began swilling.

"We've got to get a plan, Monica," Carl said. "Got any ideas?"

"Yeah. We're going to listen for an outboard motor. Then some of us are going to hike to the Missouri and wait at the boat for the grower to run. The rest of us will flush him toward the boat. Everybody got it?"

"Yeah," they all said unenthusiastically.

I grabbed a can of Chef-Boy-Ar-Dee out of my pack, opened it, and fired up some Sterno, holding it by the lid as I heated it, the way Marines and DEA operatives and homeless people do. It heated quickly and I gobbled it down. The carbohydrates were racing through my body giving me strength and alertness.

It was pitch black inside the tent with the only light coming from the moon through the mesh sides. Pat and Carl propped their flashlights up on the floor so that the light shone on the ceiling of the tent. Pat broke out a portable radio and tuned it to the local Rhythm and Blues station. Howlin Wolf was singing “Hoochie Coochie Man,” and Everybody was trying to sing along with him and swill cold beer in the semi-darkness.

Mike started the trek outside to relieve himself of fluid. The beer drinkers took turns going out, trip after trip. Ross Milton stumbled into the tent. “Man, there’s a wild animal out there. I heard it in the weeds. I don’t know what it is, but it’s big.”

“Could be the Feebs,” Ross said. “Maybe it’s that fucking Rich Moynihan spying on us.”

“Could be anything,” Pat Brown said. “But it’s probably coyotes. They’re curious creatures. Probably can’t figure out what we’re doing here on their turf.” He turned the radio down and we listened to the outside noises. There was rustling in the bush, but that’s understandable. The animals belonged here. We didn’t.

“Might be counter-surveillance,” Monica said. “Maybe somebody should go out and take a look at the patch. Any volunteers?”

“I’ll go,” I said. “I’ve got the shotgun.”

I taped my flashlight to the barrel of the sawed off, lathered up with repellant and pulled on my cammie shirt and boots.

“I’m going with you,” Carl said as he stumbled to get up. I could see that Monica and I were the only sober ones in the tent.

"No, I'll be alright. If I'm not back in ten minutes, come looking for me."

I quickly exited the tent and then slowly walked through the milkweed maze toward the dope patch. I stopped every thirty seconds and listened to the night noises, rustling and cawing and movement in the bush.

Something was definitely in the weeds, but I doubted it was human. Maybe a bear or a large coyote or wolf. I came onto the patch and visually inspected it in the existing moonlight. I watched and listened for half an hour; no one came to check on me. There was no movement around it so I made my way back to the tent.

I could hear the music as I approached, Muddy Waters singing, "Mannish Boy." How appropriate. They were laughing and I could make out Bill Yocum's deep voice. "Gargle it, Mike." The crew was laughing so loudly that any human on the twenty-six acre island could have heard them.

I walked to the tent and stopped on the outside and watched the show through the mesh sides. Mike Schweig was standing in the middle of the tent with his head back and he was gargling something.

I walked inside and he was holding a bottle of peppermint Schnapps, swilling and gargling it. He fell onto his back and sighed. "Your turn, Pat," he said as he handed the bottle toward Pat Brown.

Bill Yocum was beside himself with glee. "I love you man," he said to Mike who was still on his back.

"I'm not drinking after you," Pat Brown said. "I know where your mouth has been," he added as he handed the bottle back to Mike.

"I'm not afraid to drink after Mike," Ross Milton said as he took the bottle. He raised it and slugged a mouthful. "Gargle it, Ross," Bill Yocum said.

Ross raised his chin and tried to gargle then drank it down and sat on his rubber lady.

"I wonder what the king of belly fat, that fucking Clete, is doing right about now," Ross said.

"Eating a pizza," Mike replied.

"A pizza? Try three pizzas," Bill Yocum said.

The conversation died down. They were drinking the last of the beer. Albert King was singing "Born Under A Bad Sign." Monica was singing along, swaying and grooving.

I unzipped the tent door and walked in. "I didn't see anything out there."

"Oh, great. Thanks, Ray," Monica said as she finished a beer and tossed the can toward the entrance.

Everybody was mellowed out; everybody but me. "Ross," Monica said, "can I ask you a question?"

"Yeah, Monica, go ahead," he replied.

"Why do you always wear an ascot?" Ross was quiet for ten seconds. "Okay, I'll tell you, but you have to promise not to tell anybody else. Everybody promise?"

"Yeah, sure," they all said.

"I wear it as a form of protest. I protest being a DEA agent. I protest being one of the crowd. I'm an individual, not a team player, but I must be a team player if I want to survive, so I protest by wearing an ascot. It's as simple as that."

No one commented for five minutes. We sat in the darkness, in the wilderness listening to the rustling of animals in the bush. I didn't care about the spoiled Ross Milton and his story about how he had been wronged by the system. I had heard it a thousand times from cops who were mirrored by him.

Many of them come into this game with influential friends and relatives. They get great appointments while the rest of us "tote that barge and lift that bale."

I was concerned about the rustling in the bush. We were sitting ducks waiting for the supersonic projectile to tear into our brains. My question to myself was, "would a mere marijuana grower murder a team of DEA operatives because they were about to destroy his patch?"

I kept thinking about Henry Darby. He wasn't what he seemed. He played himself down during the interview with AUSA Sue Lee, Heidi and me. He's damn smart, sophisticated, and educated. Would he, or Viktor, or Will kill a team of DEA agents? Maybe!

I had been on the edge for my entire life: youth in east St. Louis. Marine Corps, Far East and the time off in foreign countries, police department raids, but I had never been as vulnerable as I was at this time in my strange life. Maybe it was a coyote out in the bush. If it was, it was mixed with a German Shepherd.

I was on my own if I wanted to make a reconnaissance. Everybody else was drunk. If I stated my feelings the human coyote would hear me, lay in wait and slit my throat. Maybe he's just smiling as he watches his tax dollars being wasted.

Maybe he's waiting for us to drift off into slumber land and then kill us. But if he wanted us dead, he could've done it at any time since darkness set in. If he's out there, he apparently doesn't wish us dead. I'm certain he's got a plan. At this point in time, I don't have a plan.

"I don't understand," Bill Yocum finally said. "What's so bad about being a team player?"

"Nothing, if you're in charge of the team," Ross said. "I should be in charge of the team, but I'm not, and I don't mean a DEA team. I should be in charge of a team of business executives. I almost have an MBA in marketing. I was real close to it, and then something happened."

"Something happened," Carl Robinson said. "What happened?"

"I have a relative in the business world," Ross continued. "New York City type, Wall Street, lots of money and connections. He was my mentor, sort of. He told me to take marketing and get my MBA. He also told me to join the Army Reserves so I did. I guess he thought it would look good on a resume. I got activated by the damn reserves and I had to drop out of college. When that happened, I kind of had a bad attitude, and I got in a little bit of trouble in the Army because of it. So I finally got out and my relative wouldn't have anything to do with me because another relative told him I'd had an attitude change and I wasn't the same person."

"So that's it?" Monica said.

"No, that isn't it," Ross said. "I was high and dry without a job. Another relative told me that DEA was hiring, and since I'd been an MP in the Army, I'd probably meet DEA's qualifications. The rest is history. I protest by wearing an ascot."

Five more minutes passed.

"You got activated," Pat Brown said. "What caused the activation?"

"Six little words," Ross said. "My MP commander, a Colonel, was a prick and I questioned him on a command decision once. Hell, I'd drunk beer with the guy and I thought I knew him."

"The words," Monica said. "What were the words?"

"I said," Ross paused, "What the hell is that supposed to mean?"

"That's it?" Mike said. "That's all you said?"

"Yep. I was activated immediately and sent to Germany for two years. Fucked me up! I'm still pissed about it. Now I'm getting drunk in a tent like a damn street person. See what I mean?"

"Hey," Mike Schweig slurred, "I'm a fucking graduate of

the fucking United States Military Academy, and I'm getting drunk in the same tent as you are."

"I'm a certified school teacher in the State of Mississippi," Monica said. "We're all in this together. Buck up and play the game, and we'll all get our fat pensions. That's what this is all about."

Pat Brown turned off the radio and the flashlights and everyone started making sleep sounds. I checked my wristwatch. It was 2300 hours. The night brought cool weather, down in the sixties. Thc rustling in the bush stopped. Maybe it was a coyote. I covered with my Marine Corps blanket and listened to the snoring and moaning and gas passing and realized why smart dope dealers never get caught.

The federal bureaucracy makes morons out of everybody who joins it, no matter what their potential. Except for Doc and Heidi. They've apparently got the inside track. I wondered why.

The smart dope dealers aren't mired down in bureaucracy and statistics. They only care about the bottom line--cash. They're the ones who buy the ten million dollar homes on the water in Florida and California. Yacht builders build their product for smart dope dealers and price them accordingly.

A guy who works for a living wouldn't dare pay a cool million for something that can sink at any moment.

Maybe the dope dealers have the right idea. This is America, land of the free and the free enterprise system. Maybe the system is working for the bold and adventurous, the outlaws of this era, the ones with enough chutzpa to buck the law and make themselves rich.

But, they're all such assholes! Money-grubbing weenies who snitch and cry and wet their pants when they get caught.

But I haven't seen any successful dope dealers, except for Henry Darby. Maybe he's a successful dope dealer. He's smart, and I have a feeling he's got a lot of cash stashed somewhere. He lied to AUSA Sue Lee, Heidi, and me. But most of them, they don't get caught. They're the pillars of the community. Businessmen, lawyers, doctors, politicians, professional people with a good income who want more. Insulated from the filth I deal with. They're the ones who never get caught. They're too damn smart for the feds.

"Ray," Monica whispered.

"Yeah?"

"I'm cold, Ray. Would you warm me up?"

"No," I whispered.

"I'll get on top. All you have to do is lay there and kick it back every now and then."

"Go to sleep, Monica," I sternly said.

"Is it because of Heidi? Or is it because I'm too chocolate? If I was like caramel or weak hot chocolate, would you then?"

"No, it's because of Heidi."

"You're a strange cop. I don't know how or why you came to the task force, but you're different." I wondered why she hadn't heard about Lynn Stewart.

I awoke at daybreak, mixed some powdered milk and ate some fruit and Wheaties, did my duty in the weeds, buried it, and walked back to the tent. Monica was stirring as I walked inside. She was cool to me but I didn't care. I didn't owe her anything. I never came onto her or gave her any inclination that I would have casual sex with her. It's her hang-up, her federal law enforcement lifestyle, not mine.

She walked out of the tent without speaking and headed down the path toward the patch. She started screaming. Not a terror scream, but a panic out-of-control scream like a primate calling for a mate, shrill and in bursts.

"Oh, fuck," I said. The rest of the crew started stirring and asking stupid questions like, "Where am I?" I headed out the door of the tent and down the path toward the patch and Monica.

I ran into the clearing. She was on her knees with her head down as if she was praying in the morning sun. The million dollar dope patch was now a hundred thousand dollar dope patch. Somebody had pulled up most of the plants and transported them off of the island.

"My thirteen, my journeyman grade," she moaned as she rocked on her knees with her hands clasped together. "It's gone, it's all gone."

I heard feet beating the milkweed path toward us. Pat and Bill came on scene followed by Carl and Mike. Ross brought up the rear. "Holy dog fuck," Pat exclaimed.

"I guess we were under surveillance last night," Mike moaned. "Doc's going to be pissed," Ross muttered.

"My thirteen, my journeyman grade, it's gone," Monica continued to wail.

I looked toward the Missouri River and at the large steep hill on the south side leading up to the subdivision with the four hundred thousand dollar homes. Somebody was up there watching us through a heavy lens, probably laughing and having breakfast on his deck. A smart dope dealer. One who didn't get caught.

I walked down to the Missouri and inspected the river bank. There was a cleared place on the bank with marks in the mud that a boat had been pulled up and onto it frequently. The space was about six feet wide. Probably a flat-bottomed John boat, aluminum with electric trolling motors.

Silent and efficient, but he would have to make several trips in the John boat to salvage his crop. He'd saved ninety-percent of it. A fair average in any profession. I walked back to the patch.

Mike and Ross were sitting near Monica while she grieved. Pat, Carl, and Bill were walking around the perimeter of the clearing searching for anything. "It's clean," Pat shouted. "Nothing but horseweed.

"You know," Pat continued, "horseweed looks a lot like marijuana. Same size and color, and it's not milky like that damn milkweed, and it doesn't make you sneeze like that damn ragweed."

"I don't want to hear about any damn weeds," Monica said. "I want my damn cash-weed back. FUCK!"

Monica's cell phone vibrated and she answered it. "Yes? Doc, yes, sir. No pinch yet, but we're still conducting surveillance. Zero-nine-hundred, yes, sir, we'll be expecting you. Yes, sir, good bye. FUCK! Doc's coming in with the chopper at zero-nine-hundred. He said to start burning it now so he doesn't have to spend much time here. He just wants his picture taken with the burning product, but he says to save some plants for him to throw onto the fire for the filming. Says headquarters DEA can use the film for training. I'm really fucked now." She had the look.

"We need a plan," Mike said. "Anybody got a plan?"

"You DEA guys are supposed to be the geniuses, why don't you think up a plan," Carl Robinson said.

"Yeah," Pat Brown said. "Use your brain instead of ours for a change."

"I've got a plan," Ross said. Everyone focused on him.

"Okay," Monica said. "Let's hear it."

"All Doc and headquarters are concerned about is numbers, right?" No one answered him. "Well, let's give them numbers. Let's pull up nine-hundred horseweed plants and stack them in the marijuana patch and burn them. We can save the hundred or so real marijuana plants until Doc gets here so he can have a photo op for headquarters. Nobody will ever know that the real marijuana got stolen under our noses, and Monica can still get her thirteen journeyman rating. Only we'll know, and without the king of belly fat here, nobody else will know. What do you say?"

"It's ingenious," Mike Schweig said. "Simply fucking brilliant."

"I like it, I like it a lot," Monica said with a smile.

"Let's get to work," Pat Brown said. "First pull the leftover marijuana and lay it to the side. The grower pulled nine-hundred or so last night so it probably comes out easy."

We tackled the project and the one-hundred gorgeous plants were lying safely at the side of the plot. The sun was starting to get strong and the mosquitoes began their attack as we sweated.

We went directly to the horseweed at the west of the plot and began pulling and hauling, stacking the weed on the cleared marijuana plot, crisscrossing them like cord wood. We had a stack of weeds six feet high and twenty feet in circumference. "The gasoline," Monica screamed. "Who's got the gasoline?"

Carl Robinson came running up the path with the five gallon can of gas. "It's here, I've got it," he shouted as he ran.

"Quickly, douse them. Douse them good. They're green and they won't burn real well. Doc is on the way by now." Mike made a torch and lit it and tossed it into the middle of the patch of horseweed. The fumes exploded with a whoof and the weed started burning. It burned until it couldn't be determined what type of plant it was, then died down.

"More gasoline," Monica screamed. "Pour more on it." Carl Robinson turned the can up but it was empty. The phony evidence was being destroyed, but it was starting to go out completely.

"Oh, fuck," Monica said. "What are we going to do now? What if Doc realizes that this pile of burned shit isn't really cash-weed, but shit-weed? My ass is going be up for grabs. I'll be fighting dope dealers in New York City and living in some damn tenement."

"I have another idea," Ross said. "Call Doc and ask him to bring some more gasoline. He's coming here anyway. He won't mind."

Monica frantically dialed her cell. "Doc, have you left, yet? Cool. We need some more gasoline. This weed is so green we're having a difficult time burning it. Yeah, yeah, we've got most of it semi-burned, but we left some for you to personally burn for the video. Right. I understand. We'll be waiting for you. Yes, you can land just west of the patch and then you'll be right next to the fire, I'll videotape you as you get out of the helicopter. Yes, sir. Bye."

We were staring at her. "He'll be here in about twenty minutes. He's going to get some more gas from the pilot at the hangar. We need to keep the weed smoldering and when we hear the chopper, toss some of the real weed on the fire so it can smolder and stink the place up like real weed. Got it?"

"Yeah," we said simultaneously.

Bill Yocum found a big branch and started stirring the smoldering horseweed. The fire started burning again. "Keep stirring, Bill," Monica said. "I'll reward you for this, later."

"No," Bill muttered. "I mean you don't have to reward me, I'm doing this as a friend."

"Damn, I just can't get laid for shit! I should start selling it, I damn sure can't give it away."

"I'm game," Mike Schweig said. "What about me?"

"No, that's alright but thanks for the offer. Keep stirring the fire, Bill."

"I haven't been bitten by one mosquito since I started stirring the fire," Bill said. "Maybe we came upon a natural repellant, horseweed. We could all be rich some day from this experience."

"Yeah, right," Pat Brown said. "We'll be back in the PD pretty soon, writing parking tags and working for a prick supervisor who hates our guts because we were detached to DEA. We'll be rich, alright. Monica will be journeyman grade living in Phoenix or Fort Lauderdale, and when she sees us on a damn credit card vacation, she probably won't acknowledge us."

"Never happen," Monica said. "I'll always be indebted to you guys and I'll never forget you. Toss some real weed on the fire."

Bill stopped stirring and tossed fifteen gorgeous plants onto the coals. The group huddled around the weed as it started smoldering, breathing and not speaking as the smoke filled their lungs. "Now that's some dynamite shit," Mike said.

"Yo, brother," Monica replied.

I heard the chopper off in the distance. "Chopper," I shouted.

"I don't hear it," Ross said.

"Me neither," Monica replied.

"It's coming," I said.

It was on us quickly, banking and hovering, looking for the best clearing to land. I could see Doc in the open bay door, inspecting and watching us as the chopper continued to hover.

Monica ran away from the now dead fire, grabbed the video camera from her pack and ran toward the chopper crouching and filming the arrival of Doc, her now idol, since he was trying to get her a G /S Thirteen.

The chopper was wheels down with Monica crouching

near the bay door and Doc posing until the blades stopped turning, eating up the opportunity. Doc climbed out, then turned and reached into the chopper and came out with another five-gallon can of gasoline. He stopped and posed for Monica's camera, decked out in Marine Corps camouflage, starched and pressed with First Lieutenant bars embroidered on his collar and his name boldly displayed in embroidery over his left pocket, PENROSE, which I thought was strange since he had never been in the Marine Corps, nor was he ever an officer in any military organization. He was selling used Porsches again, this time to DEA headquarters.

He continued to pose, like General MacArthur returning to the Philippines, wading onto the island of Leyte, while Monica filmed, then slowly walked toward the burned-out patch of weed, lugging the can of gasoline while the group stood back and out of camera view, all the while Doc performed his bureaucratic ballet.

He examined the quality of the marijuana and nodded his approval then started the task of stacking the plants onto the charred pile of horseweed. I could smell his aftershave and the sweet smell of his deodorant as he worked in the heat. The Missouri River mosquitoes were attacking his sweetness, he was swatting and fanning at them while he worked.

He stacked the remaining cash crop on the pile and smiled as he began soaking the weeds with the gasoline, walking back and forth with the can and splashing it onto the top and middle of the pile. The group didn't know it, and Doc didn't know it, but there apparently was one hot coal at the base of the horse weed.

The explosion sent Doc flying toward us, head over heels in the middle of a fire ball. He landed at my feet like a sack of potatoes, singed and burned and moaning with the horseweed and marijuana raining down upon us as a second explosion sent the gas can sailing over my head like a meteorite. Monica stopped filming and ran toward Doc, screaming, "NO, NO, DOC, NO! IT'S MY FAULT! IT'S ALL MY FAULT!"

Doc didn't hear her. He was out cold. Ross grabbed Monica and shook her, then spoke quietly but harshly to her, "Get a grip on yourself. The helicopter pilot is watching this show. Control yourself."

The chopper pilot came running over to us as we visually examined Doc. "Get the chopper started," Mike Schweig shouted, "We've got to evacuate immediately. Everybody get your weapons and packs. Leave everything else. Pat, you and Ray please help me get Doc onto the helicopter."

The group was scurrying around like stoned Chinamen, collecting the gear and running toward the chopper. Mike and Pat and I deposited Doc on the chopper floor and then ran back to the tent and grabbed our packs. We made it to the chopper and jumped in as it started wheels up.

It banked and I looked down onto the island and then over to the south bank of the Missouri, to a steep bank leading up to the subdivision adjacent to a county park, as we flew away from it and followed the Missouri River back to fashionable, clean, neat and trendy St. Louis County.

The chopper landed on the roof of St. John's Hospital. The medical team waited for us with a stretcher and life support equipment. Doc was conscious by then, staring at us without eyelashes or eyebrows and little hair above his forehead. The medical personnel got him off chopper and wheeled him away. "I'm staying with him," Monica said as she jumped off and followed the team into an elevator.

We took off again, hovered and banked and flew toward the airport. It landed on the tarmac by the hangar next to our G cars. We climbed out and went for our cars as if we had just been released from a torture chamber.

"There's going to be an inquiry by headquarters," Mike said. "Square Bidness is going to want to talk to us first. Everybody meet at the task force offices."

Nobody commented, just climbed into their G cars, fired them, and tore out of the parking lot. We entered the parking garage at the same time. We took the stairs and walked into the office en mass, a rag tag crew of bites and soot and body odor.

Carla and Heidi were watching as we stumbled in. No one asked any stupid questions, and we didn't offer any stories for them so everybody just went to their desks and plopped, waiting for the call that Square Bidness wanted to talk to us, as a group, or individually. Clete was at his desk banging on his laptop and trying to ignore us. Ross gave him a challenging look but Clete didn't accept it, just kept on banging.

Heidi slowly walked over to my desk but kept her distance as she looked at me. "One of the other groups did a deal early this morning," she began.

"Yeah?"

"Yeah. It was on a big expensive house in a subdivision near the Missouri River, right across from Pelican Island. They got nine hundred freshly harvested sinsemilla plants. Quite a haul, huh?"

"Yeah," I replied.

"A County cop was patrolling early in the morning and he observed a resident toting large bundles of freshly cut marijuana plants into his garage. He called the duty guy, and the duty guy called the group supervisor."

"They've got the guy in the back room, getting ready to book him."

Mike, Ross, Pat, Carl and Bill came over to my desk. "They got a guy with nine hundred plants and he lives on the south bank of the Missouri across from Pelican Island?" Mike asked.

"Yep," Heidi said. "They're getting ready to book him now, he's in the back. He had a big John boat hidden on the Missouri. He was hauling the weed from someplace near the river and dragging it up the bank and into his garage. Could be connected to your case. Where's Monica?"

"At the hospital with Doc," Ross replied.

"Doc doing okay?"

"He's conscious and breathing," Mike said. "Burned and singed and maybe some broken bones. The explosion sent him reeling head over heels."

"Square Bidness called the hangar and spoke with the helicopter pilot," Heidi continued. "He says Doc got gas from the wrong tank. He had aviation fuel, not gasoline. The pilot said he told Doc he had the potent stuff, but Doc told him we needed it because the weed was so green. The pilot told Square Bidness that Monica went berserk and said it was all her fault. What's up with that?"

"I'll tell you later," I softly said.

"Did you guys get much weed?" Heidi continued with the questions.

"Thousand plants," Ross lied. "Monica's got video of the patch. It was one of the neatest patches of sinsemilla I've ever seen. It was a million dollar patch. There's probably more like it around those Missouri River islands. I hope I don't ever have to go search for it again."

"Me neither," Mike said.

"Likewise," Carl said.

"I kind of liked it," Pat said.

"Me, too," Bill said. "It was pristine Missouri River wilderness, just like it was when Lewis and Clark explored this region. Hell, they might've stopped there and took a dump."

"Probably stopped there and grew some weed," Ross said. "Probably used it to barter with the Indians."

"They were fucking dope dealers," Carl said.

"Yeah," Mike jumped back in, "Fucking dope dealers just like everybody else in this world. They were probably the fathers of sinsemilla dope."

"I wish they were on that island," Bill Yocum said. "We could've kicked their dope-dealing asses and locked them up. Fucking dope dealing-bastards."

I intervened. "I think we should go back to the holding room and interview the other group's prisoner. Might be important to us. The guy could have another patch nearby. Anybody game?"

"Yeah," they said simultaneously.

We walked out as a group and stormed into the holding facility. He was handcuffed to a desk, big and red-faced, a giant belly with a green cammie shirt and bib overalls, jungle boots and the smell of repellant and body odor. He was about forty-five, I guessed. A country boy, semi-bald with a mustache. He looked at us smiled, then looked away.

We were surrounding him and he looked up again, then giggled, stifled it and looked down. "We need to ask you some questions," Ross began. "Your cooperation will be beneficial to you with the United States Attorney."

He looked up at Ross. "Go ahead and ask," he muttered.

"Do you grow your dope on Pelican Island?" He looked down again, and then looked up and scanned our faces. Heidi walked in and stood in the background. He fixated on her.

The agent in charge of the booking said, "Heidi, would you please hand me a print card?" Heidi complied, and stood back from the group.

"Well," Ross said. "Do you want to help yourself, or what?"

"I've got six little words for you, Ross. What the hell is that supposed to mean?" Ross recoiled and backed to the door.

"Heidi," the country boy continued, "Ray was true to you last night."

We walked out of the room and back to the task force offices. I plopped at my desk. Heidi gave me an inquisitive look. "What the hell was all of that about?"

"We had counter-surveillance on the island. He was listening to us. He knows us well. The bad guy almost won; in fact he might just win after all. I'm going home to shower. Want to ride along?"

"Yeah!"

16

We typed reports for two days: evidence reports, surveillance reports, interview reports, DEA six's and addendums; entering the tapes into the Viktor Agron case and writing our individual versions of the Pelican Island fiasco. We were wrapped up on the paperwork. I called Henry Darby on his cell.

"Yo," he answered.

"Are you out of the secret room?"

"Just. I'm in my front yard. I'm walking to my car right now."

"How do you feel?"

"With my hands."

"Funny," I said not amused. "Where are you headed?"

"To the bar. I need to take care of some business."

"Fine. You go take care of business, and then be in my office in two hours." The line went dead.

Heidi was listening. "How's he doing?"

"Surly. He's obviously pissed about the whole turn of events and wants revenge. I'm having a rough time mustering up any faith in the little asshole."

"He's got to be reassured that if he screws us around we'll put him in prison for a long time," she said.

"He's coming in today," I said.

"I heard. We'll reassure him then."

Doc walked into the task force offices, zipped by Heidi's desk, sashayed past Carla's desk and went into his office. He was wearing huge Ray Ban Wayfarers and a Cardinals ball cap. His exposed ears and nose were burned crisp and his entire face was covered with salve.

He walked out of his office and stood by Carla's desk. All eyes were on him as he removed the cap and sunglasses. His face and head looked like raw meat. "I want to get this out of the way," he began. "I'm one-hundred percent DEA and I'm not going to let a little deal mishap interfere with my career. I'm back, and I only lost one day. I'm ready to answer questions if you have any." He put the cap and Ray Bans back on. No one raised their hand. "Okay, enough of that. Heidi, Ray, go up to the big board room by Square Bidness' office. You're getting some new identity." He turned and went back into his office.

We took the steps up. A bland looking lady with thick glasses was waiting for us. "I need your current driver's licenses," she said. We complied. She examined them, then said, "Sit here." We sat in front of a blue screen as she individually took our pictures. She was going to make us new Missouri driver's licenses.

"What's your middle name?"

"Richard," I replied.

She typed into the machine and a new official license came out. She handed it to me for inspection and signature. My name was now Ray Richards, 4450 Lindell, St. Louis, Missouri. She handed me a new set of Missouri license plates, then adjusted the issue in her laptop computer. "Put these on your Corvette. Now everything is issued to Ray Richards at the Lindell address."

"Your middle name," she said to Heidi.

"Ann, but I already have a funny name. It's Sallee Jiminez." The clerk pondered her name then went through the same process with her. Heidi examined her new license. "Heidi Andrews," she said to me. "Same address on Lindell."

"Thanks," I said as we walked out of the board room and back downstairs. Doc was waiting for us at Heidi's desk.

"Come in," he said as he turned and walked away with us following him. Doc had the spare hundred thousand seized from Henry Darby stacked on his desk. "Carla," he called out.

She came running in to his office. “Yes, Doc?”

Doc grabbed a metal briefcase from under his desk and meticulously stacked the cash into it. He handed it to her. “Count these notes to insure my accuracy and then bring them back in here.”

“Yes, sir.” She took the case and exited the office.

“You guys are going undercover in south Georgia. How’s the C/I?”

“Surly. Pissed off he got caught. Feeling sorry for himself,” I replied. “He’s supposed to be here soon,” I said while looking at my Seiko. Doc nodded. He reached into his desk drawer and came out with a big wristwatch. He handed it to me; it was a solid gold Rolex. I took off the Seiko and slid on the Rolex. It fit well: twenty-thousand dollars, I figured.

Doc came up with two diamond rings. He handed them to me and I slid one on each ring finger. Gaudy and expensive, but nice. I liked the feel.

Carla returned with the metal briefcase full of money. She laid it on Doc’s desk, then walked out. “Ray,” Doc continued. “Did you know there’s a secret compartment in the Corvette?”

“No.”

“It’s under the passenger seat. The seat lays back and there’s a finger hole in the carpet. Raise that and there’s a compartment. Ten kilos will fit in there. The idiot dope dealer who once owned the car smuggled the blow that way. That was my case. I got that dope dealer in Kansas City by going undercover. He’s in the slammer, now, and you’re driving his ride. You been undercover before?”

“No.”

He stared at me through the Ray Bans as if I was a mark. “You can’t be anxious when working undercover,” he continued. "You must realize that the dope dealer desires cash. He doesn't give a damn about the dope. He wants to get rid of the dope. He wants your money and he'll take chances to get it, chances that you and I would never take in the real world. He'd kill or maim to get your money. Would you kill for money, Ray?"

"No!"

He was pondering my response. I wondered why. Is there that much difference between me and him? A city cop and a federal agent? Would he kill for money?

He regrouped and continued. "So you can see the difference between you and the dope dealer. They're anxious and desperate. You, the undercover agent, are cool and in charge. Why? Because you have the money! Money talks, Ray. Bullshit walks. The dope dealer is bullshit. He's got access to some white powder that a bunch of weirdos like to put into their bodies. It takes a weirdo low-life to do that to themselves, and it takes a weirdo low-life to deal in that white powder filth. See the difference between you and the dope dealer?"

"Yes."

"Dope dealers try to sway you with material things, big houses, boats, cars, flashy broads, physiques to die for. Most of these guys are big on body building. They have time to build that body to impress people. They're imposing; that's their shtick, but they don't have heart. They're weenies! When we take them off, they usually cry and wet their pants. They'd do their own mothers to lighten their sentences if given the chance. We take their houses and cars and boats, and their flashy broads crawl off to find some other low-life to bleed. Their suntans fade and their physiques get soft while waiting for trial, and when they show up in federal court with their expensive lawyers, they look like janitors. Get the picture?"

"Yes!"

He was surgical in his descriptive rhetoric. I knew then why he was called Doc.

"The United States Government has no money tied up in this case," Doc continued. "We're using the other dope dealer's cash. This is the last hundred thousand seized from Henry Darby. He gambled and lost, but he won't spend much time in stir. He's buying his freedom from the federal government."

He paused and stared at us as if we were school children. "I want you and Heidi to go down to Savannah. Ray, you drive the Corvette with the hundred-thousand in the secret compartment. Take three days driving down there. Touch base with me every day with your cell. When you get into town, hit Heidi on her cell. She'll be set up in a rental condo. When you guys ultimately get a face to face with Viktor Agron, I want you to make arrangements for the hundred-kilo deal. Your proposition will be that when the dope is delivered to St. Louis, you'll pay him one million. He'll balk, but he's just going to be bullshitting you. He wants the big deal. He'll probably say, 'How do I know you're going to come through with the million?' You tell him that you will give him fifty-thousand when the dope leaves south Georgia en-route to St. Louis. He'll probably barter with you on the good faith money. He'll tell you he doesn't believe you have any money. The C/I will intervene and vouch for your financial prowess. At the right time, whenever you feel it's appropriate, I want you to flash this hundred-thousand. Tell him you'll give him the hundred thousand when the dope leaves for St. Louis and the remaining nine hundred thousand when the dope gets to St. Louis. You'll have to play it by ear after that."

He paused and studied us, then continued. "Heidi will have to play second fiddle in the transactions. Ray's got to be the man with the balls. Ray, you'll already have the respect of Viktor because you're an older guy with a young vivacious broad." He paused again. "Any questions?"

"Yeah, when are we leaving?"

"You leave tomorrow morning. Carla will give you travel and expense money. Heidi will have cash for spending. Don't leave the country. We cannot cover for you if you leave the borders of the United States. If you do, you're on your own. Also, don't get on any boats if you can help it. If it's a social thing with Viktor then do it, but try to stay off of any and all boats. I'll talk to you some more before you leave. When the C/I gets here, bring him into my office." He paused again. Then said, "Excused."

We walked out of Doc's office. Carla was waiting for us at her desk. "Hold on, guys," she said. "You owe me a seizure report on the three hundred thousand dollars taken from Henry Darby. Which one of you wants to do it?"

"Ray will write it," Heidi said.

I glanced at her. She was sending me negative physiognomy-mail. It caught me off guard. "I'll write it right now," I said as I walked to my desk. Heidi ignored me as I banged on the laptop.

Carla's desk phone rang. "Henry Darby is in the waiting room," she called out.

"I'll get him," Heidi said. I continued to type. She was back in two minutes with Henry. I watched him as she escorted him into the main office and told him to wait at Carla's desk while she went into Doc's office.

He was like a kid preparing to go into the principal's office for a scolding: nervous, weight going from one foot to the other. Hands pulling on his face then running through his hair, then stuffed into his pockets. Heidi came out. "Ray." I stood and walked toward her and Henry, then followed them into Doc's office.

"Close the door," Doc said. We stood before him while he visually inspected us. Doc had taken off his Ray Bans and ball cap and was staring at Henry through his hairless, scary eyes, showing his raw-meat face. He had all of Henry's attention.

"I understand you had a little breakdown," Doc began. "Are you going to be able to continue with this assignment?"

"Yeah." His demeanor was still surly.

"I have the authority to stop this agreement, Mister Darby. Are you aware of this?"

"No, my lawyer hasn't told me that."

"Your lawyer is no longer in this deal, Mister Darby. What happens from here on out depends upon your performance as a confidential informant. Your performance is directly related to your attitude. I will not allow my agents to meet with you in Georgia for an undercover deal if your attitude is not one hundred percent positive. You'll be working for Heidi and Ray. You will not be working for your lawyer. Do you understand that?"

"Yes, sir!"

"I'll be in touch with Heidi and Ray several times a day. If they advise me that your attitude is not one hundred percent in their favor, I'll instruct them to arrest you and book you in at the Savannah field office for conspiracy to distribute cocaine. You'll be incarcerated in the County Jail awaiting arraignment. Got it?"

"Yes, sir. Not to worry. I understand," he said with his hands up, palms out. His demeanor changed to upbeat. He was the patronizing bartender again.

"Heidi, Ray, any questions for Mister Darby before this deal gets off the ground?"

Heidi didn't respond. "I have one." They looked at me as if I had the okay to ask anything I wanted. "You mentioned you were friends with some FBI agents. Is one of them named Moynihan?"

"No," he said with blinking eyes.

He knew I was watching his eye and body movements. It spooked him. I thought he was lying. Doc and Heidi didn't pick up on it. If he was lying it was time for him to try and recover.

"And they weren't my friends," he said. "They were patrons of my bar. Freebie customers who drank and ate at my place. Believe me, I got more information from them than they got from me. I wasn't their informant, if that's what you're going for. I'm not an informant for another federal agency."

Doc paused while he waited for any more questions. "Okay, Mister Darby, be in Savannah in three days. Contact Heidi and Ray on their cells. They'll instruct you on what your duties will be. You can leave, now." Henry opened the door and walked out leaving the door open. "Carla?" Doc said. "Escort Mister Darby to the elevator, please."

"Yes, sir!"

Doc was still staring and measuring, getting a feel for us as a couple of greedy want-to-be dope barons, amateurs wanting to branch out into the glamorous world of drug smuggling. "It might work," he finally said as he put on the ball cap. "How do you guys feel about it?"

"It's going be a tough one," Heidi said. "I don't know if going before Viktor for an inspection is a good idea. I'll take the background stance, but Ray has never worked undercover before. One wrong word and the deal is going to be nixed."

"There won't be any wrong words from me," I said. "I haven't worked undercover, but I've been a cop for a long time."

"Okay," Doc said. "Go and do your thing. Check in with

DEA Savannah when you get into town. Let them know when you're going into Viktor's domain. Excused!"

We walked back to our desks while Carla checked our reports and obtained travel funds for us. Crazed TFD Pat Brown sauntered over to my desk and sat on it. "I hear you're going undercover, Ray." I nodded. "You been undercover before?"

"No," I replied.

"Care if I give you some pointers?"

"No," I softly said.

"Here's how I do it," he began. "You've got to have the attitude. You've got to get into character. Like they say in Hollywood, you've got to find your motivation. Before you meet with the bad guy, you've got to imagine you own this classic Porsche convertible. The car is immaculate and everyone drools about owning it. One day you're driving it and you hear some expensive sounds coming from the engine. You know the price of a new engine is about thirty grand. You don't have that kind of jack, so basically the car is worthless, even though it blue books for thousands. Got it so far?"

"Yeah," I said with a stare.

"Now, imagine that the bad guy has been trying to get into your girlfriend's skivvies for weeks, and he's been saying bad things about you to her. He doesn't know she's been telling you what he's been saying about you. The guy has also been after you to sell him your Porsche. On the day you hear the expensive engine sounds, the guy calls you and asks you again to sell it to him. You gamble and quote him a ridiculously high price and the guy says he'll take it. You go out and drain the oil and fill the crankcase with thick, used car dealer honey oil that masks all of the funny noises. You figure the engine will last for three hard runs. The guy will run it hard when he test-drives it, and then after he buys it.

Then when he's trying to show off for some chick, it'll blow. By then you'll have his check in the bank and there's nothing he can do about it. You got him. His nose was open and you were in control because he's the bad guy and you're the good guy. Any questions?"

I didn't respond. I just stared. Agents Ross Milton and Monica Rose were shooting concerned glances at Pat, then each other. TFD's Carl Robinson and Bill Yocum were nodding their heads in the affirmative, mumbling, "Yep, that's how you do it. You follow Pat's direction and you won't have any problems."

"Come up here and get your travel and expense money," Carla said. Heidi and I walked to her desk. She gave us each three thousand in cash and several credit cards issued to a trucking company.

Doc came out of his office and waved to us to enter his office. We followed him in and stood as he sat at his desk. "Here's the one-hundred-thousand." He pushed the open metal briefcase toward me. "Count it and sign the receipt." I quickly counted the stacks of hundreds, closed the briefcase and signed the form.

"The confidential informant is a snake," he began. "But all C/I's are snakes, aren't they, Heidi?"

"Yes."

I felt they were talking around me but I dismissed it. Paranoia was always there waiting for me.

"Don't let the snake get coiled," Doc continued. "If there's any indication this deal will go sour, blow it off. Dope dealer today, dope dealer tomorrow. Understand me, Heidi?"

"Yes, sir!"

"I don't want another deal like the one in Colombia."

"Me neither," Heidi said as she looked at the floor. The paranoid ponders were attacking me again. I felt they were acting out a script for me: patronizing and poisoning me with self-serving information. It embarrassed me. I felt guilty for my feelings.

"You guys can go," Doc continued. "You've probably got some things to deal with before you leave town for who knows how long. Good luck, and touch base with me a couple of times a day. Excused!"

We left Doc's office and walked to our desks, gathered our personal belongings: tape recorders, binoculars, cell phones, Glock forty pistol, extra magazines, legal pads and pens, and headed for the door. We rode the elevator down to the parking garage without speaking. Her Bimmer was parked next to the Corvette.

"I'll hit you on your cell when I get into town. Got any idea where we'll be staying?"

"Tybee Island," she replied. "Golden Sands Hotel, little efficiencies on the beach. I've stayed there many times, it's cheap and nice."

"What happened in Colombia?" I was primed to ask the question. It was what they wanted.

"I'll tell you about it sometime. See you in south Georgia." She turned and climbed into the Bimmer, cranked it, and drove away while I stood by the Corvette.

I was unencumbered, a strange feeling for a DEA Task Force Detective. I had been compelled to be one of the boys which meant I was always under scrutiny, dissected and analyzed. My cop instincts had instantly kicked in, and I was thinking conspiracies. I couldn't stop thinking about TFD Jack Parker and his missing status. What kind of a guy would do that?

Heidi described him as a hopeless romantic, a whore, a drunk, the kind of a guy who would take a girl off of the streets and try to rehabilitate her. He was a typical cop. I wondered how he got so out of line. Cops always have strange thoughts about life and the people they meet. But rarely do they act on these weird ideas. In the task force, how could he have time to rehabilitate a whore? We were always with the crowd.

Heidi had told me Jack's dad worked as a security guard at the casino on the riverfront. I didn't know him but that's understandable. I was in an investigative job most of the time. I didn't know many of the rank and file guys. It is the pecking order of the P.D. You usually only know the people you work with.

I drove down to the casino, parked the Corvette on the cobblestones and walked to the rotting old boat. It had been called the Admiral when I was a kid on the East side. We would come over and take excursions on her. She was state of the art then. Now she's just a rusting scow with gambling tables and slot machines.

I strolled in, flashed my city cop badge at the guard on duty and asked for security guard Otis Parker. She got on her radio and called him. I stood and waited for about ten minutes, and he showed up. He wasn't smiling when I smiled at him. He was sour, and I couldn't figure out why.

He was a pale bowed over little man, bloodshot eyes, and he smelled of tobacco and booze. In law enforcement, attitude means everything. His was bad.

I offered my hand to him, "I'm Ray Arnold. Have you got a couple of minutes to talk with me?"

He gave me a cold clam handshake, and then waved for me to follow him. We walked to the fantail of the boat, he turned, and said, "What can I do for you, detective?"

"I'm detached to DEA," I began. "But, I'm a homicide cop. I'd like to ask you some questions concerning the disappearance of your son."

He was still sour as he looked me up and down. "I remember you," he said. "You were a big shot dick when I was pounding a beat. I never liked you homicide cops, your swagger, and your big hats. Who'd you piss off to get sent to DEA?"

"It's just another place to go to work. Have you heard from Jack?"

"Nope, and if I did, I wouldn't tell you."

"Why?"

"Wherever he is, he's got to be better off than being a cop or a fucking C/I with a badge out at DEA. I begged him not to join the damn department, and I begged him not to go to DEA, but it didn't do any good. Now he's gone, to God knows where, and I don't have him anymore. Damn, I miss that kid."

He was welling up. "When did you see him last?"

"The night before he went missing, he came by here. He was drunk, as usual. He told me he had a beautiful new girlfriend, rich but married. He said they were going to go away for a while, first him, and then she was going to join him. He wouldn't tell me where he was going, but I figured it was somewhere by a beach. Jack loved the beach."

"Did he say anything about the lady friend?"

He was staring at me, trying to figure if he could trust me, gauging my intentions. "Why do you want to know? Has somebody from DEA sent you here to badger me into finding Jack?"

"No! It's an instinct thing with me. People who are missing for more than a couple of months are usually dead. If that's the case with Jack, I want to know who murdered him."

"He told me she was a beautiful stripper from the East side, married to a dangerous man. He told me he was in peril at DEA and that if he didn't leave town, he'd be killed. He'd come upon some cash, and he told me he'd be okay for a long time and that he would call me when the dust settled.

It's been four months and he hasn't called. I take that to mean the dust hasn't settled yet. That's all I know."

I shook hands with him again, "Thanks, Otis." I walked to the Corvette, climbed in, and drove south. I had time to decipher the interview. I couldn't make a decision on whether TFD Jack Parker was the victim of a homicide, or just laying low. I was going to try to find out.

17

I took my time driving to Georgia. I had placed Tyrone in his most hated place, the kennel. He wouldn't look at me when I handed his lead to the attendant. He put a guilt trip on me, and I was still reeling from it. I hoped I would see him again. He was all I had in this world, all an old cop really needed. I was having second thoughts about this deal which was a normal phenomenon. If I wasn't paranoid,I would be foolish, and I had been in the business for too long to be considered foolish.

I was running through the pep talk Doc gave us. I knew it was directed mostly to me. I could see why he was a group supervisor in an organization like DEA. He was smart. A PHD by osmosis in undercover drug deals. He impressed me with his knowledge of the big-time drug dealer, a species the average person only hears about and seldom comes into contact with.

I pondered why I was instantly impressed with Doc after his speech. I mean, he should be knowledgeable about drug dealers. He's a group supervisor for the Drug Enforcement Administration, for God's sake. It's like instantly being impressed with a mechanic because his diagnosis of your engine's problem is correct.

I figured that it was because Doc was such a lowlife, and I expected more from him when I first met him. That thing with his wife and his girlfriend, and the threat to us all concerning the anonymous letter written to his wife, the one that let the cat out of the bag. In police work, a lowlife is just that. He's catalogued and pigeon holed in the cop's brain as a lowlife and nothing is going to change that. Doc was a professional, intelligent lowlife and I wasn't ready for that.

I drove all night with the top down in the balmy southern

weather just cruising at sixty, looking at nothing but the white line and the approaching lights, occasionally sliding in a Blind Blake C D. I kept thinking about TFD Jack Parker, the young missing cop I had never met. He was a drunk and a whore, but his missing was hanging out there in the open, mysteriously alone with no one caring about it. I envisioned him from the picture on Carla's desk. Why didn't anybody care? I knew the answer. It was because he was just a C/I with a badge.

Did I care? Yes! It could be a conspiracy, my reason for living. So if I cared about the missing, my mission was in St. Louis, not in Savannah, Georgia. The clue that will help me find out what happened to Jack Parker was there. I felt like I was being pulled away from the true investigation and wasting time. But it would be worth it if we could bag Viktor Agron, et al. I calmed down.

I had three days to get to nowhere in a Corvette convertible with no responsibilities and the federal government's money to spend. I had never had this kind of freedom before, and I understood why some people drop out of the rat race, buy a motor home and travel the country. It was cool.

I pulled into a Holiday Inn at dawn in Macon, got out, rented a room, and slept for six hours, got up, showered and shaved, and called Doc on my cell. "Checking in," I said.

"Where are you?" I could see his burned face in my mind and the expression he has when he is asking a question.

"Macon, Georgia."

"Cool. You going to be in Savannah tomorrow?"

"Yes, sir."

"Call me then."

"Roger, Doc. Over and out."

I drove over to Savannah and ate seafood in Thunderbolt at a restaurant frequented by the locals. I was probably pegged as an old drug dealer. I was dressed casually, black muscle Tee, and Levis, was buffed, drove a Corvette Roadster, had a twenty thousand dollar wristwatch and big diamond rings, and was a stranger. Maybe Viktor Agron would take me for a fellow crook.

The locals watched every bite I took. I was a day early. Heidi was probably already in position at the condo on Tybee Island. I could call her and she would take me in, and we would have a mini-vacation at the expense of the G, but something wasn't right in our relationship.

I love beautiful women, in fact, I worship them. To me they are a Godsend, proof that there is a supreme being who makes us the way he wants us to be. When I get struck by the beauty of one of these fantastic creatures, I thank the man upstairs for the experience. Heidi is one of the man's greatest creations. But she's aggressive and her aggressiveness makes me wary.

She doesn't give any wiggle room. The night I met her she wanted me to come home with her. I asked myself, "Why does this beautiful woman want me to follow her home? I am the prince of mediocrity; she is the princess of the Drug Enforcement Administration. Something is wrong here."

I got another room in a Holiday Inn on the Savannah River, slept like I had been drugged, showered and shaved, had a good country breakfast, and went site-seeing in old Savannah. I called Heidi's cell when I had had enough of being on my own. "I'm near. Are you decent?"

"As decent as I want to be when you come calling," she was laughing. "When will you be here?"

"Twenty minutes," I replied.

"We're in cottage number six on Eighteenth Street at the south end of the island, right on the ocean. I'll start a fire and we can cook some steaks."

"Roger." She sounded different. Uninhibited.

I drove past the millionaire real estate, parked the Corvette, and walked around to six. The mesmerizing process had already started. It always happens to me when I'm near the ocean.

The ocean breeze through the palm trees was warm and inviting. It was spring in St. Louis, but it was summer in Savannah. The smell of the ocean and the sound of the surf and the musty feeling of the salt air drugged me. I was hooked before I saw her.

She was in her black Bikini with a maroon top covering her upper torso, standing over the fire pouring more charcoal into the Weber. It was just fifteen-hundred hours and the late afternoon sun was shining on the ocean making it sparkling and inviting, but chilly. A swimmer would be uncomfortable in three minutes in the Atlantic in the spring.

She looked up at me when I walked onto the lanai, smiled and rushed me. "Ray," she said seductively, "I could hardly wait for you to get here. Is this place beautiful or what?"

"Beautiful," I tried to say with her lips on mine and her tongue darting in and out of my mouth.

"Come in here and let me show you around."

She grabbed my bag and pulled me inside the little apartment. "Kitchen," she began with the tour. "Bathroom, television, and bedroom." She kept kissing me and pulling at my clothing. Finally she took off her maroon top. She was bare from the waist up. She stood before me with a challenge. Her sculpted body was stunning. I was out of my clothes in fifteen seconds and we were in bed.

The sex was different from what I had experienced with other girlfriends. It was casual between Heidi and me, something I wasn't accustomed to. I was the kind of guy who needed to be infatuated with my prospective mate before I took the pillow plunge. There was no infatuation between Heidi and me; just lust, and I wasn't good at that.

I had worked prostitution details where the patron was arrested along with the pimp, and the whore. Some of the tricks, Johns (patrons), were wealthy businessmen. I would ask them why they had to resort to prostitutes for sexual gratification. They could have any woman they desire. Money talks in the romance/sex game.

"It's casual and fast," they would say. "There are no strings attached, no love, no return engagements, and no commitments. Just me, the pimp, and the whore."

But being with Heidi in a hideaway beach hotel was good for me even though there was no infatuation. I was always in St. Louis, always a cop, always waiting for the phone to ring or for someone to knock on my door and tell me it was time to go to work.

We were free, away from St. Louis, the office, DEA, the police department. We finished and I rolled off of her. We got our breath and I looked out at the ocean through a crack in the curtain. "I'd love to go swimming."

"Me, too," she replied. "There's a hot tub. I checked it out and it's clean and hot."

We pulled on complimentary robes and headed for the hot tub. We could have been nude; nobody was there to see us. It's one of the perks of visiting a beach retreat during the work week in late spring. We cooked like lobsters for twenty minutes. I was tired of second-guessing my attachment with Heidi. I was going to take it as it came from now on out.

I was a man first, a cop second, and I wasn't going to look a gift horse in the mouth. It wasn't as if Heidi was a crook. I was certain she wasn't, but I felt I was being set up for something. I had to let it play out.

"I bet my fire went out. Are you getting hungry?"

"Famished," I said.

She climbed out and slid into the robe. It was as if she had been made for the voyeur of feminine beauty: me. I watched her pouring charcoal on the fire and restarting it. "Strip steaks, an inch thick," she yelled at me. "Salad and baked potato." She cupped her hands as she yelled toward me. I watched her toss the steaks on the grill and then climbed out.

We had an amazing meal at the dining room window, overlooking the beach, watching the sun disappear from our view and not doing much talking. It was a magical place and we were in the groove. "I'm never leaving here," she said.

"Me neither."

We ate on plastic plates and drank out of plastic cups. She carefully extracted the knives and forks from the table and then brushed the entire mess into a trash bag. I was zoning and she picked up on it. "Thinking of something seductive, lover?" she asked.

I couldn't tell her what I was thinking about. I was wondering which one of us was the trick and which one was the whore. Doc was the pimp, I think. But maybe Heidi was the whore and the pimp. Some whores don't have pimps. That would make me the trick. But it could make me the trick and the whore.

"No," I said to her. "I was just thinking about how lucky I was to be with you, lover."

"The kitchen is clean. Now I've got to check in with Doc." She dialed her cell. I zoned in on the ocean while she waited for connection. "Hi, Doc. We're at Tybee Island. Everything's cool. Check in with you tomorrow. Got his voice mail."

We sat in solitude. The feeling of one with nature didn't last long. My cell rang. I answered it with a "Yo." It was Henry Darby. "Henry Darby," I said to Heidi with my hand over the receiver.

"Don't tell him where we are."

I nodded as I turned the cell so she could listen. "I'm staying at the Marriott Beach Hotel: Where are you guys?" Henry asked.

"We're near. What's up?"

"Viktor wants to meet with you guys tonight. He'll probably have Will the bone-crusher with him. Is that okay?"

"Hold the line." I put my hand over the receiver. "They want to meet tonight. What do you want to do?"

She was pondering. I could tell she didn't want to go back to work so soon. "I don't want to, but I think we have to," she said dejectedly.

"We'll meet you in the lobby of your hotel in one hour."

"Okay," he replied patronizingly. "But it would be easier if I gave you guys directions and then met you at a corner before we drive to his house. Is that okay?"

"Yeah."

"Okay, I'm going to make the assumption that you guys are staying on an island. Probably Tybee, so take the Islands Expressway which turns into East President Street. There's a club on your left: Savannah Golf Club. I'll be waiting for you in a blue rental Chevy. Got it?"

"Yeah. We'll see you in an hour."

"We're going to meet him in an hour at the Savannah Golf Club on East President. The little jerk knows we're staying on Tybee Island. You want to take a shower first?"

"Yeah." She stopped smiling and trudged toward the bathroom pulling off the fluffy robe. The holiday was over.

"Are we going to alert Savannah DEA that we are going into the house to make a drug deal?"

"No, it's too late. It'll be all right. I've done dozens of these things without backup."

We had the top down cruising with the trade winds massaging our faces. Heidi was exceptionally beautiful this evening, still tanned to perfection, her hair combed straight back, expensive blue designer jeans, aqua halter top showing her flat muscular belly.

I was playing the South Georgia game; khakis, deck shoes with no socks, red Polo, sports car, with a hundred thousand dollars in a metal briefcase.

We rolled up on him. He was smiling and waving and pointing for us to follow him. "He thinks we're going to bomb," Heidi said. "He's hoping we fail with Viktor so he can go back to his lawyer and tell him it's our fault the deal didn't go through. That way it's over for him and he doesn't have to do any of his other pals. The fucking creep."

"We won't bomb," I muttered. I stopped the Corvette perpendicular to his rental and rolled the window down. He did the same and had a serious look on his face as he stared. "Where exactly are we going?" I asked.

"His house is on the Ogeechee near the Canoochee. Just follow me. If you get lost for some reason hit me on my cell." I nodded and we took off.

We followed him north into the darkness where there were no street lights or street signs and then made some lefts and rights and turned into a street where the homes had big boats parked in canals behind them. We were deep in the savannahs where the water was skinny near the shore.

Most of the homes had long lighted docks reaching thirty yards into the Ogeechee River with ocean-going power boats docked at the end. He pulled into a driveway between large bushes.

The house was shielded from the front by high dense foliage. The driveway curved and he stopped in front of a split level ranch with a red brick sidewalk leading to the front door. The house was in need of care. It looked like what it was: rental property.

There were three cars parked in the driveway: an older Caddy, a Dodge pickup, and one that caught my eye, a newer Caddy with Illinois license plates. I mentally noted the tag number, silently repeating it so I could remember it. Henry got out and leaned against the rental with his blues-bar attire, trying to be tough, something he couldn't be. He stared at us. The bartender smile was gone. He was making a feeble attempt to let us know we were on our own and we should be afraid.

I read his physiognomy like a "USA Today" and dismissed it as we parked behind him and climbed out of the Corvette. I walked around and grabbed the metal briefcase from under the passenger seat as Heidi stood in front of me.

Henry didn't speak, just turned and walked toward the front door. We slowly followed him and waited a comfortable distance from him as he rang the doorbell. A striking tanned woman opened the door. She was probably Greek, and like all beautiful women, confident and smug.

She was the kind of girl who could make a grand a night stripping at a bar on the East side and another five thousand dollars a night being an escort and hooker. I wondered who she was. Henry hugged her, "Ellen, you're back. How good to see you."

She faintly acquiesced, tossed her hair back then brushed at it with her left hand. I saw the flash of a large diamond and gold ring on her index finger. A man's ring, sized like a high school girl would do, with fuzzy string. She smirked at Henry as she stared at us. "Friends of mine," Henry said with his head bobbing and eyes bulging.

I knew who she was: Viktor's wife. She didn't need the tough pimp; he needed her. She turned and walked. Henry followed her and we followed Henry through the foyer and into the heart of the house. It was Mediterranean/hillbilly.

The rug was tattered and dirty. There were pictures of Elvis and some beach scenes done on velvet, and gaudy lamps on cheap tables scattered around the house.

It smelled like a frat house that needed cleaning after a toga party. We followed her to a sunken living room with the back wall of glass and a storm door leading to a canal and dock with a large cruiser. She motioned without speaking for us to go into the sunken living room and then she turned off and went to another part of the house.

"Hi, guys." Henry kicked off the festivitics with his bartender routine as he walked down to them with body movements like a standup comic. Viktor and Will were sitting on a couch covered in clear plastic.

They blankly stared at Heidi and me, their doubtful eyes moving over us inspecting every inch. Henry started with Viktor, who was sitting in an over-stuffed chair like a pontiff, by carefully approaching him with his hand out. Viktor took it and shook it one time then dropped his hand back to the chair. Henry then walked to Will, got the ceremonial one shake and the formalities were completed.

"Enough of this shit," Viktor said. "Let's get on with business."

"No problem, Vik," Henry said with his hands up, "Not to worry, Vik. This is Ray and this is his girlfriend, Heidi. They're good friends of mine."

Heidi and I stood before them while they stared. I didn't offer to shake anyone's hand and Heidi stood behind me like a good girlfriend, acting fearful and apprehensive. I stared back at them.

Viktor made a move with his right hand, and Will got up from the couch and walked out of the living room as if he was going outside. He returned in seconds and picked up the telephone receiver next to him and dialed it. "I need an issue."

Heidi and I stood our ground. He read off the license number of the Corvette to the person on the other end of the telephone line and then slowly printed whatever the person told him. He handed the note to Vik. Vik read it and then looked up to us. "I need to see your driver's license," he said to me.

I grabbed my wallet, took out my license and handed it to him. He checked the name on my funny license and the name Will had meticulously printed on the scratch paper as I glanced around the room. Vik and Will were wearing Hawaiian shirts, different colors with the same pattern, probably shoplifted by a junky prostitute.

Typical pimps turned drug dealers. Viktor was in shape, veins bulging in his arms and neck. His chest looked solid as if he had a daily work regime. His hands were big and his knuckles were swollen as if he practiced on a heavy bag. He was a formidable foe, and he was about my size. I was older and I read him as he inspected me.

He was sizing me up as an opponent. It's what we desperate people do. We imagine what it will take to defeat the other one, physically.

"Okay," Viktor began as he handed my driver's license to me. "You're in my house, standing in my living room. What can I do for you?" I didn't answer him. I looked at Henry Darby inquisitively. Henry picked up the beat.

"These are the people I told you about, Vik. The hundred kilo deal."

"Shut up," Viktor snapped. "What can I do for you, Mister Ray Richards from St. Louis, Missouri?"

"I'm here to negotiate a hundred kilo deal," I said with a smirk. "I was told that you were the man I had to see. Obviously I was misinformed. Let's go, Heidi." I turned and grabbed Heidi's arm, and we started to walk out of the house.

"Hold up," Viktor shouted. "How do I know you aren't DEA?"

I paused and stared at him. "You're the one asking for identification. How do I know you're not DEA?" He stared meanly at me, his black pimp eyes studying me. I wondered how many young girls he had terrorized with that look. How many white hot hangars he burned them with while staring at them with those pimp eyes to make them get out and work. He glanced at Will. Will gave him a nod. He nodded back.

"I can maybe set up a deal for you," Viktor continued. "Twenty thousand a kilo, and I can close the deal this evening."

"Ten thousand a kilo is what I'm willing to pay," I countered.

He stared his scary stare again then glanced at Henry and Will. "You got some good faith money in that briefcase?"

I paused before answering him. "I'm prepared to pay fifty thousand when the dope is en route to St. Louis. The remainder when the dope reaches St. Louis."

"I don't think you got any money, Ray Richards from St. Louie. I think you're a bullshitter." He was chuckling and he looked at Will the bone-crusher, who chuckled on cue.

"He's got money," Henry replied. "He bought our last package."

"Oh, yeah?" Viktor wasn't chuckling anymore. He was as serious as a heart attack. "Show me," he said.

I opened the metal briefcase and flashed the hundred-thousand to him. He was instantly mesmerized. Will came over and looked at it then returned to the plastic couch, his black eyes blinking like a cop who has just gotten caught perjuring himself on the witness stand. I closed the briefcase and walked back to the center of the room with Heidi.

"That looks like more than fifty thousand," Viktor said.

"How much you got in there?"

"Hundred thousand," I nonchalantly replied.

"You give me the hundred thousand when the dope leaves for St. Louis, which will be tonight, and I'll make the deal for thirteen thousand a kilo."

I stared back at him. I was measuring him but he didn't know it. I figured I could take him in a hand-to-hand battle. I was on his turf and he felt superior. He naturally underestimated me, and so did his stupid employee, Will, and so many other inept criminals I had dealt with, pummeled, and incarcerated.

I wasn't imposing or scary like him. I had the upper hand. My survival of this hard life is dependent upon me being underestimated. It's how I stayed alive.

"Okay, it's a deal," I said. "Where's the dope?"

"Call Angel," he shouted at Henry, as he handed him an international cell. "Ask him where the damn boat is."

Henry dialed the cell like a madman. "Angel, the deal's in the works. Where's the boat?" I flashed back to the safe room at Henry's home. I asked him who the captain of the Corn Island was. He told me he didn't know. He knew!

He paused while Angel advised him. "Okay, muchacho. Yeah, I know where it is. The Corn Island, drifting in the Gulf Stream, coordinates," he used his chin to hold the cell while he jotted down some numbers Yeah, okay, sounds cool. Bye daddy-o."

Henry deactivated the cell and looked at Viktor as he handed him the coordinates. "It's on the Corn Island. Angel says he'll stay there for two hours, and then he's taking off for the west coast."

"The damn Corn Island," Viktor muttered. He got up from his chair and walked around the room. He was nervous, contemplating, fidgeting.

Heidi shot a quick glance at me. Henry was looking

hysteric; his eyes darting around the room, hands through his hair and then into his pockets. Viktor was still pacing and Will sat quietly on the couch taking the show in with his eyes still blinking erratically. He was in attendance to kill us: me, Heidi and Henry, if Viktor gave the command.

I wondered what Ellen would do if that happened. Would she freak and go back to East St. Louis, Illinois?

"Follow me," Viktor said. He walked through the storm door, down another red brick sidewalk and onto the dock with all of us behind him. We milled around on the dock watching the pelicans zooming over us in the dock lights.

I felt awkward carrying the metal briefcase, but I couldn't put it in the Corvette. Someone would steal it and the deal would be dead.

I did a visual on the boat. A 37-footer, a Formula with outdrives. A fast and seaworthy craft. It looked new. I knew this particular boat came with huge gasoline engines capable of cruising the boat on plane at about forty miles per hour.

Heidi, Henry, and I stood on the dock while Viktor and Will entered the cockpit and prepared the boat for cruising. Vik cranked the engines and they exploded with noise and power. They were turbo-charged diesels which made the boat worth twice as much on the used boat market. It was spotless, well cared for, and impressive; a custom cruiser for the lowlife pimp drug dealer.

Heidi, Henry, and I climbed onboard.

"Neat boat," I muttered.

"It's hot," Henry replied.

"I bet it is with those diesels," I mumbled. "It didn't come with those. What kind are they?"

"Yanmars, five hundred horsepower a piece. She'll run forty five all night long. But when I said it was hot, I didn't mean performance. She's stolen. Will stole her about two months ago from a marina in Fort Lauderdale. Viktor will keep her for about six months, then he'll ditch her. He changes boats about as often as some folks change their underwear."

Viktor expertly backed the craft out into deep water, turned it, and slowly cruised down the black canal. We stood at the transom like tourists from the Midwest, star struck by the boat. We gradually picked up speed, in the darkness, with Viktor using the spotlight looking for navigational markings. We edged closer to the cockpit to break the damp, chilly wind. We were all standing under the canopy now.

Henry acted as trip narrator. "We're in the Ogeechee River," he loudly said to Heidi and me. The boat banked and Viktor nailed the throttle. He adjusted the trim tabs then backed off the throttle. The boat planed out and the diesels hummed.

"We're on the Canoochee River now, heading for the Atlantic. The Corn Island's twenty-five miles out, waiting for us. You guys can go forward into the cabin, if you want. There's probably a fresh pot of coffee, it's gourmet. Viktor only drinks the finest coffee."

Will was checking coordinates and setting a course as he and Viktor talked to each other. I tried to listen to their conversation but couldn't make it out.

Heidi motioned to me and I followed her as she went below to the cabin. We were alone in the saloon, sitting closely. "We aren't supposed to be here," she said.

"I know, but what were we supposed to do? The dope is out here and the deal is going down."

She nodded. "We're outside the twelve-mile limit, too. We're no longer in the United States."

"I know."

"I don't feel good about this, Ray."

The conversation was going nowhere. We sat and stared

and rocked and rolled while the fast boat beat through the swells toward the scow, Corn Island. We drank a cup of gourmet coffee and didn't converse.

After about thirty minutes of the cold shoulder from Heidi, I got up and went topside still carrying the briefcase. It was a pitch black night. I could see a light in the distance and the boat was starting to slow. The tone of the engines was getting mellow.

Viktor was on the international cell phone, jabbering and screaming. I figured he was talking to the guy named Angel, the cocaine broker. In a perfect world during a perfect dope deal, Angel would have already advised the crew of the Corn Island we were on the way in a fast boat, and that the dope was to be transferred to our boat expeditiously. But there is perfection nowhere in the cop and dope business.

Viktor backed off of the diesels and the forward momentum of the fast boat faltered as if he had tossed out a sea anchor. I could barely make out the outline of the old scow and I watched it as we drew nearer, the speed getting less and less.

Viktor shined a blinding spot on it and I saw the whole ship. It was shocking. It didn't appear to be real. It was as if someone had salvaged it from the bottom of the sea and commissioned it for this dope deal.

It was large, but rusted and fearsome, the kind of craft people meet their demise on; a death ship rolling in the black nighttime waters of the Atlantic.

I started getting paranoid, and I wished we had taken Doc's advice and not come to sea with Viktor, Will the bone-crusher, and the untrustworthy snitch. I checked my crotch, feeling my crotch rocket 357. Not checking to see if it was there; I knew it was there. I touched it for courage. I felt stupid for touching it. Live by the gun, die by the gun.

We drew up to the relic, pitching and yawing in the

swells. There were Colombian Indians: long stringy hair, heavy tattered clothing like street people in the cities, skinny and bearded looking down at us. I imagined how victims of pirates must feel.

The Indians were holding automatic weapons, flourishing them at us and ordering us to back away in Spanish, motioning with their weapons. Viktor and Will talked to the Indians in broken Spanish but they weren't buying it. I don't understand Spanish but I understood what they were saying as they motioned with their weapons for us to push off.

An Indian with a cell phone and a long ponytail came to the side, shirtless, as if he just got out of a shower and ripped up like a steroid user who does repetitions for definition. He was jabbering into a cell and screaming at the other gun-toting Indians as he dressed into a shirt and jacket, and as we tried to keep the performance cruiser from colliding with the Corn Island.

The smaller boat was on an elevator, up and down, as we pushed and placed fenders on the starboard side while the boats rocked toward each other. I held onto the suitcase with the hundred thousand in it and tried to lend a hand to keep us from colliding and sinking. The scenario spelled disaster at sea, with me and Heidi being the victims.

There were two lights now: ours shooting up, and the Corn Island's massive light shooting down. "Hundred kilos, hundred kilos," Viktor shouted. The ponytail Indian grinned, shouted orders in Spanish, and the gun-toting Indians put their guns down and started tossing packages of cocaine down to us by the light of the beam spotlights. I sat the briefcase on the deck and helped bring the packages onboard. It was being stacked on the aft deck in rows of ten. I was counting it and was up to ninety five when Heidi came topside.

She walked through the light toward the stacks of

cocaine, and the ponytail Indian said something in Spanish. We were up to one hundred by then, and I figured he was ordering the Indians to stop. He put the light on her, pointed his machine pistol, and shouted, "SALLEE JIMINEZ," to her as she stood in the beam.

She looked up at him, shielded her eyes, stepped out of the beam, and didn't say anything. The Indian then shouted curses at her: "puta," which I recognized, and "dinero" and "plata," which I thought was money.

She shot off a line of Spanish toward him, using her hands for emphasis, apparently trying to hold her own. They spoke in loud Spanish, shouting and cursing at each other. They obviously knew each other, and I felt bewildered and threatened.

Ponytail was shouting at Viktor, ordering him to do something. Viktor was looking around for Heidi from the beam to the darkness. His hand shot out and he had Heidi by her arm and dragged her back into the spotlight. She was struggling to get away from him and the light.

He manhandled her to keep her where ponytail could see her as the boats pitched and yawed in the swelling sea. Will rushed over to help him control Heidi, each of them holding an arm as she struggled to get free. Ponytail was pointing his machine pistol at her as they shouted at each other in Spanish. Stay cool, undercover work is being cool, I said to myself.

Viktor was nodding as if he understood the ripped-up Indian while he held onto Heidi. In an instant the Indian disappeared, then reappeared on a cargo net clamoring over the side with two other Indians with him. They were intent on boarding the stolen cruiser; their automatic weapons slung onto their backs.

I glanced at the controls of the speedboat. I figured they were going to come onto the speedboat and take Heidi with them onto the ancient cargo vessel. I wasn't about to allow that to happen, but I didn't want to overreact and spoil the dope deal. I quickly glanced at Henry; he was panicked and looking like he was going to vomit.

I sat the suitcase on the deck and pushed as hard as I could on the barnacle-encrusted side of the Corn Island with both hands. The speedboat veered away from the Corn Island just as the Colombian Indians were about to board us. I scurried to the controls, gunned the diesels and we were headed back toward civilization, the lights of the Corn Island becoming faint.

Viktor gave me a discerning look and released his grasp on Heidi . He came to the controls and took over the running of the vessel. "Hey, man I wasn't about to let those barbarians onto the boat," I said to him. Heidi jerked away from Will, then came over to where I was standing and stood behind me.

I gave Viktor and Will a look that said if they come for her, I was going to kill them and throw them over the side which was exactly what I was going to do. Cool can only last for so long.

We stood our ground until the ride got rough and the sea started blowing over the top of the boat and soaking us. Will and Henry huddled by the bulkhead under the canopy by Viktor. Heidi remained out in the open, not wanting to get close to them.

I grabbed her hand and led her around them to the saloon. We walked in and I closed and locked the door. Surprisingly, it was quiet and warm. We were soaked. I laid the suitcase on the settee, found some towels and tossed one to Heidi. We toweled off without speaking. There was still coffee in a carafe. I poured us a cup. It was still fresh and hot. The engines were being trimmed and the boat was on plane.

I took it to her and we sat and sipped the hot brew. "I wonder where we're heading." She was perplexed.

"Back to Savannah, Heidi. Where else could it be?" I pulled out my three-fifty-seven titanium from my crotch holster and laid it on the table.

She was looking at me strangely, pointing at my titanium 357 snub revolver. "What is that, a throw-down?" I was amused at her question. Federal agents aren't privy to revolvers. They've lived in the semi-automatic world of instant death.

"My crotch rocket. I'm not going to let them harm us, deal or no deal. Mind telling me what went down back there?"

"It was an old case." She was trying to blow it off.

"What case was it?"

"Angel Perez."

"Angel Perez? What the hell is that supposed to mean to me?" I wasn't going to let this die until I got what I wanted. "So what about the case? Where was it from?"

"Colombia. I went down there right before you came to the unit. Remember my tan?"

"Yeah."

"That's where I got it."

"Oh, okay. You went to Colombia and worked on your winter tan and between rays you worked on the Angel Perez case. It's all coming back to me now. Now I know why some Indian in a death-scow cocaine-delivery ship was shouting obscenities at you and was coming over the side to board us and probably take you back to his ship with him, after he killed me because that's what he would have had to do. I wasn't going to let him have you."

Her dark eyes were penetrating me. "We had an informant down there. She was a housekeeper for Angel Perez and she'd been good for years. All of a sudden she stopped checking in. An outside agency told me she'd gone over to the other side. I got sent down there to investigate. I found out she was screwing Angel and didn't want to inform anymore. She told me that, and I tried to dissuade her and get her back on the payroll. Somebody in the gang saw us meeting and advised Angel. He asked her who I was. She said a cousin from the states. He liked my looks and eventually I got hired as a maid."

"A maid?"

"Yeah," she indignantly replied. "It was only for a couple of weeks. I had to get things arranged for the C/I to get out of Colombia. We relocated her in Bermuda. She's a housekeeper for another dope dealer now. But that's another story, another case. So, I worked for Angel and I see this giant stack of cash hidden in a secret compartment in his bedroom. The C/I is on her way to Bermuda by then so I latch onto the drug proceeds and head for the embassy. I hid out there for a couple of weeks, got the okay from DEA headquarters to bring myself and the cash back into the country, jumped on a diplomatic flight, and came back to Miami."

"How much cash?"

"Eight hundred thousand. It's all I could carry. So, I guess Angel is carrying a grudge."

"That was Angel on the Corn Island?"

"Yes!"

"The one with the muscles and ponytail and the automatic weapon?"

"Yeah, that was him," she said with a smile. "Scary bastard, ain't he?"

"Yeah, he's scary. Where's the eight hundred thousand?"

"It's a seizure. Drug proceeds. I processed it as such. That dumb dope-dealing bastard thought I was a prostitute. He still doesn't know I'm DEA. Dumb fuck!"

"What's the percentages of that happening, Heidi? I mean, running into a dope dealer from another undercover assignment while undercover on a different assignment."

"I don't know what the percentages are but it's every DEA agent's nightmare. It ranks right up there with getting your gun taken away and having it pointed at you, or having a dope dealer find out where you live."

I pondered while she stared at me. "We've got to get a secondary plan. What if the deal is blown?"

"It isn't blown, Ray. Remember what Doc said to you. Viktor wants our money. The dope is on the boat. We still have the flash money. The deal is solvent. Viktor owes no allegiance to Angel Perez. Viktor would kill his ass if he got a chance." She stopped and was pondering. "But when this boat stops and we look out of those portholes and don't see a familiar dock or house, I suggest we get ready to use your crotch rocket."

The boat was gently moving up and down in the swells as the diesels purred. We finished our coffee and I poured us another cup. "What was Angel Perez shouting down at you? Did he say, I'm going to kill you, bitch?"

"No, he was a scorned lover. He had the big-time hots for me. He was upset he couldn't consummate our relationship. He's a Latin, for God's sake."

"So you're telling me you weren't in any danger."

"Danger? Maybe. I felt I could talk myself out of my predicament. There was some danger. He didn't see me take his money. He thinks I did, but there's a scintilla of doubt in his Latin mind which grows bigger as he sees me. He didn't want to believe I took his money. He wanted to believe that I'd be his lover. The situation wasn't out of control. You handled yourself well back there. You were cool. That's what working undercover is about, cool!"

Another twenty minutes went by without us talking. We

were drying out and warmed up by the coffee. The diesels started toning down and the plane of the boat changed. I looked out a porthole and recognized the lights of the long docks on the Canoochee River. We were in the canal preparing to cruise into the Ogeechee River and Viktor's dock.

I kept watching. The boat came to a stop at Viktor's dock. The engines were idling as I guessed they were off-loading the dope and trucking it into Viktor's house. There was a tap on the door of the cabin.

"Hey guys." It was Henry Darby.

"Yeah, what's up?" I asked through the closed door.

"Everything's cool. You guys can come out now."

I slid the crotch rocket into my front pocket and kept my hand on it as I unlocked the cabin door. I opened it and Henry was standing there alone with his bartender smile and his stand-up-comic body movements. "The dope's already off-loaded and in the house. Everything's cool. Come on in and we'll close this deal and get on with our lives."

We followed him off the boat, to the house, and into the living room where Viktor and Will were sitting. Viktor was smiling; Will looked mean. I was smug and in control. I had the flash money, Heidi, and my hand on my crotch rocket. I was still pumped from the Corn Island incident. My attitude was, "Fuck the deal and fuck you too," and it showed.

Heidi was covering my back while I faced the adversaries. "Man," Viktor said with a smile. "Heidi, if that's your name, you can work for me anytime. Man, that Angel was pissed at you. He's probably pissed at me about now for not handing you over to him. But, you know, I got scruples. I stand by my business associates. You guys are fair with me, I'll protect and be fair with you. Angel might come looking for me. He knows where I live. But he knows that if he does, I'll kill him with my bare hands. He would have to snipe me, and that isn't his way. He likes to talk you to death before he kills you. It's the only way it works for him. We're all different. We all have our own ways of doing things."

It was pimp 101. He watched and waited for our response. There wasn't one. He looked disappointed. "Okay, the dope is in the trunk of the Caddy outside. Want to see it?"

"Yeah!"

He stood and walked toward thc front door. We all followed him; Heidi and I brought up the rear. I noted that the newer Caddy with the Illinois tag was gone. It had to be Ellen's Caddy. She must have flown the coop again. Viktor activated the key fob and the trunk popped open. I visually inspected the packages. Seemed to be the whole hundred. He slammed the trunk. "Give me the hundred-thou."

"When is the dope leaving for St. Louis?" I asked.

"Tomorrow morning. Me and Will and Henry will deliver it in three days. Where do you want it delivered?"

"Henry's house in the city," I replied. "Hit me on my cell when you get an hour out. Give me your cell number."

He paused, then jotted his number down and handed it to me, "I only give this to my closest friends."

I handed him the briefcase. "See you in three days. If we don't, we'll come calling."

He smiled.

18

We crashed at the beach efficiency, got up, used the hot tub, laughed, and brunched. As luck would have it, the weather turned gorgeous and the ocean was calling to me, but I didn't answer. Heidi called Doc. "It's in the works. No problems. The dope is on the way, and we're leaving this afternoon." Doc was pleased so we celebrated with one more romp in bed and one more dip in the hot tub before checkout.

We loaded into the Corvette and headed north, spent the night in Nashville and rolled into St. Louis one day ahead of schedule. I dropped Heidi off at her house and headed for south Broadway. The world is bland after leaving the beach. The Mississippi looked dead, and my little antique house seemed inadequate.

I slept hard, got up at 0600, took my time eating breakfast and showering, and walked into the task force office at 0900. Heidi was at her desk pounding on her laptop. We shot each other glances and I was just going to sit on her desk and flirt with her when Doc called us into his office.

Doc was tense and he started with the questioning. "You heard from the target?"

"No," Heidi replied. "But he's due. I expect to hear from him soon."

"What instructions did you give him?"

"We told him to contact us on my cell when he was an hour out," I replied.

"Oh," Doc said as he stared at me. "Is there an alternate plan? Can you call him?"

"Yeah, Doc. I've got his cell number, but I don't want to spook him. Let's give him a little more time."

"Who's with him?"

"His hit man, Will, and the C/I Henry Darby," Heidi replied. "They're driving up in a Caddy, blue DeVille four-door. Ray and I thought we'd do the deal at Henry Darby's house."

"I think that'll work," Doc said. He walked out of his office and stood at Carla's desk. "Everybody's on standby," he shouted to the agents and detectives. "Ray, draw me up a map with the location of the house. Nothing fancy, just something I can give the troops so they know what's going on."

"Roger."

I walked out of his office and to my desk. I drew up the map and made ten copies, then passed it around. Doc was nervously milling around in the big open office. "He's going to call, we know that for sure. We need to get some guys over there for a rolling surveillance. Pat, Ross, head over to Henry Darby's house and roll around. Don't set up, just look for counter-surveillance. This could be a rip."

"Right, boss."

My cell rang and everybody stopped and stared. "Yo," I answered.

"We're in Mount Vernon," Viktor Agron said. "Be at Henry's house in an hour or so." The line went dead.

"He hung up."

Doc was frowning. "What did he say?"

"They're in Mount Vernon, Illinois," I replied.

"That's a little more than an hour," Doc said. "Okay, everybody, you've got your maps. This is a buy bust. Bad asses coming in from South Georgia with one-hundred kilos. These guys are nobody to play cheap. They're the real deal, big-time dopers and criminals. Supposed to be driving a blue Caddy four-door. Consider them armed and dangerous. Ray and Heidi are the undercover. Heidi will be wired. Monica Rose will be in the Kell car, monitoring. Go in on her command! Got it?"

"Yeah, boss," everybody chimed in.

"Okay, let's get staged and set. Ray, Heidi, come into my office."

We followed him in. He had a sea bag which he hoisted onto his desk. "Flash money. We should be inside and placing handcuffs on the targets after you flash it, but in case we aren't, don't let them drive off with it. Understand?"

"Yeah, Doc," I said.

"This is the one that's going to make us all."

Heidi got wired. I shot a quick look at her. She wasn't impressed with Doc's promotional banter. Dave Moynihan was wrong about her. She didn't give a damn about a promotion. That was Doc's shtick.

We all walked down to the parking garage, and I tossed the sea bag with the flash money in the Corvette trunk and slammed it. Heidi and I followed the troops out of the garage and then split off and drove slowly to the buy bust scene.

Ross Milton got on the air. "The intended is circling the transaction scene. There's three white males in the car. Two of them in the front seat. The third is scrunched down in the backseat."

"Roger," Heidi replied. "The third guy must be Henry Darby."

My cell rang. "Yo."

"I don't like the exchange site," Viktor said. "You got the money?"

"Yeah!" I replied. "What the fuck is wrong with Henry's house?"

"Neighbors, nosey fucking neighbors. And the backyard is fenced. I ain't going behind no fucking fence to do a deal."

"Oh, so where do you want to go?"

"I'm thinking," Viktor replied. "Where are you?"

"We're on the way to Henry's house."

"That road that runs in front of the Arch, you familiar with it?"

"Of course," I replied.

"Take it south till it dead ends, we'll be waiting for you."

"Hold on, I got to think this out." I covered the receiver with my hand. "He wants to meet at the dead end of Lenor K. Sullivan. What do you think?"

"No," Heidi said. "It's too desolate down there. Doc might be right; this could be a rip. Tell him we'll meet him at the base of the Eads Bridge in the casino south parking lot. Tell him that's our final offer. Fuck him. Dope dealer today, dope dealer tomorrow."

"We'll meet you on the casino parking lot by the Eads Bridge."

"Okay," Viktor replied. "But be at the water's edge where I can see what's going on."

"Okay."

Heidi got on the air. "It's going to be at the casino parking lot."

Doc got on. "You sure this isn't a rip? Be careful."

"That's strange," I remarked. "Doc on a deal? He's usually at the United States Attorney's office wooing his girlfriend."

"Maybe getting blown up has changed his perspective on life," Heidi replied.

We got there first and parked by the Mississippi at the "western mast" of the Eads Bridge. We sat in the Corvette with the top down and gazed at the fishermen sitting on the cobblestones with their ocean-going rigs wedged into the cobblestones and their lines taught in the swift current.

I glanced up at the old bridge. It was built in the late

1800's of limestone and steel and was still in good shape. "One of the keys to the westward expansion," I said.

"Yeah, right," Heidi boringly replied.

There were two young men fishing just offshore on an old bass boat, the kind with sparkle paint and chairs attached to pedestals on the stern and bow. One of them looked familiar to me, familiar like I had arrested him at one time.

I noticed the engine. It was a new Mercury outboard, probably worth ten-thou. It looked out of place on the old boat under the old bridge, fishing for catfish, carp, and perch the EPA has advised against eating because of heavy metal contamination.

The men on the boat were drinking beer and laughing at their friends on shore who by city ordinance weren't allowed to drink alcohol in public. My cop instincts clicked in. The boat had to be stolen, at least the motor was hot. They didn't fit and the familiar one kept eyeballing me.

"Hey, brother," one of the shore fishermen shouted to the boaters, "Toss me one of those cans of beer." The boater cranked the Mercury and got within twenty-feet of shore and tossed a can of Stag toward him. He missed the catch and the can hit the cobblestones and burst, white foam spewing out toward the shore fishermen.

The guys on the boat were laughing and swilling the cheap beer and pointing at their friend on shore. The beer sharing turned into a game for the boaters. They inched the boat closer to shore and tossed another can at the shore fisherman, but they threw it off-line on purpose. The victim ran for it and missed it again and it blew up on the cobblestones. The haves and the have-not'; one of the games of life.

The blue DeVille was heading our way on the parking lot, Viktor at the wheel. I looked around the immediate area and didn't see any of the good guys. Heidi and I got out of the Corvette and stood by it as the Caddy pulled up to us. Viktor climbed out leaving the Caddy idling; he was all business with his flowered shirt and chest hair and his Elvis coif slicked back.

"All right, we're here. Where's the money?"

"We've got it, Vik, where's the dope?"

"In the trunk," he said with a smile in an attempt to be a businessman instead of a thug.

I glanced across the river to East St. Louis. How fitting it was that this dangerous person be taken off the streets, for good, in view of his adopted city. Henry told us Viktor still had a house there. I couldn't imagine it. Nasty man, nasty city. It was ironic and just and I liked it.

Will and Henry climbed out of the Caddy. Henry stood in the background while Viktor and Will stood shoulder to shoulder and tried to intimidate Heidi and me.

"Show us the money," Viktor ordered.

"You bring out the dope and we'll bring out the cash," I said with a smirk.

Viktor gave the nod to Will and he went back to the trunk with Henry. "Hold up," Viktor shouted to Will and Henry. "The dope's in four sea bags. How you guys going to transport it?"

Things started clicking in Viktor's gangster brain. He looked at the Corvette, and then at Heidi and me. His right hand came up with a Sig Sauer nine in it. "You guys are DEA, right?" Will started making strange sounds, like a city dweller in the woods who just stepped on a snake as he backed away and got into the Caddy. He threw it in gear and screeched the tires going backwards on the cobblestones.

Henry Darby had a look of sheer terror as he inched away from the drama. Viktor caught him crawling away and backhanded him, sending him reeling onto his back, writhing and crying. "You have to be a dope to be on either end of it" was echoing in my brain.

Heidi and I patiently waited for the troops to arrive as we stared at Viktor and his gun. "Give me your weapons," Viktor ordered.

"We're not DEA, Viktor," Heidi said.

He reached into her waistband and pulled out her Glock forty, stuck it into his shorts pocket then did the same to me. "DEA guns," he said as he backed away. "I'd kill you fuckers if it were nighttime. Where's the rest of you dirty motherfuckers? There's got to be a camera around here somewhere."

His head was jerking around while he looked for surveillance. He reached toward Heidi and tore her blouse revealing the wire between her breasts. "Shit! If I get taken off I'm going to kill you two in the process." His eyes were glazed and half-open as he stared at us and waved the Sig.

His cunning and instinct took over as he looked around for an avenue of escape. The boaters had the bass boat up against the shore, drinking beer and laughing with their landlubber friend, the Mercury idling and keeping them into the cobblestones. Viktor went for the boat. "Get out, mother fuckers." He waved the Sig at them and us.

"Hey, man," you can't take my motherfucking boat."

"Out broth-er or you're dead," Viktor slurred at him. The fishermen reluctantly climbed out and stood on shore.

Viktor backed into the boat placed it in reverse and pulled away from shore. He dumped the two Glocks into the river about ten feet off-shore. I pulled my crotch rocket 357 and ran toward the water firing at the bass boat as Viktor gunned it, heading south. He was doing sixty in about fifteen seconds and my shots were wild.

Heidi was on the air shouting for backup. "THE DOPE IS IN THE BLUE CADDY AND HE'S GOING NORTH PAST THE CASINO. WILL BLANKS IS DRIVING.

VIKTOR AGRON IS IN A BLUE BASS BOAT HEADING SOUTH ON THE MISSISSIPPI. HE'S ARMED AND DANGEROUS."

Doc got on the air. "Did he get the flash money?"

"No."

I heard the roar of the engines as Bill Yocum sped by in an SS Camaro, followed by Clete in a Dodge Hemi pickup, Monica Rose in her Mercedes convertible, Ross Milton in a Caddy Seville, and Carl Robinson in the Porsche.

Doc rolled onto the scene in his silver Mercedes sedan, parked and got out. He studied us as he walked toward us. "We thought you had it under control. Monica said you were alright."

"He pulled a Sig Sauer on us," Heidi explained. "Got the drop on us and took our guns." Doc nodded in acknowledgment.

Henry Darby got up from the cobblestones and walked toward us shaking the cobwebs. "He's going to kill me. You guys know that don't you?"

"Doc studied him, "Give him some cash for a hideout. I don't want him going home or to the bar. Better yet, meet us in the office in two hours."

Henry walked away with his head down. The bass-boat fisherman walked up to us. "You the police? What about my boat?" He was indignant and obviously blaming us for his shortcomings.

I glared at him. He was a witness to a botched drug deal. I should probably get his name and put him in the report. "Are you the owner of the boat?"

"Uh, no."

"Who owns the boat?"

He was backpedaling. "A dude," he continued. "I don't remember his name, but he told me I could use it."

"What's your name?" I asked.

"My name? Who, me?"

"Yeah!" I pulled a notebook and a pen out of my pocket.

"That's okay, officer, I'll take care of it myself."

"Okay, but if you remember who the owner is tell him to contact Detective Ray Arnold at the DEA Task Force and I'll take a report of the theft."

"Right, officer," he mumbled as he turned, walked away, then returned. "I can get those guns for you, the ones the dude dumped into the river." We stared at him incongruously. "It's only about ten feet deep there. I'll fetch them for you for twenty dollars a gun."

"Okay, go ahead."

He turned and walked away.

Carl Robinson was on the air. "We got Will Blanks, Doc."

"Where?"

"On the north side. He was stopping people on the street offering to pay them to hide him. A concerned citizen dialed 911 and said a crazy white man was looking for a hiding spot. If anybody had known he had a hundred kilos in the trunk he would've been barbecued."

"I like it," Doc replied with a smile. "Dope still in the car?"

"Yep!"

"Cool. Bring Will, the car, and the dope back to the task force. We'll meet you there."

Doc was elated. "This is a victory. Hundred kilo deal, one arrest, one fugitive. Four or five warrants will be issued by Sue Lee for Angel Perez and his counterparts. What a coup for the task force. It's a victory!"

I was watching the fisherman sounding for our Glocks. He had a rope tied around his waist and his friends on shore were holding it as he waded out and started diving into the chilly Mississippi. Three attempts and he came up with them. He was smiling as he climbed out of the stinking river and walked toward us with the guns. He handed them to me and I handed him two twenties. He walked away a happy man.

"The deal went down," Doc said as he stared at us. "Understand?"

"Yeah, Doc," we nodded in acknowledgment.

"You showed him the flash money, right? And he showed you the dope, right?"

"Yeah, Doc," Heidi replied.

Doc got on his cell phone. "The deal went down. Yeah, yeah, Viktor Agron got away. In a bass boat. Yeah, he commandeered it. We've got the Coast Guard looking for him. He won't get far. Yeah, I need you to put out a fugitive arrest order for him. Right. Okay, Sue, I'll talk to you in about an hour." He terminated the call and smiled at us. "We're all going to get promoted over this one."

His cell rang and he answered it. "Where? Okay, we'll be there in twenty minutes." He looked at us and then glanced at the fisherman. "Coast Guard found the boat. Over in East St. Louis, just about a mile downstream. He ran it up onto the shore. It's torn up and the motor is wrecked from hitting the shore so fast. Coast Guard says he must have been going twenty when he ran it up onto the rock beach. Crazy bastard. He thinks he can get away. He can run but he can't hide. I'm going over there. Give me the flash money."

I got the bag of cash out of the Corvette and dragged it over to his Mercedes. He popped the trunk and I lugged it in. He turned and walked away, then stopped and looked at us. "Good job, guys. You want to come over to the East side with me? It won't be long and Viktor Agron will be incarcerated. The dogs are looking for him right now."

An exercise in futility, I said to myself. "You've got to be a dope to be on either end" was still screaming in my ears.

"We've got to go back to the office," Heidi said. "I want to get started on the report. It's going to be a bear to write, and we've got to book Will Blanks and figure out where to hide Henry Darby."

"Okay, your call, I'll see you at the office."

Doc drove off. I stared at the river and East St. Louis. Viktor was home, a rat in the sewer he grew accustomed to while pimping and dealing his youth away, flip-flopping like so many criminals before him from the west side to the east side, then returning to his lair, Little Odessa. He'll never get caught over there. But he will resurface and we will meet again. I'm sure of that.

It's bizarre how criminal cases clash. Heidi and Angel Perez. Ellen and Viktor Agron, and East St. Louis, my hometown. It's almost like a script. I feel like I've been led and directed since I walked through the door at DEA. Weird!

Heidi and I drove to Clayton and wandered into the task force offices. Carla was watching us inquisitively. "The real bad guy got away," I said, dejectedly.

"I heard," Carla said. "Is this personal for you?" I looked at her and didn't answer. "I mean, do you hate these guys?"

"They're fucking dope dealers," I replied. "Victor Agron is mister big, the guy who's been bringing weed and cocaine into my city for decades. I want him incarcerated for life. He pulled a nine on me and Heidi. I'd kill him if I had the chance. I'd kill him for me and Heidi and for the parents of children his dope has ruined. Yeah, I hate him and his kind."

She smiled at me. My mind flashbacked to FBI Agent Rich Moynihan. "They're brainwashing you to enhance their careers." I am brainwashed but only because I have to be in order to do the job. We all are. We tell ourselves dope dealers are the cause of all evil and then we naturally hate them and try to destroy them. I blushed. Dope dealers are doing what greedy Americans have done for two hundred years. Give the masses something to alter their boring lives so they can hide in a dream world and forget about reality. Booze, sex, gambling, drugs. It's all the same.

"The boys are booking Will Blanks for you," Carla continued. "He refused to make a statement. Wants his lawyer."

"He's going need one," I replied as I sat at my desk.

We were banging on our computers when Doc came in. He was pissed, we could all read him. "He got away. The Illinois state guys and the East St. Louis police combed every inch of the immediate area. They had dogs and an airplane and a helicopter. The bastard got away. But he'll resurface. They always do. Dope dealer today, dope dealer tomorrow." Doc walked into his office and slammed the door.

I stopped typing and tried to put myself into Viktor Agron's predicament. He had to telephone someone to pick him up. Unless he had made alternate plans in case we were DEA. I dug out his cell number he had given me in Savannah and dialed it on my desk phone. His voice mail clicked on.

"I'm not taking calls," is all it said. I jotted down the Illinois tag from memory on the newer Caddy parked in front of Viktor's house. I ran it in my computer and it came back improper vehicle license. I continued to play with the numbers and letters. It was there, I just had to get it right in my damaged brain.

It took me twenty one times, but I got it. It was issued to Ellen Agron at a house on the East side. I was familiar with the area. It was once fashionable with a view of East St. Louis and downtown St. Louis. I printed the computer issue, tore it off, and stuck it in my pocket.

Square Bidness stormed into Doc's office. We all stopped temporarily and waited for the onslaught. He only showed up when there was trouble. He was in Doc's office for about three minutes and then he stormed out and exited the office without looking at any of us lowly TFD's and task force agents. Doc wandered out in about five minutes and stood at Carla's desk adjusting his Ray Bans and ball cap. We were all watching him.

"You guys remember that guy you beat up in Illinois, Jesus Rangool?"

"Yeah," the group replied like fifth graders trying to please their teacher.

"We just got word that he's selling crack out of his rehabilitation apartment down in the city. He's got the whole building hooked on it. He sits by his window and watches the street. If a strange car pulls up, he has the zombies hide him in their room. Those zombies down there are already hooked on square meds; now they're hooked on street stuff." Doc was smiling. "The irony of the dope game," he said shaking his head. "He's got an apartment on the fifth floor, number 515. I'm only telling you guys this because we're forbidden to act on this information. Let the locals handle it. Understood?"

"Yeah, Doc," the group said. He returned to his office and closed the door. We all continued typing.

Clete was walking around the room like he owned the place, his belly hanging so low that he couldn't see his penis with a mirror. I glanced at him and classified him without remorse. A fellow cop. A robber and back-shooter who's days are probably numbered.

Special Agent Jim Schwartz wandered into the office like a deadly snake seeking a warm place to hide, threatening and surly. Clete panicked and ran back to his desk and plopped down. The rest of the TFD's and special agents ignored Schwartz and banged on their laptops. I watched him.

He walked over to me and stood near my desk. "Feeb snitch," he muttered. I leaned back in my chair and stared at his giant head. He was so muscular I doubted he could handle himself proficiently in a hand-to-hand battle. He relied on the intimidation factor and the sucker punch. Just like the pimp dope dealers.

He was making serious mistakes with me. The most serious was the underestimation of me as an opponent. He was looking for someone to frighten, and I guessed he figured it wasn't going to be me so he directed his attention to Ross Milton.

He was playing the rogue biker routine, like a poorly written script that had been turned into a B movie. "I ought to snatch that ascot off of your scrawny neck and stuff it down your throat, agent."

Ross meekly smiled at him and banged on his laptop. Schwartz glanced at Heidi, who, like me stared back at him. "What's up bitch?" He snarled.

He walked to Carla who was typing as fast as her fingers would fly, trying to ignore the scene. "It's going to be you and me someday, Carla. You mark my words." He had accomplished his goal; Carla was in terror-shock.

He strolled back to Clete, who by this time was about to crawl under his desk. He spat in Clete's waste can at the side of his desk, then twirled on his left foot, and feigned accurate and balanced kicks at Clete's hog head. Schwartz was proficient in the art of kickboxing, the smooth moves were proof. I was impressed.

He was a formidable foe and opponent. I wondered if he and I would ever lock up in a death dance. It wasn't beyond the realm of reality. Doc came out of his office and stood by the door. He stared at Schwartz the way Square Bidness stared at us TFD's. Schwartz chuckled, said, "Pussies," to us and walked out.

I never liked bullies. It was probably one of the deciding factors of me becoming a cop. Jim Schwartz was a bully, carrying DEA Special Agent credentials which made it more disgusting. Even Doc was afraid of him. All of the supervisors seemed to allow him to do whatever he wished.

I had had enough of DEA for a while. I closed my laptop, locked my desk, walked past Heidi's desk and said, "I'm taking a ride." She looked at me inquisitively but didn't comment. I made my way out of the building and into the Corvette.

I was in need of some shrink time. I needed to hide in someone's artwork. I drove to the Art Museum, parked and walked in like a zombie. I was on cruise control, not thinking just moving. I never knew what painting or sculpture, or photograph I would be standing in front of when I headed for the museum.

I did know the starship I had been cruising on was on a death dive with mother earth, and the only escape hatch available to me was the museum.

I wandered freely, shadowed by a security guard who took notice of my demeanor: stiff legged, head down, within myself, feeling strange. I had been fighting the impulse to look into my damaged brain to see if there was any bleeding. I had done it when I was a kid when I always carried a concussion.

I knew when it had healed. It was like looking at a cut on your hand or arm, taking note of the scab and the colors it emitted in the healing process. I looked deeply into my head during those days and I could see the healing process.

Had I told the police department shrink that story during my pre-employment interview, I would have never become a cop. My head was up now searching the paintings, like a rich businessman looking for a new yacht. My favorite painter was the abstractionist, Phillip Guston. The museum had exhibitions of his work from time to time, and I had hidden in them before.

I was standing before a Guston oil on canvas, from the early forties, "MARTIAL MEMORY." The museum must have purchased it. It wasn't part of an exhibition. As in all of Guston's work, the painting was perfectly balanced; and it had my favorite colors, red, silver, golden brown, light blue. It was easy to enter into it, and I did so.

It showed a circle of young boys, maybe eleven years old, standing in an alley of a nasty city, much like the city I grew up in. They had discovered a cache of junk in the alley and they had made weapons out of it. Pieces of wood became swords. A teakettle and a rope became a helmet with a strap. One boy had a trashcan lid to serve as a shield.

It was apparently summertime in this city alley. The boys were dressed in shorts and tank tops, some with suspenders, but the thing I noted most, what stood out at me, was Guston's depiction of race. All of the boys were golden brown; not black, not white, not Hispanic.

One boy, with his back to the voyeur, was golden, except for his left leg; it was white. The boys who were not wearing headgear had short blonde hair.

It reminded me of DEA. There was no race issue there; we were all the same. The black people who were there were partially white; the whites, partially black; a natural balance. In the police department race governed all decisions: promotions, transfers, pay raises, benefits. We were physically, culturally, and emotionally segregated.

The transformation was complete; I was in the picture, sitting on the silver wall behind the boys, in front of the dilapidated red brick tenement, looking down. I could hear their chatter about what they were going to do to their enemy. It always came down to this: how do we destroy our enemy? The make-do weapons made them brave, and their veins bulged in their skinny arms as they wielded the wooden swords.

I could smell the stench of the alley trash and the odor of the urchin kids as I sat and watched. It was my home town, it had to be. Guston lived in St. Louis for a while. He had to have gone to the East side during his years here. But these boys weren't from my neighborhood. We didn't play with wooden swords. We had real weapons.

Guns were plentiful; my friends carried thirty-two caliber revolvers. Our swords were Army surplus bayonets, World-War-Two vintage, long and sharp. They were everywhere, easily obtainable. Italian stillettos and brass knuckles were the concealable weapons of choice for the ones who didn't cotton to firearms.

I peered at the boys' faces trying to see if I recognized them. As I strained to discern them, I realized they were in abstract, maybe not human. It struck me what message Guston was sending with his abstract talent.

Humans become sub-species when they prepare for war. We become animals, wonting for blood, and expressing the grunts and groans of mortal combat. We become readily able to punch, kick, gouge, tear, bite, stomp, and sometimes die for a stupid cause.

I felt foolish for examining the animal-like faces of the urchins, although it could have been me and my East side associates. But this painting was made decades before I was born. The problem I had was that these abstract boys and their desire to kill, like animals, were still pertinent today, getting weapons to destroy enemies, real and imaginary.

I was still one of them. My enemy on this fine day was Special Agent Jim Schwartz. Does anything change? Is there always going to be an enemy?

I snapped out of my trance, refreshed but concerned about my future. Again, my back was against a wall, in my personal life and in my chosen career. I was alone in the world preparing to go into combat with my enemy, and for once, I didn't like the odds. They were stacked against me. I strolled out of the museum and headed for the government Corvette, slid in like I was entering a cocoon, cranked it, and sat and stared at nothing.

I put the Corvette in gear and slowly drove away. I drove around the central city, reminiscent of times gone by; the fights, the arrests, the houses, prostitutes and pimps. They are all dead now. There aren't retirement homes for them; death is their retirement. The neighborhood had changed. The old nightclubs had been torn down and new houses were being built.

The disgust I felt for the DEA supervisors who allow that thief, Schwartz, to terrorize the TFD's and agents was working on me. I wished I had never come to the organization. Life was simpler in the P.D. It was much simpler in uniform working in a district. There all you do is answer the radio. The radio calls never stop coming, and before you know it, your day is over and you're turning your police car over to another robot.

I guessed that was why I was riding around my old district. It's where I had begun this strange way to make a living. What a wild and crazy place it once was. The ground was saturated with blood and false dreams. The longitude and latitude was cursed. No matter what you tear down and rebuild, it would still be the nightclub prostitute, pimp, and dope dealer part of the world.

I wouldn't want my children playing on this ground. There's no play here; just death and sorrow. But I haven't any children. I'm the child and the police department is my parent. I don't know why things worked out that way; they just did. I needed my dog. I headed for the kennel, Fetched, Tyrone and drove home.

19

We ate steak and sat on the deck watching the Mississippi slide by. I tossed the tennis ball a hundred times toward the dropoff. Tyrone pursued and captured it just before it went off the cliff then brought it back to me so I could throw it again. My house phone rang about twenty-one-thirty. I wasn't going to answer it but curiosity beckoned and I picked up. It was an old homicide dick, friend and associate. "Clete Jones bought it tonight," he said.

"Where?"

"Down by the stroll, Sarah and Olive in an alley."

"What time?"

"Nineteen-zero-two hours."

"How?"

"Gut-shot."

"Thanks," I replied.

My cell rang and I picked up. It was Carla. "Clete's been shot," she said.

"I know, I heard about it."

"I can't get hold of anybody. The TFD's are probably at the Club. Can you meet me there?"

I thought for a second. Why should I meet Carla? I didn't give a damn about Clete Jones when he was alive. But she is gorgeous. "Can't you find Doc?"

"No, he's temporarily out of the loop, probably wrapped up with his girlfriend. I left a message on his voice mail and told him I was going to the Club to tell the boys."

"I'll be there in thirty minutes." I hung up and felt the familiar feeling of being set up again. I knew redheads were bad luck from past experience, but I could never say no to them. They're unusual, inside and out.

I felt no remorse for Clete. He was a criminal hiding

behind a badge. But the little City of St. Louis didn't know his character. Dead cops are big news in this city. He was now a martyr. Special Agent Jim Schwartz had made him a hero, posthumously. In death, he gained respectability.

Was I jumping to conclusions? I was making the presumption that Schwartz shot fat Clete Jones in the gut. I observed Schwartz threaten Clete with his forty caliber pistol. They were in a partnership of no return. Either it was successful, or the TFD dies. I saw that, so in my mind, Jim Schwartz murdered him.

It was my information, nobody else was privy to it. I would sit on it until I could prove it. There had to be ballistics. I would wait for the outcome of the autopsy, and then maybe come forward and tell what I had gleaned. Right now I had no proof.

I turned on the TV as I prepared to leave the house to meet Carla. The news stations were already hyping the situation. The machine was in motion. Clete Jones, hero cop. I drove through the city to get onto the Daniel Boone to Clayton. Cop cars with lights and sirens were zooming around me.

The frenzy had begun to find the cop killer. The uninformed cops were helter skelter to follow any lead, driving eighty on the city streets, jaws set, blindly being led by the blind to locations where a suspect might be. The homicide dicks didn't have a clue. I had the clue, but I wasn't talking, yet.

I pulled into the garage and parked. The Porsche, the Camaro SS, and the Caddy Seville were parked in their spots. Carla's Chevy wasn't there. I took the elevator up and slowly walked into the Club.

Bill Yocum, Pat Brown, and Carl Robinson were doing the snake dance with three lonely secretaries who were stragglers from the after-work crowd. It was 2230 and everybody in the place had probably been drinking since 1700. The trick was to get the lonely secretaries to accompany them to one of their apartments, preferably Carl Robinson's since he lived closest.

I stood in the doorway watching as Carla slid up beside me. She kissed me on the lips and said, "Thanks for coming," then grabbed my right hand locking her fingers into mine the way a little girl does to her big brother when she's frightened. I nodded and took a long look at her.

Creamy redhead with big boobs and a chiseled ass. A gym rat with washboard abs, just what any red-blooded American cop would want. A trophy with nobody's name engraved on her. It didn't add up. And why did she kiss me on the mouth? That action means something. Is she coming on to me? I liked the thought but I had Heidi and I figured I was falling for her. I didn't need two DEA girlfriends.

The jukebox had been belting out Tina Turner singing "Proud Mary." As the music stopped, the TFD's and secretaries necked on the dance floor before going back to their tables. As they walked off the dance floor they observed Carla and me standing by the door. They walked over to us inquisitively, watching. Carla spoke before they could say anything.

"I've got some bad news for you guys. Clete's dead. Somebody shot him in the gut in some alley down by the prostitute stroll on Olive. City homicide called the duty officer after they found his credentials. I called Doc, maybe he'll show up here pretty soon. I figured I'd find you guys here."

They were intoxicated and they stared at us like ghouls while the information sunk in. "Let's sit down," Carl Robinson said. They got the telephone numbers of the lonely secretaries and dismissed them then walked to their table with Carla and me following. She released my hand

and we sat down as Pat Brown ordered another pitcher of beer.

We sat and sipped draft beer without speaking. "Clete was a lowlife scum sucker," Pat Brown began. "And it was only a matter of time before somebody killed him."

"Yeah," Carl Robinson chimed in. "But he was one of us. He was a TFD and a city cop. There's a bond there no matter what his character was. Ours isn't much better."

"Ray," Bill Yocum began, "you're the homicide dick. So what now?"

"They're working on it now and they won't stop working on it until they find who did it," I lied. The Irish wake continued as we drank and asked small stupid questions of each other and stared out at the Clayton sky line.

Doc strolled in and slowly walked to our table. A waitress brought him a glass and he filled it from the pitcher. He took a big slug. "Sorry for your loss, guys," he said with sincerity as he removed his Ray Bans and looked at us with his snake eyes. "Clete was a great detective." The TFD's nodded and slurped beer and sat. Doc was studying them and I could see the wheels turning in his big scorched head.

"It's a damn shame that a cop has to get killed in that way," Doc said. The TFD's looked at him with blank stares. "Didn't you guys hear all of the details?"

"No," they said simultaneously. Doc's hairless eyes widened and he studied them like a used Porsche dealer who was just advised by a customer that he didn't care how much the Porsche was, he had to have it.

"He was shot with his own gun. Gut shot like a mad dog and left to die. You guys ever see somebody gut shot?"

"No," they responded.

"It's the most terrible way to die," Doc went on. "If you guys ever see me gut shot, I want you to put me out of my misery with a head shot. The pain is worse than death. I don't know who did it but I do know that when I worked undercover in Mexico, that's the way the Mexicans killed their adversaries, with their own gun. Then they'd leave the gun at the scene to show their enemies they could be killed at any time if they weren't careful. It's kind of like the Italians and the fish wrapped in newspaper. It's a terrorist kind of thing. It unnerves their enemies."

"His own gun, huh," I mumbled.

"Yeah," Doc said nodding and staring with his snake eyes.

I covered my face with my hands and put myself at the scene. Clete was probably harassing the street whores in the Central West End. He didn't know it, but Schwartz was tailing him, waiting for the right moment to pull him over with the premise to have a talk with him.

Clete pulls into the alley, searching for an unsuspecting whore to rob, and Schwartz sees his window of opportunity. He pulls up alongside of Clete's DEA Durango, smiles and says, "pull over and get out, brother; I need to talk to you."

Clete, in a panic, looks for an avenue of escape. But he knew he could run but he couldn't hide from Schwartz. He takes his Colt out and stuffs it into the fat of his belly and his waistband, smiles at Schwartz and stops the Durango, turns it off, and climbs out.

Schwartz climbs out of his pickup, and they meet between the two vehicles. He terrorizes Clete, for recreation, maybe he bitch slaps him some more Then Clete figures, "what the hell," he pulls the Colt and makes a feeble attempt to pull the trigger. But Schwartz is too hip for him.

He knew Clete's tricks. He disarmed Clete, terrorized him for a couple of minutes, then shot him in the gut with his own Colt. He probably talked to Clete while Clete was dying, in excruciating pain. Why? Because Schwartz is a freak. Plain and simple. He wipes Clete's Colt down, tosses it on his body, and drives off. In that part of the world, that's a perfect murder.

"Ray," Carla said.

I removed my hands from my face. They were all looking at me as if I had flipped out and could possibly be dangerous to them or myself. "Yeah, I'm okay."

"Okay, I'll continue," Doc sarcastically said. "You know Clete, he always carried that old Colt revolver in his waistband, covered with fat."

"Old Clete, he was all fat," Pat Brown said, shaking his head.

"Mexican, huh," Bill Yocum muttered. All eyes were on him. "I wonder if Jesus Rangool had anything to do with this?"

"I don't know," Doc said. "I was just making an analogy. I didn't mean anything about Jesus Rangool or anybody else. I was just making a statement about Mexico. That's the way they do it down there, gut shoot them with their own gun."

"Jesus lives close by," Carl Robinson said.

"About eight blocks," Doc replied.

"You could walk that in fifteen minutes," Pat said.

"But," Carla interjected, "how would Jesus get the drop on Clete? That doesn't make sense. Clete would never let Jesus get that close to him."

"It's the stroll area," Doc continued. "Let's say hypothetically that Jesus asked around to find out where he could get a woman, and he was told the red light district was just eight short blocks away at Sarah and Olive. So he walked over there looking for sexual gratification and was waiting on the corner for a lady of the night. Still speaking hypothetically, Clete drives by. We all know he drives around in that area looking for informants and he loves to harass the girls. So Clete observes Jesus standing on the corner and Jesus observes him. Jesus doesn't want to mess with Clete so he ducks down a gangway and winds up in the alley. Clete drives down the alley to see what Jesus is up to and Jesus and Clete start fighting. They're fighting over control of the revolver, and Jesus gets possession of it, pushes Clete away and drills him, wipes the gun and dumps it, then walks the eight blocks back to his apartment. Clete probably pleaded for his life, begged Jesus to call 911 for him, but Jesus didn't care. He's our murderer!"

"It makes sense to me," Bill exclaimed.

"Me, too," Carl said.

"Jesus should have to pay for this," Pat said.

Doc was preying on their naivete and their drunkenness. It's what he always did to them to get them to make stats for his promotion, but this time he's poisoning them and leading them to disaster. Carla recognized it and so did I.

Doc wanted them dead, just like Clete. He was trying to get even for the letter of adultery sent to his wife. The letter that brought his chickens home to roost. The indiscretion that would haunt him for the rest of his life. He said he thought a cop wrote the letter. An agent wouldn't have done that to another agent, he said.

"I've got to go," Doc said. "Be at work bright and early tomorrow morning and we'll discuss this further." He got up and walked out.

"Euclid and West Pine, room five-fifteen," Pat Brown mumbled.

We all drilled him with our eyes: Carla and I out of anxiety; the TFD's stared for their brotherhood and the thrill of revenge and adventure. "It wouldn't hurt to interview him," Pat Brown said.

"He is a viable suspect," Carl Robinson said. "He threatened Clete's life. It's documented in official United

States Government reports."

"Don't do it," Carla sternly said. "I'm telling you guys if you go over there, there's going to be big trouble. You guys are intoxicated. You're not thinking correctly. Don't go over there. Doc shouldn't have told you guys that stuff; it's all hypothetical. Don't let it get to your brains." She was using her hands for emphasis.

"Jesus didn't kill Clete," I said.

"Oh," Bill responded. "How do you know that, Ray?"

"I've been a homicide cop for fifteen years, that's how I know."

There was silence. I dialed Heidi on my cell. "Hey, Clete got killed, did you hear? I figured you did. Can you tell me when Doc was assigned to Mexico? Okay, thanks, I'll see you tomorrow." I folded my cell and slipped it into my pocket. "Doc was fucking with you guys. He's never been assigned to Mexico. He's trying to get you riled up."

"Okay," Bill said. "You don't have to worry about us. We won't go over there. In fact it's time to go home now. I'll pay the bill."

"I can't believe you guys would even consider investigating this," Carla replied. "Clete was nobody's friend. He was ruthless. Nobody was concerned about Jack Parker when he came up missing and he was best friend to all of you. Why this loyalty to Clete?"

Nobody answered. Bill got up and walked to the bar. He came back and stood at the table. "The bill is paid; let's get out of here."

"I'll see you all tomorrow," Carla said as she stood and walked out of the bar. I followed her. She turned to me in the hall. I could tell she was concerned and upset. I again fixated on why she was single. She was gorgeous and vulnerable and she loved cops. "Can you make sure they get home alright?"

"I'll try," I mumbled, wondering why I was so weak for her. She kissed me on the lips again. I was trying to keep my composure as I walked back to the Club. The boys were milling around the bar as I walked in.

"We got to do this," Carl said. "Which car are we taking to Jesus' apartment?"

"Let's take the Seville," Pat responded. "We can all load into it and be comfortable. You coming, Ray?"

I stared at them. "There's no making sense with you guys tonight, is thcrc?"

"Nope," Carl said.

"Yeah, I'll go with you," I said, "but just for an interview, got it? No beatings or gun play."

"Yeah, Ray," Pat Brown said. "Just for an interview. Don't worry, it'll work out for us. You'll see."

I followed them out and we loaded into the Seville. Pat Brown was driving drunk and erratically, bumping parked cars and setting off alarms. We rolled onto the street and I was hoping a Clayton cop would see us and pull us over so something or somebody could put a stop to this insanity.

We jumped onto the Daniel Boone and headed east. Pat missed his exit at Kingshighway. "You missed it, Pat," Carl and Bill shouted. The sunroof was back and we were all enjoying the warm humid air blowing in.

"We haven't shot up the projects lately," Pat said. "I thought we'd do that first."

"Yeah, man," Bill and Carl replied. I sat down deep in the back seat and contemplated asking to be let out but I didn't. I was in for a penny, in for a pound. I could have begged off at the Club but I didn't. I could have told the guys that I knew who killed Clete, that it was a co-worker, a DEA agent, a steroid drugged predator.

Pat made a pass by the high-rise projects. He was begging for trouble on this fine night. I took note of him:

clean cut, blonde mullet, insane smile. He felt indestructible. Bill, who was in the front seat, pulled his Glock, racked one into the chamber, stood and fired twenty rounds of forty caliber Glock ammo at the high-rise building.

The bullets were sparking off of the brickwork. Pat sped away, the junky Caddy engine screaming. “YEAH, FUCK YEAH,” they shouted. “TAKE THAT, YOU FUCKING DOPE DEALERS.” I scrunched down deeper into the seat.

Pat turned around and made another pass by the high-rise. Carl had his Glock in his hand, stood through the sunroof from the back seat and emptied his clip. He was screaming a rebel curse and laughing, his neck veins protruding like an abstract painting as Pat accelerated toward the Central West End while the boys reloaded.

We pulled in front of the twelve-story rehabilitation center. It was state-owned and secured by a private security company. We climbed out and walked toward the front door where a security guard was watching and measuring us.

I looked up at the fifth floor and wondered if Jesus was watching us as we headed toward his comfortable and safe domain. Must be dope dealer heaven for him, I mused.

“You can’t come in here this late,” the skinny wino-looking security guard said.

“We’re with DEA,” Bill Yocum said, holding up his credentials. “We got to go to five, official business.” The guard examined our creds and waved us by. We strolled to the elevator, got on, and pushed five.

It stopped in four seconds. The door dinged and slid open. A group of hall-shuffling brain-damaged rehabbers were standing in front of the elevator door. They observed us and froze, wide-eyed and confused.

A man was crouched down in the middle of the group, his bandage turban protruding from the mass of dull thoughts. We strolled off and into the hallway and stopped.

The turban was bobbing up and down, then the man wearing it stood. It was Jesus.

"YOU FUCKING COPS AIN'T GOING TO BEAT JESUS RANGOOL AGAIN," he shouted as he pulled his snub 38 and began firing at us.

Bill Yocum caught the first round, center mass. The force of the projectile blew him back into the elevator. We all pulled our Glocks and pointed them at the group of stoned zombies trying to get a shot at Jesus who had ducked behind the shufflers again, using them as a shield.

The brain-damaged group were stoned and goofy, but they had watched enough television to know when they were about to be shot. They all hit the floor leaving Jesus without any cover. Carl and Pat shot Jesus five times each before I could get my finger on the trigger. He fell to the floor and died with his 38 still clutched in his right hand.

"BILL, YOU OKAY?" Carl screamed as Bill rolled around on the floor of the elevator holding his gut and moaning. The hall filled with curious zombies squeezing toward the elevator door trying to look inside to watch the young, bright, muscular cop die, their eyes wide with anticipation and drugs and fear while the elevator door kept trying to close.

Bill opened his eyes and stared back at the shufflers. "Where the hell am I? Who the hell are they?" The shuffle zombies were the last beings Bill observed on this earth. He died with his eyes open and his Glock still in its holster. He had caught the first round.

"GET OUT OF THE WAY," Pat screamed at the zombies as he forced his way past them. He looked up and down the hallway. "ISN'T THERE A NURSES' STATION ON THIS FLOOR?" He grabbed a zombie by the neck. "WHERE'S THE FUCKING NURSE? WHERE'S THE FUCKING DOCTOR?"

"There ain't none at night," was the response.

I dialed 911 on my cell. "A police officer has been shot, fifth floor of southwest corner of Euclid and West Pine. Officer in need of aid." I walked back to the elevator. Carl was giving mouth-to-mouth to Bill, Pat was pumping on Bill's heart. Their efforts were futile. Bill Yocum was never coming back.

Two cop killings in the same day. A television anchor's dream. I imagined the hype by the talking heads. "While attempting to arrest a murder suspect in the death of hero cop Cletus Jones, his close friend and partner was shot to death by the suspect. Police believe that Mexican immigrant Jesus Rangool murdered Cletus Jones, and then sought refuge in his medical rehab apartment at Euclid and West Pine. When detectives attempted to interview Rangool he opened up with a 38-revolver killing Detective Bill Yocum."

Jesus was now the killer of Cletus Jones, posthumously. It fit, it was tidy, and the media machine would buy it. The sirens started; they sounded like they were coming from all parts of the city. Cops, ambulance, fire trucks. A mass of uniforms invaded the fifth floor sending the hall zombies shuffling into their apartments.

EMS worked on Bill. Their efforts were just for show. They pronounced him and carted him away. The questioning began. Why? What happened? The homicide supervisor instructed us to report to homicide downtown. We drove down in the Seville.

We got our story straight on the way downtown and wrote it out for the investigators at the homicide office. We were following a lead on the murder of Cletus Jones. We thought we had a viable suspect. Time was of the essence. The guy could have fled to Mexico. We were doing our duty.

The supervisor called me into his office after reading our

statements. I had known him for sixteen years. He wore the brown off-the-rack suit that we all wore, the bland tie with the off-color shirt. He was pale because of the hours and the diet and the booze, and his hand shook as he fired up a Marlboro square and tried to suck in his belly.

He was trying to study me but my persona was too much for him to analyze. Blocking analysis was part of my new lifestyle, and no one had the tools to break through to the real me.

He looked at me as if I was from another planct. "You've changed, Ray." I ran my hand through my balding semi-mullet and smiled the used Porsche dealer smile. His eyes followed the Rolex and the diamond rings and he seemed disgusted at my black Tee and jeans, my flat stomach and muscular physique.

"Do you guys drive around in that Seville?"

"Yeah."

I was still smiling. "I've got a Corvette that I drive most of the time."

"Four guys in a Seville like that one shot up the projects tonight," He said. "I have a feeling that you're out-of-control friends heard about Cletus Jones and got drunk. Their anger mounted and they and you," he punctuated with the point of his cigarette, "decided to go and shoot up the projects. After that mission was completed you decided to go and interview a possible suspect. But it wasn't for an interview. It was for a killing. That's the way it always is when a cop gets killed. Somebody has to pay. The momentum builds. Remember, Ray. You were the one who coined that theory." We stared.

"Was it you and your little friends who shot up the projects?"

"No," I said sincerely as I stared directly into his eyes, with my dealer smile and said to myself, "It has low mileage and hasn't been hurt at all. A grandmother drove it."

"You going to be able to come back here when this is all over, Ray?"

"Oh, yeah," I said smiling. "I'll be back, someday."

"I knew I was lying to him and to myself. I thought of the Feeb, Moynihan. He warned me. I let them brainwash me, but I had no choice. It was either play the game or return to the P.D., a failure. How would he know?

Are federal agents so much smarter than us cops? It's like they can read us and manipulate us at will. Maybe it's something they teach them in the federal agent academy. How to manipulate local cops, 101.

First you give them ultimate power, then you give them money, Corvettes and Porsches, Rolexes and diamonds, and beautiful special agents to play with; next you turn them loose on the deserving dope dealers of the world. It was too late for me. I was one of them and there was no life after DEA. I was sure of it.

20

We didn't work for ten days. We would come into the office, but we didn't do any deals. Doc was cool with it, but I could see the anxiety mounting. He needed stats like a junky needed heroin. It wouldn't be long before he started badgering and threatening us to do some deals.

The double cop funeral was a media frenzy. Cops from all over the country came into St. Louis to be a part of it. Clete's relatives marveled at the emotion, tears and respect bestowed upon him in death by his peers. In reality, the tears and respect were for Bill Yocum. As usual, Clete was just along for the ride, snipping and pilfering at the emotional runoff of the event.

I sat in observance throughout the event replaying my ride with Bill Yocum back to civilization from Madison County, Illinois. I smiled to myself when I got to the part about the seat breaking in the Camaro and the beer spewing over his chest in front of the Missouri Highway Patrolman. Bill just wanted to be like his dad. Another cop's kid dead.

I was leaving the washroom when Jim Schwartz strolled in. "Feeb snitch," he muttered at me with hatred. I despised TFD Cletus Jones, but I despised Special Agent Jim Schwartz more. I wasn't afraid of him but I didn't want him to know it. I had to stare up at him, and I looked at us in the restroom mirror. I was a dwarf compared to him and I was five-eleven, one-ninety, and in shape.

"I know your secret, Jim," I muttered to him.

"What did you say, you fucking twirp?" he said to me.

"Unlike the rest of these play-cops out here, I'm a real investigator. I know your secret. You see, I've been trained as a homicide detective. I know killers and I know how to spot them."

He came out with his forty caliber Glock and put it

inches from my face. It was a typical DEA Special Agent fear tactic. I had pulled his hole card and he resented it. I was supposed to cower in fear of him, but I didn't. He would shoot me if we were in an alley near the stroll, but not in the DEA restroom in Clayton, Missouri.

"You know what happens when you live by the gun, Jim." I walked out leaving him standing alone in the john holding his Glock.

He stormed out after me, his gun now in its holster. We were alone in the hallway, "You think you're immune to my wrath, C/I with a badge? You think you know my secret, huh? I'm a United States of America Special Agent, asshole. I can do anything I want to you. You'll see." I walked back to the office and plopped at my desk.

I was contemplating my next move with Jim Schwartz. It was going to come to a head, I just didn't know when. I wasn't going to run from him. I doubted his clout within the organization, even though he was a G/S thirteen, journeyman grade special agent. I blew it off.

It was rainy and cool so we decided to eat in, which meant we were going down the hallway to the Club for lunch: Heidi and I, Pat Brown, Monica Rose, Mike Schweig, Carl Robinson, Ross Milton and Carla. Doc was circling and becoming uptight. We all could see it and we waited for the onslaught.

"That C/I Henry Darby. You heard from him lately?"

I stared at his burned and healing face and wondered if it itched. "No, Doc."

"You need to touch base with him. He might be able to give us a deal. He's got to know some dope dealers that we don't know about. Put some pressure on him."

"Okay, Doc," I said as we strolled out.

I flipped open my cell as we entered the club and seated ourselves I pressed the button to auto-dial Henry Darby's cell. I got his voice mail. I dialed the restaurant and got his manager, Gina. "Where's Henry?"

"I haven't seen him in two days," she informed. "When I last saw him he was in the cubbyhole office working late. He said he was going to work a while longer, then go home. I was thinking about calling you. I tried his cell and I only got his voice mail. He put me in charge. I'm running the business now. We're serving lunch now. You guys should come in for lunch."

"Okay," I replied. "If you hear from him have him call me." I was contemplating the worst case scenario. Heidi was watching me.

"What's up?" she asked.

"I don't know. I mean, I'm not sure. Henry Darby is off the radar and has been for a couple of days. Probably means nothing, but it might mean something. Viktor Agron is still on the loose. Henry told us Viktor was going to kill him for setting him up with us. It's a possibility."

"If I were Viktor Agron, I wouldn't be anywhere around St. Louis or the East side," Heidi commented, "He's a marked man in these parts. He can only hide for so long and then somebody's going to recognize him and call the locals. He's probably in Mexico or the Caribbean. Did Henry go to the bar?"

"Yeah."

"Bad move on his part."

We hadn't ordered yet. "Let's take a ride," I said, grabbing my windbreaker from the back of my chair as we headed for the parking garage. We climbed into the Corvette and I headed south toward Henry's house.

I drove for about fifteen minutes and we made a pass by Henry's home. There were newspapers in the driveway and the yard and the lawn needed to be mowed. I spun around and made another pass, then drove the Corvette into the driveway, climbed out and went to the front door.

I rang and knocked and looked in the windows. I used the key I had previously gotten from Gina the body and entered the house. The air was stale inside. I walked directly to the safe room, unlocked it and entered. He wasn't there. I looked in the garage from the kitchen door. His beat-up Oldsmobile wasn't in the garage, so I exited the house, locked it up, and wandered back to the Corvette. "He's gone."

"To where?"

"Don't know. Maybe he's taking our advice and trying to hide out while Viktor is on the loose."

"Sounds good to me. Let's eat."

I climbed in and we headed toward downtown. "We can eat at Henry's place; Gina said she was serving lunch now."

"Cool."

I parked the Corvette on the street, and we walked in and up and into the mezzanine restaurant. The place was packed; all of the tables were taken so we sat at the bar.

Gina saw us and came over. "Having lunch?"

"Yeah."

"Lasagna with a salad is the special today," she said with a smile.

"I'll have it with iced tea," Heidi said.

"Me, too," I said studying her. She was acting strange around us, avoiding eye contact.

"She wouldn't look me in the eye," I said to Heidi as I sat down.

"I noticed. Wonder what's up with that."

"I'm going to ask her a direct question. Help me monitor her."

I waved for Gina to come to our table. She forced a smile and stood before us like a criminal giving testimony. "Where's Henry?"

Her eyes shot down to the left; her head remained down. "I don't know," she replied.

"When you see him, tell him to contact us," I said. "Has anyone approached you asking his whereabouts?"

"No!" Her eyes shot down and to the left again.

"Okay Gina, thanks." She strolled away. "She's lying!"

"Yep!"

A server brought our lunch and we quickly ate and tried to pay the bill. Gina wouldn't take our money. She hugged me without looking at me. We walked back to the Corvette and headed for Clayton. The rain started coming down in buckets.

The Corvette's windshield wipers were banging trying to keep the windshield clear, and the windshield was leaking at the base dropping water onto our ankles and feet. I was forced to drive slowly because the sports car didn't have any traction on the wet pavement and sudden stops could result in slides. We pulled into the garage and climbed out, happy to be safely back.

Carla looked at our wet feet and pants legs as we walked into the office, and laughed. "Corvette roadster, right?"

I nodded. Heidi and I went into the sound room and stuck the tape into the machine. "She knows about the Corvette leaking," I said.

"Yeah, so what?"

"How hot and heavy was she with Jack Parker?"

"It was a thing. A DEA thing. I'm sure she felt like she was going to get her share. Everybody else did. She's gorgeous and single and probably had a thing with him."

"What about Sue Lee?" I asked.

"Probably."

"What about Doc's girlfriend, the lovely Tina Brown?"

"It's been speculated."

"Did he miss anybody?"

"Don't think so." She was smirking.

We went back to our desks. I accessed my computer to do some snooping in NADDIS. Square Bidness stormed in and went into Doc's office. That always meant trouble, and the TFD's and special agents took note of his presence. He stormed out and gave me a dirty look. Everyone took note of to whom his wrath was directed. It was me, and I couldn't figure out why.

About ten minutes went by. Special Agent Jim Schwartz, my nemesis, strolled into Doc's office. He was in there for approximately five minutes, then came strolling out. He too was giving me killer looks.

Doc came out and walked to my desk. "I knew it was you," he quietly said. "Give me the keys to the Corvette." I stared at him, then obtained the keys from my briefcase and tossed them to him.

"Give me the Rolex and the two diamond rings." I took them off and laid them on my desk. He grabbed them and walked back into his office. I wondered what had transpired in Doc's office between him and Square Bidness, and Jim Schwartz. I knew I was apparently on the outs with Doc because of something that was said about me.

I ran it back in my brain. I came to the conclusion that Schwartz must have told Doc I was the one who had written the letter to his wife informing her of Doc's infidelity. I had been set up by Schwartz. My existence in DEA would never be the same. I knew it.

I needed to get out of the office; a surveillance was definitely in my future. I wondered if Heidi would go with me. I sent her an e-mail asking her. Her computer dinged and she looked around as she switched over to the internet and read it. She looked over to me and nodded. I closed my computer and stood, preparing to leave.

Doc came storming out his office and walked to Heidi's

desk. "You are forbidden to go on surveillance with TFD Arnold." He stormed over to me, his hairless eyes, white ointment and scab-covered face, threatening me with his anger. "You Judas, you've forsaken our friendship. I'll never trust you again." He stormed into his office and slammed the door. Doc had been monitoring Heidi's computer. I glanced around the room. The agents and TFD's wouldn't look at me. I was on my own. Nobody in the task force was going to side with anybody who was on the outs with Doc.

I walked out and took the stairs down to the parking garage, walked past the Corvette, the Porsche, the Bimmers, and the Hemi and walked onto the sidewalk. I flagged a cab, got in, and looked around Clayton for an instant.

"Where to, buddy?"

"South Broadway and Bates," I said. "I'll show you the house when we get there. It's hidden behind the trees."

I paid the cabby and walked around the house to the backyard. Tyrone was in his house on the deck watching me as I made the turn.

He sauntered out and wagged at me, then got his tennis ball for me to throw. I tossed it and felt like I was skipping school, but I wasn't skipping; I got expelled. Not a new experience for cops. I was ostracized from the task force though, and that was a new experience.

I tossed the ball and had the paranoid ponders about everything: me and Heidi and my so-called friends in the task force, Viktor Agron and the missing TFD, Jack Parker. I had to capture Viktor Agron. He was deserving, and it was my job to incarcerate him. I felt guilty for allowing him to escape.

I figured if I could arrest him, it would make Doc happy, and maybe the whole mess would be forgotten. Or at least, maybe Doc would believe me over Jim Schwartz. If not, I would remain on the ostracized list for life. Man, I liked that damn Heidi.

I tossed and Tyrone retrieved. I needed something substantial to do. The address from the Caddy at Viktor's place in Savannah. It needed investigating. I searched a couple of pairs of Levis and I found the computer printout in a back pocket. 4438 Signal Hill Drive, East St. Louis, Illinois. I was familiar with it; at one time, it was the Hollywood Hills of the East side. It was where the crooked labor leaders and the crooked politicians had lavish brick homes built.

I was still a cop and I was still detached and sworn as a DEA Task Force Detective. I was a Fed and a local; Doc couldn't change that. I walked to the garage and looked at my vehicles. Which will it be? The crazy El Camino or the groovy Austin Healey? Crazy El Camino.

I got in and cranked it. The three-fifty roared and then smoothed out. Tyrone jumped in via the passenger side window. I got out and coaxed him out and walked him to the backyard, then went back to the garage, climbed in and backed out.

I made a right on Broadway, then jumped on I-55, bombed across the Poplar Street Bridge then jumped off at the first East side exit. I was on Missouri Avenue. Once the creme-de-la creme shopping area for both sides of the river. Now there are only pawn shops and massage parlors. Organized crime from Chicago and Colorado now controls the entire city. It happened because nobody cared enough to try and stop it. In Illinois, there is only one city, Chicago.

I made my way slowly through the city and up the gradual rise to 89th Street, then backtracked to Signal Hill, made some rights and a left and cruised into the part of the East side where every home has a view. I passed 4438, a brick split level built by the German immigrants in the early fifties.

It was a fortress built to last forever. There was a veranda high up decorated with tropical plants and pool furniture, and I assumed there was a lavish in-ground pool where the host and hostess would sit with their guests and sip whiskey drinks and look down at the squalor of East St. Louis.

They would look over at the struggling but still alive skyline of St. Louis and say boring little snippets like, "What a shame, the way this city turned out. St. Louis had better watch out or it's going to turn out the same way."

I looked for a vantage point where I could park and see what was transpiring without drawing too much attention. I idled around and found it at the end of the street, a dead end without any houses and some pin oaks to hide behind.

Surveillance was second nature to me. I hunkered down and watched and waited for anything, anyone, any movement that I could catalogue into my psyche until my mind picked up that right piece of data, something I could understand and make a move on. I sat for two hours without anything. An unusual experience.

An elderly lady came out into her yard and looked around the neighborhood. She looked down toward me, sitting in the crazy El Camino, bored and now obvious. I waved to her and she waved back. I got out and smiled and made my way toward her. She didn't run and I was surprised. She had to be somebody's loving grandmother: denim dress, hair in a bun, apron with pockets to keep treats in. "Morning, ma'am."

She stood her ground and looked me up and down. "You a cop?"

"No," I casually lied, "P I."

"Oh, I figured you were something like that. Why you in this neighborhood?"

I needed a false name, just to get Granny started. It was a

charade and I had to play it to the hilt. "Lauren Volz," I said staring.

"I don't know her. There ain't nobody around here by that name."

"That's her house," I said pointing at the brick fortress.

"Oh, I know her but her name ain't Lauren whatever."

It was a standoff. She was waiting for me to ask her the obvious question. The answer was going to cost me.

"What is the name of the person living in that house?"

"That depends," she wryly said, staring and smiling. "I've got some weed for sale," she continued with the skit. "Want to buy some?"

"Oh, sure I'll buy some. How much is a bag?"

"Twenty dollars," she happily replied. I reached into my pocket and came out with my wallet, ripped a twenty out and handed it to her. She retrieved a parcel from her apron and handed me a little baggie of weed. I stuck it into my pocket. "Helen Gross," she said.

I stared as if the information didn't satisfy my desires the way I thought it would. I was hooked and she knew it. This was her game now and she played it well.

"Tell me about Helen Gross. What does she look like?" She was smiling her green-toothed smile.

"More weed?"

"Yeah," I said as I gave her another twenty. She gave me another baggie. I crammed it into my pocket.

"Flashy blonde," she continued. "Some people might say she's beautiful. Body like a goddess. Rich, too."

"Rich blonde," I muttered. "What does she do for a living?" Her hand was out with a baggie in it. I gave her another twenty, took the baggie and crammed it.

"She works at the Inferno Club. She's a stripper. She ain't home much. Comes in late at night or early in the morning, just in time to shower and get fixed up, then she's out the door and into her Caddy on the way to the Inferno. She does a matinee and an evening performance. Packs them in. The marks come from all over to see her. It must be quite a show. Some of them even track her here and sit outside her house hoping to get a glance at her. I watch her house; it's better than television. Want to know what her stage name is?"

"Yeah." Her hand was out with another baggie of weed in it.

I ripped her another twenty and crammed the baggie. "Helen of Troy, Illinois." She let it sink in and then laughed as I smiled. "Kind of catchy, ain't it?"

"Yeah." I smiled for effect.

"She comes out on stage in this pure white Helen of Troy outfit with her blonde hair moving slightly in the fan breeze, then she starts her dance. The johns go crazy and start tossing cash onto the stage. Then she strips and goes into the crowd and lets them touch her and tongue her and cram money into the little pouch she has on her waist. She kills them and she makes a killing doing it."

I was envisioning Helen of Troy stripping on stage. "She had a boyfriend who she lets stay with her for a while. Give me your cell number and I'll call you when he shows up." I jotted my cell number down and handed it to her. She looked at the number and then looked at me. "What's your name?"

"Ray."

"Ray what?"

"Ray Richards."

I was all DEA, working undercover just like Doc cribbed me to do. "Her boyfriend doesn't come around very often, though," she continued.

"He doesn't?"

"Naw, her hubby came onto the scene. He put a stop to

that."

"Hubby? What does he look like?"

Her hand came up with another baggie in it. I gave her another twenty. "Foreign looking, scary guy, muscles and hair like a television preacher. Deep tan. A predator, I can tell. He comes and goes, but lately he's been here quite a lot. He's got two other predator-looking guys with him. They all look alike, but the one guy stands out. You know what I mean? He's not the oldest or the biggest, but I can tell he's the one in charge. I think maybe it's his walk or attitude. Anyway, he's scary."

"Dominant dog," I muttered.

"Right. There's one in every litter, ain't there? But you know we're all dogs from the same litter. The one who wins is the dominant one, until the next contest."

I didn't comment. Granny, dope-dealing philosopher. Only in East St. Louis. "Has the litter been around here lately?"

"Yeah. Came in late last night, left early this morning. They don't stay for long. I've got the feeling they're on the run. Probably got more than one lair to hide in. Drive old nondescript cars, Chevy's and Fords with tinted windows. They're slick, that's for sure."

"Thanks."

"Don't mention it. If you ever want some more dynamite weed, you know where to come."

I walked back to the crazy El Camino, climbed in, cranked it, and drove out of the complex. I was on Missouri Avenue but got bored with it and jumped onto the interstate and over to the west side. I tossed the baggies out of the window at the Poplar Street Bridge entrance and felt like I got my money's worth from the old lady.

Helen of Troy, Illinois. I've got to see the show. I checked my watch; the matinee was probably already in progress. I had time to go to the gym, have a steak with Tyrone, and relax before the evening performance. I needed some time to myself, something a DEA operative rarely gets.

I did a whole body, drove home, ate a big rare steak with Tyrone, and had the endorphin racing through my brain when my cell rang. I checked the caller I D, it was Heidi. I almost didn't answer. There was a possibility that Doc was monitoring her cell. I had a vision of her nude and ready and willing. "Hello?"

"Hey," she began. "What have you been doing all day?"

"I've been around. DEA isn't my life. I have other things to amuse myself."

"Yeah, right. When are you coming back to the office?"

"Maybe never."

"What? Come on, Ray," she exclaimed. "Don't be childish. You had a rift with your supervisor. Get over it and get real. Come in in the morning. Things will be back to normal. Doc was just letting off steam. He'll get off of your case. He probably feels stupid about the whole chain of events. He's an intelligent man, Ray. He's not going to let this thing between you two get in the way of progress. It's cases and stats to him, remember?"

"Is Doc listening in? Is he monitoring your cell? You don't know for sure, do you, Heidi?"

"Bye, Ray. Hope to see you in the morning."

I deactivated and tossed the cell onto the couch. "Fucking DEA."

It was getting dark, the bewitching hour when the daytime shooters from the west turn into sex ghouls and head east. Helen of Troy, Illinois. Catchy! I headed east for the second time this day and took the exit that dumped me into Rush City, a tar-paper shack neighborhood within the boundaries of East St. Louis, between the railroad tracks and the Mississippi River, a place where dead bodies show up overnight like hard-boiled eggs on Easter morning.

I wound through it, followed the gravel road to the Inferno and cruised the massive parking lot looking at cars. I did it on impulse; it's what cops do to have a feeling of ease when they go into a gathering of humans who are so far removed from reality that they squander their cash on booze and strippers. If I see a car I'm familiar with, then I'll know who and what to expect when I go through the front door.

I saw a familiar car, an Oldsmobile 98, black four-door, plain with small hubcaps and black wall tires. It was Sig Otto's car, the potato cannon C/I. I started having second thoughts about Sig. I knew he was a strange duck but I didn't peg him as a sex ghoul.

I reassessed my values. So he likes to look at beautiful naked women. That doesn't make him a sex ghoul. He's single and rich and in his sixties, so what's the big deal? In fact, I looked forward to seeing him again. I liked the guy. I parked and slowly walked toward the front of the massive building.

The structure was newly constructed out of prefabricated metal sheets, the way a modern barn or machine shed would be built. A group of lawyers in Denver, Colorado owned it. That fact had been in the newspaper. I wondered how organized crime in Chicago allowed that to happen, unless Chicago criminals actually own it and the lawyers are a front for them.

I was satisfied with that theory and continued to study the structure as I walked toward it. It was bolted together and could be dismantled and moved to another location in a couple of days if need be. The land was flood plain and not worth anything. The place probably held five-hundred crazed customers, swilling and imagining Helen of Troy, Illinois, was theirs as they tossed cash at her.

I opened the front door and walked inside. A bouncer, who was big, steroid-freaked and tattooed stood in my way as I tried to get in. "Twenty-dollars, and walk through the metal detector," he said with his hand out. I turned around, walked back outside, hid my guns in the crazy El Camino, returned, and handed him a twenty as I walked through the metal detector.

The music hit me as I went through the inner door; Ike Turner, "Feeling Low Down," catchy R & B for a stripper who was doing her thing on stage. She eventually got nude and walked into the audience as I walked toward the bar and stood. There was no place to sit. The bartender shouted something at me. I responded with a "BUD LIGHT" shout and he brought me one.

I sipped and watched the stripper do her thing for the crowd. Her moniker was Pussy Lips, and I couldn't put it together until I observed her tying her lips in a knot for the boys and then untying them without using her hands. The crowd went wild and tossed rolled-up bills at her as she continued to bump and grind and hump the seated weirdos.

I was having fragmented thoughts again, something I do when I'm stressed. I was thinking about arresting Viktor Agron and how I was going to do it. I was going to need help since he was on the run with two other criminals. Granny said there were two more and they all looked alike, like brothers.

The confidential informant, Henry Darby, didn't say anything about Viktor having any brothers involved in his criminal enterprise. Probably two more Russian gangsters from Little Odessa recruited by Viktor. Eventually they're all going to show up at Helen of Troy, Illinois' house. If I saw them and I was alone, I would be screwed. There would surely be a shootout, something I wanted to avoid.

I wondered what the Feeb Moynihan would do in a case

like this. Another fragmented thought. Why the hell am I thinking about Moynihan? He is a weirdo freak Feeb. He was my adversary, maybe that's why. But Doc is my adversary, too, in a roundabout way. And now Special Agent Jim Schwartz, the murdering thieving steroid freak is my new nemesis.

There has always been one in my life. I had always dealt with them in my own fashion. I allowed them to underestimate me and then I pounced. It had always worked for me. It will work again. But none of my past enemies were as big or as dangerous as Jim Schwartz.

All of those guys were authority figures. That's where my problem began. I hated authority figures, and I knew that I, too, was an authority figure. It was confusing. Any authority figure is my adversary if they are trying to assert their authority on me. That's the way it has always been with me which is why I have fragmented thoughts and a fragile brain. I scanned the crowd for Sig through the smoke and revolving lights.

Pussy Lips was still in the crowd. She was bumping and grinding and tying knots, and she was heading toward the bar to do her thing for us poor freaks who couldn't get a seat at the stage. She bumped and humped the guy next to me and was on me before I could kill the beer and turn around to order another.

Her fake tits were on my chest and she was humping me like a French poodle and glaring into my eyes. I gave her a fiver and she went on to the next guy as I shouted for another beer.

Moynihan would probably use a confidential informant as a backup; my fragmented thinking kicked in again. If he was on the outs with his group of agents, he would no doubt resort to a C/I as backup. It's what cops do. When they arrest the bad guy, the C/I is never mentioned in the report.

The cop or agent is a hero and his group welcomes him back with open arms.

Pussy Lips moved back to, and then off the stage, probably carrying close to a grand in her little pouch, tax-free. The master of ceremonies was on stage. He was obnoxious and trying to look and act like Tom Cruise. I wanted to beat him with my fists as he tried to get the ghouls ready for Helen of Troy, Illinois. He finally got off-stage and Helen came out.

The crowd was screaming and tossing cash at her before she could start her routine. She was dressed in a white linen dress with a gold tiara. Her long blonde hair was blowing in the breeze, and she looked as pure as the driven snow.

She took the microphone and stared at the crowd. They became quiet. She had a little girl voice as she spoke into the microphone, "I'm Helen of Troy, Illinois, and my husband can't satisfy me. Will somebody take me away from him and be my man?"

There was a new set of bouncers and they were in the darkness lining the stage. The drunk businessmen from the west were clamoring to get to her. The bouncers shoved them away as Helen started her routine. She danced and pranced to a bluesy Jimmy Smith tune and slowly removed the white linen dress.

Her body was flawless and I could see why she was so revered by the freaks. They tossed money and the bouncers picked it up for her. I watched her every move and examined every inch of her. She was no natural blonde.

She was making her way toward the steps leading off-stage and into the audience. There were two other bouncer-looking guys in the crowd approaching the businessmen and setting up personal lap dances with her. The freaks paid the two thugs and then a third bouncer would escort Helen over to them.

She would let them feel her and tongue her, and she would sit on their laps for an instant, and then she would be off to the next freak. Sig slid up next to me and nudged me with his shoulder. I offered him my hand and we shook as we watched Helen of Troy, Illinois, work the crowd.

She bled the patrons at the tables and was making her way toward the bar. She got through the spot and stage lights, and I could see her face very well as she came nearer to me. Her name wasn't Helen; it was Ellen. It was Ellen Agron, Viktor's estranged wife whom I met in Savannah, Georgia, during the undercover dope deal.

She got close to me and Sig and stared at me; she made me and her head jolted as if she had been punched. She stared hard at Sig and then danced her way back to the stage, said something to the two bouncers and then went off-stage out of sight. The show was over.

The two bouncers collecting her cash came closer to me. It had to be the associates of Viktor Agron, the weaker pups of the litter. They were getting aggressive like sharks feeding, making abrupt moves and running their hands through their long combed back hair.

They didn't appear concerned about me being in the club on official business; they weren't wanted for anything. They wanted to hurt me, probably kill me, and they didn't know how to get the job done in front of five hundred drunk lovesick West side businessmen.

I started moving toward the door. Sig followed me. I glanced at him and he acted as if he knew I was in peril. The look-alike gangsters were bouncing off customers to get to me as we moved. We got near the metal detector and I charged through the door and ran toward the crazy El Camino with Sig beside me.

I had the key out and in the lock and the door open in seconds. My 357 crotch rocket was under the arm rest. I grabbed it and turned, pointing it toward the club. The gangsters were in pursuit but they stopped and swerved behind the corner of the building as I flourished the magnum at them.

Sig stared at me as if he was my dad. "What now, Ray?"

"Get in your car and follow me."

I climbed into the El Camino, fired it and tore out of the parking lot with Sig behind me in the Olds. We drove through Rush City and onto the interstate and headed west. I drove straight to my house, parked in the garage, got out and waited for Sig to climb out of the Olds. "Welcome to my humble abode." He shook my hand again and we walked inside.

I opened the sliding glass door for Tyrone. He came tearing in and sniffed Sig then plopped down on the kitchen floor. "I don't have any alcohol in my house. Can I offer you a bottle of water?"

"Yes, Ray."

He was smiling. I got two bottles out of the fridge and handed him one. We sipped spring water at the kitchen table. He began the conversation.

"I would not have let those two thugs harm you, Ray. I could have killed both of them in an instant with Kempo Karate. They look at me and they see an old man. If they would have tried to harm you it would have been their last violent act."

I stared at him trying to figure out where he was coming from. Why this undying loyalty to me? Is it because I'm a cop? Does DEA have something to do with this?

"Do you know those guys, Sig?"

"Yes, they are pimps and dope dealers. I know their kind which brings me to a question." I stared inquisitively. "Did you and Agent Anderson act on the information I gave to you?"

"Yes. I apologize for not getting back to you with the outcome. It was a successful crusade. Several drug traffickers were taken out of business, several are still on the lam but indicted federally and are being sought. The leader of the organization is in hiding. Viktor Agron. Do you know him?"

"I have heard of him."

I was using physiognomy on him, trying to read him and he was sending me positive signals. Is he for real or just good at hiding his true intentions? He is a confidential informant, and only Feebs and old homicide cops consider them friends.

But, he might be my salvation if I can trust him. I need him more than I ever needed a C/I. I've got to get Viktor Agron. I've got to trust Sig Otto.

"We can work together on this one, if you want, Sig. You can help me capture Viktor Agron." He was reading me now staring and watching me like any intelligent human would when asked to risk his life for a cop.

"Vik Agron," he muttered. "What about Agent Anderson? Will she be assisting us?"

"No. She's working on another case right now. It'll just be you and me."

"Okay, I'll do it. When do we start?"

He paused for an instant. His eagerness gave me concern.

"Tomorrow night," I replied, thinking this was too easy. "Do you have a cell?"

"Yes," he replied. He pulled a note pad and pen from his pocket and jotted the number down. He handed it to me.

"I'll call you tomorrow evening and tell you the plan." He stood and we shook on it and he walked out. I continued to consider the possibilities, had fragmented thoughts, and then went to bed.

21

It was early when the phone rang. As usual I didn't want to answer it. It was always a hassle, always questionable news, always someone wanting something from me, usually my blood and my soul. I looked at the number on my cell, it was Heidi. I let it ring; she didn't leave a message.

I breakfasted and sat on the deck watching the Mississippi roll by, the boats going to and coming back from Florida. I watched the occupants with binoculars, and I could tell the difference between the professional yacht delivery boys and the owners.

The pros were all business. I could see it on their faces, and there were never any women on board. The private guys, the owners of their boats, were always laughing and cavorting with some dynamite gal as they drifted by. I tossed the ball and worried as Tyrone retrieved.

I had called Sig. It was 2045 and just turning dark when he rolled into my gravel circular driveway and tooted his horn. I walked out and slid in and we were off to the East side for an evening of surveillance and adventure. He was dressed strangely. He looked as if he was going to play golf or to hunt grouse or to fish for walleye: khakis, open polo and a ball cap.

"My friend," he said as I entered his Olds, "it is so good to see you again." The guy never stopped selling himself. "We will have a fine night. We will learn many things this night and hopefully catch that bastard Viktor Agron. Am I right, my friend?"

"Yeah, Sig, you're right." I watched him, still trying to run physiognomy on him and coming up empty. He was either sincere or a damn good con man. "Do you know where Signal Hill is?"

"Of course my friend. It is where the wealthy East side

folks lived. Do you know much about East St. Louis, Ray?"

"Yeah. I was born there. I left there when I was five, but my relatives all stayed there for Twenty Years or so before they moved to Belleville. I hung out there when I was a kid going to the gangster night clubs and underage drinking establishments. I got hooked on women, fast cars, blues, and jazz in East St. Louis. Head for Signal Hill, Sig. East St. Louis was a neat town at one time. Too bad it's dying."

"That's a facade, Ray. It's not dying. It's alive, but not well. You have to get into the underground of the city to actually appreciate it. I'm over here almost every night. There are great restaurants just outside of town in Belleville. I frequent them and I'm well known there. When I walk in I'm referred to as Mister Otto and I get the best table in the house. I can gamble at the casino and win at the craps tables. That's hard to do on the west side. When I get bored, I go to a strip bar like the Inferno, and see beautiful women doing their thing. Women like Helen of Troy, Illinois. Is she a beauty or what?" He was laughing his crazy laugh, the kind he used when he shot the windows out of Moynihan's G car.

"Yeah, she's a beauty."

"She has star appeal," Sig continued. "You know, she makes over a million dollars a year stripping and escorting, and it's tax-free, all in cash."

I stared at him, "How did you know that?"

"Club gossip, my friend."

"She's Viktor Agron's wife. Did you know that?"

He looked at me as he drove, "Yes, Ray, I know."

"Those thugs who were chasing us last night, they're Viktor Agron's Russian henchman. Did you know that?"

"Yes, Ray, I know."

"How do you know them?" He was forcing me to hit him with direct questions. Something I don't like to do with informants unless I'm debriefing them.

"From going to the strip bars and gambling and hanging out on the East side. It's a small community. Everyone in the underworld knows everyone else."

"You're part of the underworld of East St. Louis?"

"No," he chuckled. "It is a figure of speech, Ray. Underworld pertaining to the entertainment business in East St. Louis. The business people over here do not like Viktor Agron or his ilk. They wish they would stay in New York or Georgia. Anybody who knows them wishes they were somewhere else, or dead. Even Helen of Troy, Illinois, hatcs them, but she still has to accept them as half-assed family members."

We were approaching Signal Hill and it was completely dark outside, perfect for a surveillance. "Park at the dead end by the pin oaks, we'll be hidden down there." Sig parked the Olds and shut it off.

"He was her pimp, you know," Sig continued. "He took her from her mother when she was fifteen and pimped her around the country until they made a lot of money. Then they moved to south Florida and eventually to south Georgia."

It was getting clearer to me as he spoke that he knew more than he had previously told Heidi and me. "So you got the information about the delivery of cocaine going to the storage facility, and you thought it would be a way to get at Viktor Agron, so you called the duty number and got Heidi, and the rest is history."

"Yes, Ray. I wondered how long it was going to take you to figure that out."

"And all of the information you gave us was what you gleaned from being in the right place at the right time?"

"Yes, Ray."

"So you just gave us the scenario of the drug deal and then let us come up with conclusion. How did you know we would get to the conclusion?"

"I felt you guys out, Ray. I know quality when I see it. I knew you wouldn't let me down." Damn, the guy never stops with the flattery.

"Did you know Helen of Troy, Illinois, is really from Troy, Illinois?"

"No," I replied.

"Yep," he continued. "Born and reared there, until she was fifteen, anyway. If Viktor Agron hadn't gotten his bloody hands on her, she could have been a big star in Hollywood. California that is, not Florida. He will pay for that someday."

A dark Ford four-door with tinted windows cruised by the house, made the turn around, and headed out of the complex. "Wonder who that was," I muttered. "Think they saw us and got spooked?"

"No, I do not think they saw us," Sig said. "No telling what was going on there. Want to tail them?"

"Yeah! Can you do it?"

"You don't know my background, Ray. I can tail anybody, anywhere."

He cranked the Olds and we were off. We caught the Ford at the top of State Street and headed west toward the heart of East St. Louis.

I watched his technique as we tried to keep the Ford under surveillance and not blow our cover doing so. He was focused and excited as he drove. I could see the joy in his face, like a race car driver who had been out of the sport for a time and just got back behind the wheel.

He expertly followed the Ford to Twenty second and Missouri. It turned right and Sig went straight. A good ploy. He stopped the Olds and then turned around and faced Twenty second street and waited for five minutes.

"If they're going to a house on Twenty second we should

give them some time to park and go inside," he said. He turned down Twenty second and slowly drove while we looked at the driveways on both sides of the street for the Ford. It was at the end of the street near the railroad tracks parked in a gravel driveway of a tar-paper house with a leaning front porch. It was surrounded by weeded lots where houses used to be. I jotted down the license number as we rolled by. The rolling surveillance was expertly deployed. Almost an impossible task.

We circled the block looking for a place to set up the surveillance. Twenty second street Tee'd at the railroad tracks, and there was no place to hide the Olds. "Okay," I said. "We know where this house is. Let's head back to Signal Hill and wait for another car to cruise by."

I checked my wrist watch. It was just 2200. The night was young and we were gathering good intelligence. Sig's investigative expertise amazed me and I had to ask him about his background.

"Where did you learn to conduct a rolling surveillance?"

"A long story, my friend."

"I've got time." We pulled into our spot on Signal Hill and he shut the Olds down. It was a neat night, summertime in East St. Louis, just like when I was a kid. Muggy and breezy, fire flies blinking and buzzing and the smell of the Mississippi River gumbo and toxic waste.

"I am from Austria," Sig began. "When I was young, there were no jobs in Austria unless you were the right religion or had important relatives. I was neither. I entered the Army at age sixteen and I was tested and scored high on the written tests. I was placed in military intelligence and trained to be an operative. They gave me my first taste of Martial Arts and I grew to love them. Anyway, for two years I spied on the political enemies of the governing faction. Basically, I dug up dirt on the other side so it could be used against them during an election. I knew it was wrong but it was fun and I learned a lot. At age eighteen we came to the United States and I went to culinary school. The rest is history."

"So, you and your family, you mean your parents, migrated to St. Louis?"

"Yes. I mean we didn't come directly to St. Louis. We went to New York City." He chuckled, "I've got a story for you."

"Go ahead."

"We came into New York City and my parents were frightened, I could see it. My sister was twelve. Everyone was frightened. We were waiting to be interviewed by customs, and an agent walks out, but he is not a customs agent, he is an FBI agent. They take my dad to a room off the hallway where we were sitting and interrogate him. We were sitting on those old wooden seats and listening to them threaten him. Our last name is the same as a Nazi war criminal and the customs agent called the FBI. The FBI agent is getting louder and louder with my dad, and finally he assaults him with his open hand, slapping him across the face. My mom and sister were on the verge of hysteria and I was getting angry. I walked into the room and told the agent he had the wrong man, that my dad was just a hard-working unemployed engineer from Austria. He let my dad leave and we were granted green card status. My parents stayed in New York and I eventually moved to St. Louis. Since then I have never trusted or liked the FBI."

"Well, you got even for your dad. You got to shoot the windows out of a Feeb's G car with your potato cannon. Very few people can say they got even with the FBI."

"Man, that was fun, wasn't it?" He was laughing. I imagined the look on Moynihan's face and I started laughing. "He's a dangerous man." I laughed when I spoke.

"He's still after me, that fucking Feeb."

Sig continued to chuckle. "I'm not familiar with the word Feeb."

"It's short for FBI. DEA agents despise FBI agents. It's weird but true." I replayed my words. I didn't hate FBI agents. I was acting the way I was programmed to act. I was stone cold brainwashed and I was trying to brainwash Sig. It was pathetic. I was embarrassed.

My cell went off. It was Heidi. I thought for a moment and then answered. "Jim Schwartz has convinced Doc and Square Bidness that you're a cocaine cowboy," she blurted out. I didn't respond while I allowed this stupid information to enter my brain. "You still there?"

"Yeah. How did he manage to do that? What proof does he have?"

"I'm not certain, but I want you to come in and talk to Doc. Get this straightened out. Will you do it?"

"I don't think so," I muttered. "It's too ridiculous to pursue. I can't believe you'd ask me to defend myself over such idiotic allegations. Why would Doc or Square Bidness believe anything Schwartz said? He's insane, everybody knows it."

"This is an agent-managed organization, Ray. Whatever an agent says is considered the gospel, no matter what TFD's think of him."

"It's stupid and I won't have anything to do with it."

"Well, Doc has told me to stay away from you. I don't wish to do that, but I see I have no choice."

"So, Doc controls your life after hours. You have no private life?"

"Kind of like that, Ray. Doc is my group supervisor. I'm compelled to do what he says if I want to survive in DEA. He controls my career. A poor performance evaluation from him to headquarters, and I'll be living in New York or

Jersey or somewhere else I can't afford. Get the picture?"

"Yeah, I've got it," I said in a low voice. "I apologize to you, I'm not used to such a dense bureaucracy." She hung up.

Sig was watching me as we sat in the dark and looked at Helen of Troy, Illinois' house. "Sounds serious," he finally said.

"Yeah, maybe."

"What's up?"

I didn't wish to tell Sig what had been discussed between Heidi and me, so I skimmed the problem. "DEA group supervisor and I are on the outs. Heidi's caught in the middle and now our relationship is in peril. I've tried to like the guy, but I just can't seem to pull it off."

"Why don't you like him?"

"He's a phony bastard and he goes out on his wife. That shouldn't bother me but it does. Midwestern values, I guess. He shouldn't have gotten married and pumped out two kids if he messes around." We sat in silence for a couple of minutes.

"I have a feeling things aren't going to start hopping around here until early in the morning," Sig said.

"You're probably right."

"I've got an idea," he continued. "Let's go to Belleville and get something to eat. I'll buy!"

"Sounds great." He drove up the hill just outside of the East St. Louis City limits and pulled into a newly constructed building with a large parking lot and a sign reading GUIDO'S. We got out, and walked in, and were welcomed with, "Good evening Mister Otto. Right this way. Your table is prepared, Mister Otto."

We sat in a private section of the plush little eatery, Mediterranean-style with carpets and wallpaper and pictures and linen tablecloths. A waitress who looked familiar came over with the menu. "Steak Diane is the special this evening, Mister Otto."

"Steak Diane is it for me," he said. "Italian potatoes and a salad."

"I'll have the same."

"And a magnum of burgundy, chilled, California, 84," Sig said.

"Yes, sir. Right away, Mister Otto."

A young Italian gentleman came to our table with a large smile and the humongous bottle of burgundy. "Ah, Guido, may I introduce my friend, Ray."

"Pleased," the owner said offering his hand. We shook and he opened the wine and poured.

Sig crushed the cork and smelled and tasted the wine and Guido whisked away. I thought it unusual that no last names were thrown around, but I knew Guido, or I should say that I knew his dad when I was an intelligence detective investigating organized crime. His dad was a "fringer," a person who associates with Mafia guys but isn't a "made" guy.

He was a hustler who made some easy money in the Teamsters hierarchy and obviously left some of it for his son. There were several familiar faces around the restaurant, West County coke snorters who I had come into contact with over the years. Guido's lifelong friends, no doubt.

Crooked daddy dies and leaves some cash, and the vultures move in to eat off of the carcass until the meat is gone. I gave the place two years, tops.

We were sipping the wine and waiting for the salads when Sig started selling himself again.

"Ray, you were in Okinawa, right?"

"Yeah, fourteen months."

"Marine Corps?"

"Yeah," I said with a stare. I sipped the damn good wine.

"What was your MOS?"

"0331, machine gunner," I replied.

"Oh." He stared. "I'd take you as someone who was stationed at Camp Schwab, the northernmost camp on the island."

"Yeah." I was surprised he knew about Okinawa. He read my look.

"I studied karate from a master in Okinawa," he said. "I was in the jungle north of Camp Schwab, and I used to walk into the little town outside the gates of Schwab. Do you remember the name of the little village?"

"Yes, Hanako."

"Oh, yes," he muttered. "I remember it well. You Marines were great entertainment for me as I sat at the bars and watched your lives play out. You would be in the jungle for weeks at a time and then come into town. You were like wild animals, roaming the gravel streets of Hanako in groups, going to bars, and taking them over as your own. And the women. You took them like conquering warlords. You actually thought you owned them. It was interesting to observe."

"Those were wild times," I said as I played the mental video of my conquests in Okinawa.

"You felt invincible didn't you, Ray?"

"Yes, I thought I was invincible at the time. Young and strong and I could fight all night and never lose."

"In my observations of the young Marines, I noticed something that was interesting to me. You guys always swaggered through town in groups of four or five, but there was usually only one of the group who was the fighter. The rest of the group watched or took a backward stance. Do you remember that, Ray?"

I thought back to those ancient days. "Yes, I remember."

"You were the fighter weren't you, Ray?"

"Yes, I was the fighter of my group."

"I knew it, Ray. I can read you loud and clear. You were warrior brothers with the non-fighting Marines, even though you were the only warrior. I guarantee you, Ray, when we're warrior brothers, I'll fight with you to the death. I'm glad we teamed up."

The food came and Sig was right. It was good food. We ate and killed the magnum of wine, and I was feeling no pain as we sat and waited for the check. "You took karate lessons in Okinawa, Ray?"

"Yes."

"It's the best location in the world to take Karate. I still go back there for training and I'm way past sixty." He smiled. "You still work out, don't you, Ray?"

I wondered why he almost always emphasized his conversation by saying my name before or after the statement or question. "Yes. I work out on the heavy bag, and I go to the gym to keep strong and fit."

"It shows in your appearance and attitude. You still get stiff in the shoulder blades, and in the quadriceps, triceps, and rib cage, don't you, Ray?"

"Yeah, you mean from punching and kicking?"

"Exactly. I know a place near here owned and operated by a Mamasan from northern Okinawa. She's got some girls working there who can get your muscles relaxed and loose in about an hour. I'll treat. What do you say, Ray?"

I checked my wristwatch. The night was still young, 2300 hours. Helen of Troy, Illinois' house would be dead for another couple of hours, and maybe I could sober up after the wine. "Yeah, it sounds like a good idea."

He paid the check and we walked to the parking lot. I noticed a Ford four-door with tinted windows drive by the lot but I wasn't sure if it was the same one we saw at the house on Signal Hill. I dismissed it as Sig drove deep into

East St. Louis and to the doorstep of Rush City, no man's land, a place that makes Hanako, Okinawa, look like Epcot Center.

He pulled into a fenced-in building and used a key card to activate the sliding chainlink fence, like a storage facility, except there was no sign identifying the building. We pulled into the parking area and there were several expensive cars: Bimmers, Caddies, Lincoln's, Mercedes, and Porsches parked in the lot. Sig parked.

"I have a secret compartment at your feet," he said as he handed me his 357 Smith. "Pull up the mat and lift the floorboard up. We can hide our weapons in there." I did as he said and placed his magnum, my magnum, and my Glock forty inside, then closed it and pulled the mat over it.

We were walking toward the well-lighted front door. "Girls from Okinawa in East St. Louis. How the hell did that happen?"

"They married Americans and came to St. Louis to live the American dream with their new husbands, Ray. Romance is rocky when the husband gets back home and sees blondes and redheads. All of a sudden he doesn't want an Asian girl around him anymore. They get divorced and these beauties are on their own in a strange land. They are born masseuses. It's in their culture. They learn the art at a young age and practice it for their entire lives. It is survival, Ray, just like you becoming a cop. We do what we know. What else could you have done for a living?"

"I read you loud and clear."

His conversation brought me back to Okinawa. I was feeling invincible again. I thought about Hanako, the people and the circumstances that brought me to the little town. The locals weren't welcome there except for the bar owners and the madams who pimped the young girls.

The girls were gorgeous in an Asian sort of way. The

Marines were like animals; Sig was right about that. They used and abused the girls, then left for the states and never looked back. But the young, beautiful local girls had to stay there and wait for a new batch of young cocky Marines to show up to dominate and humiliate them in their own little town, in front of their neighbors and classmates and friends for the privilege of earning the American dollar.

It was disgusting to me then, and it is disgusting to me now, but I had lived the Marine Corps lifestyle and tried not to look back. Sig was making me look back and I wondered why.

Maybe he was trying to make me realize the Okinawa experience helped form my life. I knew someday, if I lived long enough to get out of the Marine Corps, I would be a cop somewhere. If that was what he was attempting to do, he was too late. I already knew that fact.

"Mister Otto, welcome," she said with a bow. She was dressed in a lavish white jumpsuit decorated with sequins, and her graying hair was pulled straight back. I studied her as if I might have known her as a younger woman but dismissed the thought as frivolous. She wasn't as old as I first thought and would have been an adolescent when I was in the Far East.

She took Sig's hand and shuffled toward the back of the building with me following. We came into a locker and shower area and she turned and left us. Sig was removing his clothing and he instructed me to do the same. We placed our street clothes in lockers, locked them, put on long white robes, and put the keys in the pockets of the robes.

"This way," Sig said.

I followed him into a room with cubicles opened at the top and containing massage tables. Sig went into one of them and I went into another. I looked around the little room and inspected it for cleanliness and odor, and it seemed to pass muster so I sat on the table and waited.

A small Okinawan lady walked in and said, "Hi, I'm Sheriko and I will massage you this evening." She, too, was wearing a robe which she discarded and hung on a hook on the cubicle wall. She was wearing a two-piece bathing suit and was in terrific shape, strong with sinewy muscles and a flat belly.

"Please lay on your stomach."

I obeyed.

"You must take robe off," she said with a laugh.

"Oh, yeah." I got off of the table and disrobed and then got back onto the table on my stomach. She began by kneading my entire back side from the base of my neck to my toes. This arduous task took thirty minutes, and she grunted and groaned as she worked on me, and I could feel her sweat falling on my buttocks.

"Ah, you strong," she muttered. "You know Okinawan Karate?"

"Yes."

She climbed onto the table and walked on my back, digging in with her toes at my shoulder blades and neck and shoulder muscles. I figured she weighed less than a hundred pounds and her weight didn't hurt me. She hopped off and said, "Turn over, please."

I flipped over and she strategically placed the towel over me and started kneading my pectorals and my biceps and triceps. She worked for another thirty minutes down to my toes again,

"Okay, you done. Go to sauna now."

I crawled off the table and stood while I got my bearings, and climbed into the robe, and made a right turn past Sig's cubicle as he was coming out.

"You can't get something like that on the west side," he said as he walked.

I followed him into the sauna and we sat without speaking. Ten minutes of sauna and I'd had enough.

"I'm hitting the showers." I walked out.

I was finishing and walking toward the lockers when he came out. "I'll meet you in the cool- down room, Ray."

"Roger."

I slowly dressed, walked into the cool down room, sat in a recliner, and waited for Sig. I was on cloud nine, relaxed and mellow, more than I had been in years. He came out and sat in a recliner across from mine, and closed his eyes as if he was meditating.

He sat that way for ten minutes or so, then his eyes popped open and he bounced up to his feet. "I'm ready for another surveillance."

I stood and we headed for the door, opened it and started to walk toward his Olds. It was the only car in the lot now. All of the other customers had gone. I checked my wristwatch. It was 0230. The activity at Helen of Troy's, Illinois' house should start soon if there was going to be any.

We both heard the sound at once, the sickening sound of a slide being pulled to the rear and released, and the forward momentum of it sliding forward and shoving a round of ammunition into the chamber of a semi-automatic weapon.

Instinct, training, and self-preservation kicked in at the same time for both of us as we spun to face the attackers. It was the weaker link of the Viktor Agron henchmen running toward us with pistols pointing at us at arm's length begging for us to take the guns away from them. The same two imbeciles who had pursued us the night before.

They were acting like characters in a B movie taunting us with the guns, calling us pussies and faggots. The pimp protégé nearest to me was pointing the gun at my crotch. "I'm going to shoot your balls off, you fucking DEA cop:

then I'm going to put one in your knees, and then I'm going to blind your ass and puncture your ear drums with this nail." He held up a carpenter's nail for me to see. "You're going to be a blind mute without balls, and a cripple, too."

It's one of the first martial arts moves that a person is taught. The taking away of weapons from buffoons. It's classic and second nature. We had their pistols in an instant and we both tossed them behind us. They made a skidding sound as the metal slid on the gravel into the darkness.

Sig spun and kicked the nearest one to him on the side of his head and sent him down to the gravel, still and not moving.

I grabbed the nail guy's right arm and broke it at the elbow. The break sounded like a pool cue being broken over a table. He screamed and went to his knees.

Sig kicked him below the nose sending his nose bone into his brain and causing instant death. Sig's nimrod attacker was starting to moan and stir. Sig ran to him and rolled him over then kicked him in the heart muscle causing fibrillation and death. I stared in drunken disbelief.

Sig pulled his keys out and activated the trunk release. The lid popped open. "Quick. These Asian people here are trying to run a business. They're my friends. I don't want to cause them trouble. Help me put these assholes into my trunk."

I grabbed the wrists of one carcass and Sig took his feet and we tossed him like a sack of manure into the trunk. We used the same maneuver with the other one. I slammed the trunk as Sig was getting behind the wheel. I climbed in and we slowly drove to the gate. Sig activated it and it slowly slid open.

We drove out into the neighborhood of Rush City. Sig guided the big Olds over the gravel toward the Mississippi. There was no one around, just overgrown weed fields and shot-out street lights and bare poles without street names. Sig stopped and we climbed out as he activated the trunk release.

We dumped the bodies into a drainage ditch near a street sign with no name, slammed the trunk, got back in, and drove toward western civilization. Two more hard-boiled eggs for someone to find when it gets light.

Sig was beaming. "We are brother warriors. Few people are tested the way we were tested this morning, my friend. It was textbook, precise, and I'll never forget it. I told you and Heidi that I came to America to kill the bad guy. Did you believe me?"

"I didn't know, Sig. I didn't know you at the time."

"We know each other now, my friend."

I stared at him still trying physiognomy on his face as we went under streetlights. It was no use. He was too good or too sincere.

I was back in Hanako again. I had regained my youth and I was killing the bad guy instead of fighting Marines for women. But did we have to kill them?

They were scum, cur dogs trying to kill us. They had guns; we had expertise. I was in no-man's land, not in civilization, the equivalent to a jungle where animals fight at night for survival in the summer moonlight.

The cur dogs had beaten the system long enough. Their chickens had come home to roost. They chose the wrong victims. Justice was served in Rush City.

22

I awoke late to a bright morning sun shining through my glass wall, a terrible wine hangover, and Tyrone barking wanting me to get up and toss the ball for him. I had been having nightmares about killing the Russian's henchman and dumping their bodies in a Rush City drainage ditch just like an East St. Louis hoodlum.

My feet hit the floor and I grabbed my throbbing head. The realization hit me. It wasn't a dream; it really had happened. I went over my boundaries again, and now I was going to have to live with the fact that I trusted a C/I, killed a couple of guys with him, and now he owns my ass. How stupid could I have been?

I went to the head and barfed then sat on the commode and contemplated my actions and my fate. I replayed the entire night from the moment Sig picked me up until he dropped me off at my house.

The surveillance at Helen of Troy's, Illinois house, the dark Ford with the tinted windows, the house on Twenty second street, the meal at the gangster's kid's restaurant, the Okinawan massage parlor. It was like it was choreographed, scripted, then acted out.

The entire evening was geared to the ultimate climax, the fight with the two idiots and Sig and me. The conversation about Hanako, Okinawa, and the street fighting, the karate and the Okinawan girls; it was scripted, it had to be. But by whom?

Sig and I hit it off too well. We had too much in common. I played the fight scene over in my head. I didn't kill anybody in the fight; Sig did. He caused the fibrillation in the gun-toting moron's heart with the kick. He sent the nose bone into the other idiot's brain. The fight was over. Neither moron was a threat.

My only crime was removing the bodies from the scene and dumping them in the ditch. That would be difficult to describe to a jury of my peers, and I doubted that I had any peers in East St. Louis, Illinois. But, Viktor's henchmen had intended to kill us. They just didn't have the expertise.

I climbed down and made myself some breakfast, Wheaties and fruit and strong black coffee. I devoured the bowl of cereal, sat on the deck watching the boats head downstream to Florida, drinking coffee, and tossing the tennis ball for Tyrone.

There's more to Sig than meets the eye. Not only is he dangerous, physically; he's super-intelligent and he knows how to read and play off an unsuspecting adversary. Is he my adversary? He's a confidential informant and he is my adversary! He is to be used, not trusted. I was wrong in my deployment of him.

I let him guide me into a dangerous combat situation. I think he knew we were being tailed by our enemies. I would've known had I been driving. The rearview mirror tells all. Crooks, cops, and C/I's use it constantly.

But why? If he knew there was going to be a showdown, why didn't he keep a gun with him? Is it because he wanted to kill with his bare hands? Or did he want to see me fight? Or did he want us to bond, to be brother warriors for life? A lifelong C/I friend with whom I have fought side by side and killed the bad guys. Not just any bad guys; the scum of the earth, Viktor Agron's henchman.

There was only one of the gang left on the loose, Viktor. We would have to get him tonight if he is still in East St. Louis. I had to take the play away from Sig and use him for what he is. A dangerous confidential informant.

I went to the gym in the Austin Healey with the top down and did a complete body workout. It took two hours and I was starting to feel human again when I got home. I had nervous energy and I was continually reliving the fight and the killings. Were there any witnesses? Doubtful. Unless there was a camera taping the parking lot, but I doubted it.

I cleaned my little house and then went to the outside and cleaned the glass wall facing the river. I was up on the ladder in shorts and no shirt when Tyrone started going ballistic.

I looked down to a big pretty girl with a killer body. It was my ex-girlfriend, Gloria. She just stood there looking up at me, not saying anything. Finally, I said, "Hi, Gloria. What brings you to these parts?"

She backed away from the ladder as she looked up at me. "Are you still working federal narcotics?"

"Yes."

"Oh, I just wanted to stop by and say hello. I thought maybe you were back to regular duty."

"I'm not."

"Let me know when you are." She walked away. I continued to wash windows.

I gauged my feelings for Gloria. There weren't any. Heidi had spoiled me. Leaving Heidi for Gloria would be like leaving a glamorous star and going back to the small-town girl back home. It wouldn't have worked.

I spent the rest of the day working around the house and trying to get straight. It was starting to get dark so I showered and dressed in Levis and black Tee then waited for Sig to come by and pick me up. He pulled into my circular gravel driveway. I climbed in and we headed to the hunting ground, East St. Louis.

"Tonight we will get the bastard Viktor Agron," Sig began.

"Yeah but I want him alive." He gave me an incredulous look.

"Why? That bastard deserves to die like his brothers in

arms."

"I need him alive. I need to get back in good graces with the folks at DEA. Let the system take care of him. There's no need for us to kill him."

"Okay, Ray. You're the boss."

We made the circle, Helen of Troy's, Illinois, house and the house on Twenty second street. There was no action at either place.

We set up on Missouri Avenue near Twenty-second and waited. We were there for three hours before the Ford with tinted windows made a turn onto Twenty second. We waited for two minutes and then slid by the house. We went back to Missouri and sat. Ten minutes passed. "Let's go by the house again."

Sig started the Olds and we slid by again. There was a light on at the back of the old tar paper house. We went back to Missouri Avenue and parked. "I think Viktor Agron is in that house. What do you think?"

"Maybe," Sig replied. "How can we be certain?"

"We can look through the window," I said.

"I'm game. What's the plan?"

"There's an alley behind the house. We can walk to it from Missouri, sneak into the yard, and try and look through the window."

"Okay," he reluctantly replied. "When are we going to do it?"

I checked my wristwatch. It was 0330. "Now. Have you got a flashlight?"

"Yeah." He rustled through his glove box and pulled one out. We climbed out and walked down Missouri to the alley that T'd at the end of the street. It was strewn with trash: paper, broken bottles and cardboard boxes filled with trash somebody had dumped there instead of taking them to a garbage dump. Rodents ran into our light beam and then disappeared behind boxes or ran into the lots with weeds three feet high.

The light was our guide, the lone light in the neighborhood of weeded lots shining through a slit in the room-darkening shade. We crept into the weeds and made our way to the window, past an old wooden back porch with three concrete-block steps coming down to the trash-strewn yard. The window was too high for us to see into.

"Sig," I whispered. "Kneel down so I can stand on your back and look inside." He hit the deck without question and I stood on his broad back and peered inside.

Viktor Agron was sitting in an old recliner snoozing while the television was playing reruns of "Miami Vice." He looked out of place in the squalor, dressed in his pimp flowered shirt with gold hanging off him and entwined with his chest hair and massive upper body.

The house was somebody's dream home eighty years ago. The person who owned it probably lost his job because he didn't kiss the right gangster's ass and had to abandon it. Hopefully he went west and found a good life. There's no such thing here.

I looked around the room. There was a sawed-off next to him and a semi-automatic pistol in his waistband. I stepped off of Sig and motioned for him to follow me. We stopped in the alley. "He's in there. We've got to get him out somehow. He's got a sawed-off and a pistol." Sig didn't respond: just stared at the house the way a German shepherd would stare at a hole with a rabbit in it.

"Sig, go and get the Olds and drive it down the alley past the house so it's hidden in the weeds. Pop the trunk, shut off the ignition and join me back here." He gave me a suspicious stare and then walked off. I scoured the alley for and found a cardboard box with a bottom that wasn't rotted out. I collected paper and stuffed the box with it, toted it to the sagging front porch, walked on to it and placed the box next to the front door, then walked back to the alley and waited for Sig.

I heard the Olds slowly coming down the alley, running over bottles and trash as it passed me and stopped adjacent to the rear entrance of the house. The trunk lid opened, Sig walked to me and waited for an explanation.

"I need a match or a lighter. Do you have one?"

"Yeah." He handed me an expensive cigar lighter. "What's up?"

"We're going to start a fire on the front porch. The whole house will be engulfed in minutes. Viktor's only means of escape is the backdoor. We'll be waiting for him. He shouldn't be too difficult to disarm. Are you ready?"

"Yeah." He was smiling. "I like it. I like it a lot."

"Remember, Sig. I need him alive. Understand?"

"Yes, my friend."

I walked around to the front of the house, crept onto the porch and lit the box full of paper. It burst into flame and scorched the layers of paint off of the front door. I stood back and watched as flames engulfed the entire front porch. Then I walked to the back door and waited. Sig was on one side of the steps, I was on the other.

The door opened as if it had been kicked and Viktor came out with the sawed-off at port arms. I reached out and snatched the long gun away from him and tossed it into the weeds.

He looked over at me as if he was in shock and then went for the automatic in his waistband. Sig snatched the handgun and tossed it then grabbed Viktor by the throat.

I started working Viktor's body with lefts and rights while Sig had him by the larynx. His eyes were big and he was flailing his arms trying to fend us off but he couldn't. I spoke in a low tone to him. "How does it feel, Viktor? How many people have you choked to death? How many people have you beaten while your henchman held them?"

He couldn't answer me so I continued to pummel his prison-hard body. Sig threw him to the ground and I pounced on him. I placed his hands behind his back, cuffed him, stood him up, and marched him to the waiting trunk of the Olds.

He balked when he saw the trunk. Sig kicked him in the side of the head, and he fell sideways into the trunk. I slammed it and we got in. We drove off as the tarpaper house burned to the ground.

The sun was coming up over the Gateway Arch as we made our way toward Clayton. Sig stopped the car in the garage and popped the trunk release. I got out and pulled Viktor out of it, then slammed the lid. He wasn't fighting anymore. He observed civilization and knew he wasn't going to die. He gave me a wry smile as I marched him toward the elevator. Sig drove off.

I key-padded my way past the alarm, and escorted Viktor to our holdover on the fourth floor, searched him and tossed him into the small cell. "Turn around and place your hands through the bars." He complied and I removed the handcuffs.

"Pretty slick," he said with a smile. "Did you kill my friends, too? I heard it was two guys who know karate who killed them. It had to be you and that other guy. Who the hell is he, anyway? He looks familiar. I've seen him around someplace." I ignored him and started filling out the booking sheet.

The workers were starting to drift in. Coffee pots were being cranked up and morning newspapers read. Carla stuck her head into the holdover as I filled out the booking sheet. She was gorgeous this morning: white and pink linen dress, jewelry shining like it had just been cleaned.

"Ray," she said. "I didn't think I would ever see you again." She was smiling and sipping coffee and swaggering around me. She gave the once-over to Viktor and walked out.

"I could make some money with that chick," Viktor said. I didn't respond to his ignorance.

Doc stormed in and stood in front of the cell, staring at Viktor. "Where'd you get him?"

"East St. Louis."

"Nice pinch!" He was studying me. He shot out his right hand and I took it. He was smiling. This arrest probably clinched his next promotion.

"Tell him how you got me, Ray," Viktor said. I didn't respond. "He burned my fucking house down to get me, sir. He and some other guy beat the shit out of me. I want to go to the hospital. I demand medical attention, sir. Are you in charge, sir? I demand to go to the hospital. He killed my fucking friends, too, sir, right in East St. Louis and he dumped their bodies in Rush City. Wait until I tell my lawyer what really went down."

"Come in and see me when you're done booking him," Doc said.

"I'm finished now, except for printing and photographing him."

"Great, come in now."

I placed Victor into the holding cell and wormed my way to the task force office as the agents and TFD's were wandering in. Heidi was already at her desk. Her head snapped toward me as I cruised by her and went into Doc's office.

"Have a seat," Doc said, smiling. "Now, tell me how you got him so I can relay the information to the SAC and he can relay it to headquarters."

"I had a license number issue from Ellen's car. I gleaned

it while Heidi and I were in Savannah. I went to the East side and set up a surveillance, and eventually it led to a house on Twenty second street near Missouri Avenue. I set up surveillance there and suddenly the front of the house became engulfed in flames. I drove to the rear of the residence, thinking somebody might be running out of the back door, and here came Viktor. He had a couple of guns with him, and I was lucky enough to disarm and apprehend him. There was a little skirmish between us but nothing big."

Doc was smiling as I told him my lie. "Where are the guns?"

"Still over in the weeds by the house."

"Draw me a little map of the area and a location where the guns might be."

I drew a map and marked it with notations, "sawed-off in weeds to the right of the house, semi-automatic pistol in the weeds to the left of the house."

"I wonder how the house fire started," Doc said staring and smiling.

"It was a dump, Doc, a tarpaper shack. If I were to guess, I'd say it was faulty wiring."

I was looking at Doc with a straight face. He started smiling again and then he laughed a large loud guffaw. Then he winced as the scabs on his face started pulling. I stood and we stared. "I heard about the rumor that I was a crook," I said.

He studied me, "Don't worry about it. It happens to everybody who ever works drugs. Get used to it."

I studied him. "It wasn't me who wrote the letter to your wife, Doc."

"Don't worry about it. It's history. I shouldn't have overreacted."

We both paused and studied each other. "I've got to print

Viktor and take his picture then take him downtown for arraignment."

"Yeah, okay," he said still laughing and wincing. "I'll get somebody to assist you. And I'll call Sue Lee. She'll be expecting you."

I walked into the cell room and unlocked the door to let Viktor out for fingerprinting and photographing when Heidi came in. "Doc told me to assist you."

"Oh," I muttered. "Is the ban lifted?"

"Presumably."

Viktor looked at us and smiled. "I've got to hand it to you; you guys weren't bad," he said with a chuckle. "I figured you might be DEA, but I figure everybody I meet with is DEA." Heidi ignored his comment.

"Step over here, sir," she said. Viktor stood erect and posed for the camera while Heidi took the shots.

"Over here, Viktor," I said while I was inking up the glass fingerprint pad. I took each of his fingers and placed his prints on four cards, attached the Polaroid pictures to them, and placed him back in the cell.

"What's going to happen to me? When can I call my lawyer?"

"Soon, Viktor. In fact, I'll call your lawyer for you. What's his name?"

"Fuck you, I'll call him myself. Hey, Heidi, if that's your name, you know your old boyfriend burned my house down to get me? He did, but first he murdered my associates. Fine upstanding person you're working with."

Heidi shot a glance at me but I didn't look at her. "Sue Lee is waiting for us," she said.

"Right," I muttered. "Sue Lee, the arraignment." I unlocked the cell door. "Come out, Viktor. We're taking you to the federal marshal's office. You'll be incarcerated there until your arraignment. Put your hands behind your back and face the wall." I cuffed him and we walked him down to the garage and into the back seat of Heidi's Bimmer.

Viktor sat in the back seat and ogled the scenery of summertime St. Louis as we drove to the federal courthouse. I wondered what was going through his mind as I watched him through the vanity mirror. He had to realize that a lifetime of incarceration was ahead of him.

This summertime jaunt may well be his last look at green trees and lawns, neat buildings and homes, sunshine and fresh air, gorgeous women. He caught me observing him and he read me.

"I know what you're thinking," he said. I didn't respond to his comment. "You're thinking I'm going to be locked up for the rest of my life but I'm not. I've been in this predicament before, and I've been given big time before. I always get out. This drug shit ain't nothing. When my lawyer gets through with you two on the stand, you'll be going to prison, not me. You stole Angel Perez' money, Heidi. And you, Ray, you murdered my friends. It'll all come out in the trial. My lawyer's got the best investigators in the business. All they need is a clue and they hunt and search like bloodhounds. You'll see who's going to come out on this deal. I didn't sell you the damn dope anyway. The deal was never consummated. I never took the money from you. All you got is conspiracy."

"Keep telling yourself that, Viktor. You're selling yourself pimp tales, just like you've done to the naive ladies you've tricked into prostituting themselves for you. This is the last pimp festival for you, Viktor. You're gone for good."

"Oh, yeah," he muttered. "Everybody's got to be somewhere."

Heidi pulled the Bimmer into the Sally Port, and I got

Viktor out of the backseat and marched him into the holding area while Heidi drove off in search of a parking place on the street. A United States Marshal met me in the holdover and I remanded custody of Viktor to him.

He searched him again and removed my handcuffs, returned them to me and placed him in a cell. "I'm going to AUSA Sue Lee's office." The marshal nodded.

"I want to call my lawyer," Viktor shouted as I was walking out.

I took the elevator to Sue Lee's office and walked in. She was waiting for me. "Viktor Agron case, right?"

"Yes." She was looking especially gorgeous this morning, dressed in red and white and gold, clean and neat with her Asian features and hair done up to perfection. I felt out of place being in the same room with her. I had been up all night, fighting with Viktor, burning his house, walking in a trash-strewn alley. I smelled my arm pits when she turned away from her desk. I was a bit ripe.

"Okay, tell me what happened with the arrest of Viktor Agron.

"I had a license number off of his wife's car in East St. Louis. I set up surveillance on the house in the Signal Hill area and a Ford four-door with tinted windows came by the surveillance. I followed the car and it led me to a house on Twenty second Street. I set up on the house and was there for about two hours when the front of the house mysteriously began burning."

"You mean," she said smiling, "the house caught on fire?"

"Yes," I replied straight-faced.

"Okay, go on with your story."

"I drove down the alley to the rear of the house and got out. Viktor Agron came running out of the back door. He was carrying a sawed-off shotgun and he had a semi-automatic pistol in his waistband. I tried to arrest him and we got into a fight. I disarmed him and arrested him at that time, placed him in my car and drove him to the DEA field office in Clayton."

"The guns. Where are the guns?"

"In the weeds. The house is surrounded by weeds."

"We need the guns."

"Okay, I'll go back and search for them."

Heidi walked in and sat down beside me.

"Good morning."

"Good morning."

"We need the guns," Sue Lee said to Heidi.

"Guns? What guns?"

"The guns Viktor Agron had in his possession when you arrested him."

"I didn't arrest him. I wasn't even there."

"I was by myself," I said.

"Oh." Sue Lee's slanted eyes were drilling holes in me. Her desk phone rang and she answered it. The conversation was congenial, kind of like colleagues talking about a golf outing. She hung up.

"That was Viktor Agron's attorney. He says you're a rogue agent and you murdered two of Viktor's associates in East St. Louis, Illinois, and dumped their bodies in Rush City the day before yesterday. He also said you burned Viktor Agron's house down, and when he came out the back door, you and someone else beat him and tossed him into the trunk of an Oldsmobile and conveyed him to the DEA office in Clayton this morning." She was staring and trying to run physiognomy on me. I stared back.

"Poppycock!" I replied. She nodded. Heidi was shooting glances at me; I could feel her anxiety.

"Okay," Sue Lee said. "I'm going to type this complaint and then we'll be going before Judge Saunders for the arraignment. Come to the judge's chambers in an hour with Agron. Okay?"

"Yeah."

We stood, walked out into the hallway, turned right, and wandered aimlessly, waiting for one of us to say something. I broke the silence. "I need some breakfast. How about you?"

"Sounds great."

We walked to the elevator took it down to the first floor then went to the sidewalk, and walked across the street to a café. We sat, watched the foot traffic, sipped black coffee and ate cheese bagels. I was zoning most of the time from lack of sleep.

I admired Heidi for not asking any probing questions. They were there to be asked, and a less intelligent person would have asked them. She was a cool customer.

I paid the tab and we strolled back to the courthouse, walked in, and made our way to the holding area. "Viktor Agron for arraignment in Magistrate Saunders' chambers," I said to the marshal. He nodded, went into the cell block, and returned with him.

Viktor wouldn't make eye contact with us. He placed his hands behind his back and waited for me to cuff him. I hooked him up, grabbed his right arm, escorted him out and to the elevators in the main lobby.

There was a crowd of people jockeying for position for the next elevator going up. It dinged and the door opened. "Official business," Heidi said as we stepped in front of the crowd with Viktor. "Get the next elevator."

We debarked on the fifth floor and waited in the deserted hallway for Sue Lee. We heard her heels clicking along on the marble floor before making the turn and appearing before us carrying the typed arraignment papers for Viktor. She stared at him and kept her distance. Viktor didn't look at her.

"Let's go in," she said as she pushed the wood and glass door open and went inside. We followed. I still had Viktor by the arm and was guiding him like he was a blind person. We stood in the outer office of the magistrate. His law clerks stared at us like we were from another planet.

I was sure they were trying to get a feel for us as agents of the federal government to try to put us in human perspective, classify us for future reference. They are lawyers even though they are clerks, and they will no doubt progress with their careers whether in private or with the government, and deal with agents and crooks on a daily basis.

It is the method smart people use to understand the lower level of society. They don't have to rub elbows with the dregs; they just need to be exposed to us, and they can get a feel for our lifestyle. It's why lawyers rule the world. Sue Lee went into the chambers and after about two, minutes she returned and said, "Come in."

I guided Viktor into the chambers, and we stood in front of the judge's desk. His office was adorned with pictures of presidents, his law degree, pictures of his golf exploits, a seal of the United States, and an American flag. He was a thin, elderly man with white hair and bony fingers. He didn't look up as we walked in; he was busy reading the arraignment complaint. He finally looked up at us and nodded to me. I nodded back. Viktor's eyes were down cast.

"Mister Agron," the magistrate began. "You are being charged with possession with the intent to distribute one-hundred kilos of cocaine in the Eastern District of Missouri. You will be held without bail until a bond hearing can be scheduled." Viktor still kept his eyes down. "Do you have an attorney, Mister Agron?"

"Yes. I've spoken to him once this morning. He knows

where I am."

"That's all," the judge said.

We all walked out of the office. Heidi and I walked to the elevator and Sue Lee click-clacked back toward her office. She stopped and turned toward us. "Ray, when you drop Mister Agron off at the Marshal Service, call me before leaving the building."

"Okay."

We took the elevator down, debarked at the first floor, and walked into the Marshal's service holdover. The duty Marshal removed my handcuffs from Viktor and handed them to me, searched him again, and led him back to the cell. Viktor didn't look back at us. "Here are the arraignment papers," I said as I handed them to the marshal.

I dialed Sue Lee's office on the desk phone on the Marshal's desk. She answered. "Ray Arnold," I said.

"Yes, Ray, I need you to go back to the house on Twenty second street and find those guns. When you do, they need to be entered into evidence, and a DEA six needs to be prepared relating to the arrest of Viktor Agron. I also need a surveillance report. Got it?"

"Yes." I hung up the phone, and Heidi and I walked out of the holdover, through the lobby and out into the bright late-morning sun. I pulled on my Maui Jim's and followed Heidi to the Bimmer parked two blocks away.

We headed toward the Poplar Street Bridge, jumped on it heading east. I looked down at the barge traffic and at one lone cruiser heading south. I peered at it between the bridge railing as the posts went by, like an old movie, trying to get a look at the people on board.

I wanted to classify them, get a feel for them. I wanted to be on that boat with them and laugh and watch the muddy Mississippi River go by and steer into the clear blue Gulf of Mexico.

Maybe someday, but for now I was on my way to East St. Louis, Illinois, to a neighborhood of weeded lots that had one lone house that I had burned to the ground so I could affect the arrest of one pimp, murderer, drug dealer. I would be lying about this one for years.

"Get off on Missouri Avenue," I instructed Heidi. She guided the big Bimmer to downtown East St. Louis. "Take Missouri to Twenty second and turn left." We pulled onto Twenty second and the street was blocked by an East St. Louis police car.

"DEA," Heidi said as she showed the young black officer her credentials. "We need to get through."

"Uh, okay, I guess you can go through. State police arson detectives are conducting an investigation up at the end of the street. Somebody burned the only house left on the block this morning."

Heidi gunned the Bimmer and we shot toward the burned carcass of the old house. There was an Illinois State Police arson van parked in front of the house, and a silver Mercedes convertible parked in front of it. A rare one: twelve cylinder. One hundred thirty thousand, I estimated. I guessed the Mercedes arrived on scene first.

The Illinois arson guys were standing in front of the still smoldering shack, looking and scratching their heads. There was nothing left to process, no way to tell what caused the blaze or where it started. We parked, got out, and wandered over to the arson investigators. "DEA." I showed them my credentials.

"DEA, huh," one of them said. He was an old timer, which meant he had over ten years on and thought he had seen everything and everybody. He gave us the once-over, then scratched his beard. "What brings you guys over here to the east side?"

"I made an arrest here this morning. We're back to

retrieve some evidence." He stared long and hard at us as I walked toward the back of the house with Heidi following me. I dug around in the burnt weeds to the left of the porch and came up with the sawed-off, then walked to the other side and came up with the pistol. We walked toward the Bimmer. "Thanks, guys," I said as we started to get in.

A man came out of the weed patch at the rear of the house. I recognized him from news articles. It was a big-time lawyer, probably working for Viktor Agron. He glared at us as we walked toward the Bimmer.

He was out of place in a weed patch in East St. Louis, Illinois. He was dressed in a hundred dollar silk shirt and was carrying a five hundred dollar blazer. His jewelry sparkled in the summer sun. He was perspiring and wiping his brow with a silk handkerchief.

His shoulder-length hair was wafting in the breeze and he was continually brushing it away from his sweat-covered face. He was in shape. I figured this was the first time he ever perspired while not involved in an athletic endeavor. Viktor had called him. He called Illinois Division of Criminal Investigation, no doubt.

He was already trying to build his defense against the government's charges against his client. What motivation. We climbed into the Bimmer, turned it around and headed toward Missouri Avenue. He tried to stop us by standing in the street. We drove past him and were met by another car coming down Twenty second toward us. It was Jim Schwartz. We locked eyes as we zipped past him. "Why is he here?" I asked.

"He's out to get you, Ray."

23

I crashed on the way back to the office from the East side. There was nothing left in me, no food or energy or substance. I told Heidi to take me home and she did. I slept for fifteen hours, got up early, and had a good breakfast. I was wondering if I should drive the crazy El Camino to work or the Austin Healey when my cell rang. It was Heidi telling me she was going to pick me up.

I sat on the deck and watched the river and tossed the tennis ball for Tyrone until I heard her Bimmer make the curve into my circular driveway. I got up, patted Tyrone on the head and walked around the house to the Bimmer. I climbed in and ogled her while she drove off.

"I entered the guns from the east side into evidence for you."

"Thanks," I said as I hunkered down in the seat.

"I didn't write the DEA six on it, though. And I didn't write the surveillance report."

"I understand. You weren't on the surveillance. You didn't know what really went down."

She shot glances at me while she drove. I was waiting for the question. She cleared her throat; I knew it was coming. "What did go down?" I gave her a stare and tried to figure how I could fend her off. She was chomping at the bit to know my secret.

"A lot went down." I was trying to avoid her question.

"So tell me, or don't you trust me?"

"Trust? Trust has nothing to do with anything in the dope business. You know that. It's all smoke and mirrors and conspiracies. Trust is the wrong word for us, Heidi."

She drove and I could see her in deep thought. She enjoyed the game and she wanted to be the best in it. She wanted to be the best and be in command of everything she did, from sex to driving, to being a federal agent.

"Okay. Let's say I ask you some questions, and you can answer them if you choose to."

I knew this wasn't going to go away, I said, "Okay."

"Did you go rogue and burn Viktor Agron's house down?"

"Yes."

"Who was with you?"

"No, Heidi, the game isn't played like that. You've got to pose the question so that I can give a yes or no answer. Got it?"

"Yeah, okay, sorry." She was delving deeply into herself trying to come up with a reasonable scenario. She was searching for a person. "It wasn't a federal agent," she muttered. "If it had been, he or she would've been in the forefront and you would've been in the background. You couldn't trust a federal agent, anyway, except for me, that is," she said smiling.

I didn't respond. She was still studying me with glances, trying to physiognomy me. "Couldn't be a cop, either," she muttered. "It had to be somebody who wanted to stay in the background. Somebody who was tough enough to help you nab a tough guy like Viktor Agron. Had to be a C/I," she exclaimed. "It was a confidential informant, wasn't, it?"

I didn't answer her, and I turned my head away from her so she couldn't see my face. It was a mistake on my behalf. She picked up on my body language. I shouldn't have turned away from her. I was playing her game now.

"Okay, it was a C/I," she excitedly said. "Now we're getting somewhere. But what C/I?" She was getting into the logic of the event, using her brain, and her psyche and the chain of events that led to the Agron case. She drove and zoned and continued to drive and study me.

"Sig Otto? You used Sig Otto to capture Viktor Agron?"

"Yes."

"Wow, Ray," she said in a low voice. "You think you can trust him?"

"No."

"Did you and Sig Otto kill Viktor's henchman?"

She was nervously glancing at me now. It was the kind of question I was supposed to answer. She had posed the question correctly and she was waiting for an answer.

It was obvious that I didn't want to answer her. "Let me ask you a question first, okay? Did you steal the eight-hundred thousand dollars you seized from Angel Perez?"

It was a question she didn't want to answer. The game was over. There was no winner. She guided the Bimmer into the parking garage, parked, and we walked inside.

It was 0850 when we walked into the office. It was the same song and dance. Ross Milton was back from his appointment with the silver Cadillac, and he was bragging to everybody how there was nothing to it. Pat Brown and Bill Robinson were passing around snapshots of a sexual encounter they'd had with two lonely secretaries from the Club that they had filmed covertly with a DEA camera.

Square Bidness came out of Doc's office smiling. Must be some promotion news for them. Carla stood nervously at the head of the office next to her desk waiting for everyone to settle down.

Mike Schweig walked in with a hangover, sipped coffee and made fish faces while Ross Milton took out his Boy Scout mirror and made certain his hair was combed perfectly and that his ascot was straight. Monica Rose was singing, wearing Ray Bans, and weaving like Stevie Wonder at her desk.

"Ahem," Carla said. Everyone became still and looked up at her. "Open your laptops, please. Ray Arnold, I need a DEA six from you depicting the arrest of Viktor Agron. I also need a six detailing the seizure of the guns you had to go back for. And I need a surveillance report. Okay, please begin."

We all began our chores, clicking on the laptops like good little students in secretarial college. I wrote the arrest report first. It took two hours. I hit the send key and it went to the main computer and was saved.

Carla read it on her screen and was nodding in compliance. She looked up and gave me a smile. I took a break, went to the rest room, walked back to the office, poured another cup of coffee, and entered the seizure of the guns. It only took twenty minutes because I could relate to the other report for more information.

The surveillance report was concise. I was on surveillance on Twenty second, the house started burning, I drove to the back, and Viktor Agron came out; Refer to arrest DEA six of Viktor Agron.

My cell vibrated on my desk. I grabbed it. "Yeah?"

"Is this Ray Richards, the private detective?"

It was a gravelly female voice using my undercover name.

"Yeah."

"This is the lady on Signal Hill. Do you remember me?"

"Yeah," I said with a chuckle. "I remember you."

"I been watching Helen of Troy's, Illinois' house for you," she said as if I owed her something for her labor.

"Oh, thanks. What have you come up with?"

"She come home early this morning, and she's home right now. I saw some movement through the windows and I think she's out on the veranda by the pool. Probably sunning that million dollar body," she said with sarcasm.

"Oh, okay, thanks again. Is she alone?"

"Appears to be. I haven't seen the three gangsters around for a couple of days. I heard two of them got murdered down in Rush City. I don't think she brings tricks back to her house. I've spoken to her a couple of times and she's real smart. She's real rich, too. She buys some of my weed from time to time, says it's dynamite. I've got some more for you when you come back into the neighborhood. What did you think of the sample packages I sold you?"

"Dynamite!"

"Cool, brother. I've got some stuff that'll make your hair curl. I'll save it for you."

"Thanks. I'll see you, bye." I wiped my brow with a handkerchief and thought about my youth. "I'll never get out of East St. Louis." I muttered.

I sat at my desk, zoning over nothing. Doc walked out of his office, paraded through the main office and exited toward the Club. I wondered if he and I were okay now.

Heidi was watching me and had been listening to my telephone conversation with the weed dealing granny philosopher. I walked to her desk. "We've got to interview Ellen Agron." She stared at me.

"How the hell did you find her? Why interview her? Viktor's incarcerated, what can she tell us?"

"Long story. I'll tell you on the way to East St. Louis. Do you have a snapshot of Jack Parker?"

"Yeah." She dug in her desk drawer and came out with one and held it up for me. I pocketed it.

She closed her laptop and followed me out into the garage and to the Bimmer. She unlocked it and climbed in, then released the lock for me and I climbed in.

"Take the Poplar Street Bridge and get on Missouri Avenue like yesterday, but instead of turning on Twenty second street, go all the way out to the city limits toward Belleville. She has a house on Signal Hill."

"So, this is the same gal who was in Viktor's house in Savannah when we were undercover?"

"Yeah."

"Wow," she exclaimed. "She's a prostitute, right?"

"Part-time. She's a stripper at the Inferno Club. Goes by the name Helen of Troy, Illinois. Beautiful girl, wouldn't you agree?"

"Yeah, she's cute. Helen of Troy, Illinois? Real cute! So, tell me the long story."

"That picture that you had of Jack Parker on your dresser, the one with his shirt off, on a beach, the one with his diamond cluster nugget ring. Do you know what I'm talking about?"

"Yeah!"

"Ellen was wearing a ring like that when we met her at Viktor's house in Savannah. Didn't you see it?"

"No!"

"It was a man's ring, similar to the one Jack was wearing. It had fuzzy sizing string wrapped on it, the way school girls do when they wear a older guy's ring. It's just a hunch. I want to flash the picture at her and gauge her reaction."

We slowly rolled into the neighborhood and drove by the house. "See where those palm trees are at the veranda?"

"Yeah."

"There's a pool up there. My C/I tells me she's sunning herself. She probably won't answer the front door so I think we should just figure a way to get onto the veranda and walk up on her. She'll recognize us as DEA so I don't think she'll panic and start shooting at us."

Heidi parked the Bimmer on the street and we took the steps up to the front door. I peered inside and I could see all the way to the veranda and the pool through the house. She was lying nude on a chaise lounge.

I walked toward the veranda on landscape railroad ties hugging the house with Heidi following me. We walked around and through privacy bushes until I came to a wrought-iron gate. She was lying near the gate listening to a Jimi Hendrix blues album, and appeared to be snoozing. Her perfect Greek body was oiled and firm and she had eye protectors on each eye. Her bleached blonde hair was pulled straight back and tied in a bun.

We stood and stared at her, indecisive about how we should approach. If we called out to her, she could run into the house and lock the doors, and the interview would be over before it began. If we tried the gate and it was locked and she heard us, she would balk and run.

Jimi Hendrix was singing and playing "Red House Over Yonder" and was in the part where the key to his girl's house won't fit the lock in the door and he says, "but I still got my guitar." He started with a great guitar riff as I tried the latch on the gate. It creaked and she freaked.

Ellen jumped up with a stainless forty-five automatic and pointed it toward us. We stood our ground. "DEA, Ellen," I shouted. "This is nothing but an interview. We just need to talk to you. Put the gun down and unlock the gate."

She stood still like a statue, her perfect breasts and her big bush, her nipples pointed at us like brown eyes, looking and searching. She didn't have a hard look about her like I thought she might have in the sunlight.

The sun reveals everything about a person, every imperfection, blemish, hardness. She walked to the gate and pointed the forty-five to the ground, then unlocked it and turned her back on us and walked back to the chaise lounge and lay down.

She pulled on a ball cap and a pair of Maui Jims from a table with her jewelry and a drink on it and said, "Okay, so interview me and then get the hell off my property. I wasn't a part of that damn dope deal in Savannah. I was just visiting my pimp husband. We're legally separated.

Whatever business he had with DEA is his business, not mine." We stood in the sunshine while she posed in front of us like a glamorous movie star.

"We think you might know an associate of ours, Ellen. Would you look at a picture for us?"

"No!" She wouldn't look at us. Her right hand nervously went to her abdomen and stroked her six-pack abs, then to a towel and placed it over her big black bush. She wasn't wearing the ring. I glanced at her jewelry on the table. It wasn't there.

I shot a glance at Heidi, then back at Ellen. "We need your help on this, Ellen. Viktor Agron never did anything for you. He took you at age fifteen and pimped you around the country. You owe him no allegiance." She looked at me and I could see my image in her Maui Jims.

"How did you know that?"

"I'm an investigator, Ellen. I know lots of things about you. I want to show you a picture of Jack Parker; Maybe you'll recognize him by a different name. We think you know him."

Heidi handed her the picture and she looked at it, then made a fatal mistake for any liar. She removed the Maui Jims and revealed her eyes. She examined the picture, her eyes were jumping and her face started twitching. She knew Jack Parker; that was for certain.

She slipped her Maui Jims back on and stared at me as if to say, okay, ask me something else. "Did Jack Parker come to the Inferno and watch your act?"

"Probably," she said. "Every freak in the metropolitan area comes to the Inferno. I saw you there, remember. My protection went after you. The next night somebody beat them to death and dumped them in Rush City. Was that you? You don't look that tough, but you don't look like a DEA agent, either."

"I've got a scenario, Ellen. I think Jack Parker came to the club and became infatuated with you. He approached you somehow, and you didn't discourage him. You pimped him, just like you've been pimped for your entire life. But he got to you and you fell for him. He wanted to take you away from the dark side and you were considering it. You're a wealthy gal. You and Jack Parker could have lived the good life anywhere you chose. Viktor Agron found out about it, maybe from your protection detail, and he told you to cool it with the DEA guy. But you couldn't and you told Viktor to fuck off."

"You're goofy, old cop. You should retire and go lie on a beach." She still refused to look toward me when she spoke. I was making progress.

"Jack gave you his nugget ring, didn't he Ellen? I saw you wearing it the day we met you in Savannah. Where is it now, Ellen? It infuriated Viktor, didn't it?"

She stared. "Viktor came into town and tailed Jack Parker," I continued hammering her. "It didn't take him long to figure that Jack was a drunk and a hopeless romantic. A pimp like Viktor Agron could size Jack Parker up in an hour of surveillance. Jack had a routine. Every night he would see one of his lady friends and then go to the casino boat and talk with his dad. He was always inebriated by the time he got to the boat. Then he'd walk to his Corvette which he always parked in the same spot on the cobblestones by the river and drive to Taco Bell, get loaded up on greasy food to soak up the booze, stuff himself, and drive home. A perfect victim for a tough guy like Viktor Agron."

"Fuck off, cop," she sneered.

"We know what Viktor can do to people, Ellen. We know he's a strangler, a larynx crusher. She looked at me and tears were running out from under from her Maui Jims. "You've no doubt seen him strangle someone to death,

Ellen. Not a pretty sight, is it? He's an animal, Ellen, but he kills for hate and pleasure. Animals don't do that, Ellen. Only guys like Viktor Agron. Why are you protecting him?"

"I want you to leave," she said in a low growl.

"So Viktor comes up on Jack Parker as he weeble-wobbles his way toward the government Corvette and he shouts out to him. "Hey, sir, can I talk to you a second?" Jack stops and is probably seeing two of him and he says, "Sure." He stops to talk to Viktor because he's a cop. Cops talk to people who ask them stupid questions. It's ingrained in us; it's what we do. So Viktor comes up to Jack and without fanfare, grabs him by the throat, crushes his larynx, drags him to the Mississippi River and slides him in. End of problem for Viktor. Did he tell you about it, Ellen? It's his way to terrorize people, Ellen. To destroy your will so you will do his bidding. He's the king of pimps, Ellen. It's ingrained in him. It's what he does."

She stood. The towel fell away from her bush. "I'm ordering you off of my property," she screamed. "I'm not saying another word to you without my lawyer present. Now leave."

She stooped to pick up the towel and she knocked the cocktail table over. Her jewelry and drink crashed onto the concrete pool deck. She ran toward me, her perfect breasts bouncing and her nipples staring at me like head lights on a 32-Ford Roadster. I stared at her as she stuck her finger in my face. "Get off of my property!" She dove into the pool and swam underwater to the opposite end, surfaced, leaned against the side and watched us.

"Let's go, Heidi. This interview is over." We walked through the house and out the front door, down the steps, and to the Bimmer. I looked over toward the house with the marijuana-selling grandmother. She was in her front yard, acting like she was policing the area, but she wasn't. She was prying and waiting for us to come out of Ellen's house. I motioned to Heidi and we walked over to her.

"Hi, Ray, who's your friend?"

"An associate." I wasn't smiling and she could tell I was about business on this fine summer afternoon. "I've got a picture I want you to look at."

Heidi handed the picture of Jack Parker to me and I showed it to her. "Uh-huh," she muttered. "I've seen him around."

"Oh?" I muttered back at her. "Have you seen him at Ellen's house?"

"Yeah, but not in about four or five months. He used to be there a lot. One of the few lucky patrons who got to spend the night. Sometimes he would spend days there. They spent a lot of time at the pool together."

"Okay, thanks," I said as we walked off.

"Hey, Ray," the old lady called out to me. "Want to buy some weed?"

"No, not today, granny." We walked to the Bimmer and climbed in. Heidi fired it and we worked our way back down to Missouri Avenue and headed west toward the Arch.

She was driving slowly, as if she was unsure of her destiny. She gave me a cursory look then said, "Where to?"

"We need to interview Viktor Agron. Where do you think he is?"

"Justice center."

"Okay, go there."

She had something on her mind. She was driving and trying to study me, again. I knew it was coming.

"You saw Jack's ring on Ellen's finger when we were doing the dope deal in Savannah?"

"Yeah."

She pondered for a second or so. "How did you know it was Jack's nugget ring? I'm sure there had to be more than one like it."

"I wasn't sure," I replied. "It kind of came together for me. Kind of like seeing Angel Perez. What were the chances of that? Same principle. Same drug deal. Weird. Right?"

We parked at a meter on Tucker in front of city hall, plugged it and made our way across the street to the new Justice Center. I flashed my creds to the guard. "We need to see a federal prisoner."

"Fourth floor," he barked. "But you've got to lock your guns up." He pointed to a row of lockers with keys in the locks. Heidi and I placed our Glocks in separate lockers. I dug for my crotch rocket and placed it on top of my Glock and we locked them. We took the elevator up and emptied out in a prison reception area. I flashed again to another guard.

"We need to interview Viktor Agron."

"Wait in there," he said pointing.

We walked into a stainless-steel and concrete room with a table bolted to the floor and four plastic chairs. The guard locked the door behind us with a thud, a sound I never wanted to get used to hearing. I thought about Rush City and the two dead hoodlums Sig and I rolled into the drainage ditch.

Viktor was escorted out to us by another guard who had him by the right arm and was guiding him as he shuffled along with his paper shoes and orange jumpsuit, his hands shackled to his waist by chains and a large leather belt. The ankle shackles allowed him a six inch gait which caused the paper shuffle and a rustling noise.

Viktor's head was down as he shuffled, like all prisoners. I often wondered if they kept their heads down because they were ashamed of their predicament or if they were unsure of their gait. In Viktor's case it had to be the later. He had no conscience and no shame.

He glared at Heidi and me as he entered the room. I read his look. He was thinking he would choke us to death and slide us into the Mississippi River if he had the opportunity.

"Sit," the guard ordered as if he was speaking to a misbehaving pit bull. Viktor sat on the plastic chair in front of us and glared. He was already turning yellow, the effect of incarceration on suntanned skin, and he was atrophying, his shoulders and neck were getting smaller due to the lack of high-protein food.

"I need to know about Jack Parker," I said. "What can you tell me about him?"

"Never heard of him."

"He was dating your wife, Viktor. He was a cop detached to DEA and he's missing."

"You come here and talk to me about some wayward cop. I told you, I never heard of Jack Parker, you fucking murdering cop. You think you've got me? You don't! You and some other asshole burned my house down and beat me up. You murdered my associates and dumped them in Rush City. I've got a bond hearing tomorrow morning, and I'll get bond. I'm not telling you anything. When my lawyer gets finished with you, you'll be the one sitting in here with this damn monkey suit on."

I was trying to read him. He was well informed, probably the work of some damn ex-cop legal investigator, and he was believable when he said he didn't know what I was talking about. That was a scary thing. Heidi and I stood and walked to the door while Viktor glared at us. A guard opened it for us and we walked into the reception area as he slammed it closed.

We collected our guns and were walking to the Bimmer when my cell rang.

"Yo!"

"Sue Lee here," the sexy voice said.

"Hi."

"Did you know that there is a bond hearing scheduled for tomorrow morning at ten o'clock?"

"No," I replied. "I mean, I heard there was going to be a bond hearing."

"Oh. Where did you hear it?"

"From Viktor Agron. Heidi and I interviewed him about ten minutes ago. He told me his lawyer was going to eat me for brunch. Should I be concerned?"

"Maybe. Anyway it's been rescheduled. It's going to be this afternoon, one o'clock in Judge Saunders' courtroom. Be there fifteen minutes early. We need to talk."

"Okay. Is his lawyer still Ira Brooks? We saw him nosing around over at Viktor's house when we went to retrieve the guns."

"Yes!"

I paused while it sunk in. "They've got to be in the cocaine business together?"

"Maybe, but immaterial at this point in time. He's defended him in the past. He was his lawyer of record in Florida when Viktor got some time for possession, and he was the one who got Viktor out early on a writ. He's apparently a long-time associate of Viktor Agron."

"I take it Ira is the one who got the bond hearing scheduled for today."

"Correct, he's family friends with Judge Saunders, golfing buddies at the country club and such."

"Oh, great."

"See you in court." Lawyers love to say that.

"We've got two hours," I said to Heidi; "There's a bond hearing for Viktor this afternoon, 1300, Judge Saunders' court. What do you want to do?"

"Have lunch."

We changed our tack and backtracked to the café

adjacent to the courthouse and the jail. Mexican was the special of the day so we ordered the Mexican special plato and sipped iced tea as we watched the lawyers and bondsmen and cops and agents scurry about the courthouse steps.

"Ira Brooks, huh," she muttered.

"Yeah."

"He's a damn good lawyer," she continued as she studied me.

"I know."

"He's in NADDIS," she said, matter-of-factly

"He's a documented dope dealer?" I exclaimed.

"Maybe, but not everyone in the NADDIS computer is a dope dealer. He's been associated with dope dealers, and he's been observed in third world countries associating with drug czars. It could be a professional thing. Maybe he was counseling someone when he was picked up on surveillance. I just thought you'd like to know that he is in NADDIS."

"Thanks."

The waitress brought our food and we were devouring our tacos and eyeballing our enchiladas when she asked the question.

"Have you ever testified in a federal bond hearing?"

"No."

"Humm."

"What is that supposed to mean?" I asked.

"It's different than any other court preceding. The defendant's lawyer can and will say anything to get his client out on bail. His goal is to convince the judge that you're the bad guy and that his client was framed by you. Sue Lee will probably advise you of this stuff but I thought I'd give you a heads up."

"Thanks."

She paused. I knew there was more. "It isn't going to be

pleasant, and as in every federal court preceding, it will be recorded and transcribed and be a part of Viktor Agron's case. Information uncovered in this hearing could be used in his trial, so watch what you say."

I nervously ate my lunch and the enchilada was sitting in my stomach like a brick as we finished and paid the check.

"Ready?" She asked.

"Yeah. I guess I don't have any choice."

24

We strolled over to the courthouse and took the elevator up to Sue Lee's office. We walked in as she was eating plain yogurt, an orange and drinking bottled water. The enchilada was moving inside me and I wished I had restrained myself.

"Ira Brooks is going to attack you on the stand," Sue Lee said as she studied me. "There isn't much chance of Viktor Agron getting bond, but his lawyer is going to attempt to bring damaging information out so he can use it at a later date, during the trial. Just answer the questions and don't try to be a hero. Let's go!"

She whisked out of the office with Heidi and me following as we click-clacked our way down the hall to Judge Saunders' courtroom. We walked in and sat down on the government's side. Viktor was at the defendant's table, shackled with his hands free in his orange jump suit.

He glared at us with hatred. Ira Brooks was seated next to him. My new nemesis, one of thousands I've had over the years and I'm still free and gainfully employed. I wondered where this would lead.

"OH YEA, OH YEA, BOND HEARING IS IN SESSION IN THE EASTERN DISTRICT OF MISSOURI, HONORABLE JUDGE ERWIN SAUNDERS PRESIDING. ALL RISE," the bailiff called out as Judge Saunders walked into the courtroom and took the seat at his desk.

We all stood, and then sat as the judge nodded to us. Ira Brooks and Sue Lee went to the bench and conferred with the judge. I examined Ira and ran physiognomy on his movements and appearance.

He sported a long salt-and-pepper ponytail and was wearing a very expensive, summer, black wool suit, with the hair of his pony tail sticking to it and coming out like a purebred Doberman.

The scene reminded me of my first day at junior high school. There were new faces, different students and teachers and a strange school, but it wasn't difficult to figure everybody out.

Sue Lee, the genius and motivated straight A student, determined to be a class leader. Judge Saunders, the mentor teacher recognizing Sue Lee as a potential leader and catering to her. Ira Brooks, the wealthy kid with all of the credentials. Good student, athlete, suave, and sure of himself, but there was something that stands out about guys like Ira. A dark side that only the most astute reader of body movements could detect.

His aggressiveness wasn't sincere but a learned trait. He had to make himself be aggressive and deep down inside he felt guilty about it. He was no doubt rotten to the core and would do anything to win, just like the rich and chosen guys in junior high school who would cheat on the basketball court and woo other classmates to follow and worship and beat other guys up for them.

Ira Brooks desired to be an asshole so badly that he worked at it. Maybe that's why he was associated with scum like Viktor Agron. He learned from him. Asshole 101, criminal Viktor Agron, instructor.

The smell of the courtroom was even like junior high school. The smell of books and wood and pencils and erasers. The whole scenario was depressing because I was never on the winning side like the Ira and Sue types. I was always sitting with the masses watching the Iras and Sue Lees of the world learn to lead.

I didn't give a damn who led when I was a student, and I don't give a damn who leads now; just don't try to lead me. My philosophy of life. It's why I'm where I am. Things never change. Life's a bitch and then you get murdered.

Sue Lee and Ira walked away from the bench. Sue Lee

sat at the prosecution table and Ira turned and faced the judge. “The defense calls Task Force Detective Ray Arnold, your honor,” he loudly said.

“TASK FORCE DETECTIVE RAY ARNOLD,” the bailiff shouted. I stood and walked to the witness stand. All eyes were on me, trying to read me and maybe having pity on me as the ordinary kid goes head-to-head with one of the chosen ones. I was being underestimated, again.

‘DO YOU SOLEMNLY SWEAR THAT THE TESTIMONY YOU GIVE HERE WILL BE THE TRUTH, THE WHOLE TRUTH, AND NOTHING BUT THE TRUTH SO HELP YOU GOD?” the bailiff asked as I stood before him with my right hand raised.

“I do.”

“Take the stand.”

I walked up to the witness stand and sat down. A cute blonde court reporter was sitting at my right pounding on her recording machine. She looked at me as if she was trying to size me up like a bookie sizes up a prizefighter. How many rounds will he stay on his feet?

Ira Brooks strolled up to me. His expensive suit coat was unbuttoned showing he had a flat belly, commendable for a 45 year old lawyer. He smirked at me as if to say, “You blocked my jump shot at recess, Arnold. I would have won the game for my team if you hadn’t blocked the shot. If you ever do it again, you mediocre poor kid, I’m going to have my associate and asshole mentor, Viktor Agron, beat your brains out and crush your larynx.”

His tie cost five hundred dollars. He hiked up his left sleeve, probably a nervous habit, like a ballplayer or a golfer tugging on a piece of clothing. I eyeballed his wrist watch. It was a boy toy, a Silberstein Marine-Themed Tourbillion. Eighty thousand dollars. Only an asshole would put eighty grand on his wrist. What kind of message was he trying to send with that kind of a toy glaring at people? But maybe the casual observer wouldn't know the expense of the gaudy bangle. Old cops know. We have to know the fair market value of almost anything without having to go to an expert.

"State your name and title for the court, please."

"Ray Arnold, Task Force Detective, Drug Enforcement Administration, St. Louis field office."

I glared at him, saying to myself, "You don't frighten me, you fucking charlatan. I've been in combat with dick-heads like you and Viktor Agron for my entire life." He picked up on it and back stepped one step, then resumed.

"Would you please tell the court where you were on the evening of June twenty ninth, and what you're duties were."

"I was on surveillance in East St. Louis, Illinois, trying to track down a federal fugitive, Viktor Agron."

"And you affected the arrest of my client on that morning, Detective Arnold?"

"Yes."

"Please tell the court what transpired before, during, and after the arrest of Viktor Agron."

"I was on surveillance and I observed Viktor Agron enter the house on Twenty second Street so I continued the surveillance, waiting for him to come out. While I was waiting, the front of the house became engulfed in flame, so I went to the rear of the house and waited for him to come out, disarmed him, then arrested him, and conveyed him to the St. Louis field office."

"Disarmed him, Detective Arnold? Are you saying my client was armed?"

"Yes."

"Did you have possession of a weapon when you arrived at the DEA field office in St. Louis, the location that you and my client arrived at in the morning, at approximately seven thirty A.M.?"

"No."

"Then, Detective Arnold, how do you expect the court to believe that there was said weapon if you didn't have a weapon to show?"

"I had to go back and get it after the booking. I had tossed them in the weeds during the arrest."

"Them, Detective Arnold? Now you're saying there were two weapons?"

"Yes, a twelve-gauge shotgun and a semi-automatic pistol."

"And where are those weapons now?"

"Evidence locker, St. Louis field office."

He was in deep thought holding the bridge of his nose and walking around in front of the witness stand looking down. He was planning a trap, an incriminating question I would have to answer, and that would look brilliant on the record for future use.

"Who assisted you in the arrest of Viktor Agron, Detective Arnold?"

"No one. I was alone."

"Your honor," Ira Brooks said with his pony tail hopping on his back, "please instruct the witness to answer the questions I present to him in a truthful manner. He's under oath to answer with a true response."

"Sustained," the judge replied. "Answer the question, Detective."

"I answered it, judge." I stared at him.

"He answered the question, your honor," Sue Lee said. "The defense is badgering the witness. This is a bond hearing, not a discovery hearing."

"Your honor," Ira Brooks continued. "The defense is trying to show the court that this entire case against my client is fabricated and a collusion by a DEA operative and others to discredit my client and to have him illegally incarcerated. My client needs his freedom on bond to help in the defense of himself against this collusion. My line of questioning will show this collusion."

"Continue, Mister Brooks."

"Detective Arnold," he paced in front of the witness stand, "I will repeat the question for you. Who assisted you in the arrest of Mister Agron?"

"No one!"

"No, Detective Arnold, that is not a truthful answer. The witness is purposely withholding information and continues to be evasive in his answers, your honor. I recommend he be held in contempt."

Sue Lee stood. "Permission to approach, your honor."

"Okay," the bored judge boringly said. Sue and Ira Brooks approached the bench and conferred with the judge. I could hear their muffled tones as they talked over their constitutional rights arguments.

I looked closely at Ira Brooks. I was close enough to reach over and grab his larynx and take him out. Why does he do this kind of work? He's been sleeping between silk sheets his entire life. Why strive to be an asshole? Ira Brooks is no different than TFD Cletus Jones, an asshole criminal hiding behind a title. He's the epitome of the St. Louis ruling class; never questioned, never scrutinized.

They finished conferring. Sue Lee walked back to the prosecution table, and Ira Brooks took his position in front of me.

"Isn't it true that you and an associate burned Viktor Agron's home down and when he ran out of his burning home you and the associate beat him, kicked him about the head and shoulders, and then tossed him in the trunk of your associate's vehicle and drove him to Clayton?"

"No," I lied.

"Objection, your honor," Sue Lee said. "Mister Brooks is

coming out of left field with accusations and innuendos about burning houses down, and collusion. Where is this going to end? Viktor Agron is a dangerous man and a flight risk. If he's allowed bail, he will leave the country. Bond should be denied for him." She sat down.

"Your honor," Ira Brooks continued. "My client has been wrongly accused. My client never sold cocaine to Task Force Detective Ray Arnold. I have an eye witness who will testify to that. He was denied his rights by Task Force Detective Ray Arnold when he and another person burned his home and beat him when he attempted to flee his burning home. He wasn't armed and the weapons that Detective Arnold said he was armed with have serious chain-of-evidence problems. My client needs bond to help with his defense of these untrue charges. My client is not a flight risk and will honor any bail agreement."

"Bail is set at one-hundred thousand dollars," the judge said as he hammered the gavel. Court dismissed."

Federal Marshal's whisked Viktor out of the courtroom as he smirked at me. Ira Brooks glared and then backed off as I glared back at him. The judge had left the courtroom and there was no one to protect him. He attempted to warm up to Sue Lee, but she ignored him and warmed up to me as Heidi joined us at the prosecution table. "He got a lot in," Sue Lee said.

"I can't believe he got bail," I said. "What the fuck is up with that?"

"I don't know, Ray. The better question is, who is the witness to the drug deal on the cobblestones?" Sue Lee waited for an answer. I thought back to the fisherman who retrieved the Glocks then blew it off.

Heidi was staring. "There's never a dull moment with you, Ray."

"I know. It's always been that way. I can't figure it. I

never could."

"Coming over tonight?"

I pondered. "No. There's something I need to look into."

We walked out of the courtroom, took the elevator down and walked out of the courthouse and strolled to the government Bimmer. We climbed in, Heidi cranked it, and we were westbound on the Daniel Boone heading for Clayton in two minutes.

I was zoning over the events of the day. The Helen of Troy, Illinois, interview was haunting me. There had to be a connection between her and Ira Brooks. Why would Brooks be loyal to Viktor Agron? Doesn't add up. There are certain things men strive for: sex, money, power. Brooks was born with money and power. But as Sue Lee said, "It's immaterial." I'll probably never find out. He's St. Louis insulated. Protected and coddled.

Heidi was shooting glances at me as she drove. "You lied under oath," she said nonchalantly.

I didn't respond.

"About Sig Otto when you guys arrested Viktor Agron. You protected him. You didn't have to, you know. You're legally sworn federally, and you could've used anyone to assist you in the arrest. Technically, you could have stopped a person on the street and empowered him to assist you."

"Oh, yeah, interesting," I boringly said. "I was protecting my C/I, something DEA seldom does. Remember, Heidi. The difference between me and any DEA agent is that I know the difference between the good guy and the bad guy."

"But you still lied after you were sworn."

"I was sworn years ago, Heidi. "Probably about the time you were going into grade school. The oath I took was slowly read to me by a state judge who was probably eighty five years old. He made me repeat it before he gave me a city cop badge and credentials. Part of the oath was that I would diligently protect the citizens of the City of St. Louis and the State of Missouri. After he gave me my badge, he told me there was a bad element in society that needed to be eliminated. That's what prisons are for, he said. Sometimes you have to bend the law a little to make it work for the betterment of society, he told me. I bend the law a little from time to time. The oath I took from the old judge is the only one I adhere to."

She pulled the Bimmer into the garage. We climbed out and made our way into the building and then the office without talking. She was still reading me and it was making me uncomfortable. I checked my wristwatch and it was going on 1700, the magic time when the offices at the DEA field office become deserted. There were apparently no deals tonight; the task force office was already empty.

"Do you need a ride home?"

"Yeah."

She was staring inquisitively again. Her brain was working overtime.

"We can stop and have a drink."

She was trying too hard. I wondered why. I felt myself coming out of her grasp. I wondered if she had the same feeling. I had the feeling she thought she was failing in her duty as the great mesmerizer of Ray Arnold. It had come to the point of distrust. She was up to no good. "No, Heidi. Not tonight. I just need to do some work, that's all," I was trying to calm her.

"You and Sig are going rogue again, aren't you?"

"No."

She continued to study me.

Who do you report to, Heidi girl? Is it Doc? Is it somebody from Washington? Questions I wanted to ask her. But this wasn't the right time. I didn't want her to know I suspected her of collusion against Ray Arnold. My mind was racing with possible scenarios on the ride to my house. I thanked her and got out.

I felt like I was climbing out of the dentist's chair after oral surgery.

25

I tossed and turned all night. I climbed out in the bright sunlight, made a pot, sipped and pondered. I needed a day away from the office. Away from Heidi, Doc and deals. They were consuming my life and infringing on my creative investigative endeavors. I waited until 0900, then called Carla. “I’m on surveillance. See you later in the day.”

“Okay,” she replied. No questions. I waited for my cell to go off. Heidi was bound to call to check up on her whore. But she didn’t. I sat on the deck and watched the boats as I had a leisurely breakfast. I was on my fourth cup and thinking deeply about Jack Parker. I was missing something. I had been led away from my mission. I needed to clear my mind and think unencumbered.

I needed to interview someone. There was more to this story than I was hearing or seeing. I concentrated on my previous interviews. Otis Parker. He knew something beneficial to me. He had to. Jack confided in him. He was a fellow cop; a fellow dissident in law enforcement, an attitude guy, and a dad. Otis was holding back.

I took a quick shower, climbed into the uniform of the day: jeans, black muscle shirt, deck shoes, and headed out with the top down in the Austin Healey. I was on a hunch journey. I didn’t know if Otis was working. If not, I would find out where he lived and go to his home. But I had to do something positive. I felt free and like an investigator, instead of a guided cop, a C/I with a badge.

I parked on the cobblestones, walked the gangplank, and whisked into the casino. The cigarette smoke and the sounds of the slots was offensive. I walked around looking for him. If I didn’t see him I would ask for him; then, if I had to, find out where he lived. I spied him in a corner behind a pod of slots. He was zoning out. He didn’t know I was zeroing in on him. "Otis," I said.

He jumped and stared. I didn't act phony by smiling and offering him my hand. I stared and he stared. He knew why I was there. He probably expected me. "We need to talk, Otis. Someplace we can go?"

He didn't speak. He motioned with his hand, walked away and I followed him. We walked through the haze of smoke; the large groups of hacking, morning-drinking gamblers through some doors and hallways and came out at the stern of the big casino boat. The door closed behind us and it was quiet. Just us and the nasty river. More private than the fantail.

He still stared. He had the look. It was saying, "I don't like you. I don't trust you. What do you want?" I had to be direct with him. "I need some guidance from you, Otis. Some information. Something that Jack confided in you."

"You're DEA," Otis said. "I don't trust anybody from DEA. DEA is the reason my boy's gone."

I felt compelled to lie to him. "I was sent to DEA to investigate 'Jacks disappearance." I was pleading with my words.

"Who sent you?"

"The chief sent me to DEA," I replied.

"The chief? You know what I think of that chief?" I stared. "He's a phony damn politician. I rue the day I joined that damn police department. If I had been something different maybe Jack wouldn't have joined and then he'd be here today."

"Tell me Otis. Tell me what Jack told you. What was going on? What was the scheme? Was he going to score some cash? Was it a rip? Was it big-time money? Where was it coming from? Who was involved? I know you know, Otis. Tell me. Let me solve this mystery."

It was as if I had hit him with a cattle prod. He jumped

and walked away from me, toward the dirty Mississippi River. He stopped and turned to face me. I knew what he was thinking. He was thinking about trust. Can he trust me? Why trust me? I was part of the establishment he despised, yet I seemed to care. I could be the angel of mercy to him, the one who was going to stop the pain of grief. The one who was going to settle the score. He wanted revenge for a missing son.

"I'm the guy, Otis. I can do it for you," I softly said. "You've got to trust me. I'll keep you out of it. I swear, Otis."

"He was going out of the country," he began. "Jack and two DEA agents. One of them was a chick. It was a big score. They were going to seize some Colombian's drug proceeds. It didn't work out. That's all I can tell you. I've got to get back to work."

He walked away leaving me standing on the stern of the old boat. I felt like I had been hit in the temple with a roundhouse left. I was stiff-legged and dizzy. The information was more than I had bargained for.

I wandered on the stern, watching the mud slide by, smelling the toxic fumes coming from the mighty Mississippi. I turned, walked through the doors and hallways, and made my way to the Austin Healey.

I was in another world. My concentration was solely on the case. I slowly drove around the city with the top down: shifting gears and pondering. It was good information. The best. It was toxic waste and had to be handled accordingly.

I guided the roadster over the Poplar Street Bridge and found myself cruising Helen of Troy's, Illinois house. I didn't know why. It just happened that way. I spied Granny. She smiled and waved so I stopped.

"Hey, Ray Richards, right? Haven't seen you in a couple of days. You run out of dope?"

"Yeah," I replied with a laugh. "Anything been going on around here?"

"Always, Ray. Want to buy some weed?"

"Yeah."

She smiled and reached into her apron, came out with a baggie of dope and handed it to me. I gave her a crisp twenty and she stuffed it into her pouch.

"Helen tells me the hubby's going to get out of jail on bond real soon. She says the case on him is bogus and that the cop who put it on him is probably going to get arrested for murdering his associates."

I let it sink in. It was good information. It fit. It wasn't from left field and it was sobering. "Did she say how that information came about?"

"From some high-ranking guy in DEA. Helen was told about it from some federal prosecutor on this side of the river who's a friend of hers. The cop is going to be arrested over there and transported over here. It's all hush-hush at this point."

I stared at her in disbelief. How did she know so much? Why would Helen confide in her? Why was she telling me this stuff? She must've read me. "I'm telling you because I like you, Ray."

"Thanks, granny. I'll keep in touch."

I drove aimlessly for hours, shifting and letting the wind blow my cares away. But it didn't work. My cares were multiplying. I was alone in a federal maze where all the players had a map of the maze but me.

I jumped on the Daniel Boone, took it to Boyle, exited, headed north then west, again and ended up on Euclid. I cruised and looked at the ladies who parade the street. Fashion models should look so good.

I headed west on Lindell, wound my way to Clayton, and pulled into the DEA garage. I climbed out and glanced at the surveillance camera and wondered if Square Bidness Willie Mitchell was looking at me. I came to the realization that I didn't give a damn what anybody at DEA thought about me.

I walked into the stairway and took it to the fourth floor, key-padded my way in and walked to the task force office. I went directly to my desk and plopped. Heidi was watching me. I checked my wristwatch. It was after seventeen-hundred. Doc's door was closed. It was fun and games time.

The boys were whooping and laughing. Pat Brown had apparently gotten one of Ross' ascots and had wadded it into a ball about the size of a cork ball. He was pitching to Carl Robinson who was using a broom handle as a bat. "Strike one," the crew shouted as Carl missed the pitch.

Ross was pissed. "I am a special agent with the Drug Enforcement Administration, United States Department of Justice. I order you to return my property to my desk."

"Yeah, alright, Ross," Pat said. "You agents aren't fun anymore. Whatever happened to the good old days?"

I caught Heidi glancing at me. She smiled on cue. I smiled back, but the thrill was gone. I felt she recognized it. The music began. Lightnin' Sam Hopkins was singing "Rock Me Baby," Pat Brown and Monica were dancing around the office while Mike Schweig made highballs and smoked.

Ross Milton sat and frowned. Heidi beat on her laptop and Carl Robinson was having phone sex with a lonely secretary he had met at the club.

I tried to relax. I leaned back in my chair and watched the show. The song ended, the disc jockey was on a roll. He tossed on Stevie Ray Vaughn, "Love Struck Baby." Pat and Monica picked up the beat and were flying around the room panting and laughing.

Carl and Pat wandered off like two wire-haired terrier puppies looking for another place to get into trouble as

Heidi, who had been watching me since I walked in, made her move. I was staring at the window forlornly; I saw her reflection and turned to her.

"What's up?" she asked.

I knew what she meant. She wanted me to tell her what I had been up to today. I took another hard look at her. I could get real serious about her under different circumstances.

But there was always a question in my mind when I was around her. Today's questions: Are you the DEA agent who went out of country with Jack Parker? If so, who was the other agent? Was Angel Perez the intended? Where's Jack Parker? I think you know. But those were questions not yet to be asked.

I smiled at her. "Don't worry, I'm casual. I was just zoning." She gave me her sexiest smile and meandered back to her desk. I watched her as she walked. A perfect upper body V, but not obtrusive. Firm, tight, healthy, and female.

The crew had taken their party to the Club. I watched her as she typed, went to the printer, and typed some more.

Her cell rang. "Yes?" she answered in her sexiest tone. "Yes, okay, yes. I understand, yes," she muttered. She ended the call and zoned for an instant, then as if things clicked for her, she turned to me and smiled. "You want to come over tonight?"

The conspiracy was in the works. It was coup de grace time for Detective Ray Arnold. I had to play it out, see where it led. I knew more than they thought. They had underestimated me. They weren't in control, but neither was I. "Yeah, but I need to tend to my dog," I said with a smile. "Why don't you wait for me in the office. I won't be long."

She studied me for an instant. "Yeah, go ahead. I've got paper work to do. I'll be here waiting for you."

I headed for the garage and my Austin Healey, climbed in, pulled out, and got on my cell phone. I started to dial

Sig's land-line, hesitated, and pulled into a Shell station. I climbed out and found a pay phone near the restroom, dialed his cell, and waited. He picked up after five rings.

"Hey, don't say my name."

"Okay," he said in a puzzled tone.

"Meet me in the backyard of your house in ten minutes. Wear a Tee and some shorts." I hung up, climbed back into the Healey, and cruised through the park. Scantily clad college girls were walking and jogging. The park was in full bloom, the trees full and lush. It was paradise.

I remembered Viktor Agron sitting in the back seat of Heidi's G Bimmer as we were taking him to the courthouse for arraignment. I wondered if he was taking in the sights of summer and wondering if he would ever see them again. Now I'm having the same thoughts.

I got on Kingshighway and then Lindell and then Euclid as I worked my way toward Hortense Place. I made the left and turned into Sig's palace driveway. I drove to the rear of the house and parked in the courtyard. I saw him standing in the middle of the yard under a two hundred year old oak tree, confused, wearing an old wife-beater and a pair of safari shorts.

I walked to him and raised my hands out to my sides as if I was attempting to fly. He did the same. I walked around him looking for bulges, then I looked around the yard for a parabolic dish pointing our way. There was none. I pushed his arms down.

"We need to speak lowly."

"Okay," he said with the puzzled look.

"I think I'm going to be arrested for the murders of the Rush City two." I let it sink in. He was cool to my statement, waiting for more information.

"I think Heidi told my boss Doc Penrose that you and I killed them and dumped them in Rush City. I'll probably be arrested tomorrow morning. There's an FBI agent, David Moynihan. Remember me telling you about him? You got him with your cannon."

"Yes."

"An educated guess is he'll probably take you into custody. Have you ever talked to him?"

"No."

"Has anyone approached you about the murders?"

"No."

"Okay, here's the scenario. They'll have me chained to a table at the justice center on the East side. I'll be looking forlorn, and it won't be an act. Moynihan will tell you he doesn't want you, he wants me. He'll tell you I came in on you, that I gave evidence implicating you. That'll be a lie. He'll tell you the only way you can save yourself is to come clean and tell him what he wants to hear. You must tell him you don't know what he's talking about and you want your lawyer. That's the only thing you'll say to him or to anyone else. Is that clear?"

"Yes." I turned and walked away. "Ray?" I turned and stared at him. "We'll have our revenge."

I nodded and walked to the Healey. Fired it and headed for my house. I played with Tyrone, fed and watered him, then headed for Clayton. I parked in the garage and walked into the office. Heidi was alone, and glamorous. She had made herself up while I was gone. She flashed her movie-star smile, "Ready?"

"Yeah."

We headed for the door, took the stairway down and climbed into her G car Bimmer. She headed south and I scrunched down in the leather and worried. I wondered when it was going to happen.

"Tomorrow morning," she said and then paused.

"Tomorrow morning?" I exclaimed then composed

myself.

She continued, “We should go to Sue Lee’s office and advise her about the ring you observed on Ellen Agron’s finger.”

“Great idea. Great minds think alike.” Trivial, I said to myself. It’s apparently going to happen tomorrow morning.

She stopped at a liquor store, put it in park and said, “I’ll be right back.”

I sat crunched as she zoomed inside and came back out with a package. She slid back in with a giant bottle of chilled Brut and two plastic cups. “Open this, Ray.”

I twisted the wire off and manipulated the cork, then opened the door and pointed the bottle outside as the cork popped off and the foam spurted out. It died down and I brought it back inside. She had the cups ready and I poured. She slugged her cup down in thirty seconds as I sipped mine, then refilled both of them. “Is this a celebration? I asked. “Is it your birthday?”

“No, I just felt this is a special night.”

She was melancholy with the Bud Light sign reflecting on her face and the late evening traffic zooming by and as the champagne went down and started taking its effect, I was getting melancholy with her. It would be my last tussle with her; I knew it.

We drank half the bottle and I refilled our glasses. She put the Bimmer in gear and slowly merged into traffic, southbound toward Oakville. I flipped on the stereo and tuned in an oldie R&B station. Ray Charles was singing “Hard Times.” We were singing along with him and sipping Brut as we moved through the darkness. Ray got to the part where he had a woman who was always around, then he lost his money and she put him down. I sang along while thinking about Big-Boned Gloria and the dozens like her I had known and loved. Heidi picked up on it as Ray ended his attack on my senses.

"Thinking about someone, lover?"

"Only you, lover."

Her cup was empty again. I refilled hers and topped off mine. "It's gone. Empty."

I sat the bottle on the floor and we sipped and drove and sang along with Etta James as we pulled into her driveway. We finished our wine while the garage door slowly climbed upward. She pulled in and killed the engine and we were out and walking into the house.

We scrunched our cups and tossed them as she went into the bedroom while I stood in the kitchen waiting for my invitation to join her. "Ray, you want to come in?"

I walked in and she was nude. The lights were turned down and at first I thought she was wearing a bikini because of her tan lines, but her nipples gave it away. They were big and wide and protruding and her stance was a challenge to me.

I did the expected, the tearing off of my jeans and T shirt, while looking around the room for an ultra violet, covert DEA lens. I didn't see any and we fell into bed together.

The sex was unusual in the sense that it was pure and willing. We didn't hold back; there were no inhibitions. It was like sex before a guy is going into combat or being taken away from his lover for some unknown reason.

It lasted into the early morning hours, and then she was waking me telling me to get up and shower because we had to go to the courthouse to see Sue Lee. She was dressed and ready to go.

I climbed out of bed with a wine hangover and stumbled into the shower like a zombie, used up all of the hot water and then stood in the cold water hoping to bring myself back to the reality of life; work or die.

I toweled off and stumbled into the bedroom and she had

a clean black Tee shirt for me and my Levis laying on the freshly made bed. She was standing in the doorway eating a bagel and drinking a cup of coffee, watching me as I dressed. “I poured a cup for you,” she purred.

She watched every move I made, kind of like she would never see me getting dressed again. I smiled at her and walked past her into the kitchen, slurped coffee and ate bagels while we both stood at the breakfast bar and studied each other.

“Are you ready to go?” She asked.

“Yeah.”

We strolled out and into the garage. She activated the garage door and we slid into the leather seats of the Bimmer still trying to covertly study each other as she backed out. She slid it into drive and we headed for downtown. There wasn’t much chatter, just the watching of the traffic and the listening to the morning news on KMOX.

She pulled in front of the courthouse and stopped. “Go on in, Ray. I’ll park and join you in a couple of minutes.” I slid out and watched her as she drove off. Then I walked into the courthouse and took the elevator up to Sue Lee’s floor. I got off and walked to her office and stopped at Doc’s girlfriend’s desk.

“I need to see Sue Lee.” I could see her at her desk, dressed in beige this morning, jewelry and hair perfect, makeup like a China doll’s, which is what she was, a life-like China doll with an impressive brain.

“Come in, Detective.” I walked past Doc’s girlfriend’s desk and stopped at Sue Lee’s. “You can sit down,” she said more like a directive than an option. “What can I do for you?”

She wasn’t smiling and she was acting nervous and unsure of herself. Before I could get into my spiel she said, “Excuse me for a moment” and walked out of her office to

Doc's girlfriend's desk in the outer office. She whispered to her which I thought was out of character for her. Intelligent people don't whisper. It accomplishes nothing and it draws attention that there's a conspiracy brewing.

I heard the word "marshal" in the whisper and then she came back into her office and sat at her desk. "I'm sorry for the delay," she said with a smile. "What can I do for you this morning?"

"Heidi thought I should clue you in on an observation I made when we were setting up the Savannah dope deal with Viktor Agron."

"Heidi? Oh, yes, where is she?"

"She's parking the car. Shall I wait for her?"

Sue Lee didn't answer. I sensed someone else in the room. The feel of cold steel was pressed against my temple. It's strange how the human mind works under stress. In an instant I knew the steel was the muzzle of a pistol, and in the same instant, my mind took me back to my early years as a rookie cop.

Some of the old cops were gangsters in those days. They were robbers and burglars and many of them worked for organized criminals as security for card games. They were referred to as doormen. As the department began to modernize, the new breed, the educated, politically correct cops sought to weed the gangsters out.

Some were sent to the Central West End district to finish their sordid careers, and for some unknown reason, I was the chosen one to have a few of them as partners.

They had advice for me. Advice to keep me alive in a job where combat was always lurking. One of them, a doorman, told me amateurs always stick their guns at your temple, or a little forward of your temple. They do this because they feel it will intimidate you and that you will then give up your weapon, and your life. Turn your head away from the gun, the doorman told me. That rolls the barrel away from your temple and gives you the opportunity to slap it out of the guy's hand, or to grab and use against him. In that instant all of this came back to me.

I shot a quick glance at Sue Lee who was frozen in fear, then rolled my head away from the barrel. I could feel the muzzle rolling away from my temple just like the gangster cop had told me. A worst case scenario would be that if he pulled the trigger before I could get control of it, I would lose part of my nose. Better than my brains.

I came up hard with my left hand and slapped the weapon away. It came out of the guy's hand and went muzzle over butt toward Sue Lee. She screamed and jumped to the right and the gun went over her left shoulder and rebounded off the wall behind her chair.

I had the guy's wrist and I stood and threw him down to the floor. Two more guys came in with pistols drawn. They were United States marshals, which is a fancy name for courthouse security.

"Give it up, detective," one of them shouted. I stood with the first guy's arm still in my hand and his body at my feet. I looked back over at Sue Lee.

"You've got a federal complaint in the Southern District of Illinois. Please stop resisting!"

I had to play the game. "Complaint? Complaint for what?"

"Murder. The murder of two gangsters in Rush City. FBI Special Agent David Moynihan has an informant who was an eyewitness. You might as well give it up, Ray."

She looked forlorn as I released the arm of the inept marshal. He jumped up with a vengeance, handcuffed me behind my back and retrieved his pistol from behind Sue Lee's chair. He roughly frisked me then got in my face,

"Where's your gun, asshole," he spat at me.

"In my crotch, asshole," I spat back at him.

He reached down into my trousers and came up with my crotch rocket 357.

"Neat," he muttered as he stuck it into his waistband.

Moynihan strolled in and smiled at me. He was so smug that if I hadn't been handcuffed, I would have probably tried to kill him.

"Well, this is a coincidence. I seem to remember a time when I gave you the opportunity to help yourself. It was in the evening after you and that damn female DEA agent, Heidi, had just wined and dined with one of your trusted C/I's. The night you guys shot the windows out of my G car with potatoes. Do you recall that evening, Detective Arnold?"

I didn't answer him. I stared just like so many criminals had stared at me when I had arrested them. A familiar face walked into the room. A sarge from Internal Affairs. "You're officially suspended without pay, Ray."

He walked out without fanfare. Doc walked in with Heidi at his side. They stood in the doorway and stared at me. Moynihan ignored them. "Take him down to the holdover and book him in," Moynihan ordered the Marshals.

"Yes, sir," they replied in unison. They marched me past Doc and Heidi who stared at me like I was a carnival freak down the hallway and into the elevator.

I was booked in for murder first, two-counts, federal charge, fingerprinted and photographed and put in a cell by myself. Time meant nothing to me. I was in a warp, confused and alone and staring at the walls and the bars.

They brought a heated frozen dinner and a cup of water at what must have been the evening meal. "Is this supper?"

He paused. "Yeah."

He wasn't a kid. Must have been in his sixties. Typical turnkey, military crew-type haircut and the stupid blue blazer with the seal on the pocket.

"I hear you fucked up," he said. "I used to be a cop with the city. I remember you. You were an up-and-comer, a potential big shot. You had it all. It's a shame you turned into a murderer and a dope dealer."

I didn't respond, but the words sunk in. Dope dealer? That again? I figured I needed a good lawyer. Don't overreact, I told myself. Let it play out and see where it goes.

It must have been morning. The turnkey banged on my cell and woke me. "Here," he said as he handed me a honey bun, a banana, a cup of water, and a cup of coffee through the bars. I devoured the food and slugged the coffee. The turnkey came back by. "You've got ten minutes."

"For what?"

"You're leaving for the East side in ten minutes. You're going before a federal magistrate this afternoon for arraignment."

I sat down on the steel and placed my hands over my face. I had been to many arraignments. I knew the procedure. Evidence must be presented for me to be held over. There is no evidence. There is one man's word against another. Moynihan lied. He had no informant. He was assuming he could roll Sig. He had met his match with him. Sig wouldn't roll.

A federal magistrate in the Southern District of Illinois will want evidence to hold me over. It isn't as bad as it looks. My reputation is ruined and I'll probably have to take an early retirement from the P D, but things could be worse.

The electronic lock on the cell door was activated. I dropped my hands from my face and stood. The turnkey came in and I placed my hands behind my back so he could cuff me.

"Face me."

I complied, and he placed a belt on me and cuffed me in front to the belt, then placed shackles on my ankles attached to a chain. "Follow me." I shuffled after him like a eunuch on holiday into the booking area.

There were two groups of prisoners standing and waiting for transfer or release. The turnkeys were checking our wrist bands and placing us in a group. I was in the group being transferred. Viktor Agron was standing in the group being released. He wasn't handcuffed or shackled and he leered at me.

My only defense against him would be to lie on my back and kick at him with both feet. This was his big chance to even the score. I leered back at him. Doc was right; they do look like janitors without their tans and muscles. Doc is always right!

"Viktor Agron," one of the turnkeys said.

"Yeah?"

"Come forward and sign this release form. Somebody made your bond."

He stepped up to the desk and signed the forms and was escorted to the electric door leading to freedom. The door slid open. He stopped and turned toward me, he nodded with satisfaction and rubbed his wrists. The turnkey picked up on his hesitation. "Do you want to go home?" He walked out without answering.

"This group is going to the courthouse in East St. Louis," one of the turnkeys said.

I looked out of place. I was the only white guy in my group. I was the minority, but having been born in East St. Louis and having lived and worked in St. Louis for a lifetime, I was accustomed to it.

"Follow me," the turnkey said. We shuffled after him and were led to a van parked in the sally port. We climbed in and sat on row seats without speaking. The two turnkeys got in and started the van and we were rumbling toward the east side in about three minutes.

We were on the Poplar Street Bridge. I peered out of the small window at the river below, doing what I always do, searching for the pleasure cruiser heading south toward the Gulf.

It had to be there, the one with the Captain cavorting with the scantily clad women, laughing and sipping cool beverages as the Arch and the city of St. Louis and the city of East St. Louis rolled by.

"Come on," I muttered. "Be there for me, just one more time to get me through this ordeal."

My criminal associates were staring at me as if I was already stir crazy. I kept peering through the mesh-covered window and the guard rails, it was there. A thirty six foot trawler with a giant flying bridge heading south. One guy and two chicks in bikinis.

The trawler was old but in good shape, just what I dreamed of buying when I retired, when I got out of jail, when I quit this strange way to make a living, when I even the score for Otis Parker and find his son.

My credibility was gone. How convenient for the criminals. Exactly what Moyninhan predicted. I was in trouble and labeled as a drug dealer and a murderer. I didn't know which was worse. Both were unforgivable sins.

My mind was still on the trawler as we entered the city limits of East St. Louis and wormed our way to the federal courthouse. We disembarked in the dark sally port and were placed in a bull-pen, unshackled and given a cup of coffee.

I had mine half-drank when a different turnkey came to the bars. "Ray Arnold?"

"Yeah."

I stood, faced him. He unlocked the mesh gate and I walked out to him. He brought out a pair of cuffs; I turned around and placed my hands behind my back. He took me out of the holding area, into an interview room. I had been in similar rooms for decades, interviewing prisoners, looking for information, seeking a confession.

He unhooked me and then hooked me to a steel table with a welded hook attached to it. I had one hand free. He turned and walked out and I sat there for about ten minutes, figuring I was being watched via electronic surveillance. The Feeb was probably watching with Sig and telling him how I came in on him. I had the look.

The door opened and Moynihan strolled in, still smug and victorious in his big pinch of me. He sat at the table. "You don't smoke, do you?" I shook my head. "Well, Ray. What are we going to do with you? You've been a real busy play-agent since you've been assigned to DEA. You like being a Fed?"

I didn't answer him, I just stared. It infuriated him. His expression became aggressive. "I've got an eyeball witness implicating you in the murder of Will Blanks and Robert Hasty. They weren't nice guys, but maybe, just maybe they didn't deserve to die. What do you have to say about that?"

I didn't respond. "We can still work together, Ray. I'm willing to give you another chance. I can pull this charge. You know that, don't you?" I still stared defiantly.

"You won't have a job or a paycheck when you get out of here, Ray. How are you going to make it?"

Dumb fucking Feeb. They think only they get fat pensions. I glared at him.

"I'd like an acknowledgment."

"Oh, okay, Rich, I'll give you one. Go fuck yourself!"

It was as if I spit in his face. "You'll regret that, Ray." He stood and walked out of the room. I sat there for another ten minutes when the same tired old turnkey came in and unhooked me from the table then hooked me up behind my back.

He escorted me out of the room to an elevator. We entered went up and disembarked in front of a magistrate's chambers door. We stood there, like children waiting for a school bus until I heard some clacking footsteps coming our way from a hallway around the corner. It was a young AUSA and Moynihan.

The turnkey and I were ignored as Moynihan and the AUSA walked into the judge's outer office. I was escorted in after them. They left us standing in the outer office while they walked in and conferred with the magistrate. After about another ten minutes I was summoned to enter the judge's chambers.

He was a middle-aged man, maybe fifty, who at one time had probably been a good athlete. He had the broad shoulders and developed neck of a wrestler or football player. His dark hair hadn't left him and his eyes were sharp.

He glanced at me and I recognized him. He no doubt remembered my name and face. He was a cop at one time, a city of St. Louis cop. He wasn't a friend, but he wasn't an enemy either.

He looked at the AUSA. "Is there any physical evidence in this case?"

"No, your honor," the green AUSA replied. He had been duped by Moynihan, intimidated into writing up this complaint. The arrest was bogus, but the AUSA's depended upon the FBI to bring them cases to try. It's like a doctor wanting patients.

They naturally want patients with insurance or cash. And they want patients who will refer them to other victims. They cater to the FBI. The judge knows this fact, but the AUSA doesn't. He only knows what he was told by a seasoned FBI agent.

"I don't see a statement by the accused in this complaint," the judge said looking at the AUSA and Moynihan.

"He refused to make a statement," Moynihan said.

The judge read on and then leaned back in his chair. "I'll take this under advisement at this time. A further investigation needs to be done. I need more information. This is one man's word against another. That's not enough in America, Agent Moynihan. You need to go back and further support your case against Detective Arnold. Release him!"

The turnkey unhooked me. I rubbed my wrists just like every other released criminal as I glared at Moynihan. The turnkey and I walked out and to the elevator, took it down to the holding area and I was given my property.

I had fifty dollars, my credentials, a credit card and the keys to my Austin Healey, which was parked in the DEA garage. "This isn't all of my property. Where's my gun?"

"We aren't allowed to give weapons back to released suspects. You'll have to get a writ from an attorney to get it."

I turned and walked out of the courthouse and onto the streets of East St. Louis. I hadn't been unstrapped for years and I felt naked. My Glock was locked in my desk at the task force, and I didn't have a firearm in my house.

I was never big on them but they're the tools of my trade. Kind of like a carpenter owning more than one hammer. He usually owns one at a time. You can't use two hammers at one time.

I walked toward the Metrolink, bought a ticket, and waited on the platform with the masses trying to get to the west side. It was where the commerce was. The Gateway to the West; it's what the Arch was all about, the celebration of settlers coming through the Midwest to get to California.

My train slid in and I boarded. I was rock and rolling toward the Arch and trying to think where I should get off. I could go to Clayton and get my Austin Healey. No, I didn't feel like coming face to face with my old DEA friends. Friends? Yeah, right!

Heidi knew what she was doing when she dropped me off at the U.S. Attorney's office. She knew there was an arrest order out for me. She was advised while we were still in the task force office, flirting and scheming. She had gotten that cell call. It was probably Doc telling her to keep me under surveillance and to make sure I showed up at Sue Lee's office in the morning.

It was typical DEA spy stuff. It was sickening. Nobody is loyal to anybody. But in retrospect, the agents are loyal to Doc, but only out of fear for their careers. Why should I expect loyalty from anybody at DEA? I was just a C/I with a badge, and I didn't even have the badge anymore.

I got off downtown and took the Chippewa bus to Broadway and Bates, got off and walked to my little house with a view. Tyrone, my only true friend, was glad to see me. His food bowl was empty and he was running low on water. I fed and watered him then went inside and took a long shower.

I washed my body three times, trying to scrub the federal stench off. I felt ashamed that I actually allowed myself to be brainwashed by those Geeks at DEA. Peer pressure's a bitch!

Tyrone was begging me to throw the tennis ball for him. It was about one P.M. and the sun was good, so I sat on the deck and watched the river go by as I tossed the ball toward the cliff. Tyrone never let it go over. The dog had athletic ability. My telephone rang and I answered it with a "Yo".

"I heard you got out." It was Heidi.

"Yeah," I coolly replied.

"I'm glad. We've all been terribly worried about you, Ray. Are you going to survive this thing? Are you going to be alright?"

"Yeah. I've had worse experiences but I just can't seem to think of one right now."

"You don't think anybody here had anything to do with this, do you?"

"Yeah, Heidi, I do. I think you knew I was wanted. I think you were advised to get me to Sue Lee's office so I could be arrested. Does that constitute a conspiracy against me? Fuck yeah, Heidi. You could have confided in me, but you didn't. That's not a friendly thing to do and I resent it."

She was silent for about thirty seconds. I held on in the dead air. "I had no choice, Ray. The rumor mill has you labeled as a dope dealer. Everybody here thinks you're a cocaine cowboy."

"Rumor mill? Dope dealer? That's what I've been hearing, too. Is that the Jim Schwartz information again?"

"Yeah," she replied. "He told Sue Lee you got Viktor Agron's stash after you murdered his henchman and you were selling it. The Feeb, Moynihan believes it, too."

"The Feebs, Heidi. Why is everything at DEA that's fucked up blamed on the Feebs? Are they the boogie men of the Justice Department? They get blamed for everything. I'm sick of hearing about the fucking Feebs. And I'm sick of the crazed Special Agent Jim Schwartz. I can't believe anybody would ever take anything that he said seriously."

"It's true about the Feebs, Ray," she calmly said. "They're probably listening to this conversation from a van parked on the street by your house. They're ruthless and they hate DEA. Schwartz is a nut, but he's got credibility, something I assume you don't have." I paused and thought about the phone tap, and my credibility. She was no doubt correct on both assumptions. I had been involved in several phone taps through the years, and I always heard the suspects talking about clicking on the line. I didn't hear any clicking.

"I want us to remain friends and lovers," she said in a seductive voice.

I thought back to the Angel Perez case. Why do I always revert to that case? It wasn't mine. I had nothing to do with it but it kept coming back to me. "I don't know if I can do that, Heidi."

"Tell me why."

It was a shot in the dark but I had to throw it out there for her to chew on. "The Angel Perez money seizure."

"What does that have to do with you?" she defiantly asked.

"If you legally seized Angel Perez's dope proceeds and turned them over to the United States Government, then I have no problem. But he wanted to kill you when we were on that boat with Viktor Agron. Viktor said he was pissed because you ripped him off for a bundle. Did you keep it? Did you turn it in?"

"Of course I turned it in," she said indignantly.

"Hold on. I'm getting a call on my cell." I placed the house receiver down so she couldn't hear me, then walked out into the yard, by the cliff and dialed the office on my cell.

"Task force," Carla said.

"Hey, I need a favor."

"Like what?"

"I need you to get into the Angel Perez file and tell me if there was a money seizure report."

"I could get into big trouble for that, Ray," she quietly said.

"All I want is a yes or a no."

"Okay, stand by."

I held on for two minutes. "Nope!" The line went dead. I walked back to the house phone and picked it up.

"You still there?"

"Yeah."

"Heidi, there's something I need to tell you."

"What?"

"I got into the Angel Perez file when I got back from Savannah with you. There's no seizure report in that file. You're lying. You stole the money. The rumor mill may have me as a cocaine cowboy but I'm not. I have you as a thief, and you are. A thief and a liar and that's why I can't be romantically involved with you."

I had tossed a bucket of cold water on her. I waited as she shook it off and regained her composure. "Ray," she calmly said. "You don't know what you're talking about. You're delving into dangerous territory and you aren't armed with the proper tools. You're playing a fool's game, Ray."

"You mind explaining that to me?" I asked. "I'm completely lost on that statement."

"If I explain it to you, it could cost me my career." I waited and let everything sink in and the dust to settle. The ball was in her court and if she wanted to continue our romance she would have to take a swipe at it.

"Okay, Ray, I'll clue you in, but you have to keep this confidential. Go to your backyard and call me back on your cell on the U C phone at the office."

"Okay."

Tyrone and I walked to the cliff and I dialed the undercover telephone.

"Okay," she said in answer. "Remember when I told you that the Angel Perez clue came from an outside agency?"

"Yeah."

"I lied. It came from another group within DEA. Jim Schwartz brought the case to me right after I got to St. Louis from the Miami office. The undercover operative was his C/I, and she told him Angel had tons of cash lying around and that it could be stolen or seized if DEA wanted to act on it. Jim talked with me and Doc and we agreed for me to go undercover in Colombia and to swipe his stash. Doc thought it might help him get another promotion, so we went for it."

"Promotion? I exclaimed. "Is that all anybody thinks about in that fucking agency? I wish he'd get promoted and get the fuck out of St. Louis. He belongs in Washington along with all of the other lying unconscionable bureaucrats."

"Ray, do you want me to finish?"

"Yes."

"Okay. Things went well and I flew to Miami and got set up in a hotel on Collins Avenue, undercover, and made arrangements to fly to Bogota. I didn't know Schwartz was in town. He wasn't supposed to be. We were supposed to meet up in Bogota. He kept hounding me, wanting me to go out with him. I turned him down, he was pissed. I called Doc, complained to him but Doc said to stay with the original plan, to fend him off. I did, eventually flew to Bogota and did the deal. The masses of cash the C/I had reported to Schwartz was an exaggeration, but I managed to get away with eight hundred thousand."

"Lucky you," I sarcastically said.

"Hey, it's drug proceeds," she said defensively. "It's blood money and it doesn't belong to the drug dealer. It belongs to the United States Government. It came from the states and it was supposed to go back to the states."

"The key word in that sentence is "supposed," Heidi," I calmly said. "Where did it go?"

"I'll tell you if you let me. So I globbed the proceeds and headed back to Miami and checked back into my room. I told the desk clerk that if anyone was inquiring about me that he should tell them I was indisposed at this time and to leave a message. A good hotel will provide that service."

"Yeah, I've heard."

"So, I'm in my room, and the desk clerk called me on the house phone and told me that a gentleman had inquired about me and that he was told I was indisposed. The gentleman then said, "Okay," and then walked to the elevator and took it up presumably headed for my room. He described him to me. It was Schwartz."

"He couldn't get in, could he?"

"Just listen, please. I cranked on the shower and went into the bathroom. I thought I'd hear him knock on the door, but I didn't so I peeked out and saw him standing in my room. He apparently had one of those room-entering keys like the Feebs carry. I watched him as he went directly for the cash. It was in a big duffel bag, kind of like a sea bag except this one had shoulder straps. It probably weighed a hundred and fifty pounds. He strapped it on and left."

"Interesting," I muttered.

"So I called Doc and told him my story. Doc said he was probably going to turn the cash in himself since it was his snitch and his case. I felt weird about it because it was my work and I was a DEA agent so it should have been my seizure. I told Doc I didn't like it. What if the cash isn't turned in? I'm going to get accused of stealing it. Doc said not to worry, and that if I'm asked about it, to tell headquarters that Schwartz took it after you got back. He said he'd be in headquarters by then anyway and that he'd intervene if there was a problem. Well, there's a problem and Doc hasn't been promoted. I had Carla get deeply into the DEA super-secret computer and to check on the seizure report. There isn't one. Schwartz stole the money."

"So Schwartz is a thief. What else is new? I'd like to have some kind of proof. It's easy to accuse a thief of stealing, but this is America. You should have something to back up your story."

"I do. I took his picture with my cell phone as he was leaving my room with the duffel bag. He didn't see me. I just stuck the phone out of the bathroom door and clicked it. I was lucky. It took it clear, caught him in flagrante. If you actually would have gotten into the file you would have seen the picture. You lied to me. I knew you were lying but I care enough about you to tell you the truth anyway. You figure out what you want to do about us. Call me when you decide."

The line went dead. She always wins! Is it because she's so damn much smarter than me? He who has the information controls the situation. The intelligence creed. She has access to the information. But she has access because she's a federal agent. She's a federal agent because she's smarter than me. Can something like that be taught? Damn it!

But I could have pulled her hole card. She didn't know that I was in possession of information that TFD Jack Parker, the missing cop, had gone to Colombia with her and Schwartz to work on the Angel Perez case. I didn't know the other DEA agent was Schwartz at the time, but I do now.

Heidi told me half-truths. They went to rip off Angel Perez for millions. I wondered if they got millions. Otis Parker said it was a bust. I wondered why they really went down there.

I walked back to the deck and sat in the sun. There were a plethora of boats going south, and I ogled every one of them and placed myself in them. It was summer and the folks from Chicago and the Great Lakes were taking their toys down to Florida. I guessed they lived on their yachts, cruised, played golf and went out to eat, then headed back north when the hurricanes threatened.

The picture of Schwartz walking out of Heidi's hotel room with a duffel bag full of drug proceeds haunted me. I longed to view it but I wasn't sure if Carla would buy this one. I dialed the task force office. Nothing ventured, nothing gained.

"Task force." I wondered if she ever tired of saying that. The same phrase every time the bell sounded. A Pavlov's dog reaction, and there was always someone on the other end wanting something from her, baiting and challenging her to perform and show her intelligence. She is intelligent and a performer.

"Hey," I warmly started out.

"Yes?" she cautiously replied.

"I need one more favor." She didn't respond. "I swear this is the last one. Just one more time and then you'll be done with me." She was still thinking and I had hope.

"What is it?"

"The Angel Perez case."

"Yeah?"

"There's a picture in the file. Can you make me a copy of it?"

"Maybe. Why do you want it?"

"Investigation." She was thinking again. "Do you know the picture I'm speaking of?"

"Yes."

"Will you do it?"

"Probably." She sighed.

"Okay, great." I was thinking fast. "When you get it, just slip it in my Austin Healey. It's still parked in the garage. You know what it looks like, don't you?"

"Of course, Ray, who could forget that?"

"Is that a compliment?"

"Take it any way you want."

"Thanks. I owe you."

I was still sitting on my deck throwing the ball and watching the boat show, but the sun was losing its sting and falling quickly, and I was feeling the urge to eat red meat.

I walked into the house and got two large porterhouse steaks out of the freezer, ran hot water on them, seasoned one of them, and walked back to the deck and fired up the Weber.

Tyrone was watching me intently; he knew he was going to get a porterhouse to maul. I tossed the ball for him, went back into the house, made a salad and tossed a baking potato in the microwave then returned to the deck and tossed the tennis ball some more for Tyrone.

I kept envisioning Angel Perez on the rotting cargo ship shouting and cursing and waving the machine pistol down at us. Typical Colombian Indian, muscular, dark, square features with the long ponytail, erratic and dangerous. Every cop's nightmare: a nut with a gun.

The microwave kicked off. I tossed the steaks on the grill and set up a place for me on the deck. We devoured the meal as the sun went down and the yachts stopped going south.

I had been in fight-or-flight mode for the past year and it had taken its toll on me. I was suddenly bone tired, emotionally drained, done in. I walked inside and cleaned up the kitchen then sat in front of the boob tube to watch sports updates on ESPN.

I dozed off in the recliner with Tyrone sleeping next to me. He nudged me at about 2200 wanting to go outside. I stirred and let him out and waited at the slider for him to come back in. He slid in, I turned off the tube, climbed up to the loft and into bed. I was instantly asleep.

For some reason, in one of my fragmented thoughts, I regressed back to a time when I was a rookie. I had gotten a call for a shooting. A man was lying on the sidewalk bleeding from a chest wound. "He's coming for me," the man said.

"Who?" I asked.

"The grim reaper. He's coming and he's smiling." The man died.

I was sleeping and dreaming. The grim reaper was coming for me. I was in my fighting stance waiting for him to make his move. It was Angel Perez and he was smiling, which is what grim reapers do when they come for you. I've got proof!

He got close enough for me to attack so I kicked him in the head with my right foot and came around with a straight left hand to the temple.

Both shots connected with precision but I couldn't get my foot or hand back. They stuck where I aimed them and Angel was still smiling and reaching for me. I was assessing the situation when Tyrone woke me to go outside again. The endorphins in the meat was working on him, I figured so I crawled out, pulled on a pair of Levis, climbed down the ladder, slid open the door and waited in the darkness while he went out and did his thing.

The realization of my dilemma attacked me. What's my next step? I don't have a job but I've got a damn good pension. I could retire, get Big-Boned Gloria and head down to Florida and forget this DEA thing ever happened. Do the retirees in Florida give a damn about what happened in St. Louis, Missouri? I doubt it.

My problem was I had never given up on anything. It wasn't in my nature. If I quit, Jack Parker and DEA would haunt me until I died.

Doc, Heidi, Schwartz, Angel Perez, Jack Parker. They're all connected. There's money and death tied to all of them. I can spot a conspiracy ten miles away. It's what I had always done, root out conspiracies. It is my personality, my reason for existence. I couldn't stop now; I needed to get back to the basics of investigation. I had to know more about my adversaries.

It's what intelligence is about. Information. The creed. Tomorrow I start my investigation. I start my investigation, unhindered by DEA, Jim Schwartz and the Feeb, Moynihan. I had the super-snitch, Sig Otto. He wanted to help. Helping me was his hobby and he was good. But can I trust him? He hadn't let me down yet, but I had been affiliated with DEA. I was a lone wolf now. It was a chance I had to take.

26

The morning was crisp. I walked around my backyard with Tyrone, a cup of coffee, and a head full of investigative ideas. I needed to get my Austin Healey from the DEA garage.

I caught the downtown bus at the edge of my driveway, transferred over to the Metro Link at Union Station, took it to Clayton, and waltzed into the garage at DEA without detection.

I was back home with the Healey in the garage, walking around my backyard with Tyrone, drinking my fourth cup in an hour. Tyrone perked up and pointed toward the house. Someone was on the property. I had no gun. I looked around the yard for a weapon, a limb or a rock, something that would give me a chance to attack an intruder, get him off-balance so I could get my feet and knuckles into vulnerable body parts.

Sig came walking around the house, still wearing the wife-beater, safari shorts, and a puzzled look. He approached me with his arms out like wings. I laughed.

"Put your arms down, Sig, you look like you're going to soar off my cliff." I walked his way and met him in the middle of the yard. I shook hands with him: "Coffee?"

"Yes." He smiled.

We walked to the deck. He sat at the deck table while I brought a cup and the pot out to him. I poured a cup for Sig and topped mine off..

"I apologize for coming in on you unannounced. I was afraid to telephone you. I think my line might be tapped. Yours probably is too."

"Probably."

"I wanted to tell you what transpired after I spoke to you in my backyard." I nodded in acknowledgment.

"Special Agent Moynihan came to my house early the next morning. He took me into custody and transported me to the justice center in East St. Louis. Just like you said. He grilled me for about an hour, just like you said. He told me you came in on me, implicated me in the killings of the two scum suckers. I told him I did not know what he was talking about. I told him I wanted my lawyer. He showed me you on a closed circuit television, shackled to the table. You did look miserable, like a broken man. I could tell it wasn't an act, but I stuck to my guns. I believe in you. You could have implicated me. It was actually I who killed them. I thought back to my experience with the FBI when the agent beat my poor dad. I drew strength from it. I didn't make a statement. How did I do?" He was smiling but teary eyed.

"You did great, Sig. That episode is over and done. The Feds shot their best stick and lost. It's time for our investigation to begin."

"What can I do? I want to help. I'll do anything."

I paused for five seconds. I was balking. Why was I balking? He was reading me, watching me emotionally withdraw from him. He wasn't hurt; more like amused. It was one of the reasons I liked him. He didn't make stupid utterances. He had the intelligence to wait things out and gather the information as it comes.

"I don't know where the investigation is going to lead, Sig. I have some computer work to do. Hopefully I'll know something soon. Just stand by and I'll get back to you."

He waited the appropriate five seconds before responding

"Okay, Ray."

I studied him. He was as calm as a preacher on Easter morning. He had made his bones with me. We'd tested each other. We were a good team. But I was a loner; always had been. I did my best work alone. That's the way it had to be for now.

He stood, shot down his last swig of coffee, shook my hand, and walked toward my circular drive. I sat and watched him wondering if there was anyone else like him. He was an original, too good to be true. That's what bothered me. Snitches are never that good.

I needed more information. My nemesis, Jim Schwartz, was the one I had to worry about. Doc was no threat. He only wants to be promoted. FBI Agent David Moynihan had shot his wad at me and missed.

Schwartz was eaten up with something. Steroids, for sure. Maybe some speed. Big-time steroid rats use speed. Steroids and speed go hand in hand. I wondered if Schwartz had ever come into contact with Helen of Troy, Illinois.

I climbed the ladder to my loft and accessed the computer. I had the Missouri Department of Revenue web site in seconds and crashed into driver's license records in sixty more. Schwartz's ugly head was on my screen. I printed it. Grainy, but recognizable.

I climbed down, went to the garage, climbed into my Austin Healey. I compared the in flagrante picture Heidi took with her phone camera to the one I printed. The one Carla got out of the file and tossed in my car. It was the same asshole. My photo was better.

I headed east with the top down. I was doing eighty as I took the Missouri Avenue exit. I idled into the East side toney neighborhood and parked. Granny came waddling toward me, smiling. "Hi, Ray."

"Hi, granny."

"What brings you to these parts this morning? Run outta dope?" She was grinning like a possum with her hand in her apron.

"No, granny. I need you to look at this picture." I handed it to her.

"Wanna buy some weed?" She was uttering a baggie at

me. I peeled off a twenty and reluctantly handed it to her.

"That's the guy I've been telling you about, Ray. He's the one who spent a lot of time here."

It was too pat, too easy. I figured she was telling me what I wanted to hear so she could sell me weed. I had to test her. "How tall is the guy, Granny?"

"He's a giant," she replied. "Big and mean looking. I could tell by his walk he was dangerous." She'd passed muster. "He tried to get rough with her and she ran him off." She handed the picture back to me.

I heard someone walking toward us. "Oh, oh, here comes trouble." She had a worried look on her face. I quickly climbed out of the roadster, looked over my shoulder, and saw Viktor Agron closing on us. He was starting to get his tan back and he was pumped up again.

He looked like what he was; a dangerous pimp and dope dealer, shirt open, hair slicked back, gold on neck and fingers. He'd probably been pumping and lying in the sun on his wife's pool deck. Once you're in shape it doesn't take long to get it back.

I faced him, prepared to go the distance. "DON'T TALK TO HIM, GRANNY," Viktor shouted. "HE'S A NARK AND A DAMN COP."

"A NARK? YOU A FUCKING NARK, RAY?" she loudly asked.

"Kind of, granny. Actually, I'm an ex-nark."

"NARK, EX-NARK, IT'S ALL THE SAME TO ME."

Viktor stopped before he was near enough for me to strike. I patiently waited for him to enter my zone.

"YOU FUCKING MURDERING COP. YOU CROOKED COP. YOU MURDERED MY FRIENDS AND YOUR AGENT FRIEND MURDERED ANGEL PEREZ'S MAID DOWN IN COLOMBIA. I JUST GOT OFF OF THE PHONE WITH ANGEL. HE TOLD

ME THE WHOLE STORY. AND SHE STOLE HIS CASH. BOTH OF YOU BELONG IN PRISON. IN FACT, I'M GOING TO BEAT YOUR FUCKING BRAINS OUT FOR GANGING UP ON ME WHEN YOU BURNED MY HOUSE DOWN. YOU AIN'T GOT YOUR FRIEND WITH YOU NOW. IT'S JUST YOU AND ME," he shouted.

He leaped at me, throwing his big right hand, which I parried off as I pummeled his big face with straight lefts and rights. He staggered back; I gave him time to regroup. I wanted him to think he had a chance against me. I wanted him to keep coming so I could punish him for all of his sins. It is what I had always done.

He came at me again; I body punched him until he went down on one knee. I could have kicked him into unconsciousness but I didn't. Every punch I landed on his hard body was redemption for me.

I felt them up into my shoulders pulling and jarring my deltoids, my triceps, and my pectorals. It's what every cop dreams of, evening the score for past victims. I was going to take him apart punch by punch.

He got up and kicked at my knee; he missed. Granny made a quick movement to my right and I glanced at her. Viktor took advantage of the opportunity. He came at me with his full body and slammed into me. We went to the ground. He was trying to get his claw onto my larynx.

He was making sounds like an animal mauling his prey, but he couldn't get his hand on my neck, I had his claw and I was out muscling him. He was frothing and moaning and cursing. I pushed my hand into his face and pushed as hard as I could.

We were locked in a death battle where strength and conditioning would determine the winner. His strength was waning. I could feel it. I broke the hold and he reeled backward. We were on our feet circling and getting our breath.

I could read the fear in his eyes. He wanted to break and run for Helen of Troy's, Illinois house, but he knew I would run him down and finish him off before he ever got there. I wanted to kill him, but I was no longer a cop killing bad guys. I was back to my Hanako mode. Fighting for fun instead of killing for glory.

He was a human punching bag for my punches and kicks, unable to fight back. I beat him about the face and shoulders and chest until he went down. He lay on his back and sputtered blood while I climbed into my roadster, fired it, and sped away from the scene.

I checked myself out as I drove across the Poplar Street Bridge. He had only gotten a couple of shots on me. I was lucky. He wasn't. I wondered how granny was faring.

I hoped she wasn't having a heart attack. That was a lot of excitement for an old gal. "Oh well, fuck her. She's just another dope dealer," I muttered as I tossed the baggie of weed out into traffic.

I drove straight to the gym, had a light workout and then hit the steam room. I had it all worked out before I left to go home. I cruised to my little house feeling good, parked and strolled in. Tyrone and I sat on the deck as I tried to figure my next move.

I tossed on a couple of steaks, and we sat on the deck and watched the Mississippi roll by. It was dark before I got up and moved inside.

Viktor said Heidi murdered Angel Perez's maid in Colombia. Where the hell did that come from? I plopped into my recliner and watched the evening news. No scoop. No cop killings. No dope seizures. An uneventful day for the talking heads. I climbed up the ladder and went to bed.

27

It was a morning of lethargy. Mortal combat does that to me. I mope for a couple of hours until it wears off. I was sore, real sore. I thought I had worked it off but it was there. The muscles of a damaged old cop. I thought about the cop business. What a strange way to make a living. But one positive note on being a cop, if you drop the ball, the way I did in homicide, the powers that be will give you a chance to scramble for it, regain control, and resume play.

Had I solved the Lynn Stewart murder, the beautiful young blonde waitress, I would have gotten a second wind. But I didn't. I was scrambling and I was sore, but I got to punish Viktor Agron, super-pimp and lifetime criminal. Not many people can say that.

I altered my breakfast hoping to get some protein to my freaked muscles. I chopped up strawberries and banana and blended them into a quart of plain yogurt. It slid down real easy and I was starting to feel like a younger man.

I walked around my backyard in my bare feet with Tyrone chasing the tennis ball as I pitched it while the Mississippi rolled by.

I had something this morning that I didn't have yesterday morning: clues. Clues about Special Agent Jim Schwartz, murderer, whoremonger, and number one nemesis. He was intense and a prick and he hates me. But most of the DEA agents are pricks and hate cops. At least that's been my observation. Being a prick comes with the job. They probably have classes in the DEA academy on how to hate and manipulate cops and be a prick.

But Schwartz was obviously insane. And worse than that, he was a rogue agent and a dangerous man. He was like Clete Jones, hiding behind his credentials and being a crook at the same time. He would murder for money. Almost any federal agent would. He would murder for fun. He's a back shooter, not a warrior. I'm sure he murdered Clete Jones, but Jesus Rangool from Tijuana, Mexico, went down for that murder. I had better watch my back.

Who is the professional here? Who is the criminal and who is the good guy? I studied the conundrum. It took the usual five seconds. I'm the professional and I'm the good guy. Schwartz is a criminal. Granny said so. I've witnessed his escapades. He tried to defame me with that phony dope dealer rap and probably succeeded.

An amateur can't beat a professional at his game. Schwartz didn't know that I knew about him and Helen of Troy, Illinois. He didn't know I knew he was a sex freak. Rough stuff with a prostitute? That just indicates that he prefers rough sex, period. But he does know I figured he'd murdered Clete Jones. I told him that fact.

And this DEA thing. My friends there, my so-called friends, had been leading me by the nose since I walked into the task force office. I don't know who orchestrated the mesmerizing of Ray Arnold but he was good. Could it have been Doc? He's definitely intelligent enough and he's in charge. He runs the task force with an iron hand. Did he orchestrate the Angel Perez case? Heidi put it on Schwartz, with Doc's blessing.

Viktor Agron, in a fit of rage, said Angel Perez told him Heidi killed his maid and then ripped him off for a bunch of cash. He didn't say how much cash. Maybe there was more than eight hundred thousand. Maybe there were millions.

Heidi said there was a C/I maid involved, but she didn't say anything about her being murdered. Heidi was keeping Jack Parker out of it. Is it because he wasn't supposed to leave the United States? Or is there more? Why Jack Parker? What expertise did he bring to the table in Colombia? Why have him violate the rules to assist in the

Angel Perez case? Heidi, the undercover. Schwartz, the connections to the alleged maid; C/I TFD Jack Parker; St. Louis Metropolitan Police Officer, detached to DEA to work in the confines of the United States. A TFD in Colombia? He was the third thumb on the pair of rubber gloves.

I climbed back to the loft and accessed the computer. I paused and tried to let the energy flow, thinking naturally. I grabbed a calendar and looked at the date I had been detached to DEA. It had only been a little over a year.

Seemed like a lifetime. Heidi said she was in Colombia when I came to the unit. That would have been in early March. A good time to go to the tropics. Jack Parker went missing about the same time. That's a correlation.

I started prodding and clicking on the search engine. "American Airlines," I typed in. "Tickets and seat assignments for." I stopped. Heidi wouldn't use her real name. She was going on an undercover assignment to a third world country. I envisioned Angel Perez calling down to her as he pointed the automatic weapon on the boat next to the Corn Island. "SALLEE JIMINEZ."

I typed in Sallee Jiminez, departing for Miami. It popped up; March fourth, seat assignment 55-A. I printed and stared at it. I wasn't satisfied. There was something I was missing. I typed in seat assignments for seats 55-B and 55-C then pressed enter.

The search engine stalled out on me. It now knew I was focused on pertinent flight information. It requested my credit card information to continue. I was hooked. I typed in the credit card information. I was back online.

Jack Parker was in 55-B, Jim Schwartz was in 55-C. I printed it and sat with my hands covering my face. So Jack Parker went to Miami with Heidi and Schwartz. That didn't mean he went to Colombia. TFD's are forbidden to leave the United States. Otis Parker told me Jack went to Colombia with two DEA agents, one of them a chick. So he must have gone there. I violated that rule when we went to meet the Corn Island.

There is a connection between Schwartz and Jack Parker besides DEA. They both knew Helen of Troy, Illinois, dope-dealer Viktor Agron's prostitute wife. That's a correlation. I wondered what town they actually went to in Colombia. Heidi said Bogota. Is she a liar? Hell yeah, she is.

I continued to badger the search engine: Aces Airlines, seat assignment for Sallee Jiminez. It blinked for a minute, then popped up. 4-A first class to Barranquilla.

Heidi didn't say anything about Barranquilla. She always just said Colombia, or Bogota. She's such a damn liar. I typed in seat assignments for the entire plane. It came up. I carefully examined it. Jack Parker was 4-B, Jim Schwartz was 10-C.

I clicked onto the map section of the search engine and typed in Barranquilla, Colombia. It popped up, south of Cartagena, on the coast. Probably a beautiful place. Great beaches, mountains in the background, healthy dope economy. It would be neat to interview Angel Perez, but that wasn't going to happen.

I grabbed a calendar. Jack Parker went missing shortly after he returned from Colombia. He knew something. He witnessed something and took off in a panic because of it. He witnessed the murder of the maid in Colombia. Or maybe he murdered her. He was a witness and then a missing. Was Heidi a witness? Why is she still around?

Besides being Special Agents for the United States of America and working for the Justice Department, what did Heidi, Doc, and Schwartz have in common? TFD Jack Parker! Not to mention the obvious; they are all unconscionable. That's not a bad trait in law enforcement. I allowed those federal creeps at DEA to lead me around.

Their cunning overwhelmed me. I admit defeat but I don't accept it.

I continued to mentally run the information I had gleaned on Jack Parker. Maybe he wasn't unconscionable. He was a hopeless romantic and a drunk. It takes a conscience to have those traits. Having a conscience probably got him listed as missing.

Having a conscience might get me killed if I'm not careful. Heidi told me I was delving into something I knew nothing about and it could be dangerous for me. Was she trying to tell me something? Is the man coming for me? Probably!

Damn, I liked Heidi. I liked her looks. I liked having sex with her and I liked her moxie. But she wasn't who I thought she was. She was a different person, an actress, pimping and smiling and getting the most out of an old cop-detective playing a young cop-detective's game.

A TFD at my age? What the hell was the chief thinking? I was in way over my head. He should have seen that. I was the wrong person to detach. They were waiting for me at the door with aluminum ball bats. I felt foolish for allowing that young woman to manipulate me, but what man has a defense against a young beautiful willing woman? None that I know of. There's no fool like an old fool.

I needed more information. I'm as much a junky for information as Doc is for stats. I needed to speak to someone in Barranquilla, Colombia, maybe a cop. I dialed information on my cell. "The country of Colombia, please."

Another operator got on. "International information How may I assist you?"

"The local police in Barranquilla, Colombia."

"One moment, please."

She didn't give me the number, just connected me and the phone started ringing.

"Barranquilla, Policia," the female voice said.

"I'm a police officer in St. Louis, Missouri. Do you speak English?"

"Si, a little, sir."

"Do you have a narcotics unit? Or a homicide unit?"

"No comprendo, Sir."

"Narco, murder, killing?" I waited the five seconds for a response. I heard her shouting for someone and emphasizing the blast of Spanish with "Gringo."

A man got on. "Si, how may I assist you?"

"I'm a cop from St. Louis, Missouri. I need to speak to an investigator."

"Si, how may I assist you?"

I was shocked that I was actually getting somewhere. I was smiling, and it must have bled over to him. "Do you work narcotics or homicide?"

"I do it all, sir. How may I assist you?"

"Oh, wow, thanks. You speak real good English."

"I was a cop in Miami for a while," he explained. "I speak four languages, fluently. It helps to be multi-lingual while doing business in international cities."

He already had the ups on me. Americans assume that if you aren't American then you must be ignorant. He was born in Colombia and speaks four languages. I was born in East St. Louis and I speak one. Who is the ignorant one? It's part of the ugly American syndrome. No wonder everyone hates us.

He patiently waited on the line for me to state my business. He didn't ask any stupid questions. I liked this guy! He was cool and sure of himself, and I wanted to glean information from him and maybe be able to touch base with him again. Colombia is apparently where my investigation leads me.

"Oh, Miami. It must have been a culture shock leaving

Miami and returning to Barranquilla."

There was silence. I had done it again with the ugly American routine. In my American mindset, no place in Colombia could be as neat as Miami. If that was the case, then why did he leave? It was ignorant on my behalf.

He respectfully cleared his throat. "No, Miami is quite like Barranquilla. Beaches, expensive real estate, beautiful women, fine restaurants, drug dealers, and lowlifes, and we have mountains as a backdrop. Actually, Barranquilla is nicer than Miami."

"Oh," I stammered.

"How may I assist you, sir?"

"I'm a detective in St. Louis, Missouri," I started all over again. "My name is Ray Arnold."

"My name is Corporal Jose Pedro. How may I assist you?"

It was time to get right to the matter at hand or I was going to lose this guy. All he had to do was hang up the receiver and my investigation in Barranquilla, Colombia, would be over before it began.

"Do you know a dope smuggler named Angel Perez?"

He didn't answer after the law enforcement five-second pause and his silence wasn't as if he was searching the cockles of his brain for information. It was as if he had been asked this question via telephone many times before by a gringo and was growing tired of answering it.

"Yes, I know who he is."

I didn't want to come off as anxious so I waited the five-seconds for effect. We were dueling; he no doubt wanted to know why I wanted to know about Angel Perez, but he didn't want to come off as anxious either. At least I know he's a good investigator. He knows how to play the game.

"Was one of his employees murdered? Maybe in early March of last year?" He was pausing for effect again. En guard, Corporal Pedro!

"Yes, on the fifteenth." He was silent again. He was inviting me to lunge at him with my foil but I had to be coy.

"Was it his maid?"

"Yes it was," he replied with a parry, without offering detailed information.

"Did the murder happen at Angel Perez's residence?"

It was time for a thrust from him. He should be aiming his blade at my heart and pushing himself off balance.

"Why do you need to know this information, Detective Arnold?"

I needed to parry his blade and engage him. "I'm investigating several murders in St. Louis and the name Angel Perez has come up. An informant advised me the Perez's maid was murdered in Barranquilla, and I just wanted to check on the credence of my informant's information." He was pausing again. My parry must have worked.

"Your informant is correct, Detective Arnold." We were disengaged at this point in the match, staring at each other with our swords in the air, both of us waiting for the feint, the trick move.

"Can you tell me about the scene? About the victim? Time of occurrence?" He was still pausing.

"The victim was a beautiful young woman, Detective Arnold. The scene was a bedroom of a wealthy drug smuggler's hacienda. She was beaten to death. Screams were heard about 1200 hours. Her name was Rita Guiterez. A vile man did this to her."

"Any suspects? What about Angel Perez?"

"There is no communication between this office and Angel Perez, Detective Arnold. He refused to speak to us. He hired an attorney and that was the end of his involvement."

"Was the scene processed?"

"Yes, the house was processed and photographed."

"Were there fingerprints?"

"Yes."

"Will you fax them to me?" The defining question. The thrust to the eyes.

"I've already faxed them to St. Louis, Detective Arnold, to a special agent in the Drug Enforcement Administration, Delbert Penrose. Can you get them from him?"

It was a riposte, a thrust after my parry. It sunk into my heart. He has the information. Interview and interrogation 101. The creed. Corporal Pedro knows the creed.

I was trying to recover and he was waiting with his sword up and at the ready. He was slicing it through the air and making sounds of victory as he looked down his nose at the ignorant gringo from East St. Louis, Illinois.

"I'm not in a position to request any favors from a federal agency, Corporal Pedro." I was trying to get my sword back up to engagement.

He politely cleared his throat again. "I see." There was amusement in his voice. "That is an interesting remark. Have you been a police officer for a long time?"

"Yes, for a very long time."

"Then you must have seen many troubles in your lifetime."

"Yes, many troubles." The ugly American was on his knees begging for pity.

"You are now in trouble with the establishment in St. Louis, correct?"

"Yes." I was amazed at his insight.

"Where shall I fax the prints?"

"To St. Louis homicide, 314-444-3210. And I'd like to be able to contact you again if I need to. Is that okay?"

"Si, Detective Arnold, and te veo luego."

The line went dead and I paced my little house. Tyrone wanted outside; I slid open the door and he ran out. I grabbed another cup of coffee and went out after him, pacing and placing my ducks in order in my bare feet, watching the Mississippi, searching for boats, and assimilating the information I had gleaned from Corporal Jose Pedro.

Delbert Penrose is Doc. Why the hell would Doc want fingerprints from a murder scene in Barranquilla? For the same reason I wanted them: an investigation. But why is he investigating it? I doubt he cared who killed Rita Guiterrez. I didn't think he cared Jack Parker was missing. I was almost sure of that. He probably hoped he was deceased.

28

I dialed homicide on my cell and stopped near the cliff, fixated on the river as I waited for someone to answer. A familiar female voice said, "Hello?" The unit secretary, Becky.

"Hey, Ray Arnold here; How have you been, Becky? I haven't seen you in a while." I was pimping her and she knew it.

There was the five-second pause, "Okay, Ray what is it?"

"I need a favor."

"No doubt, Ray. Every time this telephone rings someone needs a favor. I could get into trouble doing favors for you. The word is that you went to the dark side. Is it true?"

"No, baby, you don't actually believe those department rumors, do you? I'm being attacked on all sides because of something I worked on at DEA. I'm the same guy, believe me." Another five-second pause.

"Okay, I believe you. What do you want?"

"There should be some fingerprints coming over the fax from Barranquilla, Colombia." She interrupted me. "They're here now. Good prints, too. Great likeness and clear. What do you want?"

"I need those prints run through AFIS. Will you do it for me?"

Another five-second pause. "Yeah, I can do it for you." I heard her breathing as she scurried between her desk and air tube that shoots the print requests to the fifth floor with the receiver crammed between her jaw and shoulder. I heard the whoosh of the tube being sent on its way.

"Okay, they're in. It says here they came from a doorknob and a bedpost and the boarding of the floor, all in the upstairs bedroom of Hacienda Perez. It'll take five or ten minutes. Want to call back?"

"No, I'll hold."

I wandered and waited and dreamed about Big-Boned Gloria as I walked around my yard, sipped coffee and ogled boats. She enjoyed walking in the yard, nude. I enjoyed watching her walk. It had been fifteen minutes.

"Okay, are you ready?"

"Yeah."

"The bed post is a smudged hand-print with just enough of the right thumb and index finger to make an identification. It's from a guy named James Q. Schwartz. I've got his DOB and social if you want it."

"No, I've got it."

"Okay. The floor print and the door knob consist of a right thumb and index finger, and the floor is a palm smudge and a left index finger. It belongs to John J. Parker. I've got his DOB and social if you want it."

"No, I've got his, too, but does it say if the doorknob print came from outside of the door or inside of the door?"

"Umm," she purred as she read. "Outside."

"Thanks, darling, I owe you."

I wandered into my house and sat at the kitchen table. "Beaten to death," I muttered. Beautiful woman beaten to death in her drug-smuggling employer's hacienda. Dick Schwartz and Jack Parker were there when it happened. Where the hell was Heidi? Where was Angel Perez?

I covered my face with my hands and imagined the scene. Jack Parker opened the door to the bedroom which meant he was the first person in the room. The victim was probably already there. Maybe it was where the money was kept, maybe hidden in a closet or in a compartment under the bed.

Maybe the maid surprised them and she started screaming. Maybe she tried to run out of the room and Jack Parker grabbed her and they both went to the floor and his fingerprints were from him kipping up like wrestlers do when they are on their backs. That would be consistent with the prints.

What about Schwartz? Let's say he slapped her and sent her reeling onto the bed while Jack frantically searched for the dope proceeds. The victim would regain her composure quickly from a slap. Schwartz was probably yelling at Jack. "HURRY UP AND FIND IT."

The maid was probably screaming at the top of her lungs. Schwartz started beating her. He stopped her screaming. He was looking into her saucer eyes, big brown beautiful Hispanic eyes as he began beating her with his giant fists, holding her with his left and pummeling her with his right. He enjoyed it and he gave her one last punch.

He crushed her skull like a grape and the beautiful maid was dead. He tossed her away from him and lost his balance. He grabbed the brass bedpost to keep from falling. The dirty bastard!

Jack Parker, the romantic drunk, probably panicked and ran out of the room and the house. He headed for the American Embassy, probably. It's what spies do. The deal was a bust, whatever the deal was. Was it a dope rip for the government? Was it a dope rip for Schwartz and Jack? One thing for sure. Rita Guiterrez will never tell.

I climbed back up to my loft and activated my computer. "Search engine;" I typed in and one flashed on. Aces Airlines, departing flights from Barranquilla, Colombia to Miami, March fifteenth to the twentieth. "Do you wish to use the same credit card information?" It flashed at me. "Yes," I typed in.

Schwartz came back by himself on the fifteenth at twenty-hundred hours. Five hours after the screams were heard coming from the house. Heidi didn't come back on Aces.

Neither did Jack Parker. They would come on a

diplomatic flight if they had contraband to bring to the federal government. Eight hundred thousand dollars, or more, is a lot of baggage.

I needed a contact within DEA. Carla had been my go-to gal in the past. I thought I could trust her. She's one-hundred percent DEA but she's not an agent. She's a civilian employee. Doc gives her carte-blanche because she's so intelligent and she runs the office for him.

He trusts her if a guy like Doc can trust anyone. Trust for him is a sign of weakness. It means he needs someone to rely on and I doubt that's a good feeling for him. He's a predator, the natural leader of the pack. He and Heidi are almost too good to be true for DEA.

They're too slick! Why waste talent like theirs in sleepy old St. Louis? Carla could clue me on them. She acts like she likes me and wants to get something going with me. She's gorgeous and I wouldn't exactly be sacrificing, but she's a redhead and I know they're bad luck.

I had fiddled the day away talking and thinking, walking around in my backyard on my bare feet, looking at boats. But I did have pertinent information. The day was a success. I dialed Carla. It was Friday. She's always in a good mood on Friday afternoon.

"Task force." Her voice was melodic and seductive. I paused too long. "Task force!"

She was stern and business-like.

"Hey, it's me."

"Oh, hi, Ray." She was warm again. "I've been getting some strange calls lately, breathing and hangups. I'm sorry I bit at you."

I decided to get right to the point. "Will you meet me for supper?" She gave me the five-second shot.

"Yeah, Ray. You want a favor, right?"

"I always want a favor, Carla, but I also want your

company. I like you and I want to get to know you better."

"What about Heidi? Is it over between you two?"

"It's over!"

"Does she know it's over?"

"Yes."

"Where do you want to meet?"

"Lombardo's at Union Station. Is Italian okay?"

"Yeah." She paused, probably looking at her wristwatch. "Is six okay?"

I looked at mine. "Great, I'll meet you there. Bye!"

The investigation was still fragmented. I had to bring it together. Schwartz and Jack Parker, too many unanswered questions.

I checked my wristwatch again. Sixteen-thirty. I pondered. It was a fragmented long shot but I wondered if Henry Darby knew Schwartz.

Henry Darby was the driver of the dump-truck full of dope. The one who caused the crash of Angel Perez, Viktor Agron, his associates, and Heidi and me. Not to mention the other players involved in this accident; dead and alive. Especially Jack Parker.

Henry Darby was the catalyst of the conspiracy. He emphatically denied he knew Moynihan, but he was a liar and a dope dealer. Nothing he said would have much credence unless the United States Attorney had him by the balls and was squeezing. But Henry Darby was in hiding. He wasn't available to me.

I pulled off my black Tee and slipped on a Polo then made my way to the garage and the Austin Healey. I fired it. The 350 blasted to life and idled and lobed as I backed out and headed for downtown. I was there in fifteen minutes, parked, and strolled into the blues bar.

Gina the body, Henry's manager, was behind the bar smiling as I walked in. It wasn't a bartender's smile; it was sincere, like I was an old friend she hadn't seen in a while. I smiled back and walked to the end of the bar where the bartender hangs out between servings, away from the ears of the drinking patrons.

She approached me and gave me a juicy kiss on the lips. "I'm glad to see you, Ray. It's been weird around here since Henry disappeared. I don't know who to trust so I don't trust anybody. You know what I mean, Ray?"

"Yeah, I know the feeling."

I took a survey of her. Real blue eyes, a dark blonde ponytail, hip huggers revealing her flat belly. Tight ass, hard body, good skin and bones. She had possibilities but I didn't need another woman in my life right now. Maybe later when things got back to normal.

I came here for answers. I didn't want to start firing on her without warming her up a bit. Business is always a good place to start. "What's going to happen to this place? What if Henry turns up dead or just is never heard of again?"

She gave me the pause before answering, as if to say, "Why do you want to know?"

"It's in Henry's will that I run the place and the proceeds go to his young illegitimate children. I got a real good raise and I don't mind the responsibilities. I think it's going to work out. Business is good! We had a killer lunch today and I expect a big supper crowd."

"Great, I'm glad to hear it."

"Can I get you a drink, Ray?"

"Yeah, Diet Coke."

I pulled the in flagrante picture of Schwartz out of my pocket and slid it across the bar to her. "You ever seen this guy?" She took a quick look at it and tensed up.

"Yeah, all the time when Henry was around. He ate lunch here almost every day, even before we served lunch. He'd go to the kitchen and make his own sandwich, and he drank here almost every night, gratis, of course. Cheap bastard wouldn't even leave a tip. He's an asshole, but Henry said to give him anything he wanted so I did. He's persona non grata as far as I'm concerned. He's a sick guy."

"How sick?" I anxiously asked.

"He came onto me. I rebuffed him and he took it personally. He tried to get Henry to fire me and he followed me home a couple of times, not to mention the telephone calls."

"Telephone calls?"

"Yeah, he's got some kind of a speed dialer on his phone, and he'd call me constantly at night, keeping me awake. I had to unhook my phone to get any sleep. He's a creep!"

"Is he married?"

"Married?" She said with a laugh. "Hell no. Who'd marry that creep? He doesn't even have any kin. He said they all died of something, I don't remember. You meet all kinds in the bar business. I'm sure I'll meet worse than him before I'm finished."

"Would he say anything to you when he called?"

"Yeah, at first he'd ask me to meet him. Then when I said no, he'd curse at me and say sexual things. Like what he wanted to do to me. I'd hang up and then the calls and the breathing would begin. He even called me here with his speed dialer. Henry said he was a speed freak and he took steroids to body build, or something. Stone freak. He hasn't bothered me since Henry left. I hope he doesn't. I heard through the grapevine he was bothering another barmaid in the downtown area, too. I don't know how she got rid of him, though."

"Do you know what bar?" I quickly asked. "Was it the Purple Grape? I knew a gal at the Purple Grape who had trouble with a guy." I must've sounded anxious. She gave me the once-over. Cop detectives aren't supposed to be anxious. We're supposed to know the answer before we ask the question. At least that's what we want our snitches to think.

"No, it was just bar talk. I don't even know how it came up. It was just silly bar talk. I figured it was bad information, anyway. Most of bar talk is. But I did hear him bragging to Henry he had some new kind of designer drug that can't be detected in urine tests. He laughed at the Justice Department. He's scary!"

"What did Henry think of him?"

"They started out as adversaries. Henry was always pimping him and he would pimp Henry. Then, gradually, they became friends. They were always talking about the dope game and gleaning from each other. They'd have private conversations at a booth or table, serious conversations. Henry started acting like he was afraid of him but he continued to talk to him. Henry's priority was cash flow. If he thought he could make a fast buck, he'd talk to the devil."

"He may have been talking to him," I muttered.

I got a goodbye kiss and headed out to the street and the Austin Healey. I had left the top down and felt foolish for doing so. A street person could be sitting in it. There wasn't anybody in it and I was feeling lucky as I slid in, fired it and cruised toward Union Station.

I parked in front and gave the security guard ten bucks to personally guard my roadster. He crammed the ten and nodded to me. I wandered in. Carla was sitting at the bar. She waved as I approached her, then greeted me with a warm kiss on my lips. That's three kisses in the past thirty minutes from two different gorgeous young women. Luck is with me.

She was sipping a martini. I could taste the vermouth and gin. She was giddy and already tipsy. I wondered how long she had been there, but she was freshly showered. I could smell the fragrance of perfumed soap on her neck. She was dressed to attract attention: pale red blouse, unbuttoned far enough down to reveal her creamy cleavage; beige skirt, tight-fitting and short, enhancing her rock-hard body and tight buttocks.

She was gorgeous in this atmosphere, different than at the task force office. She was happy, uninhibited, smiling and open. I thought I could get used to her being around. A dangerous thought. I wondered why there weren't a plethora of men in her life.

We were escorted to a table by the manager and took our time looking at the menu, and each other, as we sipped vino. It took half a bottle but I caught up with her. I was mellowing as the evening progressed.

She had Italian and I had my usual steak with Italian trimmings. We were still sipping the vino when she helped me out by asking the obvious question. "Okay, Ray, what do you want from me?"

She was staring and smiling and as usual she controlled the situation because she had the information. She drilled me with her big green eyes.

"I need to know about Doc."

She stopped smiling and continued to stare. "Like what?"

"Like everything."

"What's to know? He's a DEA group supervisor with ambition. End of story."

She was trying to blow it off. I didn't need her to tell me something I already knew. I had to get her talking about the players so I started with Doc. There was always something new to find out.

"Hey, Carla, I know you're loyal to him, and I know you respect him, but you must remember; I'm trying to figure out why a cop is missing. A cop who was a close friend of yours. Jack Parker might be dead. Doc might be a suspect. I need to dismiss him or pursue him. I don't have time for blind alleys. If he isn't viable I want to dismiss him and get on with my investigation."

She gave the five-second pause for effect. Since I asked her a direct question, the pause effect for this application meant she was trying to be sincere with her response, or she wanted me to think she was.

"Loyal? That's a descriptive word pertaining to the present," she said. "When Doc is in his office and I'm trying to keep the office together and running smoothly, the reports written and filed, the telephone answered, and the TFD's and agents happy, yes, I'm loyal to him. But right now I'm not loyal to him. He'll be gone shortly, promoted and going to another powerful position in the United States Government. I'll still be at my desk trying to keep things running smoothly. He probably won't even remember my name. DEA secretaries are a lot like TFD's. The agency takes what it can get out of you and then dismisses you. If you're not a special agent in DEA then you're expendable. Respect? That's a strange word for any DEA agent or TFD. Doc's a panderer, a super-intelligent pimp/whore. He'll jump in the sack with anybody. How could I respect that? Besides, Ray, I've been wooed by the best of them. I might as well be wooed by you." She smiled and I liked her a lot.

We were staring again. I knew what I wanted and she was giving me a window to ask her. "I need to know more about him. Like his career. What can you tell me about his career?"

"He's been to a lot of schools. Is that what you're talking about?"

"Yeah, maybe. Like what kind of schools?"

"Weird schools. One of them is called the Americas, or something like that."

"School of the Americas?"

"Yeah, that's it."

"Why would a DEA Agent go there?"

"I don't know, Ray, I'm just answering your question. He went to another one, uh, Escape and Evasion School? Does that sound right?"

I was staring at her. "Did you know that Manuel Noriega went to School of the Americas and Escape and Evasion School?"

"You mean that general from Panama who just got out of prison? No! I didn't know that."

Her green eyes were penetrating my soul. "Those are schools for assassins. Government schools for government killers, Carla. You sure Doc's just a DEA Agent?"

"As far as I know, Ray. He comes and goes a lot. He travels for the government. He has big ambitions. That's all I know about him."

We sipped the vino and made measured glances at each other.

"What about Heidi?" I asked.

"You mean as far as schools?"

"Yeah!"

"Same schools, different dates of enrollment."

"Holy fuck," I mumbled. I paid the check and we strolled out to her car. I kissed her passionately and walked away.

"Ray." I stopped and turned.

"You want to come over?" She was sincere. Not smiling.

"Yeah, I'll follow you." I quickly replied.

I walked to my Austin Healey, still in paranoia. Am I a whore like the rest of them? Am I passionate for her because she agreed to assist me in my investigation? If that's the case then I'm unconscionable just like the rest of the other cops and agents.

But I do have a conscience. I'm a one-percent guy. What

if she would have told me to fuck off? Would I have kissed her so passionately?

I climbed in, cranked it, sitting and waiting for her to drive to me. It's just that she's a redhead. I get wrapped up with a gorgeous redhead I might as well give it up. Big-Boned Gloria won't be able to save me. I didn't want to think about it.

She drove past me and I followed her. We jumped on the Daniel Boone and she got off in Clayton. Then we drove through Clayton to the beginning of University City. It was a neat little house with a two car garage.

She pulled into one side, got out and motioned for me to pull in beside her. I complied. I couldn't get over how her car resembled a government car. A plain-Jane Chevy four-door. A fleet car. But DEA secretaries don't get government cars, only Special Agents and TFD's. I dismissed it.

She pushed the button and the garage door came down as she nervously looked outside. I looked at her inquisitively. "I've been having trouble with a guy. I don't want him to vandalize your car, It's such a neat car."

"Thanks."

She was still dressed in evening clothes. I wasn't expecting that. I was so used to Heidi and her get down-and-dirty quickness.

I sat on the couch and fought my subconscious attacking me about redheads. I shook it off. Maybe she isn't a true redhead. I must be looking weird. I can see she's amused with me.

She walked over to me, knelt down and kissed me on the mouth. I kissed her back. She took my hand and led me to the bedroom. "Don't worry, Ray, I won't hurt you." I followed her like a good little cop.

It was 0200 when the telephone started ringing. She answered the first time and then refused to answer it anymore. I picked it up; a guy was breathing and mumbling. He finally spoke, "Either you're my friend or you're my enemy. Trust me, you don't want to be my enemy."

The line went dead. She was up with the bedside light on scrambling for the wall phone connection. She gingerly pulled it out, turned off the light and came back to bed. "He won't bother us anymore tonight."

I recognized the voice. "It's Jim Schwartz, isn't it?"

"Yeah, he's a freak, but you knew that, didn't you?"

I studied her. She was frazzled. "He apparently doesn't know I'm here. That's good for us, bad for him. I think he killed Jack Parker. I think he killed a girl in Colombia, and I'm certain he murdered TFD Cletus Jones. Jack Parker witnessed the murder in Colombia and fled back to St. Louis. Schwartz tracked him and did him in. Do you know anything about this stuff?"

"Maybe. For now let's get some sleep."

"Maybe? How can it be maybe? Either you do or you don't."

She turned the light back on. "I'm in a position to hear things, Ray. I don't hear whole sentences or whole paragraphs. I hear bits and pieces. I heard Doc and Heidi talking in hushed tones in Doc's office. It was right after you got beat up. The killing in Barranquilla, Colombia, was the topic of the morning. I heard the term, "fucking nutty Schwartz," bantered about. He's a plague to our office; walking in here and threatening the TFD's. Anyway, I knew Jack Parker and Heidi went to Colombia, and Schwartz was the source of the information. Jack and I were on the outs at that time because of Heidi. I didn't want him gallivanting off to the tropics with her, deal or no deal. He told me he was going to make some money, and that we could go away for a long time on it."

"Make some money? That's interesting. And Heidi was

his handler?"

"Strange terminology, Ray, but I guess you could call it that."

"TFD's aren't supposed to go out of country," I said. "He must've been going covertly, illegally as a representative of the United States Government."

"No, he said he was sanctioned to go. I don't know what transpired, but he went, came back, and went missing. He didn't tell me what went down in Colombia but from what I gleaned from eavesdropping, he witnessed a woman getting murdered and it freaked him."

There was a banging at the front door, then someone going around the house, knocking on the windows. Carla looked out through the peephole in the front door. "It's him. I just saw him." She was clutching her gown, terrified.

He was trying to kick open the back door. I ran to the kitchen and grabbed a butcher knife. "If he comes through the door I'm going to kill him." The kicking stopped; a car screeched away from the house.

"I think he's gone," she said. She was hanging on me and sobbing.

"Does this happen very often?"

"Yes, two or three times a week," she sobbed. "I think he wants to kill me for rebuffing him."

"Don't worry, red," I said stroking her hair. "Nothing is going to happen to you when I'm around. Let's go to bed."

"I can't sleep now, Ray. I'm all out of sorts. I'm too scared to sleep."

We sat in the living room and didn't speak. My mind naturally went back to the investigation. Gina said Henry Darby and Schwartz were friends. Business partners? Maybe. How is it that Gina the body didn't know more about their collusion? They spoke in front of her.

They had to have said things in front of her she could

pick up on. There was booze involved. People talk out their ass when booze is involved. There has to be a reason Gina didn't confide in me.

Carla was seductively watching me. "What's up?"

"I was thinking about the case. It consumes most of my life and it will until I get it solved and pigeon-holed. The case is fragmented, a lot like my thought process. Henry Darby; Viktor Agron; his henchman; and Helen of Troy, Illinois. Jack Parker, Schwartz, Doc and Heidi, who seem to be onlookers, guiding but not joining in.

It's kind of like two cases collided with all kinds of witnesses, and I'm the one who has to sort it all out. The collision occurred on that speedboat next to the Corn Island on a warm night when Angel Perez shined his light down onto our boat and shouted, SALLEE JIMINEZ. Everything was logical up to that point. Two completely different conspiracies collided at the crossroads of the dope game."

"Tomorrow I need you to go to the office and run some computer stuff for me." I had my hands over my face trying to think of Gina the body's last name. "It's Phelps," I muttered.

I'm online here," she replied. "I work from home some of the time."

"Gina Phelps. Can you check something in the computer for me?"

"Yeah, maybe. What is it?"

"You wouldn't have informant information available to you, would you?"

"No, Ray, sorry."

"What if you ran a name for a voucher pertaining to government funds? Everybody has to sign one of those, don't they?"

"Yeah!"

"Gina Phelps. Run her."

Her fingers blurred as she typed in the information. She paused. “Gina Phelps has received funds from the United States Government. There are code numbers here.” She typed one in. “This one is from DEA, five thousand dollars. It was paid to her by Doc. There’s another payment; it came from Justice, but it’s an account number I’m not familiar with, it was before Doc’s.”

“Gina the body was snitching to Doc? That’s interesting. She was snitching to somebody in Justice, too. This has got to have something to do with the Barranquilla caper. She could’ve gleaned it from Henry Darby and Schwartz’s covert conversations. But why did Heidi and Jack Parker go to Barranquilla with Schwartz? See what I mean. It’s fragmented. Tomorrow I’m going to interview Gina the body again. This time I’m forearmed.”

29

We slept late, breakfasted on Carla's tiny private patio at the rear of her house and made small talk about our co-workers at DEA. It was a glorious Saturday morning in St. Louis. Crisp clean air, gorgeous foliage and bright sun.

We didn't shower together which I thought was strange. It is almost a ritual for two new lovers. It was a walk-in shower, big enough for both of us, but she didn't come in. I climbed out and she climbed in. I shaved, pulled on my black Polo and Levis, and said "Goodbye."

"I want to go with you," she said. "Can I go with you?" Her green eyes were pleading. She was probably afraid to be left alone. The boogie man was afoot.

"Okay, you can go." She smiled and kept shooting glances at me. I got the feeling she was telling herself I was easy. She was right!

We were in the Healey in five minutes slowly cruising through Forest Park, down Lindell with its turn-of-the-century mansions, built for the World's Fair and still gorgeous. We entered downtown heading toward Henry Darby's blues bar searching for a meter to park at.

I changed my mind and rolled into the parking garage. We climbed out, casually strolled into the empty saloon holding hands, just like Heidi and I used to do, and headed for the cubbyhole office.

The door was ajar. I pushed it open and looked inside. Gina the body was at the desk crunching numbers. She looked up, smiled, glanced at Carla then looked confused.

"Carla, Gina," I motioned with my hand; they both nodded. Carla was pink and white and as clean as the Board of Health. Gina was cute, tight and preened, but she was no Carla.

"I need to ask you some questions, Gina." She picked up

on my business demeanor and struck a defiant pose behind the desk. I was on her turf. She wasn't going to allow me to push her around without a battle. I just needed one innuendo to soften her up and she would be easy to manipulate.

"Where is Henry Darby?" I started with the hammering.

"I don't know." She was frightened and she stared at me. Her eyes were going crazy, darting around and rolling. She was a poor liar, unusual for a sexy woman.

"Gina, I'm trained to detect a lie. You're lying. Carla is a federal agent with the Drug Enforcement Administration," I lied. "She'll make a telephone call and have a lie detector machine here in one hour. Start telling me the truth or you'll be on the box. Now, where is Henry?"

She locked up. I thought I would make it easier for her. I didn't really care where Henry was, or if he was dead or alive. It was just a ploy to get her softened up for the other information I needed. "Have you heard from him?"

"No, he won't telephone. He's afraid our phones are bugged. He won't even call on my cell."

"Who is he afraid of? Viktor Agron?"

"No," she nervously replied. "Jim Schwartz." She looked at me as if to say, "your move." But she gave me an opening. Schwartz was the reason I was there. She had opened the door to him.

"What were his instructions to you when he left?"

"He told me to run the business and to make sure his kids are taken care of financially. He said he may never come back, but that when things get cleared up, he might come back. I have a contract drawn up by his attorney. It gives me carte-blanche to run the business the way I see fit. Percentages are stipulated; I get a percentage, his kids get a percentage, and a percentage goes into an escrow account." She stared, frightened.

"Tell me about Schwartz."

She was terrified; her hands were shaking. Was she in fear of Schwartz or for something she had done?

"What's to tell? Schwartz and Henry were friends. Schwartz referred to Henry as a client. I never could figure out what that meant. The agent ate and drank in here and didn't pay. FBI agents would be at the bar, drinking, gratis, and the big freak Schwartz would be at a booth. It was like a private club for federal agents, and the FBI guys didn't even know a DEA guy was in the room. Schwartz didn't know they were FBI either. It was weird. All they cared about was free booze and bar food."

"There's more, Gina. You're holding out on me. I know there's a lot more."

She locked her jaw up, the muscles were bulging. I needed leverage. She had overheard something between Henry Darby and Schwartz. She snitched to Doc. It had to be good information, or Doc wouldn't have given her five-thousand dollars. Uncle doesn't pay out that kind of cash unless something is as good as gold. I was searching the synapses of my brain trying to picture the scheme. A shot in the dark scenario.

"I'll level with you, Gina. We know you overheard a plan between Schwartz and Henry. Schwartz wanted to rip somebody off, a drug dealer. You telephoned Washington, Justice and told them you had information about a crooked DEA agent in St. Louis. Whatever you told the guy in Justice, he paid you some cash for the information so it had to be good. The crook was Schwartz. Justice referred you to Agent Doc Penrose. You told Doc about Schwartz and his plan. What did you tell him, Gina?"

"You seem to have the answers," she defiantly said.

"I have them, Gina. I'm trying to give you a chance to be my friend. Tell me. What did you tell Doc about Schwartz?"

She stared, red-faced but not teary. "That he was a freak,

a murderer and that I thought he was going to murder me."

I paused and let it sink in. It was better than I had expected. "A murderer, Gina. Who did he murder?"

"A girl, a downtown barmaid. He told Henry about it and I heard him. He said he beat her to death because she rebuffed him. Tossed her out of his car on a downtown street like rubbish. He laughed about it and Henry laughed, too, mostly out of fear."

It took me off-guard. Is this what it was all about? Stagger through the job until I stumbled onto the clue I had been looking for? The clue that would redeem me, return me to the real world. "Did she work at the Purple Grape?"

"I think so."

Her response humbled me. It was as good as gold. I paused and had flash backs. I was zoning instead of interrogating. The information calmed me and made me vulnerable. I had paused for too long. Gina and Carla were both staring at me as I mentally dilly-dallied with my new enlightenment. "This is good information, Gina, but there's more. Keep going."

She froze up again. I had to get her talking. "You know, Gina, I know Henry Darby as well as you. I haven't known him as long, but I know him well. He was an easy guy to figure out. He's always played both ends against the middle. He was being badgered by Schwartz to set up a dope dealer for him to rip off. But he didn't give Schwartz Angel Perez's name. He'd hold that in abeyance, his ace in the hole. But he told you about Angel, didn't he?"

"Yes!"

"And you told Doc, right?"

"Yes!"

Heidi had lied to me again. The Barranquilla caper didn't come from Schwartz, it came from Doc. Doc orchestrated the scheme and invited Schwartz into it. Then he sent TFD

Jack Parker, Schwartz, and Heidi there to rip the dope man for the United States of America. "They're United States funds," Heidi had said. "They belong back in America."

Doc sets the deal up but it doesn't go as planned by Doc. Everybody comes back to St. Louis, and Jack Parker takes a hike. Doc's got information on Henry Darby, now. It's part B of the master plan.

He brings in Sig Otto, and Heidi and I go through the song and dance with him and get information on the cocaine delivery by Henry. It's all about stats now. Doc wants to bleed every deal he can get his fangs into for his promotion.

Sig Otto wasn't the catalyst. Gina the body was. She started the ball rolling with her greed. She wanted the restaurant, and she knew that if her boss, Henry Darby the cocaine dealer got into trouble, she would get to run the business as her own.

But in the dope business there's always a catch, something the Docs and the Heidis of the world weren't expecting. This time the fly in the ointment was Angel Perez in the rotting dope ship, peering over the side, ripped and stoned, long stringy hair, and an automatic weapon, shouting "SALLEE JIMINEZ". Nobody expected that.

"You learned from the master, Henry Darby, Gina. You played both ends against the middle and now you're running things and making a good living at it."

She was looking scared and guilty again. "You're not going to tell Henry's lawyer, are you?"

"No, Gina, not just yet. Good bye, Gina."

We walked out of the office and made our way through the restaurant to the parking garage, climbed in, fired it and headed for the street. I drove aimlessly, slowly cruising with the top down and a luscious redhead next to me. I went by my house, fed Tyrone, tossed the ball for him, put on clean underwear, Polo and Levis and we were off again.

Carla was watching me as I drove. "You did well back there at the restaurant. Your interview skills are superior."

"Thanks. Anywhere you'd like to go?"

"Just drive. I'm feeling the pressure leave me. I'm being rejuvenated by the sun and the wind and the sound of the motor."

I headed west, jumped on the Daniel Boone, took it to route 94 then headed west some more. We slowly drove the crooked, scenic back country roads to Jefferson City, stopped, and used the facilities, filled up and headed back the same way.

We stopped at a winery in Herman and had supper, a glorious supper: German food, Rhine wine, chocolate cake for dessert with the Missouri River in front of us and the rolling hills of wine country behind us just starting to turn colors.

I had answers to some of my questions, and I wasn't haunted by the Lynne Stewart murder anymore. I knew who did it, at least I thought I did, but how was I going to prove it? Justice will prevail, somehow.

We stayed on the back roads all the way to Carla's house. I pulled into her driveway and she got out activated the garage door, then shut it behind me as I tucked the Austin Healey away for the evening. It was going on 2200 and I was feeling the effect of driving a sports car on winding roads all day with the top down.

Carla jumped into the shower and I was sitting on the couch waiting for my turn when the telephone started ringing. She answered it in the bathroom, screamed and hung up. She came out frantic. "It's him again. He says he's coming over and that he's coming in whether I open the door for him or not."

She quickly dressed, pants; sweatshirt and tennis shoes. She paced and pulled on her lower lip like a little girl. She was the angel of peace being terrorized by the devil. I became a cop to stop things like this. The brutalizing of the weak by the strong. I felt it was what I was born to do.

The telephone kept ringing, then stopping and then ringing again. I envisioned Schwartz's face as he speed dialed the number. A car stopped outside; Carla looked out of the peephole. "It's him, and he's coming this way." She ran to a corner and cowed.

He pounded on the front door, then followed his terror routine of going to all of the windows and banging on them, then pounded at the rear door. He kicked it, not real hard, just hard enough to terrorize. He could have kicked the door off of its hinges. It's what cops and agents do and it's not difficult.

One swift kick above the lock and the door flies open. Most times it lands on the floor and we walk over it. Schwartz just kicked and terrorized not knowing what was waiting for him when he finally gave it a true kick and sent it flying. I heard the door hit the kitchen floor and his footsteps coming in.

He chanted her name, "Carla, Carla, I know you're in here. Where are you, my Carla?"

He made it into the living room where Carla was cowering in the corner, and I was sitting on the couch, patiently waiting.

He was spook-like, freshly stoned, wobbly on his feet, crouching and smiling when he observed me. He recoiled, stood erect, and pulled his Glock forty, pointing it at my face as he scanned the room. "Ray Arnold," he said with sour grapes. "Carla, what's he doing here?"

He was rabid, the combination of meth and steroids taking its toll on him, but I didn't feel sorry for him. He wasn't in Carla's living room waving a Glock forty because he was seeking help. He was primed to kill. I had seen it a dozen times and he was a classic example.

He closed on me with the Glock. "I'm gonna kill you, Ray Arnold." I was disappointed in his tactic. He should have known better. He did the normal thing. He underestimated the old cop.

He got within five feet of me and I sprang. I had the Glock out of his hand and sailing across the room toward Carla. He was surprised but he got into a fighting stance and held his ground, more wobbly and vulnerable. He was smiling like the madman he was.

He started throwing kicks at my head, but I was waiting for them. I knew he was going to use that tactic. I had seen him feint kicks at Clete. He was missing and wide open, his face and solar plexus begging me to pummel them, so I did.

He was big and slow because of his huge, fake muscles and the dope. I couldn't miss with my punches. I started working on his liver and staying out of the way of his kicks and punches. I was picking at him, circling him, digging in at his liver with straight accurate punches.

It didn't take long until he started losing his composure. Liver shots do that. He became infuriated and charged me, a lot like Viktor Agron, trying to use body weight to overpower the smaller opponent.

I moved away from him and he almost fell to the floor. He didn't go down but he was moving slowly and he was hurt, I could sense it. I thought he would have had a backup pistol. Almost everybody does. I expected him to flourish it at me, or just pull it and kill me with it so I gave him a flurry of straight punches to his heart. He went to the floor moaning and trying to get up.

He didn't have one. I wanted to get it over with. I got down to business. I kicked him in the temple. He went completely down. I jumped on top of him and locked up on his throat with the crook of my arm. He was fighting and kicking and trying to get away.

I whispered in his ear, "Lynn Stewart, Lynn Stewart, Rita Guiterrez, Jack Parker, Purple Grape, Purple Grape," as he kicked and tried to survive. I choked him out, stood, and stared at him. He was in the last stages of life. His larynx was crushed; his brain was shutting down. An eye for an eye, a tooth for a tooth.

Carla came over and looked at him. "Is he dead?"

"Yeah!"

She picked up the telephone and dialed a number. I figured she was calling the University City Police. I had some explaining to do, but the evidence was in my favor, and I had a witness, Carla. He came to kill us. This wasn't a lover's triangle. It was a doped-up DEA agent with death in his heart. I'd probably have to hire a lawyer. Damn!

"It's done," is all she said, then hung up.

I sat on the couch while she went as far away as she could from Schwartz's carcass. We were waiting for something, I didn't know what, but we weren't communicating, just staring and waiting. I listened for sirens, first responders, nothing.

It took about twenty minutes, but finally there was a knock on the front door. She opened it and stood back. Doc and Heidi walked in. Doc was smug and nodded to me. Heidi acted professional and in charge. Doc sat down and played second fiddle to her.

Heidi walked past me and looked at Schwartz's corpse. She felt his carotid artery then nodded to Doc. "Make the call," she said.

Doc flipped open his cell, hit a speed dialer. "You can come in now," is all Doc said.

Heidi surveyed the scene like a homicide cop. She studied Carla. "Carla, pull your car out of the garage and park it on the street then leave the garage door open." Carla responded like a robot. She stood and walked out without acknowledging.

Heidi and I stood by the corpse and looked at each other, not speaking. It was starting to play out for me, but I didn't put it all together until a man with coveralls came into the room and put Schwartz's body into a body bag.

He secured Schwartz's gun in a separate bag, then he and Doc muscled the bag out to a van that had been parked in the garage. Doc came back into the room by himself. I heard the van crank up and pull out, and I heard Carla's car come back into the garage and the door close.

They had played me to the max. They got three hundred fifty horsepower out of a two hundred horsepower motor. It all fell in place for me, "Jack Parker was supposed to do this for you in Barranquilla, right?"

They didn't deny it; they just gave me the federal stare and the federal smile. Carla walked back in. She was stone-faced as she stared at me. She was a machine. She was a Rolls Royce and I was her spare tire.

"What were you going to do for Jack Parker? What was he going to get for eliminating an insane, drugged-up, murdering DEA agent? Was he going to get some of the drug money at Angel Perez's? Or did he get all of it, and then split?"

Doc was still smug. Heidi looked like she had just pulled off a big coup, one that was going to shoot her to the top. She wasn't a DEA agent. I didn't know what she was. I didn't know where she came from. But she was damn good at what she did. Manipulation. She had manipulated a kill for someone in Washington. Got rid of an embarrassment. She had a murderer murdered through her wit. Smart! Smooth!

I was feeling used and I didn't like the feeling. Heidi sensed it. She was eyeing me. She had me read well enough to know I could harm her and Doc at the same time in an instant.

"Don't do anything foolish, Ray," she said.

"Foolish, Heidi?" I said through clenched teeth.

"We have the power to contract out, Ray," she said.

Doc kept his head down, hoping I wouldn't pummel him to the point he would have to kill me with his Glock. But he was prepared and ready to do it. I could read his every move.

"Jack wanted money, Ray," Heidi continued. "He wanted to get away. A mad dog had to be eliminated. It is part of what we do, Ray. We gave Jack the opportunity but he didn't have the stomach for it. He did what some of the TFD's do, Ray. He snatched the cash and left a pittance for the United States Government and came running back to St. Louis to the booze and the broads and the protection of his dad. It didn't help him, Ray. Schwartz tracked him and tried to kill him. Jack left for greener pastures. He'll probably come back now that Schwartz is on the missing list."

She stared at me to give me time to assimilate the information. It had come at me fast and furious. The set-up began with the first dope deal. The one I got beat up in. The old brain concussion thing coming back to haunt me. I was so vulnerable, so easy, trying to be one of the boys to appease Doc. I followed their script to a Tee. For once in my life, I was a perfect student.

"Our assignment was still current," Heidi said. "We waited for the right opportunity and then you got transferred in. We knew somebody was coming in to replace Jack, but we didn't know it was going to be someone with your talents. Your arrival was a coup for us, Ray. You were the real deal. We were fortunate to have you to work on. I figured you'd finally get enough of me, so we got Carla to entertain you a little and it worked. Lord knows I tried with everything I had."

I shot a look at angelic Carla. What man could resist? "You expect me to be quiet about this?" I calmly asked.

"It's the right thing to do, Ray," Heidi replied.

"It's the only thing you can do," Doc said still smiling. "Who can you tell, Ray? Are you going to tell your chief you murdered a DEA agent? Are you going to the press? All of the bases are covered, Ray. All you can do is play the game."

"You guys used me like a whore," I spat at them. "You pimped me from jump-street. I resent it."

Heidi frowned at me, "Grow up, Ray. It was a good experience for you. You got to kill the demons you acquired in homicide with the Lynn Stewart murder. We did that for you, Ray. You should thank us. You can get on with your life, now. We know everything there is to know about you, Ray. Get your little girlfriend, retire, go to Florida, and forget about DEA and St. Louis, Missouri. We're all dogs from the same litter, Ray. I was the dominant dog this time, you'll be the next time."

That was Granny's philosophy, almost word for word. How did Heidi know about Granny's weed dealer snitch philosophy? I was alone when Granny hit me with that one. Granny was a plant. A manipulative plant!

Sentences and phrases were slamming my brain. Things I had said during the investigation. I was naive. I should have caught on. Sig Otto knew me too well. He had probably studied my Marine Corps file. They had me coming and going. I didn't stand a chance. I was reeling from information overload. I had to get out of there. I stood and walked out without looking back. I'd been had, how could I have been so easy?

I cranked the Austin Healey, backed out and tore down the street, jumped on the Daniel Boone, did ninety across the Poplar Street Bridge, got off on Missouri Avenue and cruised into the Helen of Troy's, Illinois neighborhood. I parked in front of Granny's house. There was a light on. I walked to the porch and heard a television. I knocked. A fat man with a wife-beater came to the door. "What?"

"I'm looking for Granny."

"She ain't here and she never will be here again." We stared at each other.

"Isn't this her house?"

"No, she was a renter. She left abruptly. Some guy with a mullet driving a Mercedes picked her up last night. I don't know where she went." He slammed the door.

"Doc!" I got back into the Healey and sat. I could see lights on at the veranda of Ellen's house. She probably just got home from work and was watching Viktor lift weights on the pool deck. She had no intention of meeting Jack Parker in paradise.

I cranked it and headed west. Granny for sure wasn't real. She was a definite plant. A person to manipulate me, guide me the way Doc and Heidi, or someone in Washington wanted me to go. Slick! The slickest!

I took the Boyle exit off of the Daniel Boone and headed for the Central West End. I turned on to Hortense and cruised by Sig Otto's mansion. The house was lighted. Sig couldn't be real. He had to be a plant, too. They had everything tied up; all the angles covered.

I stopped, got out, walked up to the porch and knocked on the front door. No answer. I peered into the foyer, then walked around the porch to a window. Bare. The place was cleaned out. The lights were on but nobody was home. How appropriate! Life's a bitch and then you get murdered!

30

I bounced out of bed on Monday morning wondering if what had happened to me the day before was real. It was. Nothing had changed in the world of smoke and mirrors. Bad guys were still being killed by the good guys, and crime still flourished. The crooks disappeared like that when I was a rookie cop.

Am I on my way to disappearance? People forget. I could be gone for six months, and nobody would even know I ever existed. I didn't even have a gun to protect myself.

I called the Marshal's Office in East St. Louis, lied and told them I was reinstated to the police department and I needed my gun back. The old marshal said, "Sure, come over and get it." I had my usual breakfast, kibitzed with Tyrone, then drove over in the Austin Healey with the top down.

I was on the Poplar Street Bridge on the return trip, my rocket gun tucked neatly in my crotch holster when I decided to make a move. I dialed the Chief's Office. An aide answered when I asked to speak to him, they put me on hold. I envisioned the antics transpiring. The aide goes into his office, "Sir, Ray Arnold is on the phone."

"Oh, God, I knew this was coming. He wants his job back, right?"

"Probably, sir."

"Get his number, tell him I'll get back to him."

I flashbacked to reality; the aide requested my cell number. He called back as I was getting onto south Broadway. "Chief, here."

"Hi, Chief. I wanted you to know that my mission at DEA is complete. Justice was served. I need my old job back."

"Mission? I don't follow you, Ray. Aren't you

suspended?"

"Yes, sir, a suspension that's the product of my investigation into my mission."

"Mission? I don't recall any mission. I didn't send you to DEA on any mission. What are you suspended for?"

"Investigation of a couple of murders. Trumped-up charges, sir. The federal government was trying to discredit me."

The pause, the five-second pause, then the clearing of the throat, the hand over the receiver, then he was back. "Report to homicide tomorrow morning. I'll get you reinstated. Welcome home."

"Thank you, sir."

I was smiling. It was a new experience for me. I tried to think of the last time I had actually smiled. There were no catastrophes in my life at this particular point in time and I was smiling. I felt like an idiot.

It was noon. I drove straight to the gym, did an entire body, then headed back to the antique house with a view. I checked my closet and pulled out my least drab blue suit. I couldn't imagine putting it on. It wasn't me anymore. I picked out a tie and a pair of hard shoes, an off-color shirt and laid them on the bed.

This was like a World War Two freedom fighter preparing to pull on a Nazi uniform. I hung them back up and walked around my backyard throwing the ball for Tyrone.

The day was shot. Dusk was upon us. I fired up the grill and tossed on two steaks. We ate on the deck. I was in bed by 2200.

I was up at 0600, bustling around the house, showering and eating and downing cups of coffee, excited about my return to homicide. It came time to get dressed and I felt down. "Stop it," I shouted. I pulled on the shirt, the trousers,

the tie, the hard shoes and carried the suit
coat. I felt like I was in a strait jacket.

I found my soft-sided briefcase, tossed my gun, camera, handcuffs and writing material, and headed out the door. I put the top up on the Austin Healey. I didn't want anybody to see me dressed this way.

I parked at a meter and trudged into the building. The elevator crowd was waiting in the lobby. It was a déjà vu junior high school experience: everyone dressing alike, smelling alike, acting alike. We waited for the next car. The door opened, we exited like cattle and I got off on the fourth floor.

I wasn't smiling as I walked in and searched for an empty desk. I found one, tossed my bag on top, and sat down. The detectives were wandering in. I didn't know any of them. They were all young; I felt real old.

My old associate, Detective Sergeant Jason Allen, strolled in. I stood up to shake his hand. He didn't offer his. "Stay at your desk, I'll get back to you," is all he said, then he whisked away. I sat there, went to the rest room, and then sat some more. I tried small talk with the young cops; they weren't buying it.

I left the office to plug the meter. I had a twenty five dollar tag. I plugged it again and trudged back up to the office. I was at my desk; Jason approached me. "Where were you?"

"I went down to plug the meter. I had a tag, twenty five dollars, can you fix it?"

He stared while the youngsters went out to lunch. "I told you to stay at your desk."

"Okay, but why? Tell me why I have to sit at this desk with nothing to do while everyone else comes and goes as they please?" He stared some more.

"You've got a jacket, Ray. The word is that you went to

the dark side, that you're a dope dealer, a cocaine cowboy, and a killer. You got suspended for killing two guys on the East side and dumping them in Rush City. Right?" I just stared at him. "It'll blow over, Ray, just give it some time. If you're at your desk, the young guys won't suspect you of being out making dope deals. They'll warm up to you eventually, you'll see. But in the meantime, just sit there."

I sat all day. It wasn't healthy for me. I kept thinking about DEA, the task force, and Heidi. Carla was always on my mind. I even missed Doc.

My heart fluttered whenever I imagined our antics together; the deals, the beers, the cars, and glamour of being a federal nark. I dialed the task force number, expecting to hear Carla answer. Mike Schweig answered instead. I smiled as I envisioned him, hung over with a cheap suit or sport coat, smoking squares and pushing his lips out when he tried to concentrate, subconsciously making fish faces.

"Hey, Mike, Ray Arnold here. Let me talk to Carla."

"Oh, hi, Ray, Carla isn't here."

"Oh? Where is she?"

"Gone! Transferred."

"Transferred? To where?"

"Nobody knows for sure, Ray. She's gone. So is Doc and Heidi. It's weird, they all came here at the same time, and now they've all left at the same time. It's almost like they were a team. I'm in charge for now."

My heart sank. I'm in the cold and there's nobody who can bring me inside. "Carla is a civilian employee. You should know where she went." I was grasping at straws.

"No, actually she was a special agent, but not with DEA. Heidi, too. I just found this out. They were both assigned here for some covert operation from some Washington spook tank. If I hear from her, I'll tell her you inquired about her. So long, Ray."

I felt sick. I was in enemy territory with no backup. I examined my dilemma. Stockholm Syndrome! Brainwashed by the best brainwashing machine in the world. I blushed. What chance did I have? One little old cop against the system. I did their bidding. They won.

1700 rolled around. I was the first one out the door. I had another tag on the Healey. I took my tie off, pulled my shirt out, and removed it, then tossed the top back. I felt like a mental patient who just talked his guards into removing his restraint.

I drove slowly home my mind wandering about DEA. I thought about the evening Heidi and I went to Sig Otto's house. I imagined the potatoes going through the Feeb's windows and the look on Moynihan's face.

My cell rang and I answered it. "Ray," the familiar voice said. It was Sig Otto. "I want to apologize for what I had to do to you, Ray. I was under the gun."

"What kind of a gun, Sig? What did they have on you?"

"It was an IRS beef, Ray. I had to work it off. I worked it off by assisting Heidi and Doc with you. I feel ashamed and I sincerely apologize. I hope you'll forgive me."

I gave him the federal pause. He did what he had to do. How could I hate him for that? "Don't worry about it, Sig. It's history. So long, Sig."

"Ray, we'll have our revenge."

"No we won't, so long, Sig." I hung up and wondered what kind of federal beef Granny was working off. I would never know. I thought about Henry Darby and Jack Parker. Henry was in hiding. Heidi will never testify against anybody in St. Louis. Henry got a free ride, so did Viktor Agron. No telling where Heidi is.

The United States Attorney wouldn't go forward with the Viktor Agron case. He was going to skate again. No wonder the dope game flourishes. Another bad experience in law enforcement. Why was I surprised?

I flashed back to the interview in the street after Moynihan pulled Heidi and I over. He told me there was no life after DEA. I told him to fuck off and climbed back in with Heidi.

My cell rang again. I checked the I.D. it was Gloria. I answered with a "Yo."

"I heard you came back to the P.D." She paused and waited for my response.

My mind was racing, flashing back from Heidi, to Carla, and then to Gloria. Heidi and Carla were quickly fading away like the morning fog. The picture in my brain was Gloria walking around in my backyard in the nude; Big-boned, strong and firm. I wanted Gloria back, but I had to be cool.

"Yeah," I replied. "I'm back in homicide, for now."

"Okay if I come over for a while?" she asked.

"Yeah, I'm heading for home right now. See you in a couple of minutes?"

"Yeah!"

For some reason, Heidi again beamed into my mind. I had to decipher why. I knew it was all a part of the brain washing process. I had to be able to shake her off. I had to realize that she wasn't real, just something manufactured by the government. I was an assignment for her. She would forget me and move on to the next target.

I imagined her gorgeous Hispanic features as I asked her the question. Is there life after DEA? She scrunched her nose and looked at me. "Doubtful," she replied.

About The Author

The author, Timothy C. Richards, is a retired St. Louis police detective. He served in the Intelligence Unit, investigating organized crime. He also served in the Homicide section and the federal Drug Enforcement Administration. He is highly decorated and awarded as a federal drug agent and as a police detective. A graduate of the University of Missouri, he was inspired to write about his experiences. He has written one true cop/detective book, 'CROOKS KILL, COPS LIE.' Dope is a D.E.A.d Man's Game is his first fictional novel featuring protagonist, Detective Ray Arnold. Several of his colleagues refer to it as 'factional'.

CPSIA information can be obtained at www.ICGtesting.com
Printed in the USA
LVOW04s1025050914

402621LV00012B/211/P